A Song for
the Road

A Song for the Road

♦ *A NOVEL* ♦

KATHLEEN BASI

alcove
press

Copyright © 2021 by Kathleen Basi

All rights reserved.

Published in the United States by Alcove Press, an imprint of The Quick Brown Fox & Company LLC.

Alcove Press and its logo are trademarks of The Quick Brown Fox & Company LLC.

Library of Congress Catalog-in-Publication data available upon request.

ISBN (trade paperback): 978-1-64385-690-2
ISBN (ebook): 978-1-64385-691-9

Cover design by Melanie Sun

Printed in the United States.

www.alcovepress.com

Alcove Press
34 West 27th St., 10th Floor
New York, NY 10001

First Edition: May 2021

10 9 8 7 6 5 4 3 2 1

*To my husband Christian, who has walked
every step of this journey with me, and who
has helped me understand the beauty and
complexity of love.*

Part 1

Atlanta, Georgia

If your heart is a volcano, how shall you expect flowers to bloom?

—Khalil Gibran

◆ 1 ◆

O<small>N HER THIRTY-EIGHTH BIRTHDAY,</small> Miriam Tedesco received flowers from a ghost.

She didn't need the blatant reminder that the universe hated her. She'd known for a year. And if she'd had any doubts, they vanished the moment she got called to lead music for a funeral on a day she should have been at home, nursing her own loss.

"Miriam!" the hospitality director greeted her at the door of St. Gregory the Great Church. "Thank God you're here. I need the key for the janitor's closet. A kid threw up in the cry room."

"I—"

A second volunteer touched her shoulder, not quite meeting her eyes. "Miriam, the reserved signs are missing. Do you know where they are?"

"Hey, guys!" said one of her choir members. "Somebody's gotta talk to those readers. They both have the same Scripture. It's getting ugly up there."

Miriam tried to point out that a Catholic funeral included two readings, and it shouldn't be that hard to satisfy everyone, but her voice wouldn't work. Heart pounding, roaring ears—was she having a panic attack? And why didn't anyone seem to notice?

Usually, she relished the way people at St. Greg's counted on her institutional knowledge, her competence, for things beyond her musical expertise. She'd worked here long enough to know a music director in a Catholic parish did much more than play music.

But it sure seemed like the good Lord could've cut her a break on the first anniversary of the day her husband and kids had died.

Too many colors—flowers burying the altar, and more arriving every minute. Too many people—the hushed conversations like a mosquito she could hear, but not see well enough to swat. The walls wouldn't stand still. If she didn't know better, she'd swear the stained-glass saints ringing the church were laughing at her.

A firm hand gripped her elbow from behind, and a crisp voice addressed the volunteers. "Gentlemen!"

The men snapped to attention. For twenty-five years, that voice had tolerated no nonsense in St. Gregory parish.

"Becky," Miriam gasped, clutching her best friend's arm.

Becky Lindon, parish secretary and at sixty, a silver-haired force of nature, tightened her grip. "Gentlemen," she repeated. "A little space, for heaven's sake!" She fixed her fierce gaze on each of them in turn. "I realize everyone's freaked out about hosting a funeral for a congressman, but it's still just a funeral. You've all done this a hundred times. The reserved signs are in the front pew. I can see them from here. Here are my keys. Go clean up the puke yourself. And as for the readers, ask Father Simeon. Miriam doesn't need to be dealing with that. Go on—scoot!"

The volunteers scattered. Becky turned to Miriam. Her embrace made the walls stop undulating and the stained glass stand still. "I'm so sorry you got called in today," she murmured. "I won't wish you a happy birthday, but I'm praying hard it doesn't completely suck."

Miriam snorted. "Too late."

Becky's grip tightened briefly. "Come on. You don't have to sing. You don't have to say a word. You just have to play the piano. It's just another Mass, okay? Let's get this thing done. The choir's already warmed up." Murmuring about a last-minute change the widow had made to the music list, she marched Miriam past two more floral delivery guys and a funeral home employee. In the music area, the ad hoc group of volunteers who sang for funerals awaited her leadership. Miriam gathered her scattered wits and started bookmarking her accompaniment books. Like Becky said, it was just another Mass. She could do this. She'd been doing it since high school. She could do it in her sleep. She'd be fine.

Naturally, that was the moment the flowers arrived.

"Excuse me, I'm looking for—"

"Just find a place on the stairs," Miriam told the delivery guy, waving toward the bower around the altar.

"Um, actually, they're not for the funeral." He looked embarrassed. "I'm looking for Miriam . . . Teddy . . . skoo?"

The choir went abruptly silent.

And Miriam knew. She didn't need to look; she could smell them. Mock orange and larkspur. The same arrangement Teo had presented her with nineteen years ago on the way into the courthouse—and every anniversary and birthday since.

How could she have forgotten? Talia had set up the auto-delivery on her father's behalf, right in front of Miriam, at the dinner table two years ago last night. They'd all gotten such a laugh out of it.

Becky, trim in her polyester suit, set her hymnal aside and went over to the delivery man. "I'll take those, thank you." She turned to Miriam, who stared at the clumps of rounded white blossoms pierced by pink and blue and purple spears.

"They're so pretty," said an alto who'd joined the choir only a few weeks ago. "Who are they from?"

A moment of dead silence. Miriam didn't have the energy to explain the nuances. "Teo," she said. "They're from Teo."

At the sound of her dead husband's name, silence fell. "But—" the alto said.

"Yes. Teo's dead. My whole family is dead. I know." Miriam shoved her freak-out into a deep, dark corner of her mind she never visited during daylight hours. Or at night, if she could help it. But the niggling thought stuck its foot in the door, preventing her from slamming it shut: *If she'd forgotten this, what else might be lurking on the calendar, waiting to ambush her?*

It's been a year, she told herself. *If there was anything else, it should have happened by now.*

Still. It wouldn't hurt to get into Talia's computer and poke around. Just to be safe.

Having a plan eased the tightness in her chest, but she wasn't going anywhere near those flowers. "Just put them on the organ, would you, Bec?"

Becky complied briskly, as if there were nothing freak-ish about a floral delivery from a dead man, and returned to her seat in the alto section.

Time to redirect. For all their sakes. "So," she said. "I hear we have a change in the opening song."

Several people exchanged glances. She could see them asking each other: *"Are we really going to just pretend that didn't happen?"*

Miriam made eye contact with John Merrick, a bass who'd been singing with them since the day she and Teo arrived at St. Greg's. Like Becky, he got things done. She gave him her best beseeching eyes.

John sat forward. "Y'know," he drawled, "I don't know why we bother havin' a music list if we're just gonna change it anyway."

Anemic laughter rippled through the choir as the joke spread. "Oh, come on, you know the list is more like—"

"Guidelines than actual rules!"

The laughter fizzled. That had been Teo's joke. Usually delivered in a hilariously lousy Captain Barbosa imitation. In John's mouth, it just underscored how everything had changed.

The smell of mock orange teased her nostrils. Miriam gripped the music stand as the choir eyed her nervously. What would they do if she stood up and screamed, "Do this without me. I hate this damn job, and I hate all of you!"

Keep it together. That's not true and you know it.

It felt true, though. Eighteen years ago, she and Teo had come here with twin babies in tow. The parish hadn't been expecting to hire a young married couple to fill a single staff position, but they'd risen to the occasion. They'd offered the family a shabby but solid house two doors down from the church, recently bequeathed by a parishioner, as part of their compensation. Miriam and Teo had been more than codirectors of music here. This parish had been their home, a place where she could shake off the scorn with which her family had always viewed her passion for music. A place where she'd blossomed.

If she couldn't handle this work anymore, where would she go? What would she do?

The sound of footsteps in the back of church signaled the arrival of the dead congressman's family. It was time to work. Miriam sat on the piano bench and nodded to Becky to announce the opening song.

Don't think, just play.

She put her fingers to the keys and began. After so many years in ministry, playing "Amazing Grace" was nearly automatic. Which was great, except it left more space to think.

Teo had been so conflicted about that floral delivery. He almost canceled it—he only left it in place because he didn't want to hurt Talia's feelings. But it had felt wrong to him because he loved giving gifts. He wanted to do it himself.

He was good at it too. Every year she thought she was impervious to surprise, and every year he'd managed it anyway—often with the help of the twins. Three years ago, he'd planned a scavenger hunt that covered half the metro area. Miriam ended up at the nicest restaurant in Atlanta, the one that was supposed to be impossible to get a reservation for and that they couldn't possibly afford. He'd met her there, holding a duplicate of the bouquet now perched on the organ.

It had never occurred to her he might be able to surprise her from beyond the grave.

He'd always loved her better than she'd loved him.

The funeral went on: music, prayers, Scriptures, more music. So many people. So unlike the average funeral, where the mourners barely occupied a quarter of the church. St. Gregory seated a thousand, and today every pew was crammed elbow to elbow. People standing in the back, as if it were Christmas Eve. Three news cameras panned the church.

All this for a bigoted, ethically challenged, old-fashioned bully of a congressman who'd cheated on his wife repeatedly before landing with that young thing perched in the front pew?

Miriam took a deep breath to discourage her rising blood pressure. The locket around her neck chilled her skin. She could almost hear Teo whisper, *"Be nice, Sassafras."*

Hard on its heels came another voice: her daughter's, calculated to wound. *"No heart,"* Talia had said in their last fight. *"You can't fight with someone who has no heart."*

Miriam clenched her fists, but the shaking had spread to her whole body now.

"Miriam." Becky's hiss brought her back to reality. Miriam glanced up at the altar, where Father Simeon, her boss, stood looking at her with his eyebrows raised. She'd missed a cue. She launched into an acclamation, keenly aware that not only was she failing at her job, she didn't even want to do it.

She had to get herself together. Before people realized the only good thing about Miriam Tedesco had been her husband and kids.

Communion took forever. The choir finished singing and joined the procession; Miriam kept playing, her butt cheeks going numb as her rage grew, fed by the never-ending crowd that proved power and fame meant more than integrity. Today of all days, with the loss of her family so close at hand, that reality burned.

Burning . . . now there was an intriguing thought.

She ought to give this congressman a tribute of her own. A little Johnny Cash, perhaps. If she did it right—played around with the rhythms, stretched out the melody—no one else even had to know she was celebrating a funeral with a song about a man descending into a burning ring of fire.

Miriam snickered as she made the transition. Becky, returning from Communion, frowned at her, but Miriam pretended not to notice. Her body relaxed as she flexed her improv muscles. Burning. Genius. It was perfect on so many levels. She didn't mean it . . . exactly. It was more a little joke, to get her through this day. Surely the good Lord would forgive her a private joke.

At least, she thought it was private until, a chorus or two down the line, a hand slammed down on the grand piano. "What the *hell* do you *think* you are *doing*?"

Startled, Miriam lifted her hands from the keys. She looked up to find the congressman's young widow standing beside her, quivering with rage.

Silence fell in the church. She'd been so absorbed by her musical exercise, she'd failed to notice that the Communion line had finally cleared. A glance around the building revealed a thousand faces turned toward her. A few hid smiles. Most looked confused; some, angry.

But none as angry as the widow—a woman who, Miriam remembered too late, had been up-and-coming in Nashville before she left it all behind to marry Atlanta's longest-serving congressman.

Of course she would recognize "Ring of Fire," no matter how Miriam dressed it up.

Well . . . Okay, she hadn't dressed it up *that* much.

Ordinarily, Miriam tried to follow the third commandment. But at this moment, only one word properly expressed the depths of trouble she'd just landed herself in.

Shit.

♦ 2 ♦

No MATTER HOW MANY times Miriam pulled into the driveway, the sight of the little blue bungalow sitting cold and silent was always a shock. It had always been overrun with noise: piano in the front room and cello in the first bedroom, Teo's Argentine jam sessions on the porch, with June bugs flinging themselves against every glass surface. Music spilling through leaky windows, sparking impromptu dance parties among the little girls next door. And always Blaise and Talia, working together, shouting at each other, fighting and making up, their tempers no match for the bond of the womb.

Miriam slung the white shopping bag—the only thing she had to show for this whole day—over her shoulder and slammed the car door.

A figure separated from the porch swing and said, "There you are!"

Becky was the only person in the universe who could wear jeans and a pink flowered "Grandma" sweatshirt without looking like a slob. Maybe she starched her clothes to get them to maintain that shape. "What are you doing here?"

Her friend held up a bottle and a flat box. "Birthday treats?" She shrugged. "After today, I figured wine and chocolate were more appropriate than cake."

Despite herself, Miriam's lips twisted to one side. "Not gonna argue with you there." She started up the walkway, inhaling the scent of Teo's herb garden, which she hadn't managed to kill yet.

"You disappeared after the funeral. I was worried."

Miriam stopped at the top of the porch stairs. She looked down at the gray-blue boards and kneaded her forehead. "I, well, Father Simeon called me in for a come-to-Jesus meeting."

"And?"

"And what? Are you asking if I got fired?"

Becky looked sheepish.

Miriam leaned one shoulder on a support. "Well, no. But I think it's safe to say I'm on probation. He made it clear I'd better not ever pull a stunt like that again."

"Were you intending to?"

Miriam gave that smart-ass comment the eye roll it deserved. "Anyway, I knew I wasn't going to be of use to anyone today. Better to clear out and . . ."

"Soul search."

Wallow was the word she'd been thinking of. Becky's take sounded better. She shrugged. "Simeon . . . suggested . . . I go out to the grave site," she said.

"Oh, Miriam." The sympathy in Becky's voice nearly undid her. "You should have called me. I would have gone with you."

Miriam picked at some peeling paint on the porch support. "I couldn't get out of the car," she admitted in a low voice.

Becky hugged her again, the box and bottle bumping the post behind her. "You shouldn't go out there by yourself," she murmured. "Let the people who love you help you."

Miriam melted into the touch of another human being. She couldn't get used to the lack of human contact—as a wife and mother, someone had always been touching her.

For one moment, she considered unburdening herself to Becky—telling her the ways in which she'd failed Teo, the last fight with Talia, the secret that should have felt less burdensome now that they were all gone, but that felt heavier than ever.

But Becky would never look at her the same way again.

No. She had to figure this out on her own.

Miriam straightened, and Becky released her. Away from that human touch, the spring night held a chill.

Becky sighed. "Well, it's just as well you weren't in the office today. Ella came in looking for you."

Miriam shuddered. "Ella Evil would have been the cherry on top of this day."

Becky's lips twitched. "One of these days, you're going to slip up and call her that to her face."

"Bring it on." For months after Ella Emil, the "online voice of Atlanta," featured Miriam's quest to memorialize her children with a fine arts addition at St. Gregory the Great High School, her life had been hell. Everyone read Ella's gossipy blog, even if they'd never admit it. Miriam had taken to grocery shopping at one AM to avoid running into people who thought they were entitled to hug her and pat her cheek and share their own sob stories.

She should have known better than to talk to that woman. Should have known Ella would make her look like a saint; it racked up blog hits. Should have known trying to live up to that image would crush her soul. But Mom had insisted publicity would help the cause and that talking would make her feel better.

She'd been right on point A. Point B, not so much. "What's Ella want now?" she asked.

"An update."

Miriam groaned. "'Grief-stricken widow goes crazy at funeral of congressman.' You have to admit, it has a certain ring."

"Nobody thinks you're crazy, Miriam. We're all just worried about you."

Miriam moved toward the door, shuffling with her keys. "I wish people would chill. It's not like I've spent the last year holed up in my bedroom refusing to shower."

Becky cocked her head, giving Miriam a Look. The kind that required capitalization. "I hate to break it to you, but there's more to living than showing up showered."

"Brilliant, Becky. Put it on a meme."

"Miriam, you know I love you. But you can't go on like this."

Miriam swung on her friend. "You think I don't know that?" Her words bounced off the house across the street; she winced.

"Everyone knows what you've been through." Becky spoke softly. "Nobody should have to do what you had to do today. It was a terrible set of circumstances. But, Miriam, honey, you can't take it out on your volunteers."

"I didn't yell at anyone."

"Not today, you didn't."

Miriam winced. The sound guy still flinched every time she looked his way, and it had been, what, six weeks since that spat?

No wonder her volunteer ranks were getting thin.

She rested her forehead against the wall. Sometimes she woke in the night with her pulse pounding, crucified on the knowledge that everything she'd sacrificed had been for nothing. Sometimes the anger caught her off guard in the most inappropriate moment. Like when she stood before the choir, her hands raised, their eyes on her, trusting her, and she longed to launch a microphone stand at them, javelin-like.

But most of the time, she just felt dead. As if the emotion that had fueled her music and given purpose to her days—everything that made her good at her job—went into the ocean with her husband and twin teenagers a year ago.

She'd been certain nothing could be worse than the crushing weight of grief that had paralyzed her for months. Every day, every hour, every minute.

She'd been wrong. Feeling nothing at all was much worse.

Miriam swallowed. "I hate everything. I hate my job, I hate playing piano, I hate dealing with people. I . . . I don't know if I can do it anymore, Bec."

"Oh, Miriam," Becky said softly, "don't lose yourself in this. Teo would never have wanted this for you." She bit her lip but couldn't quite swallow the chuckle. "'Ring of Fire,'" she said, shaking her head. "Where did that even come from?"

"The devil made me do it," Miriam muttered, only half joking.

Becky sniffed, held her hand out, and wiggled her fingers. "Let me see the card."

Miriam didn't pretend to misunderstand. She pulled the floral card from in front of the photo in her phone case and handed it over. Becky took it, and Miriam ran her finger over the photo of herself and Teo standing beside the piano at St. Gregory's. Teo's hand rested on the neck of his guitar; Miriam pointed to something in the accompaniment book. She didn't remember what. Only that they'd been in the middle of a spirited discussion about it when the kids had told them to look and snapped the picture.

They were making faces.

Miriam loved that picture. It was quintessential Teo: that big Italian-Argentine nose, the glasses that made him look like a geeky professor, right from the day she'd first met him at the national convention for liturgical music.

From day one, he'd made her feel like she belonged. What had she ever done for him?

"'Happy birthday, love of my life,'" Becky read. She looked up. "Pretty generic for a message from beyond the grave."

"It's an auto-delivery for my birthday and anniversary," Miriam said dully.

Becky's eyebrows shot skyward. "Auto-delivery doesn't sound like Teo."

"Two years ago, the night before my birthday, he realized at dinner he forgot to call the florist." Miriam passed her hand across her eyes. She could still see Blaise's sardonic thumbs-up at Teo's exclamation. *"Way to keep a surprise, Dad!"* he'd said.

Talia had rolled her eyes and whipped out her phone. Miriam could hear the timbre of teenage exasperation in her daughter's voice, clashing with the glow of pride at the chance to show off her expertise.

"Talia set it up, to show off for her Luddite parents," she said now.

"You're not a Luddite," Becky said with a tolerant smile, but then frowned. "But if it was an auto-delivery, why didn't it didn't happen last year?"

"It did. But on my birthday, when the flowers arrived, they hadn't . . ." She couldn't say it. The car accident that had killed her husband and twin teenagers—hit head-on by a drunk driver as they drove down the highway toward a beach on the other side of the country—hadn't happened until later in the day.

Thankfully, she didn't have to say it; Becky nodded her understanding.

"And on my anniversary . . . Mom was here then. I remember a delivery truck, but . . . I was in such a fog then." Miriam shoved her key into the front door lock. As usual, it wouldn't turn. Her locket bumped against her breastbone as she wrestled with the door.

"You think your mom got rid of them before you saw them?"

"Seems like a safe guess." She wrenched the lock again. "Damn it, you stupid door. Open!"

Becky tucked the wine under her elbow, took the key from Miriam, and unlocked the door. Of course. Even inanimate objects obeyed Becky.

It swung open, and the smell of old house—slightly acrid, slightly spicy—rolled out to meet them. Becky handed the key back. "Miriam, talk to me."

Miriam stared into the darkness of the house, a darkness perforated by the silhouettes of even blacker objects: the baby grand, Teo's armchair, the tree full of coats that lost the scent of their owners months ago. Everything where it had been a year ago this night, when she'd turned all the lights off, powered down her phone, and tried to pretend she'd died too. "I can't live like this anymore," she whispered. "I'm surrounded by ghosts. They talk to me, you know." She sensed Becky's hesitation. "Not like that. I just always know what they'd say if they were here. Or I remember what they *did* say. It's like I have a built-in Greek chorus."

She rested her head on the door frame. "And yet still, I was totally blindsided by a delivery of flowers I should have known were coming." She shook her head. "I'm stuck, Becky. What if it's because I'm still here? Living in the middle of a life that doesn't exist anymore?"

"He's been so unhappy. Why do you always push him away?"

Miriam shuddered at the echo of the words Talia had flung at her the night before her family left for California, never to return. Had Teo really been unhappy? Why hadn't she noticed?

Becky put a hand on her shoulder. "Miriam, don't be so hard on yourself. You've got to give yourself some time."

"I've had nothing *but* time, Becky. And look what happened today." She shook her head. "I can't go on like this. At the very least, I've got to get into Talia's computer and close her accounts. If this got by me, there's no telling what else might be hiding out there. I can't handle any more surprises. I'll lose my job if there's another day like today." She pulled out the roll of trash bags from the shopping bag. "I figure, if I'm going to purge the computer, I might as well just keep going."

Becky's eyes narrowed. Her mouth too. Then she nodded and gestured with the wine and chocolate. "We're going to need this more than I thought."

★ ★ ★

Becky stepped over the threshold and flipped a light switch. Her footsteps creaked across the old hardwood floor. Teo always joked that the kids could never sneak out of the house, those floors made so much racket.

Her friend went straight for the kitchen to open the wine bottle and pour a couple of glasses. Miriam wandered more slowly, stopping—as she so often did these days—at the piano, where Blaise's spiral notebook lay open on the music stand.

She'd known, the way mothers know, that he'd been writing a piano sonata for her. He never worked on it while she was around. But she recognized the look of one sunk deep into his own mind, circling the core of his muse, trying to cajole a spark to light. Too many times, she'd heard unfamiliar music as she approached the house after work, and by the time she'd fumbled the door open, he'd be practicing Liszt or Beethoven again. Once—only once, but once was enough—she'd seen the handwritten scribbles peeking from behind published scores.

She'd found it when the police sent the boxes back from California—boxes containing the things most important to her husband and children. The things important enough to take with them on such a highly anticipated trip: Talia's cello and laptop, the satchels full of music, the suitcases, and a spiral music notebook with the words *Sonata—for Mom* scribbled across it in Blaise's handwriting.

It was months later before she found the folded e-mail printout tucked into the manuscript notebook. The pinpoint of vivid, scarlet rage that note had aroused in her was one of her few clear memories of that time. Rage at the universe. Rage at her impotence—and her cowardice. She should have dealt with this years ago. When it could have made a difference.

One e-mail. That was all it took to trigger her insecurities—and a familiar craving to prove herself. To gain the notice of a man whose opinion shouldn't matter at all.

She'd resolved to finish what her son no longer could. But she'd done it for all the wrong reasons, and she'd been regretting her rashness ever since. Sure, she'd written music—small forms, responses meant for use on Sunday mornings. Nothing like a major piano work.

And how anyone else had found out about it remained a mystery. She didn't remember talking about it. Then again, she'd spent so long in a fog, that was hardly surprising. Her mother, convinced the key to surviving loss was staying busy, had talked her into starting the capital campaign for the fine arts wing. Surely the sonata must have had something to do with that.

Still, to this day, Miriam couldn't say how the sonata ended up being the headline of a concert benefiting the campaign. She just knew she'd spent December in a haze of writing, only to discover in January that every note she'd written was complete, utter, derivative drivel. Christmas carols! She'd managed to write Christmas carols into it!

Miriam ran a finger over the pencil marks. Blaise's handwriting was better than hers. *"You should have been a doctor,"* Teo used to tease.

She slid onto the piano bench, smoothed the notebook flat, and began to play.

The themes were lyrical, a window into the beautiful, sensitive soul of her beautiful, sensitive boy. The sinuous melodies massaged her heart, only to be repulsed before evoking any emotion. What remained of her heart sat beneath her sternum, slowly compressing like coal, getting hotter and hotter. Much longer and she'd either lay a diamond egg or blow like Mount Vesuvius.

If she had loved Blaise, surely a few of the notes pouring from her fingers should have sparked an answering call in her heart. And if she hadn't really loved Blaise, who had been a mirror of her own soul, how could she hope to look Talia's ghost in the eye and say she'd loved Teo?

Miriam found her hands at a standstill on the keys, her gaze fixed on the last measure Blaise had written. "Come on, Miriam," she growled, starting in again. He'd laid out all the material. She only had to develop it. Motive,

sequence, inversion, secondary dominant. She closed her
eyes, trying to let her fingers find a path forward. Instead,
she found her hand drifting toward the e-mail that barely
protruded from the manuscript:

"Is that it?"

Miriam snatched her hand back and looked to her left.
Becky leaned against the archway between the kitchen and
the living room, holding two glasses of wine.

"It's beautiful," Becky said.

The sonata. Becky was talking about the sonata. Not
the e-mail. "Sorry," Miriam said. "I should be . . ."

"Don't apologize. Do you want to talk?"

"No." Miriam switched off the piano lamp.

"Okay, then." Becky held out a glass. "You ready to get
started?"

Miriam took a sip. "Not even remotely." She got up
from the piano and started down the hallway toward Talia's
room. She hadn't been inside in eleven months. Not since
she'd received an overdue notice from the library. She'd gone
in but left without searching. Paying the fine seemed easier.

The moment she pushed open the door, ghosts darted
out. She could hear it so clearly: the sound of six-year-old
Talia, banished to her room for punching Blaise, throwing a bouncy ball at the ceiling. When the sound stopped,
Miriam thought she'd gone to sleep. But then she'd found
Blaise on the floor of his room, whispering into the old
heating vents, keeping his twin sister company through her
incarceration.

"You can't fight with someone who has no heart."

Miriam had heard Talia's words in her head a hundred
times since her daughter shouted them at her. What she
wouldn't give to hear them in reality now. To have a chance
to make amends.

Becky stood watching her anxiously. Miriam edged
over the threshold and turned on the light.

Just inside the door lay two music cases: Teo's guitar and
Talia's cello. Yo-Yo Ma and Steve Jobs still looked down

from the walls; award cups covered every surface. Books, sketch notebooks. Stuffed animals Talia had relegated to a hammock but couldn't bear to get rid of.

Talia's laptop case lay on the bed. "You start with the accounts," suggested Becky. "And I'll take the stuffed animals. How many do you want to keep?"

All of them. Miriam twitched a shoulder. "Maybe just Blue Beary. He was her favorite. And the unicorn. You think we can send the rest to a children's shelter?"

"I don't know. We can ask." Dust showered down as Becky unhooked the hammock. She set the two privileged animals on the bed and started stuffing the rest into a trash bag.

It made Miriam ill to watch. She opened Talia's computer. After a year, it was dead, of course. She plugged it in. Blaise's interest had been composing; Talia's was programming. She and Teo had been forced to concoct increasingly complex rules about screen time to make sure they honored her gift without losing her to the online world altogether.

"Closet?" Becky said.

Miriam looked up to find Becky awaiting permission. Behind her hung an array of flowing skirts, loose blouses, and bright scarves: Talia's lovely, bohemian wardrobe. Her daughter could work magic with a scarf tied into her dark curls.

Why on earth had Miriam ever thought this was a good idea?

Becky put a hand on her shoulder, her voice gentle. "I'll tell you what. For now, let's just lay it all out and take inventory."

Miriam's fingers crept toward the rainbow of scarves Becky laid across the bed. She picked up one embroidered with baby blue. Talia had always made fun of her mother's penchant for no-fuss slacks and soft cotton blouses. How many times had Talia tried to get her to wear some of these beautiful, feminine clothes?

Miriam tied the scarf into her hair, the way Talia had, with the long tail hanging down her back. She regarded her reflection in the mirror. It didn't look as ridiculous as she'd feared. She was only thirty-eight, after all.

Miriam turned back to Talia's laptop. They'd required the kids to share all passwords with their parents. *Cellista00!* she entered, and the familiar background came up: a close-up of the twins, taken after a high school choir concert. Miriam clutched her locket, then took a swig of merlot. She could do this.

As Becky murmured and sorted and laid things in piles, Miriam found the floral delivery and canceled it. Then she headed for Talia's e-mail, reading and deleting, forwarding to herself anything she wanted to keep. The wine helped. Her brain felt fuzzy.

"I don't remember this one," Becky said, and an inky black dress with huge red flowers dropped into Miriam's lap.

Miriam recoiled. It was the dress Teo and Talia had bought for her birthday. After the fight, Miriam couldn't bear to look at it. She'd forgotten she'd hung it here.

"It's gorgeous," Becky said.

Miriam shoved it toward her. "You take it."

Her friend laughed. "Oh, honey, that ship sailed long ago." She turned to the mirror, holding the dress against her body. "Twenty years ago I could have pulled this off." She pursed her lips and turned back. "Well . . . maybe thirty. But not now. You, on the other hand . . ."

Miriam turned her back. "I'm done for tonight."

They'd barely started, but Becky didn't bat an eye. "Sure. Just let me finish pulling these last few things out."

As Miriam navigated to the laptop's shutdown menu, the cursor flashed across a desktop folder she hadn't noticed before:

Project Parents.

She hesitated. What could Talia possibly have been working on for her parents? Did she even want to know?

She clicked it open. The contents of the folder fell off the bottom of the window. Video files, spreadsheets, documents with complicated programming code names, others labeled "heads" and "tails" in a series of numbers, and still others with names as inexplicable as "Ketchup." And at the top, what appeared to be a program titled *Projectparents.exe*.

She hesitated, then double-clicked.

The computer spun for a few seconds. Then a video box sprang up, and Miriam found herself staring at the last thing she'd expected.

Her children.

3

9:20 PM

"Hey, there, mom and Dad."
  "Mom. Dad."
Miriam recoiled, her hand accidentally smacking the keyboard. The video froze Talia and Blaise in time. They were stretched out across this very bed, resting on their elbows. Talia's beautiful hair, thicker and darker than Miriam's, was tied up in the same scarf Miriam now wore. The fresh sweetness in those brown eyes took Miriam's breath away. The way her mouth buttoned up on the beginning of her next word. The single zit on her cheek.

And Blaise, with his thick-rimmed glasses, the fine stubble around his jaw, and the deliberately messy state of his hair, which he worked so carefully to achieve every morning.

They looked so much like *him*. How had she never noticed?

Miriam closed her eyes against the reminder of everything she wanted to forget. The pit yawned before her, waiting to suck her back down. She could feel the ground sliding away. She was so tired of resisting.

The mattress compressed beside her. Becky's hand spread warmth in a circle around her back. "What did you find?" she asked.

With effort, Miriam pulled herself back from the breach. "I'm not sure." The fog was descending again. She clenched her fists—a physical reminder that she was alive, that she had both the ability and the responsibility to carry on.

Miriam examined the frozen image on the screen. It was winter in this video; they were both wearing sweaters, and Talia wore her jingle bell earrings. So long before the fight. Months before they died.

"Are you going to watch it?" Becky asked.

Swallowing, Miriam hit "Play."

"So if you're watching this, we're obviously at Interlochen." Talia's eyes danced. She and Blaise had been so excited about getting to spend six weeks at one of the world's preeminent music camps. They'd missed it by two months. "Blaise is probably hogging a piano someplace to avoid talking to anyone—"

Blaise shoved his shoulder into his sister's. "And Talia's flirting, I'm sure."

Talia laughed—the dusky, silvery laugh that delighted everyone who ever heard it. "I don't flirt."

"Do too."

"I just like people. Unlike *some* people I know."

Blaise looked straight at the camera, raising his eyebrows and dipping his chin with an eloquence that rendered words unnecessary. Miriam's heart skipped. Actually skipped. How long since it had done that?

"Anyway"—Talia elbowed him—"the *point* is, we know very well you guys are useless without us around. The last thing we need is you stalking us, showing up every weekend. Blaise and I have an assignment for you while we're gone."

"It's a road trip," Blaise said. "And don't try to weasel out of it by claiming you don't have the money. We're working our butts off to get scholarships, so pull out the tent and camp if you're that worried about it."

"And no using the 'work' excuse either." Talia pointed a finger at Miriam. "You said yourself, Mom: there are very few liturgical emergencies."

Miriam chuckled. She'd forgotten how alive these two made her feel. No, not forgotten, exactly, but the visceral reality of it was electrifying.

"So," Talia went on, "here's the deal. This is a special kind of road trip, and I'm warning you . . ." She leaned into the camera until only her eyes were visible. "It's gonna be a stretch for you, Mom." She retreated. "This is called a flip-a-coin vacation."

Blaise mimed holding a microphone to his mouth. "What's that mean, Miz Tedesco?" he asked in a game-show-host voice, and thrust the imaginary mic in front of her.

"I'm so glad you asked, Mr. Tedesco. It means at every stop you'll flip a coin and open the corresponding file, which will take you to a Google map leading to your next destination. Every file is locked until the one before it is opened. And once you open it, you can't go back, whether you like what you see or not!"

"Oh, lordy!" Becky laughed out loud. "She sure pegged you, didn't she?"

"Rules of the game, guys," Blaise said. "This is serious. Talia's been working for weeks to figure out that programming gem."

"Don't try to second-guess it," Talia said. "You can't predict it, so don't try. You're going all the way across the country, from coast to coast, and it's completely out of your hands. You're just along for the ride."

"But," Blaise said, "we promise the last stop will be someplace nice and romantic."

"Ugh, Blaise, seriously. Did you really need to say 'romantic'?"

Another shoulder shove. Miriam laughed even as she brushed at her eyes.

"You gotta give them some hope, or they won't go at all," Blaise told his sister.

Talia made a guttural noise of disgust. "Fine," she said. "We're going to find you the most beautiful beach on the West Coast. See? I'm not completely unreasonable."

"Darling girl," Becky told the screen, "you are a wonder."

Miriam put an arm around her friend and squeezed her thanks for expressing what she couldn't say herself.

"By the way. You have to do this, because I have plans for this baby. I'm going to sell it once you guys have tested it for me, and pay for my college tuition." Talia made a kissy face. "You're welcome. Now, get packed for your summer vacation, parental units. Over and out!"

The video ended with fanfare and the words slowly writing themselves across the screen: *Love, Talia and Blaise.*

Miriam sat on the edge of the bed, savoring the sensation for a long moment before recognizing it.

Joy. It was joy.

The time these kids had invested in this project! Miriam could see from the number of files—some of them recognizable formats, most of them not—the complexity of this undertaking. And all while they were practicing for the finals of their scholarship competition in San Francisco. The one they'd won just before departing the world forever.

"A flip-a-coin road trip," Becky said. "Genius."

What Talia might have accomplished if she'd lived. Miriam's joy was draining fast. Trying to hold onto it was like trying to hold the sea in a sand castle moat. Her gaze caught on something beyond the laptop, a family photo tucked into the corner of the dresser. It was taken after Talia subbed as principal cellist with the civic orchestra—a high honor for a sixteen-year-old. They'd gone out for ice cream afterward. Blaise and Talia had shot water at each other through their straws. She'd gotten so mad at them, especially when Teo joined in. *"It's like I have three children!"* she'd snapped.

"I never deserved them," she said softly.

Becky made a soft tutting sound. "Miriam, you know better than that. We all admired your family. Envied you, even."

Miriam looked around the shabby bedroom they could never afford to update. The idea of Becky, with her pristine house with gleaming stainless steel kitchen appliances and vaulted ceilings, envying her was laughable. Yet Miriam understood. Teo and the kids had a gift for happiness.

She knew she'd done right by her children. By scrimping and saving, she and Teo had given Blaise and Talia the opportunities they needed in order to find out who they were meant to be. Which was more than she'd had; her parents had tried so hard to discourage her from pursuing music, right up to the day Dad died. She'd promised herself she'd do things differently. She'd let her children find their passion and follow it. She could cling to that, at least.

But she'd always cherished a little regret for the life that could have been. How could Teo compete with that? Teo, who had always greeted her with a kiss and a hug, while she responded with a stream of logistics and scheduling conundrums. Teo, who'd come home every few days with some inexpensive token of affection. She'd never managed to offer him more than a semi-clean house and a good meal.

The truth was, she was a fraud. Talia had figured it out, in the last few months, when Miriam had begun to look forward to the day the kids left home, and had started dreaming again. Her whole life had been about her.

The edges of the room whispered silence to the shadows. Miriam longed to get away from it all—from the too-quiet house and the incomplete sonata languishing on the piano; from the need to hide from the world all the ways she'd failed her family.

But she didn't deserve a respite from this torture. She needed to stand face-to-face with the tempest and let it batter her until she felt *something* again. Something other than resentment and bitterness.

Suddenly, everything seemed crystal clear. "I'm going to do it," she said. She walked over to the closet and stood on her tiptoes. The house was so small, they'd had to store suitcases on Talia's top shelf. She pulled one down and threw it open on the bed, gathering up Talia's blouses and skirts and tossing them in helter-skelter.

Becky watched, frowning. "Do what? Get rid of it all?"

"Huh?"

Becky gestured at the clothes piling up in the suitcase.

"No," Miriam said. "I'm going on the road trip."

Becky grabbed her arm. "Honey, you're not thinking this through."

"I'm thinking just fine. I can find somebody to cover me for a weekend. I'll be gone, what, a week? Ten days?"

"A road trip across the US? You'll be lucky to be back in a month!"

"So what? I can't go on like this. You said it yourself."

"I did," Becky said slowly.

"Simeon told me to take all the time I needed." He hadn't meant an extended vacation, but she didn't really care. She'd been wearing the mantle of the grieving widow so long, it felt shellacked onto her spirit. She wanted it gone, and it never would be as long as she stayed here.

She would point herself toward the west and a beach her family had died trying to reach. And when she stood in that place they'd never gotten to see, she'd be able to look her ghosts in the eye and say that once, at least, she'd given Teo everything she had to give.

4

Thursday, April 28
7:50 AM

"**A**RE YOU ABSOLUTELY SURE about this?" asked Becky as she set the tent into the trunk of the Sonata.

At this point, Miriam didn't think it mattered if she was sure or not. They'd been up until midnight, taking care of details: calling Simeon to approve the time off, stopping the mail, finding subs to cover the next few weeks' music at St. Greg's. And of course, getting Talia's app loaded onto Miriam's phone. They'd had to call in John Merrick, who worked as an IT specialist. He'd figured out the transfer, but it had taken a while.

She was committed now. She flashed Becky a cocky grin. "Are *you* sure you want me taking your car?"

"That van of yours won't make it, and you know it." Becky sighed and shook her head. "Just call me, all right?"

"I will."

"And follow the speed limit."

Miriam chuckled and slid Talia's cello into the back seat of the Sonata beside Teo's beat-up guitar case.

Becky winced as it smacked the frame. "Why do you need the instruments, Miriam?"

"It just feels right." Miriam sucked in a deep, fragrant lungful of air. It was a perfect morning, the sky a flawless blue, the air vibrating. Every bird and bee in the greater

Atlanta area seemed frantic to make up for lost time. The sweetness of spring made poetry of every indrawn breath. This was going to work. She was going to California to lay down her guilt at the edge of the ocean.

"Miriam." Becky pulled her around and faced her. "I need you to be honest with yourself. Look at you. You've packed yourself a single suitcase full of your *daughter's clothes*." She fingered Miriam's—Talia's—white peasant blouse.

Miriam's shoulders tensed. She knew it looked weird, but deep down she also knew she wasn't brave enough for this monumental an undertaking. She was hoping wearing Talia's clothes would let her imbibe some of her daughter's fearlessness.

Of course, it wasn't working so far. One more gentle protest from Becky, and Miriam might just fold. But then again, she was still standing outside her own house. If she could just get on the road, momentum could carry her.

"I need this, Becky," she said softly.

Becky's nostrils flared; she sighed and nodded. "All right. But promise me you won't pretend to be someone you're not. It won't make the pain go away."

"I'll be fine." There was a nervous, flighty weightlessness to knowing she was leaving all responsibility behind for a couple of weeks, nothing ahead of her but an unknown adventure planned by the children she'd lost. Miriam swiped her phone and pulled up Talia's app.

Welcome to your #GreatAmericanAdventure! read the home screen. *Upload photo to begin.*

Screw that. Miriam swiped upward and found two icons: one of the profile of George Washington; the other, an eagle.

"Well, here goes nothing," she said. She pulled out one of the wheat pennies Blaise had collected over the years. It slid off her finger twice before she managed to flick it into the air. She didn't catch it so much as trap it against her white blouse, chasing it downward and around her back until she managed to stop its momentum. "Shut up," she said to Becky, who was trying not to smile, and smacked it on the back of her hand. "Heads," she said, and tapped the icon of George Washington.

A gif of a wagging finger popped up, and the screen reset to the words *Upload media.*

"Seriously?" she muttered.

Becky bit back a smile. "That girl was good."

Miriam scowled. "She knows I don't do selfies."

"Well, you're doing one now." Becky pulled the phone out of Miriam's hand and tapped on the camera icon.

Miriam put her head down.

In the photo, of course, Becky looked genteel and refined, not a single hair out of place. Miriam, as she'd intended, showed only the crown of her head. Was that a gray hair? Gah! As if she needed more reasons to loathe selfies.

She uploaded it. *Say something about this photo,* the screen prompted. She sighed.

Commencing Great American Adventure. Here's hoping my programmer knew what she was doing.

BTW I don't do selfies. Just sayin'.

The phone played a five-second snippet of "The Best I Ever Had," flashing *Congratulations! Your post has been sent! Time to flip a coin!*

Becky laughed and pulled out her own phone, her finger navigating busily. "It's connected to your Facebook account," she said. "And . . ." Another tap. "Yep, it's cross-posting to a dedicated Facebook page." She showed Miriam the phone, which boasted a header photo of mountains in the sunset, with the title *#Gr8AmAdven* below it. "I'll forward this around to the choir, now that we know you'll be forced to update regularly. That girl . . . amazing."

Miriam was a little impressed herself.

Becky embraced her briefly. "I feel better knowing she's going to force you to keep in touch. Explore that app so we can keep tabs on you."

"My dream come true." Miriam hesitated. "All right. I'll see you in a few weeks."

Becky exhaled, closing her eyes for a moment. Miriam was certain she felt the feather-light brush of a prayer skitter over her shoulder. "All right. You call me every day, you hear?"

"You already said that."

"I'm worried about you."

"I'll be fine." Miriam paused. "But thank you."

Miriam got in the car. She checked the mirrors, adjusting them to just the right angle, and paused at the sliver of her own reflection—the tip-top of a pasty, heart-shaped face surrounded by dishwater-blond hair and a pair of hazel eyes that showed just a bit more fear than she wanted to admit. An uncharted road, and no control at all: the story of her life.

She flared her nose and set her teeth, then tapped George Washington. "Okay, kids," she said. "Let's rock and roll."

Part 2

Green Bank, West Virginia

The regret of my life is that I have not said "I love you" often enough.

—Yoko Ono

Blaise's video intro to the Green Bank Telescope

Hey there, Mom and Dad. This first stop was my pick, so congrats on your good taste. Or luck. Y'know. Whatever.

    So, here's what you need to know: you're going to visit the world's . . . lemme see if I've got this right . . . the world's largest steerable radio telescope. Four hundred eighty-five feet high, in the middle of a valley in West Virginia, in a teeny little town called Green Bank. The dish is supposed to be so big it could hold two football fields, and they say it can measure the energy given off by a single snowflake hitting the ground. Cool, huh? But I gotta warn you, it's kinda in the middle of nowhere, so I hope you packed the tent because I doubt they have a Motel 6. Sayonara. Have fun.

◆ 5 ◆

Thursday, April 28
Rural West Virginia

Six hours into the Great American Adventure, Miriam had learned one thing and one thing only: she hated that damn headrest.

Up, down, lean the seat forward, lean the seat back, angle her body like the Leaning Tower of Pisa to avoid it altogether—nothing worked. It was made to coddle people with bad posture. By the time she left the interstate for the two-lane roads of West Virginia, she had a headache.

The scenery was fabulous, though. At the top of a mountain, she pulled off at an overlook to stretch, squat, and generally bring her butt back to life. The wind whispered in the pines. Before her, the ridges lined up, marching across the landscape in neat rows, each one bluer and hazier than the one in front of it.

Miriam massaged her neck and pulled out her phone to snap a picture, then uploaded it to the app. *Alleghenies,* she typed. *Like folds of cake batter. #Gr8AmAdven.*

The photo took forever to upload. At last, she got back on the road and pressed on with only the radio for company. If you could call it "company" when it kept dipping into bursts of static. Anyway, it kept her mind occupied. And right now, that was a very good thing. She could feel panic nosing around back there, looking for an entry point.

The next static break went on and on. Miriam's breaths shortened. The worst thing about anxiety was the way it made a person feel claustrophobic inside her own body.

She punched the Bluetooth. "Call work," she said, and the static flipped over to her cell connection.

"St. Gregory the Great, this is Becky. May I help you?"

"Becky, it's Miriam." Already the pressure behind her eyes had eased.

"Hi! How's it going? I saw your post. Pretty picture."

"Yeah, it's beautiful." Miriam glanced at the sunlight flashing between the trees—still mostly bare at this elevation—that crowded either side of the road. "Very remote too. I don't think I've passed more than a dozen cars since I got off the interstate."

"Aren't you glad I made you take my car now?"

Except for the headrest. "Yes, thank you." There, that was an appropriate response. She wasn't a complete sociopath. "So how are things at work?"

"Oh, the usual. Overflowing toilet. Complaints about Father's homily."

Miriam chuckled. "I won't miss that. Have fun."

Silence.

"Becky?"

Miriam picked up her phone and punched the screen. *Call failed.* She redialed before she saw the words *No signal* in the corner. Well, crap.

She dropped the phone, and the speakers reverted to the static on the radio dial.

She glanced at the string of beads hanging from the rearview mirror. She could always say a rosary, but she suspected the lulling rhythm of prayers would either put her to sleep or enable the panic. She needed distraction, not meditation.

She hit the "Scan" button on the radio. The screen flew through the numbers. When it rounded the dial and started over, Miriam grabbed the top CD on the stack she'd brought.

The static disappeared into the jaunty sound of Teo's favorite Argentine folk recording. Miriam's heart expanded and contracted at the same time, which mostly meant it hurt. So much in her life had become foreign territory since her family died, it seemed almost criminal to feel such a pang of loss for the Friday night jam sessions. Teo and his group of expat Argentine musicians had packed themselves onto the front porch till there was barely room to squeeze through. Women sat in fold-up chairs on the lawn, chatting while their kids ran around the yard with Popsicle-stained T-shirts. The folding table bowed in the middle with the weight of the potluck, and the smell of beer and liquor flavored the hot air.

Talia would squeeze in beside Teo on the porch swing and sing while he strummed. Blaise claimed a tenuous perch on the railing, where he'd use his thighs, or even the spindles, as drums.

Miriam spent those nights running in and out the door, ferrying ice and refilling glasses. Like her mother before her, she'd been driven to *do, do, do.* And yet while she was pretending to be the perfect hostess, the music had seeped into her bones.

"Come sit a spell, Sassafras," Teo used to say. Why had she never done it? It would have meant so much to him.

Miriam twisted the volume knob until the rhythmic melodic energy almost overwhelmed her. She'd never hear her GPS over it.

Come to think of it, the GPS hadn't spoken for quite a while. She glanced down. The satellite image had reverted to the green and tan of a traditional map. The dot indicating her location moved slowly along the blue line.

By the time Miriam drove into Green Bank—little more than a handful of buildings strung along the highway—she was famished. She pulled off at what looked like the only convenience store in town. On the curb in front sat a young biracial woman, her wiry hair corralled into dozens of short pigtails. She was flanked by a ridiculously large green backpack and a roll-around suitcase plastered with travel stickers. Waiting for a bus, maybe.

Miriam went inside and grabbed a prewrapped sandwich and a Pepsi. The clerk seemed too caught up in his conversation with another customer—a conversation about the state of one marriage or the other; Miriam couldn't tell whose—to notice that Miriam wanted to ask a question. So she went back outside.

"Excuse me," she said to the young woman with the suitcase.

The girl raised her head. Only then did Miriam notice the bump around her middle, big enough to force her knees apart. And the bleak expression in her dark eyes.

Miriam knew exactly how it felt at the intersection of those two particular qualities.

She locked her knees to keep from bolting. "Sorry to bother you, but they seemed kind of busy in there." Amazing. She sounded cool and calm and totally put together. "I'm trying to get to the telescope, but I lost my cell signal." She held up her phone and quirked a smile. "Guess I'll have to have a talk with my provider."

The girl's expression did not change. "Nobody has cell service here. This is the radio quiet zone."

"Oh." Miriam wondered what precisely a radio quiet zone was, but she didn't really want to extend the conversation. That lost look scared her. "Well," she said, gesturing with her phone, "Google doesn't seem to have lost me yet, at least."

The girl shook her head. "You better turn that off. It's illegal to use them here. It screws with the telescope signals. Anyway, you don't need it. The center's on up the road a couple miles. You can't miss it." She waved a hand.

"Okay. Thanks." Miriam hesitated, torn. Maybe she should offer the girl a ride. Buy her a bottle of water . . . well, not a bottle of water; the side pockets of the green backpack both had bottles sticking out the top already.

Maybe a snack. Or dinner. Or just ask if she needed help. That's what Teo would have done.

But Miriam couldn't even deal with her own problems, let alone take on anybody else's. "Well, have a nice day."

"Yeah, you too." If the girl noticed Miriam's happy-clappy tone, she didn't give any indication. She just hunched back over her knees again.

Miriam got back in the car. She gripped the steering wheel and closed her eyes for a moment, but she could feel Teo sitting like Jiminy Cricket on her shoulder as she pulled out.

She'd barely eaten half her sandwich before the trees gave way to a parking lot fronted by a big white sign proclaiming "Green Bank Observatory." After the long hours spent traversing undeveloped mountain country, the spreading concrete complex came as a bit of a shock. Miriam parked in front of the visitors' center and got out. A lifetime in Detroit, then Philly, and finally Atlanta had not prepared her for such quiet. The noise of her own chewing felt deafening. She'd never noticed that the background rumble of traffic and air conditioners and human noises exerted a pressure on the eardrums. Not until this moment, when the pressure vanished.

It was a bit unnerving.

She finished her sandwich and tossed back the Pepsi. Maybe if she ignored the shaky, weak feeling in her fingers, it would go away. She stuffed the trash into the holder in the bottom of the door and squared her shoulders. "Well, here goes nothing," Miriam said to the stillness, and headed inside.

★ ★ ★

"Sorry." The man at the front desk didn't look sorry so much as tired. "You just missed the last bus tour. If you want, you can walk out there yourself." He pulled a brochure from a stack and held it out. "Here's a map. There are several other telescopes along the way. But you'll need to turn off your cell phone past the gate. Totally off."

Miriam blinked. "Really? You can't even take a picture?"

"Not out by the telescope."

"But—" Miriam stopped; what could she say? *I have to have a photo before my dead daughter will tell me where to go next?*

He'd think she was crazy. And he might not be wrong.

"If you'd like, the gift shop sells disposable film cameras."

Miriam bit back a snarky response. It wasn't his fault, and anyway, she was supposed to be proving she was a functional human being, capable of empathy and appropriate social interaction.

Had the kids known about this? Probably not; otherwise, they'd have made note of it.

Unless it was Talia's idea of a joke.

Or punishment.

Miriam closed her eyes, willing away her paranoia. The road trip videos were recorded before the fight. Besides, this place was Blaise's pick, not Talia's.

"Ma'am? You all right?"

She opened her eyes. The man still held the map in his hand. She took it. "Fine, thanks."

Miriam bought a camera and went back to the car to stash her phone in the glove compartment. She grabbed the wide-brimmed straw hat sitting on the passenger seat and paused, fingering the white lining printed with bright flowers. A matching ribbon trailed from the brim. The last person to wear this hat was Talia. Could Miriam really just stick it on her own head, right after she'd practically accused her daughter of trying to punish her from the grave? She might as well invite a haunting.

Which she didn't believe in, anyway.

Don't be an idiot, Miriam. She was already wearing Talia's clothes; what difference could a hat make? Miriam shoved it onto her head and slammed the car door harder than necessary.

Miriam shared the walk out to the telescope with a number of people power walking or jogging. Every so often she passed smaller machines. None of them looked like she'd expected; she'd been picturing, well, telescopes. A domed building with a slide-open hatch. At the very least, something with a long tube and a viewfinder. Instead, they looked like big satellite dishes, bright white against the newly greened grass. One of them reminded her of a sousa-phone with a tube wrapped around it.

There was no mistaking the main attraction, though. The Green Bank Telescope towered over everything in sight, like something out of a James Bond movie—four hundred something feet high, hadn't Blaise's video said?— and a reflector dish wide enough to hold two football fields side by side. It rested on an enormous base of white cross-hatched metal webbing, with a matching arm stretching toward the sky. The telescope took up half her peripheral vision, its long shadow enveloping acres of grass and pine. Slanting sunbeams formed a cross behind the white scaf-folding. Miriam stopped a few feet shy of the tall chain link fence to snap a couple of photos with the disposable camera.

Check. *Now what?*

The wind whispered low in the pines. In the distance, a car hissed down the highway, its sound quickly swallowed by the stillness. The quiet expanded, hunkering down around her, as if it wanted the space she inhabited. She shiv-ered and pulled Talia's sweater closed across her chest. But that only pressed her locket hard against her skin. The cold burrowed inward, piercing her breastbone and clamping down on the hard, angry spot at her core.

Miriam's eyes were so dry they stung. Had she really driven nine hours to gawk at a telescope? To take a picture, throw it up on social media, and drive nine hours to the next place to do it all again? Weren't road trips supposed to be a symbol for a journey of the heart, or some such psychobabble?

Miriam clasped the chain link fence. The emptiness around her, the emptiness within, cried out to be filled, the way she'd filled the endless ticking seconds of the past year. Mom had been right about that, at least.

Of the days and weeks following her family's death, she remembered very little. She could rattle off everything they sang at the funeral, every well-meaning but insensitive comment. But the events themselves had vanished from her memory. For weeks, every waking moment had been devoted to the struggle to draw breath, and every sleeping one, to surviving the nightmares. It was like being pinned to a dartboard, never knowing when the next projectile would come squealing out of the mist.

And truthfully, there wasn't much of substance to remember. For years, her life had involved a planner tightly packed with school presentations and doctor visits, rehearsals and camps. With informational forms paper clipped onto certain weeks and lists tucked into the cover. Baking breads and meals and desserts, deep cleaning the house, learning accompaniments for solos, and drawing up music lists for church while waiting at cello or piano lessons. Bullying the twins—and sometimes Teo—into helping her grow and weed and harvest and can vegetables, the pressure cooker intensifying the heat of oppressive Georgia summers. Because with only one income, they needed to save every cent they could.

Madness—always madness—and then suddenly, nothing. No one to talk to, no one who needed her. Nothing to fill the emptiness, nothing to occupy her mind or her hands. Just never-ending nights, waiting for the sun to rise, and never-ending days, waiting for it to set again. Memories. Memories and self-recrimination.

Getting busy had changed all that. And one morning, when the maple tree outside her window was just beginning to blush, and school-bus brakes were shrieking along the residential streets, Miriam woke to the realization that she'd slept through the night. A few days later, she'd smiled at a video on Facebook. And she'd thought, *I might actually survive this.*

For the first time, Miriam recognized the magnitude of what she'd done at the funeral yesterday. The congressman's widow had only just set sail into the maelstrom of that vast, crushing emptiness when Miriam callously exercised her own musical wit at the expense of the deceased—and those who loved him.

When had she become capable of such willful, self-indulgent cruelty?

The breeze settled into stillness. Such a vast, quiet emptiness. She dropped her forehead onto the diamond-hatched fence. Once, she'd been pliable—able to roll with the punches, however inexpertly. Music had helped her connect with the divine, and through it, with others. When even music failed to move her, what hope did she have?

A cow mooed, the sound muted by distance and echoing faintly off the telescope. If she sang out here, amid this great emptiness, would the silence swallow her voice, or would it, too, echo off that vast white dish and reverberate in her own heart?

The cool breeze sighed through the pines, causing her gauzy skirt and the ribbon trailing from her hat to flutter. Like the little thing with feathers, perched on her soul and just now pulling its head from beneath its wing.

Miriam glanced behind her. The road stood empty. She faced the telescope, raised herself into proper singing posture, and let the air vibrate her vocal cords.

For the beauty of the earth, for the glory of the skies,
For the love which from our birth over and around us lies . . .

It was one of Blaise's favorite hymns. But in this great, vast emptiness, her voice sounded small. Hesitant. She put a little more muscle behind the sound.

For the joy of human love, Brother, sister, parent,
child—

Her voice cracked. Silence swallowed the sound as if
it had never been. Miriam wove her fingers into the fence
again and bowed her head. "Please," she whispered. It was
the best she could come up with.

Silence. What had she expected? A cosmic event? An
angelic visitation? Communing with landmarks couldn't fix
what was wrong with her.

The little bird in her soul dove for cover. Miriam shoved
backward and shook her fist at the telescope. "You're just a
stupid inanimate object! What the hell am I doing singing
to you, anyway?"

Her words bounced off the dish, like a mischievous
sprite poking fun at her temper tantrum, and disappeared
into the great emptiness.

And then, with a hum of electricity and the whirring
of motors, the white behemoth beyond the fence began to
move.

♦ 6 ♦

M IRIAM TOOK TWO STEPS back before her intellect caught up. The telescope couldn't hear her; it was just responding to instructions from its command center. The wheels beneath the superstructure rolled slowly counterclockwise, and the massive reflection panel tilted its head back, half a degree at a time. Miriam stared, awestruck by the sheer power required to change the trajectory of such an enormous object.

The sound of a diesel engine crescendoed, replacing the noise of the motors. Miriam turned to see an old white pickup turning in at the gate. The driver killed the engine and got out. "Afternoon, ma'am."

Miriam forced her hunched shoulders down. "Am I . . .?"

"You're just fine, ma'am. I'm coming out to do some maintenance." He gestured to the camera in her hand. "You want me to take a picture for you?"

"Oh . . . that's all right. I don't really like pictures of myself."

"Aw, come on. Come on. Surely you want some proof you were here." He wiggled his fingers.

Miriam shrugged and handed it over. "I don't know where to develop it. I can't even get a cell signal to look it up."

"Walgreen's." Then he scowled. "You don't have a phone out here, do you?"

She tensed again. "I left it in the car, I swear."

He relaxed. "Sorry, ma'am. Some people think the law don't apply to them. We're always having to drive around and figure out where the interference is coming from. The telescope picks it all up, you know. Wi-Fi, microwave . . . seems like everything puts out radio signals these days. And this monster"—he gestured beyond the fence with an affectionate smile—"measures radio waves from space. Very, very faint ones."

"Like really distant stars?"

"More like the gas and dust clouds between them." He cocked an eyebrow. "Didn't you look around the visitor's center?"

"No, I missed the last tour. The guy gave me a map to walk out here on my own."

"So . . ." The man dragged the word out, his lips twitching as he ticked the points off on his fingers. "You didn't check the schedule before coming; you didn't know this was a cell-free zone; and you weren't even interested enough in astronomy to poke around the visitors' center before coming out. Which begs the question: Why *are* you here?"

Miriam managed a crooked smile. "You wouldn't believe me if I told you."

His eyebrows skyrocketed. "Try me."

All right, then. "My kids sent me on a flip-a-coin road trip across the country. This is the first stop."

"No kidding!"

Not the reaction she'd expected. Although what she *had* expected, she couldn't say.

"Well, if that don't beat all." He raised the camera to his eye. "We do have pay phones, so you can use a card to call them. Let them know you haven't fallen into some man trap in backwater West Virginia."

She didn't have to tell him. A simple thank-you would suffice. But something inside her craved hearing the truth

aloud, here in the shadow of this great white monster Blaise
had wanted her to see. "Actually, they passed away."

He lowered the camera again. Now he'd get all weird
and figure out some awkward way to extricate himself from
the conversation. Loss seemed to turn a person into an
allergen.

But to Miriam's surprise, he stepped toward her instead
of away. "I'm so sorry," he said, touching her elbow. Just
like she would have once done when a family came to plan
a funeral. "I lost my wife three years ago. I know you probably hate for people to say they understand, but . . . I understand. And I'm sorry."

"I'm sorry too." Damn it, this trip was supposed to be
about *her*. Her family, her demons, her chance to grieve—
alone. She hadn't come out here to sympathize with a ran-
dom stranger's personal tragedy.

But she'd lived long enough in Georgia to know the
demands of Southern hospitality. "How did she die?"

"Cancer. Long, drawn out. Horrible. With just enough
hope to keep you from letting go. You know?"

No, she didn't know. She hadn't had the luxury. Only a
knife to the gut, and the long, slow bleed ever since.

The technician went on. "I always pictured the two of
us at eighty years old, sitting in rocking chairs on a porch,
holding hands. And instead, . . . you know, by the time it
was over, I wouldn't have recognized her as the woman I
married." He turned the green camera over and over in
his hands. "But I'm grateful for that time too. In those last
few months, I was able to love her in a way I'd never imagined was possible. It was intense. I thought sometimes it was
going to about kill *me*. It was a long, hard goodbye, but it
was a gift too."

Miriam tried to imagine sitting by Teo's deathbed. Or,
for that matter, sitting in twin rockers, holding hands. She
couldn't do it. She'd never been able to sit still for long. She
wanted to be doing—making lists and checking things off
them. Just like her mother.

"Come sit, Sassafras. The work will wait."

Of course, the work could have waited. It was just dishes and balancing checkbooks and cleaning the bathroom . . . and fixing the toilet. It all would have waited. But it hadn't felt that way all those times when Teo stretched out a hand and asked her to come cuddle on the couch. How many times had she turned her back on him and resented the hell out of him the rest of the night? Resented them all, actually, for watching reruns of *Knight Rider* when they'd all seen the to-do list stuck to the refrigerator.

Was this how Mom had felt, all those years: drowning under the weight of too much to do and too many unfulfilled dreams? Had Dad ever asked her to stop and just spend time with him?

Maybe it was better that Teo was gone. Otherwise, there might have come a day when, like Miriam's parents, she and Teo started throwing around the word *divorce*—a word that could never be taken back. Even if, in the end, like her parents, they stuck it out.

The technician stood silently, his gaze fixed on something only he could see. She ought to reach out—offer a warm hand clasp or a gentle hand on his shoulder. One thing she'd learned from doing pastoral work: for life's toughest moments, words were useless. But here, on the far side of her own loss, helplessness walked in lockstep with her stifled, guilt-ridden grief.

The technician shook himself back to reality. "What am I doing, standing here all afternoon? Here, let's take your picture."

He snapped the photo, handed the camera back, and walked toward the gate, whistling and jingling his keys. Miriam headed back the way she'd come, turning to walk backward for a few steps, staring up at the first landmark of her journey.

Maybe her life wasn't so different from this telescope: ponderously heavy, fixed on a given point in time and space. Maybe it took something massive and powerful to shift the trajectory of her life too. Something like a flip-a-coin road trip.

As frightening as this vast emptiness felt, it belonged to her alone. Out here, she had a chance to discover what she needed, with no one else offering opinions on whether it was right or wrong. To dig deep for the strength to become whole again.

Her hand crept to her locket. She traced the engravings on the antique silver and fingered the latch. It would be so easy to give up and go back home to the comfortable misery of the familiar. But the wind in the pine trees seemed to whisper, *"Be bold, Sassafras."*

Letting the locket fall, Miriam squared her shoulders and strode back along the road toward the highway.

✦ 7 ✦

April, one year earlier
Atlanta, Georgia

ON THE LAST DAY Miriam ever spent with Teo, he brought her flowers.

She hadn't slept well the night before. Not with Talia's words rattling in her brain: *"Are you cheating on Dad?"*

It wasn't the accusation; Miriam knew her own innocence. It was the fact that Talia even thought it possible.

Teo, of course, had slept fine. Teenage drama always slid off his back; he'd been singing Argentine folk songs all morning. They'd set aside this day for home improvements: touching up the paint on the wraparound porch, nailing down a board that had sprung free over the winter, and installing landscaping stones.

It was a lot to accomplish before Teo and the kids caught a late-afternoon flight to San Francisco. Tomorrow the twins would rehearse with their competition accompanists, and on Sunday they would compete for ten-thousand-dollar scholarships—the final round of a competition they'd been working their way through all school year.

Miriam had her own list of things to do. Practicing the concerto she was to perform with the local symphony this weekend, for starters. Double-checking the kids' suitcases, to make sure they hadn't forgotten anything. And squeezing in as much of the camping gear as possible, so that when she joined them on Monday for their low-budget vacation, they wouldn't have to rent too much equipment.

When she got inside, she found the breakfast dishes piled haphazardly by the sink. "Teenagers," Miriam muttered. She opened the dishwasher only to discover it hadn't been emptied. She washed her hands and started putting plates in the cabinet.

She felt Teo's presence behind her before he touched her—the warmth, the smell of dirt and sweat. He pressed his body into her back and put his arms around her. "Hey, beautiful."

"Stop it, Teo. I'm gross. And you're dropping dirt clods all over the floor."

"I'll clean it up." He lifted her ponytail and kissed the juncture of her neck and shoulder. "Come on, Mira. How often do we get a day off work together without the kids around?"

Her body wanted to respond, but she really wasn't in the mood. Even so, her lips curved upward. "It's the wrong time of the month for that, unless you want another kid."

He chuckled. "I know. Doesn't mean we can't have a little fun." His hands went exploring, and Miriam's knees went weak.

She maneuvered her shoulder up and shoved him away. "Cut it out, Teo. I still have work to do. And so do you."

But she couldn't mask her smile, and as he retreated, she heard him chuckling. Miriam wanted to be annoyed, but it seemed stupid to cling to negativity if she had the choice.

When Teo came home a couple hours later, after picking up Talia and Blaise, he brought with him a bunch of wildflowers he'd picked from the ditch in front of the school. He presented them to Miriam, wrapped gently in his coat, like Juan Diego before the bishop.

It wasn't eagerness Miriam saw in his eyes—they were far beyond that; he no longer expected her to respond like a woman being wooed. It was simply devotion, devoid of expectation.

And as she'd stood there, her lips forming a tolerant query about how many bugs he'd just brought into the house, she caught Talia's eye. Her daughter stood at the sink, running a glass of water and glaring at her. The air between them thrummed with the previous night's parting shot. *"You can't fight with someone who has no heart."*

Talia was right. The thought came like a sucker punch to the gut. Miriam had fallen into a pattern of negativity, and no matter what Teo did, he couldn't break it.

But there was barely time to have the thought, let alone ponder it.

"Talia, you left your backpack on the piano bench again!" Blaise called from the front room, and Talia dropped her cup in the sink and tore from the room, screaming: "Don't you dare throw it on the floor—it has my iPad in it!" Followed soon thereafter by "Where's my charger?" and "Who took my purse! I need my license for airport security!" And then even Blaise was showing his nerves, his normally placid demeanor dissolving into a cutting remark that caused his sister to burst into tears. Miriam snapped at her son, and he flung himself onto the piano bench and launched into Beethoven's *Tempest* sonata with the fury only a persecuted seventeen-year-old could summon.

And then Talia was dragging *her* to the piano for one last run-through of Grieg, and snapping at her about tempos. "I'm doing that on purpose," Miriam said. "You don't know what your competition accompanist might do. You have to be ready." Talia mumbled something Miriam chose not to hear. And Teo was shoving microwaved burritos at them and interrupting half a dozen times to ask about things she'd packed hours ago.

By the time Teo got the suitcases and the music satchels and Talia's computer bag and the cello loaded in the van, Miriam was ready to wash her hands of them. Let Teo deal with the teenage hormones for a couple of days.

"Let's go! We've got a flight to catch!" he bellowed from the doorway, and a minor stampede ensued.

Miriam walked them to the security gate at the airport. Blaise went first, his flighty kiss burning her cheek. Talia rushed past with barely a glance, only to be stopped by Teo. "Hey," he said. "What do you think you're doing, leaving without giving your mother a kiss?"

Talia's eyes flashed, but she never argued with Teo. She turned back and gave Miriam the most thin-lipped, least satisfying peck on the cheek ever.

Teo sighed as Talia glided forward, nose in the air, all poise and grace, and handed her boarding pass and driver's license to the TSA agent. "I'm sorry, Mira," he said. "It's just nerves. It'll be better after the competition."

It wasn't, and it wouldn't, and they both knew it. She summoned a wan smile. "Have fun."

"We'll miss you, but it'll be good for you to have this time to yourself. Good luck with the concerto. I know you'll do great."

"Thanks."

"I love you." He kissed her, shouldered his duffel bag, and headed into the line himself. He caught up with Blaise and said something to him. Blaise turned back and cupped his hands around his mouth. "Play pretty!" he called, echoing the words Miriam had said to them before every one of their performances. "We'll see you on Monday!"

When Miriam got home, an hour later, the flowers were still waiting, spread on Teo's jacket on the old, metal-legged kitchen table, a relic of the 1970s. Tiny blue irises and a pale yellow bulb-shaped flower, violets and something feathery white whose name she didn't know. They'd already started to wilt. She fingered the stems as she put them in water. She should have done this before they left for the airport. Teo probably thought she didn't like them. Like all her responses to him, this one had been half-assed.

I need to do better by him. The thought had the familiarity of knowledge that had lain dormant for months—years, perhaps, waiting for her to take notice. It was time. Past time. Once her performance was out of the way—on

Monday, when she flew out to join them in California—she would turn over a new leaf.

Two days later, when she saw Simeon get out of the police car in front of the house, she didn't at first connect what it must mean.

Unlike the weeks that followed, almost everything about that moment remained crystal clear in Miriam's memory. The unusually cool April day. The boards from the porch swing striping her jeans. The warm fatigue in her fingers following an hour of practicing. The cardinal that cut a slash of crimson across her vision as Father Simeon and the policeman came up the walkway, stirring up the pungent smell of the chocolate mint growing on either side. The car that backfired on the next street, and farther away the high whine of a circular saw punctuated by hammer blows. The way the setting sun gleamed on Simeon's bald black head as he sat down beside her.

She remembered it all except the words. The words were gone long before their meaning sank in. The look on Simeon's face told her everything that really mattered, anyway.

She had waited too long to love Teo, and now it was too late.

♦ 8 ♦

Friday, April 29
Green Bank, West Virginia

BY MORNING, MIRIAM WASN'T feeling bold so much as battered. Spring came late to the mountains; when she finally got settled in her tent with an arrangement of blankets and a sleeping bag that kept her warm enough to drop off, the parade of memories started up, yanking her back from the edge of consciousness, with her heart pounding.

It had been quite a while since she'd experienced a night like this. Right after the accident, it had happened regularly: she'd lie awake, playing God, trying to rearrange the sequence of events of the last few days before her family died, to see if she could change the outcome. If she'd been with them on the trip; if she'd gotten them moving sooner, so they were already on the beach before the man, drunk from a business lunch, crossed the center line as they drove down the highway toward it. If she'd said no to the concerto performance. If she'd never tried to start a performance career at all.

It always seemed like she had to go further back, further and further into the past. Back to the beginning, even, to college and choices she'd never realized could have such earth-shattering consequences.

Tonight, the exercise in futility did a tarantella in her brain opposite Teo's invitations and Talia's accusations.

And always, the niggling thought of the e-mail tucked into Blaise's manuscript notebook. Out of sight, but not out of mind, like a scratchy clothing tag that kept rubbing: half itch, half pain, all aggravation.

And then, just for fun, a gut-hollowing tune—more motif than melody, really—emerged from the darkness, sinuous and haunting. She couldn't identify it, no matter how many times she hummed it through, trying to wrap it around to its beginning. Two measures, circling in her head all night long. It was the earworm from hell.

The sun hadn't yet risen when Miriam decided enough was enough. She gathered her toiletries and headed for the campground shower house.

The water stayed stubbornly tepid. Shivering, Miriam showered in record time and slipped into a pair of Talia's leggings and a tan, cable-knit sweater with lace sewed to the bottom. She liked the look, but the longer she wore these clothes, the harder it became to shake off her daughter's ghost.

Miriam hadn't thought about that when she'd packed the suitcase full of them.

Or maybe, somewhere in her subconscious mind, she'd planned it this way.

She wiped down the tent with her towel, the locket like a drumbeat against her chest. She couldn't wait to rejoin a world that had Wi-Fi and cell signal and plenty of distraction.

Shortly after eight, she pulled out and headed back south, retracing yesterday's route. She couldn't handle the energy of the Argentine music this morning. Until she got back within range of an NPR station, which could occupy her brain with discussions of other people's problems, her own memories would have to do. Mom wasn't here to scold her for wallowing, after all. Besides, she'd spent all night self-flagellating. There were no memories left except good ones.

There was Talia, six years old, presiding over a birthday tea party at the kitchen table. Miriam had filched the gauzy royal purple drapings they used for Advent decoration at St. Greg's and camouflaged the cracked, dingy walls. Everything was purple that year, from the girls' pipe-cleaner crowns to the cupcakes. She remembered feeling like a real grown-up, doing a lot with very little, like her mother before her.

There was the impossible softness of Blaise's cheeks, the little-boy kisses she mourned to this day. The evening she kissed him good night and realized his cheek was stubbly. And the day he folded himself into the space between the top step of the kitchen stool and the carrying handle. He was all arms and legs, still skinny enough, but too tall to really fit. It must have been so uncomfortable, yet he sat there for fifteen minutes while she cooked dinner, because he needed to talk through a situation at school.

Memories took no time at all; Miriam was only a couple miles south of town when the sight of a bestickered suitcase and green backpack recalled her to the present. It took a moment to realize why it looked familiar. Then she remembered the pregnant girl who'd been sitting outside the quick stop yesterday. The one she'd thought was waiting for a bus.

Clearly, she hadn't found one. And now she was walking. *Walking* through the back country of back countries. Hadn't this girl ever seen *Deliverance*?

More to the point, where had she slept?

Teo would already have hit the brake. *"Come on, Mira. Shelter the traveler, right?"* He'd elbow her, give her his big, goofy grin, making a joke out of the works of mercy to deflect attention from how effortless he made them look.

She couldn't just drive past. She knew too well how it felt to be pregnant and alone.

Miriam stopped in the middle of the deserted highway. The girl was a quarter mile behind her already. She muscled the car into reverse and let her foot off the clutch, promptly killing the engine. Good thing Becky wasn't here to see Miriam abusing her car.

By the time she made it back to the hitchhiker, the girl had her wary face on. "I'm fine, thanks," she said before Miriam even opened her mouth.

Miriam put the car in first to coast alongside. At least, that was the idea. A standard transmission in first gear wasn't built for rolling; the car moved in fits and starts. "Running away from home?" she ventured.

The girl didn't stop walking, but she did shoot Miriam a withering look. "Please. I'm twenty-two. I'm not running away from anyone."

Well, maybe that hadn't been the best approach. But Miriam knew desperation when she saw it. The girl was definitely running from *something*. Miriam studied her a moment. She was lovely, with that tawny beige skin and her myriad short, puffy ponytails. It was like looking at Talia, only a year or two older and biracial. "Please let me give you a ride," she said.

"I don't need help."

Miriam sighed as the girl walked on. Teo would have already coaxed her whole history out of her. He'd always been better at that sort of thing.

Wait a minute. Was that leaf debris stuck to the girl's jacket? And her socks? And her hair?

Miriam had the engine off and the door open before she realized she'd decided to act. "Did you sleep in the woods?"

The girl whirled. "Who the hell are you?"

Miriam stopped, raising her hands in a nonthreatening gesture. "I'm not following you! It's just, you're covered in leaves. And you're . . . you're pregnant."

"Really?" The girl released her suitcase to flutter her hand over her heart. "Is *that* what all that kicking around in there is? Good thing somebody finally explained it to me!"

Miriam eyed the bump in the girl's midsection. Six months, maybe? What on earth could have made this self-possessed, self-reliant young woman desperate enough to sleep in the woods?

Whatever it was, she clearly had no intention of letting herself be cowed. Miriam liked her already.

Even if she was stubborn to the point of cussedness, she thought as the girl started walking again. The psychedelic suitcase bumped awkwardly along the uneven shoulder.

Miriam hurried forward. "Look," she said. "I'm not a psycho. I'm a church music director and a—"

The reality of her loss crashed down again. A child who lost its parents had a name: orphan. But what did you call a woman who had lost her entire family? She'd lost even her identity. "Well, I *used* to be a mother," she said quietly.

A look Miriam couldn't decipher flitted across the girl's face. Finally, she'd made an impression.

Miriam rallied. "Look, it's sixty miles before you're going to hit an interstate, let alone a town where you can get a hotel room or a reasonable bite to eat. Think about your baby. Let me give you a ride."

The girl stared her down. Then something seemed to give way. For a fleeting moment, Miriam saw again the lost look that had tugged at her heart yesterday. Then it disappeared into a casual shrug. "Fine, whatever."

It took a little rearranging to make room for the huge suitcase in the trunk. The backpack the girl kept in the front seat, her arms wrapped around it. She wore a bright blue metal bracelet on her wrist. It had writing on it, but Miriam couldn't see it well enough to read it. As the Hyundai started moving again, the girl glanced around the car. "That's a guitar, right?"

"Mm-hmm."

"What's the other thing?"

"A cello."

A beat, while the girl waited for an explanation Miriam had no intention of giving. Then: "Okay," she said.

Now it was Miriam's turn to make conversation. "So where are you headed?"

"Charleston."

"South Carolina?"

"West Virginia."

West. Not south. Miriam hadn't realized she'd been hoping for an excuse to turn around. "Is Charleston home?"

"No, it's the nearest bus station."

"Oh."

"What about you? Where are you headed?"

"Who knows?"

The girl gave her a quizzical look.

Miriam shifted through the gears and settled into sixth. She cleared her throat. "My kids wanted me to see this part of the country."

"Your kids are . . .?" Clearly, the girl didn't want to be the one to say it.

"They died."

"How?"

"A car accident." Miriam had no intention of going into further detail. "They wanted me to take a trip across the country. A flip-a-coin road trip with a bunch of stops along the way."

The girl sucked in a gasp that unceremoniously launched a coughing fit. A bad one. Miriam was starting to worry by the time it finally settled. The girl pulled an enormous water bottle from her backpack and took a swig of water from it. "Sorry," she said. "I'm Dicey, by the way."

"Miriam. Miriam Tedesco."

"Nice to meet you. And . . . thanks for the ride."

"You're welcome." She bit her lip as Dicey coughed again—a hard, forceful cough—but only one.

The engine revved as they started gaining elevation. The silence stretched on for a bit. "So," Miriam ventured, "how far along are you?"

"Thirty-two weeks."

Miriam frowned and sized her up again. "Really? Wow. You're so tiny! I was a whale at thirty-two weeks. Then again"—she sighed—"I was carrying twins."

Dicey shuddered. "I can't imagine. My hips hurt all the time."

"Ligaments loosening up, getting ready for labor."

"Don't remind me."

Miriam would have liked to inquire further, but they'd only just met. How would Teo have done it? She racked her brain, but before she came up with anything, Dicey spoke again.

"I'm sorry you lost your kids." Dicey traced the outline of the air-conditioning vent. "But your road trip sounds cool." She cocked her head as if thinking. "How many stops have you done?"

"Just the one." Miriam shrugged. "It was kind of a bust. I missed the tours. I just went out and sang to the telescope."

"You sang to the telescope, and you call it a *bust*? Did you get a video? Oh, wait, I guess you couldn't."

"Right. No phones allowed."

"Too bad. That would've been awesome!"

Once again, Miriam was reminded of Talia. She smiled. "I'm glad you approve."

Dicey coughed again. "So, Tedesco," she said. "What is that, Italian?"

"Argentine-Italian. I'm impressed. Most people don't guess Italian."

"I like names," said Dicey. "Interesting names especially. Figuring out what they mean, where they come from. Names should mean something."

"Interesting hobby."

"Probably comes from having a name as boring as Smith."

"Smith has a meaning."

"Yeah, yeah, blacksmith, I know. But you have a pretty badass name."

"Um, thanks?"

"Oh, come on. A church choir director oughtta know who Miriam was. Baby in the river, fooling a princess into letting his own mom raise him, singing by the Red Sea?"

Miriam laughed, and for one blessed moment the tightness in her chest eased. "All right, all right. Yes, I know who Miriam was. Did you know Miriam is the Hebrew form of 'Mary'? Even *the* Mary might have gone by Miriam."

A glance showed Dicey scowling, but it was a half-hearted one. "You're stealing my thunder."

Miriam laughed again. "So what about Dicey? That's the most not-boring name I think I've ever heard."

"It was a nickname for Laodicea Langston. She was from South Carolina, and she spied for the Patriots during the Revolution."

"No kidding? So is your name Laodicea?"

"No, just Dicey." Dicey expelled a breath, leaning back against her headrest. Apparently it didn't bother her the way it bothered Miriam. "So sleepy. It wasn't a very good night."

Miriam had intended to ask about baby names, but now she detoured. "I can imagine. I don't understand how you didn't get hypothermia."

"Found a bunch of dry leaves to burrow down under. Blanket on top. But it was still cold."

The warmth of the rising sun dropped in a line across Miriam's forearm. The quiet seemed companionable. Dicey stuffed her backpack between her shoulder and her head and rested against the window. A mile unfolded. Two. Then, into the silence, she said, "You're still a mom, you know."

Miriam looked over. "What?"

The girl's eyes remained closed; her words were soft, but they carried in the quiet. "You said you used to be a mother. But you'll always be a mom. Even after *you're* dead."

Miriam's breath caught. Her vision blurred. She ran a finger over the puffy skin below her left eye. It came away wet. Just one tear—but a tear. How long had it been since she'd cried?

She looked over at the girl in the passenger seat, but Dicey's chest rose and fell in a slow, even rhythm. Miriam faced forward again.

The miles unfolded in silence.

WHEN HER PHONE FINALLY dinged, Miriam almost ran off the road. It hadn't made a sound in eighteen hours; she'd readjusted to life off the grid.

The sound effects tripped over each other in their haste to alert her to everything she'd missed: *ding-ding-bloopety-bloopety-ding-ding.*

Dicey's phone buzzed too; she jerked upright with an audible gasp, blinking at the rock-and-tree-covered slope outside her window. "Crap, that scared me."

The sound effects continued. Miriam pulled onto the shoulder across from a wide field tucked into the valley. She turned the engine off and rolled down the windows. The mountain breeze carried the cool scent of pine and the same quiet that had unnerved her at the telescope yesterday. But at least this time she had something to occupy her.

"All right," she said, "time to play catch-up."

"Uh-huh." Dicey unzipped her backpack and pulled out a can of Pringles and a bottle of water and started crunching as she navigated her phone. Miriam swallowed a bit of envy. If she ate that much fat and salt, she'd gain a pound a day.

Miriam turned her attention to her own device. Nine texts, six missed calls, and a handful of voicemails.

"Why haven't you called me? I specifically said call me every day!" Becky sighed. "Call me when you get this."

Delete. Next message.

"Miriam! Where! Are! You! You're scaring me!"

"Seriously, Becky," she muttered. "Chill."

"Mira, it's Mom. What's this about a road trip? I thought you were going to get serious about finishing Blaise's sonata. Please call me. I haven't talked to you in weeks, and I can't help thinking you're avoiding—"

Miriam felt slightly guilty deleting this voicemail. She'd e-mailed Mom instead of calling to tell her about the trip because, she'd told herself, it was too late at night. And because she knew Mom would bring up Blaise's sonata. Mom's enthusiasm on that subject seemed singularly unfair when her parents had worked so hard to discourage Miriam's own musical ambition.

But none of that was the real reason.

The last voicemail was from her brother. "Mira, it's Brad." He sounded tired. Probably Mom or Jo had awakened him while he was recovering from a brutal day in the world of Hollywood face-lifts and breast implants. "What's going on? Jo called, but I really didn't follow it . . . something about a road trip?" He sighed. "Anyway, Mom's a wreck, and Jo thinks you're mad at her about the Easter thing. Can you just call one of them so they'll leave me alone?"

Miriam growled; Dicey glanced up from her phone. "Everything okay?"

"Do you have siblings?"

"Four brothers."

"Whoa." Miriam regarded her with new respect. "Are they always in your business?"

Dicey raised her eyebrows. "Well, duh." Her lips quirked. "You?"

"One of each. I guess my mom's freaking out about this trip. Apparently she and my sister elected my brother to reel me back in."

"Let me guess. You're the youngest."

"Yeah . . . why?"

The girl pointed at her own chest and then spread her hands with a wry smile.

Miriam looked back at her phone, but she couldn't concentrate. Mom was right: embarking on this road trip did feel like abandoning her commitment to Blaise.

"No heart," Talia's voice whispered.

Miriam shuddered. If she'd loved her family better—loved them so they were in no doubt of it—surely Talia could never have entertained such a thought. But Teo and the kids were all demonstrative in their love, while Miriam—well, Miriam was her parents' child.

And that was the real reason she'd avoided calling her mom. The reason she'd been dodging her mother's calls for months. Ever since Miriam's subconscious started dredging up Talia's accusations and Teo's pleas for time and attention, she'd been seeing more clearly the parallels between her own marriage and her parents'.

For years, she'd buried the question now bubbling up, but it felt too important to ignore any longer.

Why *hadn't* Mom and Dad ever gotten divorced?

Had they decided it was too much hassle? That it wasn't worth becoming the talk of the church? Of course, once Dad got sick, it was a moot point. What kind of person would leave a dying man?

For several long moments, Miriam stared at the "Call" button beneath her mother's name. But she couldn't imagine having that conversation in front of Dicey.

Cursing her cowardice, she navigated to her text messages. There were five from Becky and a handful from other choir members, at least two of which seemed to include the words *Ella Emil*. One from Father Simeon, short and sweet: *God go with you.* What a good guy.

And of course, one from Josephine. It started with the un-word *Srsly?* Miriam flipped over to e-mail, where her social tab was filled with notifications about friends and choir members who'd mentioned her in their comments. "Well, at least I know the app works," she murmured.

"What app?" Dicey didn't look up from her own screen.

"Talia's app."

"Who's Talia?"

"My daughter. She wrote the road trip app."

Dicey looked at her then, her hands frozen. "Hang on. Your daughter wrote an app? For this road trip?"

"Yeah. Why?"

"Can I see?"

"Sure." Miriam returned to her home screen and tapped the nondescript green icon. *Welcome to your Great American Road Trip!* it read. *Upload photo/video to unlock your next destination.* She turned the phone toward the younger woman.

Dicey's lips parted. "Whoa. This connects to social media?"

"Uh-huh."

Dicey reached for Miriam's phone, then paused. "You mind?"

"Go ahead."

Miriam watched, bemused, as Dicey punched and swiped. "Look," said the younger woman. "Up here, she has access to all the accounts, so if you want to post on one of them individually, it'll take you straight there. Which means, I guess, if you post in the main tab—here—it goes everywhere. Where's the list of . . . oh, there it is!" She was working on both phones now, pulling up apps and typing so fast, Miriam couldn't keep up. "I'm following you, in case you're wondering," Dicey said. "That's the worst selfie ever. No one would even recognize you."

"Good."

"This trip was seriously cool—and that was before I knew about *this*! I can't believe you didn't mention it in the first place." Dicey handed Miriam's phone back, but her thumbs continued to move busily. "So who's this Ella Emil person?"

Miriam froze. Then she went back to her texts.

Josephine's read, *Srsly? I have 2 find out from Facebook?* Miriam tapped on the pasted link and found herself looking at Ella's blog, *Atlanta Attaché.* The headline read: *A year after her family's death, Atlanta widow sets off on cross-country pilgrimage planned by her dead daughter.* "Shit," she said.

Dicey's eyebrows skyrocketed. "Such language from a church choir director!"

Miriam gave Dicey her best "Mom Look" and then shook her head. "I can't do this trip with Ella Evil staring at my backside."

Dicey snorted. "Ella Evil?"

Miriam threw her phone in the center cupholder and turned the car back on, easing out onto the road. "She's a glorified gossip columnist in Atlanta. She did a write-up after Teo and the kids died."

Dicey flipped her phone end over end as the car got back up to highway speed. "That sucks," she said. She tipped her chin upward and stared at the passing scenery for half a mile before continuing. "Still . . . this isn't about her, right? It's about your family."

Miriam shuddered. She pulled off again, resting her forehead on the steering wheel. She wasn't working very hard to prove she loved her family if one post from Ella Evil could make her turn tail and run. "All right," she said. "All right."

She picked up her phone again and sighed at the "Upload media" button.

"What's the matter?"

"I have to upload a picture of the last stop in order to unlock the next one. But all my pictures are on here." Miriam tapped the disposable camera tucked into the cupholder.

Dicey dropped her forehead in her palm, shaking her head. "Oh, Miriam. You could've taken a picture from the observation deck."

Figures.

"It really is too bad you couldn't get a video of you singing to the telescope," Dicey mused, staring out the window.

The guitar and the cello in the back seat seemed to whisper her name. "Well . . ." She scanned the scenery:

trees, fields, mountains. Beauty everywhere. "I suppose I could do something right here. You could take a picture for me." She twisted her neck to look at the hard black cases in the back seat.

Dicey followed her gaze. "You actually play those?"

"Some. I mean, I'm not bad. I played cello in high school."

"Okay, then let's go." Dicey opened her car door.

Miriam got out too. Was she really doing this? Maybe she *had* absorbed some of Talia's courage. Playing on a stage was one thing. Playing to a bunch of trees and fields beside a road felt somehow far more conspicuous and threatening.

But Talia would have done it. No question.

Miriam opened the car and grabbed the cello before she talked herself out of it. She'd sung for Blaise yesterday at the telescope. Today, she'd play for her daughter.

★ ★ ★

Miriam braved the tattered remains of last year's under-growth, getting Talia's leggings and lace-lined tunic full of sticktights for her trouble. She perched on a stump over-looking a newly plowed field. It wasn't a cello chair, but it could have been worse. Miriam settled on the stump, extended the end pin, and set it on the ground between her feet. She wondered what Talia would have thought about all this—the peg in the soft dirt, Miriam getting ready to play the instrument that had been her pride and joy.

Who was she kidding? Talia would have loved it. She would probably have materialized an accompaniment track and made a slick, high-production video of the experience. Where had that girl gotten her flair for the dramatic?

Miriam knew exactly where. *Keep it together, Mira. Focus on the details.*

Rosin the bow. Tune the strings.

Talia's cello sounded terrible. Miriam couldn't fix it by adjusting the fine tuners below the bridge. She closed her eyes and reached deep inside for her almost-perfect pitch, then bowed the A string with one hand while twisting the peg at the end of the neck with the other. She'd never heard this instrument so far out of tune. Then again, it had been sitting in its case for a year. What else could she expect?

And once again, she could barely breathe. Had the sun gone behind a cloud? No . . . she knew this feeling, this sensation of falling in slow motion down a long tunnel, farther and farther from the light.

If she'd harbored a hope that leaving home would deliver her from triggers, she'd clearly miscalculated. A cello, of all things. But a cello that, until a year ago, only saw the inside of its case when Talia was on her way somewhere with it. When she got stuck on a programming conundrum, she played. When she was ticked off at her parents, she played. She'd even taken it with her to Argentina last year—no, two years ago—when Teo took the twins to meet his extended family.

Miriam hadn't gone on that trip either.

"Miriam? Are you okay?"

Miriam blinked. The sound of birdcalls returned; sunlight still filtered through baby leaves fluttering in a cool, pine-scented breeze. She looked up to find Dicey peering at her. "Sorry," she said. "I'm, um . . . I'm here." Not okay, but still here, among the living.

Dicey seemed to be debating whether to push the issue, but she pursed her lips and moved on. "You ready to go all *Sound of Music*?"

One thing about this girl: she made Miriam laugh. Or, well, chuckle, anyway. "All right."

A car passed and slowed to gawk. Miriam tensed, expecting them to stop and accuse her of trespassing.

Dicey glanced at them as they accelerated away. "Just ignore them," she said. "And ignore me. I'll walk around and take some pictures so you have several to choose from."

It felt awkward and slightly forced, but Miriam squashed her antipathy and nodded. She stared across the field, tilled but not yet planted, and the old hills rising beyond it. In the trees around her, birds competed to fill the morning.

She didn't know what to play. The only thing in her head, thanks to Dicey, began with the words "The hills are alive."

And of course, the melody that had kept her awake last night.

Well, why not? She closed her eyes and began to play. It was a pretty melody, soaring and plaintive. She wished she could place it. This wasn't like her. On the long car trips to visit Mom and Dad in Detroit, they used to play *Name That Tune*. Miriam had an almost photographic memory for melody; nobody could beat her, whether they sang classical, pop, show tunes, country, or liturgical music. Once in a while, Teo had managed to stump her by starting in the middle of Tchaikovsky, borrowing from himself. Otherwise, she was invincible.

What *was* this melody? There was more to it now than in the darkness last night, but still, twelve bars in, she came up blank. The bow faltered. The vibration of the strings faded away. The birds took up the slack. In the distance, Miriam heard the hiss of tires on asphalt.

A touch on her arm. "That was gorgeous, Miriam," said Dicey. She crouched to examine the sleek lines of the cello. "I wish I could've learned to play."

"Never too late."

That twist to Dicey's lips might have been a smile. "If you say so." She handed Miriam's phone back to her and started fiddling with her own.

Miriam laid the device on her leg and gazed across the valley. She wasn't ready to put away the cello. The melody filled more than her head; it seemed to be spreading out inside her heart, connecting her to the profusion of green all around. Playing that melody here, in this space, had felt like . . . healing.

Her phone dinged. It was her sister: *I don't get it. You couldn't take one weekend off to spend Easter with the family but you can take who knows how much time for a road trip? How do you think that makes Mom feel?*

Miriam growled. "I *work* on Easter, Jo," she told the device. "It's my *job*." But they'd been through all this four weeks before Easter, when Jo tried to buy her a plane ticket to Albuquerque. Mom understood. Or at least she claimed to. Perhaps Jo knew better. She and Mom had always been close. When Jo lived at home, they'd go shopping together or get nail treatments at the beauty school. Miriam would beg to tag along, but Dad always said she was too little. Once Jo left for college, Miriam thought she'd get her chance, but Jo called to talk to Mom every day, so maybe Mom never felt the need.

Miriam scrolled through the pictures. Dicey had a good eye. She chose one and uploaded it, then packed up the cello and headed for the car. The burn in her calves as she hauled the instrument up the hill felt . . . good. *She* felt good. That bubbling sensation beneath her locket surprised her. She'd forgotten music could make her feel this way: alive, humming with potential. If she could make music at one stop on this Great American Road Trip, why not at all of them?

Maybe she really could find redemption out here.

The women got back in the car. "I'm totally sharing this with all my friends," Dicey said.

"Do I even want to know how many friends you have?"

"A bunch." Dicey shrugged, a smug twist to her lips. "So now what?"

Miriam smiled and pulled out Blaise's wheat penny. "Here goes nothing," she said, and flipped the coin.

Part 3

Cincinnati, Ohio

I spent a lot of years trying to outrun or outsmart vulnerability by making things certain and definite, black and white, good and bad. My inability to lean into the discomfort of vulnerability limited the fullness of those important experiences that are wrought with uncertainty: Love, belonging, trust, joy, and creativity to name a few.

—Brené Brown

Talia's intro

So, one stop down! Wouldn't you like to know how many are left? Guess what? I can't even tell you because we're figuring this out and recording videos as we go too. How fun is that? Almost makes me want to go on the trip with you.

Wait a minute. What am I saying?

Anyway.

So . . . drum roll . . . your next stop is . . . Cincinnati, Ohio! It's a date night! There's all kinds of stuff to do there. You can take a steamboat ride, you can rent bikes, you can walk a labyrinth, see a baseball game. Maybe there'll even be a concert. Who knows? Anyway. You're welcome. Have fun, kids. Don't call us. We really don't wanna know.

◆ 10 ◆

Friday, April 29
Eastern Ohio

DICEY SLEPT MORE THAN anyone Miriam had ever met, including her teenage son. She slept through five counties and over an hour of *All Things Considered*, after which Miriam went looking for a pop station because listening to presidential politics was doing nothing for her existential crisis.

As she drove westward, humming, the sun disappeared into a cloud bank. The afternoon darkened, making it feel later than it really was. Dicey woke up coughing in Middle-of-Nowhere, Ohio. She reached into her backpack and pulled out a fast-food napkin, covering her mouth until the hacking finally stopped.

"You okay?" Miriam asked.

"Fine. Except this isn't the interstate." Dicey folded the napkin and tucked it away.

"Yeah. Construction zone, followed by an accident. Google rerouted us. Unfortunately, it also bypassed Charleston."

"Oh."

"I figured I might as well take you as far as Cincinnati. You can catch a bus there too."

"Wow. Thanks."

"Sure. I'm glad for the company." On the radio, Taylor Swift was whining about her boyfriend. Miriam started singing softly again; Dicey pulled down the corners of her mouth to hide a smile. "You listen to TSwift. Really?"

"What can I say? It helps me get my teenage angst out."

"Ugh. That's totally a Tweet." Dicey tapped out a post, speaking it out loud: *So now I know what church choir directors listen to. TSwift. Explains a lot, I think.*

"Lovely." Miriam shook her head. "So keep me company. Tell me about yourself."

Dicey shrugged. "What's to tell? Pregnant, no degree, no future."

Miriam pried her jaw open. "I don't believe that for a minute."

"Suit yourself."

She gripped the steering wheel hard. "My daughter would have turned eighteen in February. Don't tell me you have no future. You're alive."

Dicey slumped. "I'm sorry," she said. "That was supposed to be a joke. I didn't think. I'm sorry."

Miriam eased up on the steering wheel. "Thanks for that."

Dicey coughed again, drank from her water bottle, and screwed the cap back on. "My mama's amazing," she said, and the sardonic note in her voice was gone, replaced by sincerity. "She raised five Black boys in south L.A., and every one of them got himself a college degree."

"Wow."

"And my dad came around just often enough to keep from having to pay child support. Till I was about five, anyway. Then Mama told him he better hang around for good or else don't bother coming back at all. Soon enough, she was sorry she ever did. He was an ugly drunk. Breaking things, calling names. All that yelling. The first time he laid a hand on her, though, she packed us all up and moved up to the Bay Area. We haven't seen him since."

"Wow," Miriam said again. It seemed a ridiculously inadequate response. She knew all about men who weren't father material, but she couldn't quite bring herself to say so.

Dicey twirled a string of beads hanging off her backpack. "When I was five, Mom went to get her nursing degree so she could . . ."

Miriam waited a beat before venturing, "Have a career of her own?"

Dicey gave a noncommittal shrug.

A ring tone interrupted the radio. The dashboard screen flashed *Incoming call from: Becky Lindon.*

Miriam answered. "Becky! What's up?"

Her friend's voice filled the speakers. "Finally!"

"I didn't have a cell signal."

"Yes, I saw your post. Well, I'm glad to hear you sounding so . . . chipper."

"It's been interesting."

"You want to talk about it?"

"Um . . ." Miriam glanced over at Dicey, who was pretending not to listen. "Not right now."

"All right. So, you know about . . . um . . .?"

"Ella Evil? Yes, I know about it."

"Well . . ." Becky sounded disconcerted. "That wasn't what I meant, but since you brought it up, you seem surprisingly calm."

"It's me," Dicey said. "I'm giving her sedatives."

A brief pause. "Uh . . . hello," Becky said. "I didn't realize there was someone else in the car."

"Yeah, I figured I better announce myself before it got weird."

"Dicey, meet my friend Becky. She's one of my choir members. And our social director. Becky, this is Dicey Smith. I'm giving her a ride to the bus station."

"Oh."

Monosyllables were not Becky's style. "What's going on, Bec?"

Becky hesitated. "Well, there's a comment you need to see. On Blaise's video."

That didn't sound good. "What is it?"

"You need to read it yourself."

"Hang on." Dicey's thumbs danced over her screen. "Here, this must be it—it tags about a bazillion people."

Miriam clenched her fists on the steering wheel. "So what does it say?"

"It's a link to an old Instagram post." She peered at it. "It's a picture of two boys. I guess one of them must be Blaise. This guy says, 'When I saw this video, all I could think of was those two fairies at science camp who got caught outside together after curfew. Went looking and guess what? This is one of them! You figure those queens—'"

Dicey stopped abruptly, but the lid had already blown off the hot, hard scab covering Miriam's heart. "Finish it," she said.

"Uh, Miriam—"

"*Finish it!*"

Dicey hesitated. Sighed. Clicked her phone off. "The gist of it is this prick questioning whether either of them . . ." She redirected. "If they were . . . actually equipped to have sex."

Miriam's rage raised the temperature in the car ten degrees. She had to open the window and let in the cool of the approaching storm, just so the cabin didn't spontaneously combust. "Let me see."

"Miriam—"

"Now."

Dicey thumbed the phone and held it out. A quick glance showed her Blaise and another boy holding hands and looking into each other's eyes with an intensity that leaped off the screen.

Miriam returned her attention to the road, breathing hard through her nose. What kind of person went after someone who was *dead*?

Dicey peered at the screen. "The original post got a lot of interaction." She hesitated. "These comments are horrible. It went on for days. Can you imagine living with that for a whole week?"

"I thought the same thing," said Becky softly. "Did Blaise tell you anything about it, Miriam?"

Her rage vanished beneath a wave of pain so powerful, Miriam felt as if her guts had been yanked out of her body and thrown on the pavement. "No," she said.

She pulled off on the shoulder and bent over the steering wheel. She remembered that camp. Blaise had been so excited—a whole week devoted to astronomy. Yet afterward, he'd had nothing to say. He was quiet by nature, but this was different. For weeks afterward, he'd been moody and withdrawn. He'd only perked up when Talia brought home information from her cello teacher about a tiered competition whose final winners would earn ten thousand dollars in scholarships, payable to a music school of their choice. He threw himself into preparing for the first round, and Miriam breathed a sigh of relief and let it go.

She'd given him space and privacy when what he needed was love. Why hadn't she dug deeper? He'd been suffering, and she'd done nothing to help him bear it.

"Ssssooooo . . ." said Dicey, "your son was gay?"

Miriam shook her head, the steering wheel rolling across her forehead. "I didn't think . . . I don't know."

The music in her suitcase mocked her: the manila folder, the printouts, the manuscript notebook filled with her pathetic attempts to finish what Blaise had begun. No wonder she'd failed so miserably.

The clouds hunkered down, sucking wattage from the day. It couldn't be. He would have told her.

Wouldn't he?

Her body craved motion. Miriam sat up and accelerated back onto the highway. "I can't talk about this right now. I gotta get off the phone, Bec."

A long pause. Then Becky sighed. "All right. Call me tomorrow."

"Okay." Music replaced her friend's voice in the speakers. The perky beat grated like sandpaper. Miriam punched the radio off.

Of all Miriam's family, she and Blaise had understood each other best. Why wouldn't he have told her? Did he think she'd be angry? Reject him?

Maybe he'd told Teo. Teo never got angry about anything. It was his most maddening trait. He never let anything get to him.

A fat drop of rain splattered the windshield. Another. And another. Miriam turned on the wipers, but they only smeared the dust. She punched the wiper fluid dispenser.

She had to finish that music. Find whatever message Blaise had left for her there.

"Um, Miriam?"

She glanced to her right. Dicey had a slightly strained look on her face.

"Sorry, but I need to pee. And eat. And I need a couple of prescription refills."

Miriam winced. She knew what it was like to be pregnant. She should have been thinking about this without Dicey having to ask. "Of course," she said. As the rain started in earnest, she flipped her turn signal and headed down the next exit ramp.

♦ 11 ♦

THEY DROPPED OFF THE disposable camera and Dicey's prescriptions at Walgreen's before taking refuge from the downpour at the McDonald's next door. By the time they headed back to pick up their purchases, the storm had passed, or at least, paused. Traffic hissed noisily on wet pavement. The sky spat small, hard raindrops.

"How'd you meet your husband, anyway?" Dicey asked as they hurried across the parking lot to the Walgreen's.

Miriam hunched her shoulders against the rain. "At a convention for Catholic music ministers."

"Love at first sight?"

Miriam snorted. "Not hardly."

"Oh, come on. You said he was Italian-Argentine, right?" Dicey infused the sentence with the worst fake Italian accent ever. She had the hand motions and all. "You must-a had a spicy relationship-a!"

The laugh caught her by surprise. "Yeah, well, Teo missed out on that particular gene. He was more the nerdy professor type." Talia's ghost bared its teeth at her, but Miriam stared it down. He'd said it himself a hundred times.

Dicey sighed. "Oh well, I suppose it was too much to hope for."

Thinking about that convention provided welcome distraction. "I expected to be miserable that week. Everyone I knew had always thought I was a weirdo."

"Why?"

"I don't care about sports, and I don't keep up with TV shows. I had nothing in common with people. I got laughed at when we did those 'all about me' worksheets and I said my favorite music was Rachmaninoff. And my parents thought studying music was a waste of time. They worked the assembly lines in Detroit. They wanted us to get out, and they didn't see classical music getting me there." The darkening air flashed blue; a clap of thunder signaled an uptick in the rain. The women picked up the pace. "I mean, I get it. We always lived hand to mouth. I remember one day the day care was closed and Mom had to work, so she sent me to stay with a family from church. They spent most of the day shopping for clothes. It was hard pretending I wasn't jealous. I'm sure that's how my parents felt all the time. But still."

The doors to the Walgreen's swooshed open. Not a moment too soon. Miriam glanced over her shoulder at the steady, driving rain once again pounding the asphalt. "Anyway, all those church music people 'got' me."

"They were classical musicians?"

"Not necessarily. They were just really good at what they did." They wandered down the first aisle. "Making music together has a way of building community. When you've got three or twenty or a hundred people all working on the same piece of music, it's like all the things that divide us don't matter. You *need* high voices and low voices. The guy with the power voice who can't read music ends up being the anchor for the guy who reads music but isn't as good at matching pitch. And the guy who can't sing at all rocks the accessory percussion. Music lets us connect with each other at a level so deep, you can't even put words on it. You know, after all the years my choir has been singing together, they'll pick up a brand-new piece of music and sing the exact same wrong rhythm? How does that happen?"

She paused to catch her breath and stole a glance at Dicey, self-conscious. She'd gotten carried away. "Anyway. When the music is centered around something else you share in common, like faith, it's really powerful. Teo was helping with the youth track at my first convention. A lot of the people I met that week became our friends. A bunch of them came to Atlanta to do the music for the funeral."

"So was Teo a piano player too?"

"No."

Dicey drew a soft breath. "The guitar. That's his guitar. Right?"

Miriam smiled and nodded. "He taught me to play it . . . a little."

"How many instruments do you play?"

Miriam shrugged. "I can get by on several. But the piano's my thing."

"Then we need to find you one." Dicey stopped walking to devote her energy to a single, forceful cough.

The store rattled beneath another clap of thunder.

Dicey pulled out her phone and tapped the weather app. The radar screen was red with purple specks. She zoomed out twice before the green came back. "Maybe this is a good time to stock up on road trip snacks."

They wandered toward the snack aisle. "So what *was* Teo like?" Dicey asked.

Miriam had never had to describe him before. Everyone she'd known had also known him. Except in college. She'd kept her church life totally separate from school. "He was kind," she said. "Thoughtful. Totally authentic. Rarely said a bad word about anyone."

"Not super sexy, in other words."

Miriam shoved down a swell of defensiveness. "There are more important things."

Dicey heaved a sigh. "That's true. I should know." She rested her hands on her round belly.

Time to focus on Dicey now. "Have you picked a name?" Miriam asked.

Dicey scowled.

Miriam raised her hands defensively. "Sorry, I just thought, for someone who's into names, that would be a big deal."

"It is a big deal. It's a big decision." The younger woman stopped walking, surveying a shelf filled with scrapbooks and supplies. She picked up a book with a pink cover and a photo frame on the front. "I should make a scrapbook for her. So she knows what I was doing these last few weeks. Like meeting up with you. One of the coolest things that's ever happened to me."

"You're sweet." But Miriam didn't miss that Dicey was trying to shift the subject away from herself.

She tried again. "What did you study in school?"

"Film and media studies." Dicey fingered the selection of pens as she went on. "Well, until this." She patted her swollen midsection, her face darkening.

Miriam wanted to tell Dicey she understood the younger woman's frustration and fear. But it was more important to get Dicey talking about herself. "Where do—where did—you go to school?"

"William and Mary." Dicey shook her head. "I just wanted to get as far from home as possible. I should never have taken on that much debt."

"But . . ." Something didn't add up. "Then what were you doing in Green Bank, West Virginia?"

Dicey's face shut down. "Breaking up with an ass-hole. Anyway"—she turned away from the scrapbooking paraphernalia—"you know what? I'll bet you can do scrap-booking online. That would be easier in a car."

A phone dinged; Dicey had hers unlocked before Miriam identified whose it was. "Come on, Mom," she murmured, typing with her thumbs.

"I'll just be over here." Miriam motioned toward the snack aisle. Dicey didn't acknowledge her.

Miriam loaded a cart with trail mix, whole-grain crackers, and protein bars. Then she got in line at the photo counter. She opened her phone case; the photo of her with Teo peeked over the floral card. Hesitantly, she slipped an older picture from behind it—a poor-quality snapshot of the two of them, arms draped over each other's shoulders, taken the last day of the convention.

He looked so young. He'd been three years older, but his face was still a little round, a hint of baby fat clinging to cheeks that would hollow out into middle age but would never see wrinkles. That big nose.

Young Miriam still had that awkward adolescent look. The terrible hair, a few prominent zits. But she liked this picture anyway. In it, she looked calm. Safe. That was how she'd always felt around Teo. Even when she was furious with him for leaving his shoes in the middle of the floor.

She'd arrived at the convention feeling raw and unsettled. The situation at home was strained, her parents' silences brittle, their bright conversations even more so. She'd been certain by the time she came home, Dad would be gone. She'd tried to back out of the trip, but the church music director who was mentoring her had insisted she go.

Teo was the first to greet her when she walked into the glacial ballroom that had been home base for the youth that week. For some reason she couldn't explain, when he said, "I'm so glad you're here," she believed him. By the end of the second day, she would happily have stayed at this convention center forever, talking chord progressions and ensemble and ministry.

The night before she went home, she broke down during evening prayer. Quietly, seated in the back row, so no one would know. Yet amid the chorus of voices singing responses, she felt a warm hand rest on her back. She looked up to find Teo sitting beside her. He never stopped singing.

He never even looked at her. But his concern projected a force field of security around her.

They stayed in the hall talking for hours: the uncertain situation awaiting her at home; the loneliness he felt living with his uncle; the little brother who barely knew him. His parents' dreams for his future as a well-to-do American; her parents' bafflement with her musical aspirations.

When she returned home, her parents seemed back to normal. Except for that one spectacular blowup—the one they still didn't know she'd overheard—Miriam had never seen her parents fight. But now Miriam recognized tensions she hadn't seen before. The way her parents avoided being alone with each other. The way they never quite met each other's eyes. The self-aware courtesy and deference they demonstrated when making plans.

The peace felt fragile, and the last thing Miriam wanted to do was upset it. Her parents eyed her correspondence with Teo, a college student, with suspicion. Miriam started leaving his letters lying around so they could accidentally read them and be reassured nothing creepy was going on. The tactic seemed to work; at any rate, they never tried to stop her.

It was Teo, then in his third year at Temple University, who'd learned of the Curtis Institute's generous scholarships and encouraged her to apply. He helped her move into her apartment in Philadelphia. She was a little nervous that the easy friendship they'd shared at convention wouldn't transfer to real life—a needless worry, it turned out. Their conversation picked up as if they'd left off last night, not last year. He recruited her for the music group he coordinated at a parish in downtown Philly.

From then until the day he died, they'd been inseparable. Even in those few delirious weeks she'd spent with Gus, her one and only boyfriend—if he even deserved the title—Miriam had spent Saturday nights at church with Teo. Once, Gus tried to get her to skip Mass to go to a show with him, but Miriam wouldn't budge. When she played music with Teo, she felt more herself than anywhere else. Music let her express the things she didn't know how to put into words. Playing with Teo, she didn't need to. He just understood.

Thunder rattled the roof again. Miriam touched the photo. Here in this chilly Walgreen's, with the rain pounding the roof, it seemed impossible that Teo could be dead. That she couldn't tap his name on her phone and hear his voice on the other end. He'd had a way of making her feel safe. Wrapped up in security. Teo had felt like . . . home.

Even now, the echo of that feeling settled on her shoulders like a cozy blanket. She could still feel the warmth of his hand on her back. Still hear his voice, calling her Mira—or, when he was feeling particularly affectionate, Sassafras. She didn't even remember where that nickname had come from. Like everything else about Teo, it simply was.

She'd spent so long blaming herself for what she'd failed to give him, she hadn't really let herself realize what she'd lost: her best friend.

"Can I help you?"

The cashier's voice recalled her to the present. "Oh," Miriam said. "Um . . . last name Tedesco?"

"Just a sec."

The clerk returned. Miriam laid the photo and her phone on the counter while she paid for the groceries and the photos. As she punched in her PIN, her phone rang, showing a number with a 415 area code. Who could that be? She swiped the "answer" bar. "Hello?"

"Hello, is this Miriam Tedesco?"

"Yes?" Belatedly, she realized why the voice—strong, baritone, rich as butter and soft as silk—sounded familiar. No. Just no. It couldn't be. She couldn't have conjured him by a single fleeting thought.

"Great! I've been trying to reach you for days. I left a message at your work, but it just occurred to me that I probably had your mobile on an emergency contact form. I wasn't sure it would work."

The air felt as heavy and muddy as Play-Doh. Miriam couldn't get it into her lungs.

"I'm sorry, where are my manners?" he said. "I should introduce myself."

She couldn't talk to *him*. Not now, with Teo's face staring up at her.

"Hello?" she said loudly.

"Hello? Can you hear me?"

"Hello?"

"This is—"

Miriam punched the red button and flipped the phone to silent, then turned to find Dicey staring at her, a question poised on her lips. Miriam knew very well the volume had been too high to disguise the fiction she'd just perpetrated.

Why did he have to call at *this* moment? This moment had been Teo's. For once in her life, she'd had her mind focused where it ought to be. Why did he have to pick *this* moment to upend her life yet again?

Damn Gus von Rickenbach.

◆ 12 ◆

Twenty-three years earlier
Detroit, Michigan

THE DAY MIRIAM MET Gus, she was performing at a regional competition for high school students. He sailed into the room where everyone was waiting to perform, wearing a bright fuchsia shirt so neatly pressed, the creases could have sliced her open.

Miriam was too busy running through her music in her head to notice him making the circuit of the room, cracking jokes and introducing himself as if he were the host instead of a fellow competitor. She was the youngest of them all, and the only one without a string of awards to her name. It was all she could do to squash the devil in her head.

I am Mira Lewis, and I belong here. I am good enough!

"Hi," said a voice, rich and warm like butter and cream and sugar fresh out of the oven.

She looked up and found herself face to face with the most gorgeous guy she'd ever seen: thick black hair, straight nose, and a smile that said no one else in the world mattered.

She blinked stupidly at him.

He stuck a hand out. "Gus von Rickenbach," he said. "I'm from Chicago. More or less."

Nobody that gorgeous had ever talked to her before. Or anybody that old, for that matter; at school, people looked right past her. Miriam's brain went completely blank.

Gus von Rickenbach raised his eyebrows, giving her a teasing smile. "This is the part where you say, 'Oh, hi, my name is . . .'"

The stage door opened, and the previous competitor, an Asian girl with an immaculate bun, tapped out in her high heels, wearing a bright smile.

"Mira Lewis." The room monitor read from his list in a bored voice. "Mira Lewis."

Miriam leaped up. "That's me." She hurried through the heavy soundproof door, through the wing, and onto the stage. But she'd lost her concentration; all she could see was Gus von Rickenbach's handsome face and that smile—oh, that smile!

She had a memory lapse halfway through her first piece. It went downhill from there.

Miriam barely held herself together long enough to get off the stage. She couldn't go back out into that room like this. Instead, she melted into the shadows of the wings, stifling her tears while the next competitor filed out onto the stage and settled on the piano bench.

When the music started, Miriam stopped crying. She'd never heard playing like that in real life. She looked up to see a neatly pressed fuchsia shirt and glossy black hair. She watched Gus's entire performance through the gaps between the vertical wood panels, mesmerized by the beauty of the music; the beauty of his face, rapt with concentration; and the beauty of his body swaying as his hands flowed over the keys.

From that moment, Miriam Lewis was smitten.

She came in fourteenth that day. Out of fourteen. Gus, of course, won. Miriam went to congratulate him, but he barely looked at her as he shook her hand and went on whispering in the ear of the second-place finisher, a blonde bombshell who'd draped herself over him.

Miriam felt she'd been patted on the head by a rock star. It was exhilarating—and humiliating.

For the next several years, what kept Miriam's butt glued to the piano bench—and her body moving on the job when every neuron screamed for rest—was the determination to be good enough to challenge him. But it made no difference. No matter how hard she fought—and she never, ever again had a memory flub—he was always better. His bio kept expanding. He took lessons from famous players. He won awards. He went to camps.

Miriam only knew she ought to be doing any of those things because he'd already beaten her to it.

It took her four years to beat Gus in a competition. By then they were both at the Curtis Institute—no small thing for a blue-collar girl whose parents not only had no money to send her to a high-level performing arts school but had no desire to do so.

By then, she finally understood why he acted like a Kennedy: he sort of *was*. Not literally, but he had that kind of history. Money, talent, charm. Oh, the charm. Even the teachers eyed him from behind as he walked down the hall.

And her classmates? They had no chance. The female student body fell like dominoes before him. Long, long rows of dominoes. Every six or seven weeks, he had a new girl. Tall, short, white, brown, black—he liked them all. Except, apparently, Miriam. He'd walk right past her on nights she worked as an usher at the downtown concert hall, and show her the same charming, remote smile he bestowed on her at school—the one that made her question whether he even knew her name.

Well, fine. Let him run through all those other girls. Miriam had no intention of being one of them. She intended to be the one who made him realize there was more to love than being fawned over by the masses. Like Elizabeth and Mr. Darcy, when Gus noticed her, it was going to be because she was different. Worth committing to. When he noticed her, it would be as his equal.

Which meant she had to beat him.

And finally, in the spring of her first year at Curtis, she did.

That night in Boston, she wore a shimmery gown she'd found in a secondhand shop that was revealing, but not trashy. Gus played right before her, and as they traded spaces in the wings, he did a double take. She paused and gave him her Elizabeth Bennet smile—*I am not like all those other shallow, simpering girls*—and swayed out onto the stage, aware of his eyes on her body the entire way.

The bench still radiated the warmth of his body. She took the energy of that sensation and channeled it all into her performance. And when she finished, with fire and desire blazing through her, she'd known—*known*—that this time, this one time, she'd bested him.

"You were amazing!" he greeted her in the wings, putting both hands on her shoulders and kissing her cheek. "I've never heard Piazzolla played like that except by a professional. Come on—I'm taking you to dinner."

Cheeks burning, blood racing, Miriam said yes before she had time to consider playing harder to get. What else was she going to do tonight? Go back to her cheap motel and eat the Ramen noodles she'd packed to keep expenses down? Call Mom and Dad and have the sweet triumph of beating Gus—not just beating, but absolutely clobbering him—ruined by their lukewarm compliments?

She finally had his attention, here in a city far from his sycophantic fan club. No way would she blow that opportunity. Time to embrace the moment.

Dominoes.

◆ 13 ◆

M IRIAM SAT IN THE car by herself for nearly ten minutes, wet and shivering, before the rain eased off and
Dicey came out. The whole time, her phone, upside down
in the storage area between the seats, kept lighting up, causing the stack of CDs below it to glow.

Dicey closed the door and maneuvered her backpack
into the space at her feet. "I found a scrapbooking app," she
announced. "Already got started. Want to see?"

Miriam oohed appropriately at the simple layouts Dicey
had created while waiting inside.

Dicey clicked her phone off, plugged it into the charger,
and fixed her gaze on Miriam. "So what's up?"

"Nothing."

Dicey adopted a cocky demeanor. "Please. I mean, I
know I've only known ya for, like, nine hours. But I gotta
say . . ." She dropped the act. "Are you okay?"

"I'm fine."

Dicey stared at her for a long moment. Then she
coughed into her shoulder. "Okay, then, if you're not in a
talking mood, we might as well get going."

Miriam started the car and backed out. She merged onto
the highway, where the spray from big trucks turned the
taillights ahead of her into long streaks of red. She twisted
the dial on the windshield wipers to keep up.

Dicey was annoyed with her. The silent treatment, the folded arms, the conspicuous lack of phone usage—it was classic passive-aggressive teenage crap. Talia had been a pro, but Miriam had eventually learned how to ignore it.

Of course, look where that had gotten her with Talia. Teo had never ignored Talia's moods. He'd always cajoled her, made her laugh, pulled her out of it. No wonder she'd been so fiercely loyal to him.

Maybe this was a chance to redeem herself. To be more like Teo. To meet someone on their terms instead of hers. She cleared her throat. "Look, I wasn't prepared for that phone call. That's all."

Dicey regarded her coolly. "Bad news?"

Gus von Rickenbach *was* bad news, categorically, but not the kind Dicey meant. "It was the coordinator of the competition my kids went out to California for last spring."

"Oh." Dicey's body language softened. "They both went?"

Miriam nodded. "They both won their divisions in a regional music competition last year—"

"Define *division*."

"Blaise won piano solo, Talia won strings."

"Okay."

"So they went to nationals together. It was kind of a big deal, having two kids from the same family there. And twins, no less."

A semi roared past, kicking up a curtain of water. Miriam grabbed the wheel as the draft tried to suck her in. "I found out a few months ago that Blaise e-mailed Gus—the coordinator—ahead of time. He was asking for feedback on this sonata he was writing."

"The one you're supposed to be finishing."

Miriam cut her a glance. They hadn't talked about that, had they?

Dicey spread her hands. "I Googled you."

So Dicey had seen Ella Evil's write-up. "What wasn't in that story is that I was supposed to join them afterward. We were going to celebrate my birthday with a camping trip. But . . ."

But then Gus happened.

"I got sick," she said. The lie wormed its way around her belly. If she couldn't tell the truth now, when would she? But Teo had come up with that particular fiction when they realized going to California would mean confronting Gus. It all would have come out then.

"This isn't how they should find out," he'd said, and even now she agreed. But she would forever regret not having the chance to do it right.

Was it possible Blaise suspected? Surely not.

She couldn't decide whether to be proud of him for having the guts to reach out to someone with as high a profile as Gus von Rickenbach, or pained that he'd done so without telling her. Which, it hurt to admit, seemed to be a pattern.

This is exceptional work, Gus's e-mail read. *You have a lot of potential. I'd love to sit down with you and talk after the competition, but let me point out a few things to be thinking about in the meantime . . .* He'd proceeded to do a detailed analysis of the sonata's every weakness. Miriam wanted to scratch his eyes out for criticizing her child, but she couldn't. Point for point, he was on target. Every time she worked on it herself, she heard his voice saying *"derivative . . . fresher harmony will take you to unexpected places . . ."*

Dicey sat in the passenger seat, waiting patiently. "Anyway," Miriam said, "that weekend in San Francisco, Blaise apparently hit it off with Gus."

The phone lit up again. Dicey eyed it. "That's probably him."

"Of course it is."

Dicey frowned. "I don't understand why you're so freaked out about talking to him."

Miriam shifted her weight. "He's kind of a big deal these days. He's written . . . some music." Well, it was true, wasn't it? "He teaches at the San Francisco Conservatory along with his wife. She's an opera singer. I just don't like feeling overshadowed, okay?"

"But why would you feel over—oh. You know him, don't you?"

Miriam's shoulders tightened. "I *knew* him. A long time ago."

"Ooh." Dicey regarded her with a speculative gleam in her eye. "Were you a *thing*?"

Miriam scowled.

Dicey clapped her hands. "Oh, now I get it! Were you in school together?"

"Yes."

"Was he better than you?"

Miriam's fingers hurt. She relaxed her grip on the steering wheel. "Not always. Not at the end."

"Hmm. And he doesn't remember you?"

"Apparently not."

"Ouch."

Understatement of the year. How could Gus not know who she was? He'd managed to find out she was trying to finish the sonata, so he must have done some research. But if he'd connected Miriam Tedesco with the Mira Lewis he'd slept with at Curtis, surely he would have led with it!

She hated this slimy feeling. Hated how it had glommed onto her now, when she'd been truly focused on Teo. For one moment, back there in line at Walgreen's, she'd been on the verge of something profound.

And Gus just barged in. How typical.

Dicey twirled the string of beads on her backpack. "So he's a big deal, and you were as good as he was. So that means you were, like, a real musician."

Dicey had a way of sparking her sense of humor at the most unexpected times. Miriam felt the corner of her mouth twitch. "As opposed to a church musician, you mean?"

"Woman, don't you go putting words in my mouth. I'm *trying* to say, if you're freaked out because your ex-boyfriend doesn't realize who you are, then tell him already. He'll be so embarrassed, you'll have the upper hand."

Miriam chuckled mirthlessly. *Tell him already,* Dicey said, as if she hadn't been wrestling with exactly that question for seventeen years.

"I'm just saying, if that's what's bothering you—"

"That's not what's bothering me." Not exactly. For twenty years, she'd known everything about him that could be gleaned from a web search. When he canceled a performance or won an award, she knew. When his parents got sick, she knew. What if she'd been so insignificant on his playboy radar that he didn't remember her at all?

Dicey tapped her phone on her palm. "Y'know," she said, "I don't want to be pushy, but you're being dumb."

"Don't pull your punches now. Tell me what you really think."

"I'm serious. What if he can help you get your son's music out there? You don't want to squander the opportunity."

Having said her piece, Dicey disappeared into her phone. Rain hissed beneath the tires. All at once, weariness descended like a veil, burying Miriam's ability to think. In the past twelve hours, she'd picked up a hitchhiker, found out her son was gay—maybe—and was bullied—definitely—and fielded a phone call from the person she'd been simultaneously stalking and trying to avoid for twenty years.

No wonder she was exhausted.

Maybe Dicey was right. Maybe she *should* talk to him. Just get it over with, so she could finally move on.

But she couldn't be sure right now. And she'd already wasted so much emotional bandwidth on Gus von Rickenbach. All of it at the expense of a man who'd loved her with a devotion she'd never returned.

"No," she said now. "I'm not getting distracted this time. I'm not out here to obsess about Gus. This time is for my family."

Dicey looked up, raised her eyebrows, and shrugged. "Okay."

Miriam focused her attention ahead, relieved for the reprieve. Gus wasn't going anywhere. In a day or two, she could try to sort out that rat's nest. Tonight and tomorrow, she had one purpose: to honor her family.

◆ 14 ◆

THEY'D MISSED THE LAST Greyhound of the day, so the women decided to split a hotel room in Cincinnati. As soon as they got inside, Dicey lugged her suitcase and backpack into the bathroom. The shower turned on, soon followed by loud music. Very loud. What in the world? Did she think Miriam was likely to abscond with all her earthly possessions?

It was not the first time Miriam had found herself befuddled by the younger generation.

She threw her keys and wallet on the nightstand and, drawn by a need stronger than reason, pulled out Talia's laptop.

She'd never posted photos from Green Bank. The visit to the giant radio telescope already seemed like the distant past, but she'd spent the money, so she might as well upload them. Then she turned her attention to tomorrow's itinerary. Miriam went down half a dozen rabbit holes while investigating the possibilities. Teo had often done this at the dinner table, clicking one interesting and semi-related link after another while she scolded him to put the phone away. She never won because the truth was they all enjoyed it.

Miriam clicked a new post.

Fun facts about Cincinnati: The Reds always open the sea-son at home, because they were the first pro baseball team. The suspension bridge that crosses the river here was the model for the Brooklyn Bridge. (Take that, New York!) And—are you ready for this? There is a house here shaped like a mushroom.

She attached a link to prove it, smiling as she posted. But the words looked frivolous on the blue-and-white screen. The real reason the computer had called her was farther down the page.

Reluctantly, she opened the photo of Blaise and the unknown boy.

She could see why people interpreted it as romantic. They were wholly focused on each other, oblivious to who-ever had snapped the picture. But the expression on the other boy's face could have been despair as easily as roman-tic longing. What if the photographer simply interrupted Blaise trying to comfort a friend in distress?

There was no way to know the real story, short of the other boy surfacing—and why would he?

Had Blaise really been gay, or had he and the other boy been victims of some teenage tribal power play?

The photo had racked up dozens of replies, with mov-ing dots at the bottom promising more to come. A small part of her took comfort in seeing the number of exclama-tion points; it meant plenty of other people were surprised. Maybe that meant it was bullshit. Surely if Blaise were gay, someone would have suspected?

The foulness of the caption set the hot, hard spot inside her boiling. The bigotry. The cruelty of publicly assaulting the human dignity of someone who was *dead*. The fact that her child had been bullied, and she hadn't even known it. Most of all, the bitter acknowledgment that she'd never, ever know the answer to the question raised by that post.

Rabbit holes were a nice distraction, but right now what she needed was authenticity.

She clicked the white box on the browser. Stared at the flashing cursor. Listened to the water running in the bathroom, the hip-hop rattling the fixtures. The whole room seemed to be vibrating—more than the volume really justified. She cocked her head toward the door, listening. It sounded like there was a machine running in the bathroom. Well, Dicey *had* taken her whole suitcase in there. But what could make that racket? She couldn't think of any beauty apparatus that made a noise like that.

"Procrastination," she whispered, and turned her attention back to the computer.

Everyone thinks I was so devoted to my family, but the truth is I resented them as much as I loved them. This wasn't the life I planned. I was supposed to be stamping my passport every week, playing recitals and concertos all over the world. Not hauling kids to music lessons and club meetings, tied to a husband, having to consider his needs instead of touring Europe.

And now they're gone, and I'm not even sure I knew them, let alone loved them. Can you imagine what it's like to live with that? To know that, no matter what you do, you can never—

Her phone dinged. She looked down to see Gus's name.

Sorry we got cut off earlier. If you're interested, I'd love to talk with you about your son's music. I don't know if you know this, but he showed it to me last spring. Call anytime.

Huh. That was surprisingly not pushy.

How many times *had* he tried to contact her today? She opened her texts and found . . . nothing from him. Plenty from Becky, from Jo, from Mom. But from Gus, only this one.

It was not what she'd expected. Come to think of it, there had been something different in his voice earlier. He'd sounded less . . . cocky. Slightly vulnerable. Maybe even a little needy.

What could have changed someone like Gus so much? If he really had changed, having a real conversation might help her discern what, if anything, she owed him.

In the bathroom, the shower went off, and Dicey turned down the music to a socially acceptable level. If that didn't constitute a sign, Miriam didn't know what did.

She dialed before she lost her nerve.

"Hello?"

"Hello, this is Miriam Tedesco."

"Hello! Oh, I'm so glad you called me back! My name is August von Rickenbach. I'm sorry, I know this must feel like it's coming out of nowhere, but I was the coordinator for your son's—"

"Yes, I know. You and Blaise e-mailed each other. About his sonata. Without telling me."

"Oh." He sounded startled. Score one for her. "I . . . he reached out to me. I want to be totally clear on that."

"Easy, Mira," Teo would have said. She wanted to know what kind of person Gus von Rickenbach had become. She couldn't accomplish that if she put him on the defensive. She took a deep breath to settle her nerves. "I know," she said. "He had your reply in his manuscript notebook. I'm sorry—I didn't mean to accuse."

"Oh. Well, it's okay." He hesitated, regrouping. "I just want to start by saying your son was extraordinary, Mrs. Tedesco. I mean, I'm sure you knew that."

"Yes," she said softly.

"I can't tell you the last time I was so excited about a young player. He was the real thing, a star in the making. So understated until you put him at the piano, and then— that intensity!"

This was the irrepressible, irresistible Gus she remembered. Miriam leaned back against the bank of soft pillows and stared at the blank TV screen, listening.

"We were spellbound," he said. "The judges and every-one else in the room. He walked off the stage, and we looked at each other and said, 'What just happened?'"

The funny thing about grief was that sometimes it resembled joy. Miriam ran her finger over her lips, smil-ing as her vision blurred. "I wasn't . . . able to be there," she said. "I had . . . a professional commitment." Just a solo performance with the local symphony. And unpaid, at that. But at the time, it had seemed like an opportunity she couldn't pass up.

No. She needed to be honest. She hadn't *wanted* to pass it up. How many events had she driven them to? How many hours had she sat around waiting for them, bored, handing them opportunities she'd had to pursue with a tenacity beyond common sense? It was her turn.

It had never occurred to her she might miss their final performance.

". . . beautiful sensitivity," Gus was saying. "Extraordinary passion and extraordinary magnetism. I just felt this *connection* with him, you know? Of course not. It makes no sense. But I did. And for his sister to win the string division!" Gus laughed. "They brought the house down at the showcase concert at the end of the festival, you know. They put on a full-fledged comedy routine. I've never seen anything like it."

"I know. My husband posted it on Facebook." Miriam laughed too. "They were quite a pair, weren't they?"

"I have never wanted any student in my studio as much as I wanted him." Gus's voice settled into something more appropriately somber. "I—I know I'm talking too much, but I wanted you to know my interest is entirely sincere."

Interest in what? Miriam wondered. Behind the muted hip-hop strains, she could hear Dicey packing up. She didn't have much longer. "I believe you're sincere," she said carefully.

He exhaled softly. "I'm glad. You see, I . . . a few years ago, when I turned thirty-five, I realized I'd already achieved so many of the goals I'd set for my life. And it was amazing, reaching the top of that mountain, but once I got there, I just felt . . . alone."

Again, the hint of vulnerability. Brokenness, even. Miriam tucked her elbows against her ribs.

"I woke up one day going, 'Now what? I have everything, and I have no one.' Eventually I got married, and . . . well." He cleared his throat. "Meeting Blaise gave me a purpose. I realized *this* is what I want to do with the rest of my life. Help kids who don't have the advantages I grew up with— kids with potential. But when he died . . . I know it makes no sense, but I felt like my dream died too. Until a few days ago. I was in Atlanta to meet with a movie director about a soundtrack, and I heard a PSA about the concert coming up, and they mentioned Blaise's sonata. I realized I probably had your phone number, so when I got home today, I went looking." His energy was returning. "I have sponsors lined up. My friends in the film industry love the idea. We're starting a foundation. We're putting on a big concert gala in a couple months to kick things off, and I'd like to use Blaise's sonata."

Of course he wanted something. This vague disappointment was irrational. "Why not use some of your own music?"

"Oh, you know my music?" He sounded unreasonably pleased.

"Everyone knows your music."

He laughed. "Well, not everyone knows who wrote it. But then, I shouldn't be surprised you do. I understand you're involved in music yourself."

Nothing stung like damnation by faint praise. "I'm a church musician."

"But you write music—I read online somewhere that you were going to finish the sonata. A blog—*Atlanta Attaché*, I think it was called."

So. He'd seen a picture of her, and he still didn't know who she was. Maybe she shouldn't be surprised. But it was humiliating.

"Is it finished?" he asked now. "The sonata, I mean? Because—I mean, I'm sure you want to premiere the sonata at your own concert, but afterward, if it turns out well, will you let me use it for mine? We'll publish it, distribute it, under his name or yours—whatever you want. I have the contacts. I'm not worried about the money. It's yours. You do whatever you want with it. My lawyer can set up a fund, a scholarship fund for young artists—I just want to record it."

It was a stunningly generous offer, characteristically grandiose, yet his casual stipulation—*if it turns out well*—made her writhe. Her mediocre accomplishments stood in the wings, laughing at her. "Well, I don't really feel comfortable talking about that until it's finished . . ."

"So it's not done." He sounded disappointed. "But your concert is soon, isn't it? So you must be close. The second movement was just lacking a recapitulation, and then it just needed a third movement. It wouldn't take much."

Just another movement. Her work, these past years, had impacted a lot of lives, but it paled beside Gus's achievements. She felt her old competitive instincts heating up again. Now she had another reason to finish Blaise's sonata. "I'll get it done," she said.

"Wonderful! I'm glad to hear it." In the background, Miriam heard a feminine voice. "Oh, that's my wife calling. I'll be looking forward to hearing from you."

"Sure—"

"Good night, then."

Miriam pulled the phone away from her ear and stared at the *call ended* screen. He'd changed in some ways, but the man still thought he was the center of the universe.

And she was like a moth; even knowing what happened when one got too close to Gus von Rickenbach, she craved his notice.

If it turns out well? She'd show him. She'd write something worthy of Blaise if it killed her.

No time like the present. She'd seen a piano in the lounge downstairs. Maybe she could sweet-talk her way into using it until the late-night crowd came in.

Miriam leaped up and heaved her suitcase onto the bed, digging to the bottom for Blaise's music. She shoved aside scarves and artfully wrinkled blouses until she saw the edge of the file folder peeking from beneath a swatch of crinkled black fabric splashed with red flowers. Even the contents of her suitcase were determined to underscore her failings.

Miriam yanked the music out and slammed the suitcase shut. She stalked out the door, sending Dicey a text on her way downstairs.

★   ★   ★

The lounge was quiet, and the manager gave her permission to play. But Miriam felt more stuck than ever. *Derivative,* Gus had said of two measures on the second page, but she loved them just as they were. She'd keep every note her son had written. Take that, Gus von condescending Rickenbach!

Except something about the seam between Blaise's clean, deliberate script and the few measures she'd written in her messy scrawl caused her to freeze up.

He'd had problems with that spot too. The paper was worn by multiple erasings, the layers of pencil marks still faintly visible. In its current form, the music charged over a cliff and stopped. Blaise had left half a page blank and gone on to the recapitulation. But he hadn't gotten far there either.

She played it again. Maybe it was just because she'd been thinking of Gus, but tonight she thought she heard something of Gus's compositional style in these measures.

Miriam tried another variation. It should be so simple: restate the original themes, except without changing keys. Maybe it *was* simple for Gus, but in her current emotional state, Miriam found it baffling.

"If it turns out well."

". . . remember those two fairies at science camp?"

"Can't fight with someone who has no heart."

Amazing sounds were coming from the piano, melodies that riffed quite nicely on Blaise's themes. But the moment she focused on them, the path forward, which a moment ago had seemed inevitable, disappeared.

She chased it backward, but like a dream, it evaporated too quickly to catch hold of, despite her hands suspended above the piano, poised to hitch a ride on the slightest inspiration.

"Excuse me, young lady."

Miriam glanced up to see an elderly man in a suit. "Hi?"

"Are you taking requests? It's my anniversary, you see. I'm wondering if you could play 'Someone To Watch Over Me' for us. It's my wife's favorite song."

"Um . . . sure."

The small crowd applauded politely when she finished. More people were arriving. She should go, but now she was wound up. She'd never sleep until she bled off some energy. She embarked on a set of improvisations on simple folk tunes. "Shenandoah." "Simple Gifts." "Suwanee River."

When she looked up again, the lounge was full. She saw Dicey, casual in a flowing sweater and sweats, sitting at the nearest table with a tumbler full of what looked like cranberry juice and a bowl of peanuts. She had her phone trained on the piano. *Keep going,* she gestured.

Miriam obeyed. The requests kept coming; she got sucked into a stint of 1980s pseudo-karaoke with a crowd of tipsy women on a girls' weekend.

But after an hour and a half, her brain was shutting down. Dicey came up as she started stacking her music to put back in Blaise's satchel. "Bedtime already, Lounge Lizard?"

"More than," Miriam said, yawning. "I'm two hours past."

"That is lame," Dicey said. "You know that, don't you?"

"Says the woman who slept half the day in the car." But her mouth quirked. Dicey made her feel like she was with Talia again: the irrepressible spirit, the need to stay on her toes.

"I don't suppose I could interest you in a regular gig?" asked the lounge manager, a trim woman in a blue suit.

"Sorry," Miriam said. "One engagement only. I'm just passing through."

"Too bad. Where ya headed?"

"Oh . . . just a road trip."

Dicey peered at the woman's name tag. "Athena. That's great. Named after the goddess of wisdom."

"And war," Miriam added. Dicey frowned at her.

"The wisdom is knowing when not to make war," said Athena. "What's the reason for the road trip?"

It was too late at night for that conversation. Miriam said, "Who needs a reason?" at the same moment Dicey said, "She's honoring her husband and teenagers who died."

Miriam's muscles locked up; Dicey's eyes widened as she realized her error.

"Wow." Athena shook her head. "Teenagers? That's so sad. But at least you had them for a long time. My cousin miscarried at thirty-five weeks a while back. She was a *real* mess."

Dead silence in the lounge. Miriam sucked in a slow, deep breath, focusing on the weight of the locket against her breastbone. Teo wouldn't want her to lash out. No matter what kind of asshat thing was said to her.

She pasted on a smile: "I'm turning in," she said, grabbing Blaise's music satchel.

Dicey caught up with her in front of the elevator. She wrapped her arms around Miriam from behind. "I'm so sorry, Miriam."

"Sorry about that woman being clueless and insensitive? Or sorry for presuming you had any right to tell my story for me?"

"Both," Dicey said quietly.

Miriam sagged. She hadn't realized just how starved she was for human contact. She could feel the younger woman's embrace in her calves and her toes and the center of her brain. *Lonely,* her body cried out as they stood there, rocking. *I'm so lonely.*

"I don't think she meant it like that," Dicey whispered into her shoulder. "Most people are just too caught up in their own tragedies to realize when they're making other people's worse."

Miriam stiffened and shook her off. "What do you know about tragedy?"

It was grossly unfair, perhaps even cruel. Nobody hitchhiked at thirty-two weeks pregnant, let alone slept outside with nothing but leaves to keep her warm, unless she had tragedy to spare. And Dicey had just as much reason to be angry at Athena's tactlessness as Miriam did. Talking about miscarrying at thirty-five weeks, in front of a pregnant woman? Who did that?

But Miriam was too sore on her own behalf to sympathize much. She was sick of pretending she wasn't angry and bitter, and Dicey was not her daughter. Not her responsibility.

Dicey took the verbal blow with her arms hung at her sides, but the brown eyes stared back with a quiet certainty beyond reproach. "Everybody's got tragedies," she said softly.

The elevator dinged, the doors whooshing open to the sound of Muzak, the pathetic approximation of music meant to offend no one, which therefore offended everyone.

Just as Miriam had offended Dicey. She ought to apologize, but her nerve endings reeled from the sudden loss of human contact. She could still feel the younger woman's hug warming her back. She craved that touch more than she wanted to admit. It was hard not to be charmed by this girl who had Talia's vibrance, Talia's zest for life, with none of the baggage.

"*No heart,*" Talia had accused her.

Miriam shuddered. Had Talia thought about that fight in the last moments of her life? Regretted it?

How she longed to slip these new memories she was making with Dicey over her memory of Talia. To bury the misunderstanding that must now remain forever unresolved, and pretend she had never lost her daughter at all.

No. No! Why invest in this trip at all, if that was to be the outcome? She needed to put Dicey on a bus. Tomorrow morning, Miriam would refocus on the reason she'd embarked on this trip in the first place. Alone.

"Come on," she said wearily. "Let's just get some sleep."

◆ 15 ◆

S HORTLY BEFORE NOON THE next day, Miriam found herself
on a shaded metal swing, looking across the Ohio River
at the south side of the Mason–Dixon line while Dicey bustled around her. Miriam still wasn't sure how it had happened. She'd gone to sleep intending to put the pregnant
woman on the first bus headed west this morning, with or
without apologizing for last night. Preferably without.

But by the time she woke up, Dicey had the whole
day laid out: the best time for a video shoot, where to put
Miriam, how to set up the shot. Dicey was like a freight
train when she got going. It didn't even occur to Miriam to
ask when they'd decided to start making videos.

Besides, her conscience seemed more verbal when well
rested. Maybe by the time the afternoon bus left, she'd
manage to apologize.

The crowds on the riverfront streamed by, a sea of red
headed toward the Great American Ball Park. Miriam laid
Blaise's notebook and a pencil on the swing beside her
and removed Teo's guitar from its case. Behind her, the
city roared; in front of her, a steamboat chugged beneath a
bridge, its decorative wheel chopping the water.

But the slow, languid movement of the swing resisted
the chaos. It felt good to sit here and just *be*.

"I need your phone," Dicey said.

Miriam unlocked it. She'd missed quite a few notifications, including an Amber Alert. Something about a kid in a stolen car. Poor parents.

She cleared the screen and handed it over. "I hope it's legal to play music down here."

"You worry too much."

She slid the guitar strap over her shoulder and adjusted Talia's straw hat. While she tuned, Dicey rigged the phone on a stone planter behind her shoulder. "Don't look at me," the younger woman said.

Miriam fingered the wireless mic clipped to her lapel, which Dicey had materialized this morning. "I'm not sure about this, Dicey . . ."

"It'll be great, I promise. Film studies, remember?"

Miriam sighed. "What do you want me to do?" she asked meekly.

"I don't know, play something. Didn't you say you wanted to . . . what was it you said?"

"Work on chord progressions."

"Yeah, that. Do that. Whatever it is."

"It's the structure of—"

"Yeah, yeah. I don't care, just do your thing."

Miriam smoothed the notebook open in front of her and started analyzing chords. If she could get a sense of the big picture instead of getting lost in the interplay of melodic themes, maybe she could sketch out a road map.

She stuck the pencil between her lips and strummed the chords. She wished she could recall the snatches of brilliance that fell from her fingers last night. If only Dicey had been recording *that*.

"One of these days, we really should do a livestream," Dicey said.

We. Not *you.* Miriam cursed her heart for the way it leaped at the idea of keeping Dicey with her. She should have done this with Talia while she was alive. Not now, with a near-stranger.

She'd forgotten what soul-killing work analyzing chords could be. Maybe a few of Teo's Argentine folk tunes could help get the creative juices flowing.

On those sticky summer nights, Teo and his jam buddies used to go through five gallons of sweet tea and a cooler full of beer. She'd been so focused on hosting, she'd never realized how relaxing it could be just to sit with the music. She closed her eyes to summon the melodies she'd never seen written, but had only absorbed, the music seeping in as perspiration seeped out.

Miriam couldn't match the flair and style of Teo and his band of Argentine expats. But she heard the ghost of their presence in the vibration beneath her fingers. One night, when Talia was about eight, she'd suddenly started singing harmony on this song.

Blaise never sang. He had a lovely voice, but it made him self-conscious to use it. He just . . .

Wait a minute. That chord progression resembled a spot on the second page of the sonata. How had she never noticed it before? Of course; it made sense that Blaise had absorbed the Argentine music, just as she had.

The mystery melody bubbled up again. She began to hum, playing with chord variations. It worked for the sonata, but it cried out for voices. She could almost hear the words. Almost. And she really could hear a voice singing it back to her as she paused to scribble ideas.

She looked up. A small child, three or so, stood nearby, dressed in a Superman shirt, mimicking her. Perfectly on pitch. Uncannily so.

She took the guitar pick out of her mouth. "Hello there. Where did you come from?" She was startled to realize she'd attracted a handful of listeners. But their body language didn't indicate that he belonged to any of them.

Dicey, who had left Miriam's phone to record, circled the perimeter with her own in hand. She motioned to keep going.

The boy stared at the guitar, rocking gently. Miriam started another Argentine folk song, and the rocking stopped. The moment she finished singing, he sang it back, note for note, but without words.

Amazing. What about opera? She hummed a snippet of Puccini. Again, perfect. She'd never seen anything like it.

The crowd was growing, people stopping to watch and listen. They seemed appreciative—all except one woman. She held a plastic cup in her hand, and she kept looking at her phone, scowling at Miriam, and looking again. It made Miriam nervous.

But the boy had started rocking again. She hesitated. He didn't seem verbal. Was he autistic? Had he wandered away? There had to be a panicked parent somewhere on the waterfront.

But at least he was safe while he was with her, and as long as he remained riveted to the music, he wouldn't wander elsewhere. A child in one place would be easier to find.

Besides, she was curious. Just how good was he? She knew how to find out: Mozart's Queen of the Night aria. She couldn't sing it—she'd always thought it sounded like Mariah Carey hopping mushrooms in some video game—but she picked the notes from the strings.

He nailed it.

Miriam's insides felt squirmy. Squirmy in a good way. Happy! That's what this was. She felt like doing a little dance . . . until she caught the eye of the woman with the cup. She hadn't imagined the hostility there.

Miriam returned her attention to the boy. Just one more. And only because of his shirt. If the parents hadn't shown by then, she'd find a policeman.

Teo used to play the Superman theme for Blaise at bedtime, to ward off the monsters under the bed—a ritual Miriam found irksome on days when she felt strung out and stretched thin, and Teo had worship commission or ministry training at church. But she'd learned to do it. Not with Teo's flair, but enough to banish the monsters.

She started the iconic theme. Instantly, the little boy stood up straight and put a fist out, turning a slow circle as he sang along.

She finished with a cheesy flourish; the crowd laughed and applauded. People started throwing coins and bills in Miriam's guitar case. She hadn't anticipated that. "No, no," she said, rising. "You don't need to—I'm not—"

"You are despicable," came a voice right in her ear. Miriam whirled. The hostile woman.

Not hostile. Drunk. Miriam took a step back and bumped into the swing. The guitar strings vibrated as wood contacted metal.

"Exploiting a child to get people to give you money!"

Miriam glanced at the boy—or, more accurately, where he had been a moment ago. Because he was gone.

She dropped Teo's guitar in its case and sidestepped her antagonist. The child hadn't gotten far, fortunately, but he was wandering down the lawn toward the riverbank. "Kiddo!" she called. "Superman!"

The woman followed. "You can't get away. I've called the police on you!"

The woman was drunk *and* crazy. Miriam hurried after Superman, hoping Dicey would get back soon, since she'd left her belongings unguarded at the top of the hill.

But someone else was streaking toward them now: a twenty-something man who looked frantic enough to be searching for a lost child.

Miriam waved him over. "Is this your son?"

"My sister's kid," he said, gasping for breath as he pounded out a text. "He has autism."

"I thought he might. I have to warn you—"

The drunk woman weaved toward them, waving both her glass and her phone while she raved about circles of hell.

"—about that," Miriam sighed.

"Who are *you*?" demanded Drunk Lady. Beer sloshed out of her glass, dousing both Miriam and the boy's uncle. "Cops didn't know you had an accomplice, did they?"

"Look," Miriam said, "I wasn't using him to make money. His uncle has him now. Let it go."

"Oh no." Another slosh, this time dousing the boy, who wailed. "You ain't goin' nowhere, sister. I called—"

"The cops," Miriam finished with her. They couldn't get here soon enough, as far as she was concerned.

"We don't need cops," said the uncle, putting his hands on his nephew's shoulders and tucking the boy close against his legs.

"Hey!" Drunk Lady raised her voice. "Hey, everybody! These two are the kidnappers! This is that kid from the Amber Alert!"

Miriam and the young man both froze, staring at each other open-mouthed. Then his face crumpled into fury. "Back off, you crazy bitch," he snapped. Superman began to hum, his body rocking. "This is my nephew, and I'm taking him back to his mother."

"Nice try. Everybody! Everybody!" The woman pointed to the boy. "The kid from the Amber Alert! Help! They're going to get away!"

The man began to steer his nephew away. He didn't see the punch coming.

But Miriam did. Instinctively, she leaped into its path.

For being drunk, the woman packed quite a wallop. Without time to brace for the impact, Miriam staggered backward into the pair she was trying to protect. The man nearly fell on his nephew.

When he regained his balance, he swung on the drunk woman, shoving her backward with a snarl. She retaliated with what had to be self-defense training, both of them red-faced and shouting, both oblivious to the child rocking and keening in the danger zone between them.

Damn it, somebody had to think of that poor kid. Miriam reached down and scooped him up to pull him out of harm's way.

And all hell broke loose.

Screaming. Thrashing. Beating on her. Kicking. Talia's hat went flying. It caught the stiff breeze blowing off the Ohio River, but before Miriam could go after it the woman slammed her fist into the back of Miriam's ribcage. She nearly dropped the boy. Her maternal instincts kicking in, she managed to get him safely to the ground.

Then she turned to the drunk woman and punched her in the face.

Which was, of course, the moment the police arrived.

The drunk woman took off running. Why was she running? She was the one who'd called the cops in the first place!

A female officer sprinted after her. In the distance Dicey, laboring down the sidewalk with a panicked expression on her face, nearly got run over. She staggered as the drunk woman shoved her aside and continued on. "Dicey!" Miriam ran to help.

Or at least she tried. Because then there were hands on her elbows, restraining her. More shouting.

And then, the icy burn of handcuffs.

THE TINY, WINDOWLESS ROOM had a one-way mirror and a table with two chairs. Normally, fluorescent lighting didn't bother Miriam, but this one flickered visibly, and with nothing else to listen to and nothing to think about except how she was going to pay for a lawyer who could convince a judge and jury she hadn't done anything worse than lose her temper . . .

Well, that electric buzz had her skittering on the end of her last nerve.

She propped her elbows on her knees and rested her head in her hands. If Teo had been there, he would've figured out a way to de-escalate the situation, drunk woman or not. Probably he'd have stopped the impromptu mirror-mirror musical revue before it started, in favor of packing up and finding the boy's parents. Which clearly would have been the wiser course.

The door clicked open. Miriam's adrenaline surged as the detective who'd questioned her came in with his hands in his pockets. "You're free to go, Mrs. Tedesco."

She gaped at him. "Just like that?"

He sat down across from her. "The video corroborates your story."

Thank God for Dicey's videography! That video was getting deleted the moment she got her phone back, but still, thank God!

"What about the boy?" she asked. "Superman? Is he okay? Did his mother find him?"

"Yes, they're all fine. Apparently he wandered away from the playground up by the Roebling Bridge. So at least we don't have *another* missing child to find."

"I don't understand why she fixated on me."

He shrugged. "You fit the same general description as the suspect."

Miriam pressed the heels of her hands to her temples and groaned.

He stood up. "Come on. Your friend is waiting for you."

Her friend. The friend who'd saved her butt and whom she'd resolved to drop off at the bus station at the first possible opportunity. The friend she'd been rude to last night.

Now she *really* needed to apologize.

Miriam almost burst into tears when she entered the waiting area and saw Dicey, looking pale and drawn, struggle to her feet.

Dicey *did* burst into tears. "I'm so sorry!" she wailed. She threw her arms around Miriam, the hard swell of her belly like a punch in the gut. "I had the livestream running, and I thought I'd go get some panoramic shots, and I didn't realize it had all gone to shit until too late. They confiscated the phone and the guitar and everything. It took me an hour to convince them to talk to me!"

Miriam patted her back. "It's okay, honey. I'm just so grateful you didn't bail on me. Especially after I was such a bitch to you last night."

"You weren't a bitch."

Miriam opened her mouth to argue, but then Dicey's earlier statement sank in. "Hang on," she said slowly. "Did you just say 'livestream'?"

Dicey coughed hard, once only, and blew her nose. "Uh, yeah. I'm sorry. I know I didn't ask, but when that boy—"

"Livestream."

"Yeah. I mean . . ." Dicey's shoulders hunched. "You didn't say no, so I figured . . ."

"Shit."

"Yeah." Dicey looked at the floor, fiddling with her blue bracelet, her shoulders hunched. She clearly thought Miriam would bite her head off.

A tempting idea. If only Dicey hadn't just saved her butt.

Miriam sighed and rubbed her forehead. This day just kept getting better and better. "Do his parents know their kid was livestreamed?"

Dicey looked like she wanted to crawl in a hole. "Um, yes."

"And they said what about it?"

"Well . . ." She shrugged. "They're more philosophical than anything."

"Did you apologize?"

Dicey gave her a withering stare. "Of course I did."

"A lot?"

"Profusely."

Miriam sighed. Nothing to be done about it now. "All right," she said. "Let's get going, then."

They stepped toward the door, and traffic noise swept over them in a warm, humid wave. Becky's Hyundai sat in front of the station, loaded with all the equipment. Miriam turned to Dicey. "You loaded it all by yourself?"

Dicey shrugged. "Somebody should have been livestreaming *me*. I probably looked like a camel with a hump on *both* sides." She gave Miriam a mischievous look. "Race you to the car."

Miriam's eyebrows skyrocketed. "You're kidding, right?"

"Totally serious. But you run. I'll waddle."

Miriam chuckled. "Fine."

"On the count of three. One—GO!" said Dicey, and took off down the stairs, giggling.

She did look pretty comical waddling down the steps of the police station. Miriam laughed out loud as she followed. She hadn't had a good belly laugh in a long time. It lifted her spirits, but she didn't know why for a moment.

When her brain caught up, everything became clear. Why not?

As Dicey settled into the passenger seat, her laughter spiraled into coughing. Miriam reached over with alarm. "Are you okay? Dicey, honey—"

"Okay," she gasped. "Just go." She shoved Miriam's arm away.

Miriam put up both hands and left her to her coughing fit. She nosed her way out into traffic.

By the time she merged onto the highway, Dicey's hacking had eased. The younger woman leaned back against the headrest and closed her eyes. Miriam stole a glance at her. "Are you okay?"

Dicey nodded. They both knew the itinerary: a short jaunt to the bus station and a farewell Miriam no longer wanted. Maybe she didn't have to do this alone.

She cleared her throat. "So, Dicey, I was thinking."

"Yeah?"

"Wondering, really, where exactly it is you're headed. And how much of a hurry you're in to get there. Because, if you've got a little time, you're welcome to ride with me, as long as it's generally on the way."

The slow smile was so unlike Talia's quicksilver grin, it underscored how alike the two girls were in other ways. "I'm headed home," Dicey said. "To California. And I'd love to tag along."

Miriam pulled Blaise's wheat penny from her wallet. "Well, you're in luck, because I'm going to California too. Care to do the honors?"

Dicey grinned and took the penny. "I thought you'd never ask."

Part 4

St. Louis, Missouri

Such is my experience—not that I ever mourned the loss of a child, but that I consider myself as lost!

—Deborah Sampson

Talia's intro

So, have you got the hang of this yet? Here's hoping. Though Mom's probably a lost cause. Dad, you'll have to walk her through it.

Your next stop is Cahokia Mounds. You'll like this one, Dad. The Almighty Wiki says this is a . . . "pre-Columbian Native American city, circa 600–1400 CE, situated directly across the Mississippi River from modern St. Louis, Missouri." It's got eighty mounds, and one of them is really big. Like, a hundred and fifty-four steps high. Hope you packed your walking shoes.

◆ 17 ◆

Saturday, April 30
En route to St. Louis, Missouri

THE MILE MARKERS FLASHED past unseen, Miriam steering for St. Louis on autopilot. She'd planned to camp tonight, to save money, but the thunderheads gathered above, flashing blue without ever revealing a single lightning bolt, changed her mind. As usual, Becky saved the day, texting her the number for a Benedictine monastery in north St. Louis that offered rooms to travelers in need.

And now, with Dicey absorbed in her scrapbooking app, there was nothing to keep her mind occupied except Talia. Beautiful Talia and her unbeautiful crack at Miriam's discomfort with technology, now on display for everyone to hear.

It made no difference, knowing the video had been recorded long before the big fight. It still felt like a poisoned dart.

Her phone rang through the Bluetooth. Miriam glanced at the screen and groaned.

Dicey looked up. "What's wrong?"

"Nothing," Miriam said, and answered. "Hi, Jo."

"Miriam," said her sister. "Please tell me you told Mom."

"Told Mom what?" Too late, Miriam heard the defensiveness in her own voice. Jo had always known exactly what buttons to push.

"Hello? You got arrested on Facebook Live?"

Miriam stole a glance at Dicey, whose shoulders hunched. "Ease up, Jo. It was all a misunderstanding. Everything's fine."

"Ease up? *Ease up?* My kids found out about it at school! They were terrified. These are your nieces! Did you even *think* how this might affect your family? Of course not. You just went off half-cocked on a trip across the country, no planning—"

"Hang on," Miriam interrupted, focusing on the part that would not cause her to lose her temper. "Why would the kids have heard about it at school?"

It might have been the first time Miriam had ever silenced her sister. When Jo spoke again, her voice was much lower. "Do you really not know?"

"Know what?"

"It went viral."

Dicey and Miriam exchanged a wide-eyed glance. Then Dicey leaned over her phone, navigating furiously. "She's right, Miriam. Holy crap."

The connection hissed in silence while the word looped in Miriam's head, *viral viral viral viral*, like the teacup ride at Disney World. If you didn't hold onto the wheel, it got completely out of control, centrifugal force plastering you to the wall, powerless over your own body.

"This is exactly why you should be calling off the whole trip," Jo said, and the edge was back. "If you'd thought about it for half a minute instead of going off half-cocked, you'd never have left home."

Miriam locked her jaw to keep from responding.

"I–it's kind of cool, actually," Dicey ventured into the silence. "Most of the comments are really sweet. Most of them."

"I'm not looking at comments."

"But—"

"Not happening, Dicey."

"Okay," Dicey said meekly.

"Well, that's the first thing you've said that makes any sense," Jo said.

Since she'd said almost nothing, that wasn't saying much. Jo had a way of making Miriam want to run out and do exactly the thing she was told not to do. Jo was the only person in the world who could get that reaction out of her. "Not helpful," she said through gritted teeth.

"Look." Jo's voice softened again. "I know it's been hard, but this won't change anything. Just come home. Please. Before anything worse happens."

Miriam rubbed her forehead, examining her motivations. "No," she said. "I'm going on. Because it's what they would have wanted."

"Mira—"

"Will you please talk to Mom for me?" Miriam asked.

"You need to talk to her yourself."

"You're probably right, but—"

"Of course I'm right."

Miriam counted to three to settle her irritation. "Please, Jo. I'll call her in a day or two. I promise."

Jo was silent for a long moment. When she spoke, her voice was tight. "Fine," she said. "I'm holding you to that."

"Fine."

"Good night then."

"Bye, Jo."

Dicey exhaled when the music returned. "Wow."

"Yeah." Miriam sighed.

"Is she always like that?"

"Pretty much."

"Wow."

"Yeah." Miriam sighed. "Viral, huh. Talia would have loved that. Imagine the stories she could have told her kids about it."

Dicey dimpled. "Like my mom kicking my dad out of the house wearing nothing but a pair of boxers and black socks, with a slice of anchovy pizza in his hand."

Miriam chuckled.

"You really don't want to look at the comments?"

"Nope. What I'd like you to do is tell me about your scrapbooking."

"What does that have to do with anything?"

"Nothing. That's the point." Miriam reached over and tapped Dicey's phone. "Do you do a lot of it?"

"This is my first time. But my mom made each of us a homemade baby book."

Miriam's mother hadn't done anything like that for her. But then, she hadn't done it for Jo or Brad either. It wasn't her way. But that didn't stop Jo from being fiercely protective of Mom. What critical piece of empathy was missing in Miriam? Because Jo was right. It hadn't even occurred to Miriam to let Mom know what happened in Cincinnati.

She shook her head clear. She was trying to focus on Dicey, not herself. "Are you close to your mom?" she asked.

"Well . . . let's just say I had a pretty intense childhood. You don't have a choice but to get close."

"Intense in what way?"

"Health stuff."

"She know about the baby?"

"Yeah."

Miriam hesitated. "I don't want to stick my nose in, but . . . what's up with the baby's father?"

"Not in the picture, not gonna be."

"Okay."

Dicey fiddled with her blue bracelet. Miriam wondered about the significance of that piece of jewelry. "I'll tell you, but you have to promise not to judge, okay, church lady?"

Miriam blinked. "Um . . . okay . . ."

"I had a work-study job at school, working for a professor in astrophysics, and I was stupid."

Miriam nodded once; she got the picture. "Um . . ." *Brilliant, Miriam.* "How does one . . . get involved with a professor?"

Dicey snorted. "How does anyone 'get involved' with anyone?" She put air quotes around the euphemism. "A little too much alcohol, a little too much ego."

"I'm assuming he was married?"

"Naturally." Dicey made a face. "It never occurred to me I could get pregnant. I shouldn't have been able to get pregnant."

"Everybody thinks that until it happens."

Dicey gave her a dirty look. "Anyway, by the time I realized, I was way far along, and he was out at Green Bank for a stint. He didn't answer my calls for weeks. All I had was a cell number."

"And he was in the no-cell-signal zone." Miriam nodded. "So you had to go there to talk to him. I take it he wasn't interested?"

"The asshole wrote me a check and told me to 'take care of it.'" Dicey blew out a breath. "I'll use it to start her college fund. And there you have it. My whole sordid history."

"I'm sorry." How would Dicey support herself and her baby? "Will your brothers help you? Like, with taking care of her?"

"Oh, sure. They've got kids already. She'll have cousins by the dozens."

"That's good."

"Yeah . . . she's gonna need all the help she can get."

Miriam frowned. It couldn't be easy to be a single parent, but Dicey's comment seemed to imply something more.

But Dicey redirected before she could formulate a question. "Anyway, what about you? That was your sister, right?"

Miriam nodded. "Jo's nine years older than me, and Brad's seven years older. Nobody's ever said it, but I think I was probably an 'oops' baby. Dad passed away and Mom moved to Albuquerque a couple years ago."

"You see them often?"

Miriam shrugged. "Holidays." She felt rather than saw Dicey's disapproval. "I mean, we talk occasionally. And Mom came and stayed with me a while after . . . last year."

Dicey remained silent. Miriam squirmed. "Teo always said my parents weren't so different from his. They just wanted the best for us. But Mom is hard to please. She's like a whirlwind. She never wears down. She comes in with a long list of things to do, and all the while she's crossing things off it and coming up with new ones."

"Use the left two lanes to take the Interstate 55 south Interstate 70 exit toward St. Louis," Siri interrupted.

Miriam flipped her turn signal on. "They're not bad people," she added quickly. "We're just different, that's all. The things I thought were important, my parents never did. When I was little, we'd go to all Jo's basketball games. Even the away games. But when I had my last middle school choir concert, somebody gave them Pistons tickets. So they went to the game instead. I know it sounds petty, but we only had two performances a year, you know?"

"That is pretty sucky."

"Yeah." Come to think of it, even after her parents' relationship soured, they still went to sporting events together. That, and church activities.

"Did you ever say anything?" Dicey asked.

Miriam shrugged. "I did what every middle schooler does when their parents hurt their feelings. I was a butthead."

Dicey smiled, but two miles of flat fields, dotted with oil wells turning lazily, passed by before she spoke again. "My mom's a rock star," she said. "I always knew that, but I wonder if I appreciated it. I remember this one day—it had been rough for a while, and when we got past it, Mom let me skip school to celebrate. She *never* let me skip school. She said I missed too much as it was, 'cause I was always sick. I got every virus that hit a classroom."

Miriam glanced sharply at her, thinking of the cough, but Dicey carried on.

"Anyway, we went down to the waterfront to celebrate. Did all the tourist things. Rode the street cars. Drove down Lombard Street." She laughed. "She even let me have ice cream at Ghirardelli's—for *lunch*. You have no idea how big a deal that was. She always gave me the healthiest, most tasteless lunches you can imagine."

"Is that why you put salt on everything now?" Miriam couldn't resist the little dig.

"Ha ha. Anyway, family is a pain, but they're also, like . . . everything. I just hate to see you with no one at all."

Miriam braced, expecting the pit to appear in front of her, but the siren call of despair sounded muffled. It took a moment to think why that might be. She squeezed Dicey's hand. "I'm not alone, am I?"

Dicey smiled and squeezed back. "So tell me about your siblings."

"Brad's a plastic surgeon in California and Jo has a corner office in Manhattan. That's what my parents wanted for us. It's what they worked for all those years on an assembly line. They hated that Teo and I lived this life where we were tied to the church community at holidays and not making a whole lot of money."

"You said she came to stay after . . .?"

"After the funeral." She made herself say it. "She decided I needed distraction, so she made a to-do list for me. She's the one who called Ella Evil. Thought it would help me to talk it out."

"That sucks," Dicey said again. She turned her phone end over end. "Grief must be hard enough without a spotlight on you."

Grief. Miriam supposed what she'd been suffering through for the past year was grief. Mostly she'd felt buffeted: by regret, self-recrimination, unwanted notoriety, and by the echoes of her husband and daughter—though not her son. Never her son. That was a pain all its own.

If Mom hadn't driven her so hard, would she have allowed herself to dip into the well of anguish and deal with it properly? Instead, she'd buried it all, distracting herself with tributes and busy work until she'd almost convinced herself Mom was right, that this whole grief thing could be contained and controlled.

She knew better now. Grief was messy. It didn't make sense.

Beside her, Dicey was humming. Miriam would have loved to have that silky, dusky voice in her choir. But once again, the melody seemed familiar, and yet Miriam couldn't place it. What was up with her inner ear?

Then, just like that, it clicked. "How do you know that tune?"

The humming stopped. "Huh?"

"The one you were just humming. My son wrote it. How do you know it?"

Dicey hesitated, frowning. "It's that thing you played back in West Virginia."

Miriam opened her mouth to argue and then closed it again as she heard it. Of course. That was why she couldn't put a name to her ghost melody. It didn't have one.

But it wasn't quite right, somehow. "Sing it again," she said.

Dicey looked a little self-conscious, but she complied. There. That's where she'd gone wrong: the third note was a step lower than what Blaise had written. A subtle difference, but—

Without warning, the whole next strain opened up in Miriam's head. It was like merging onto a freeway—melody, chords, registration, all charging in the same direction.

She pulled off on the shoulder and punched the hazards. Blaise's notebook was in her suitcase, in the trunk, but she couldn't take the time to get it. She could sense the freight train of inspiration rushing by. "Paper," she said. "Quick. Paper and a pencil."

Dicey looked at her like she'd suddenly sprouted a third eye. "I don't have any paper."

Miriam made a disgusted sound as she grabbed a pen and the hotel receipt from Cincinnati. She smoothed it over the steering wheel, slung ten lines across the back, and started scribbling.

"Um, Miriam?"

"Shush." She ran out of room on the first set of lines. Had to draw another one. It angled down the page like a melting ice cream cone. A third set. Her fingers itched to feel keys beneath them, to bring the sound out of her head, off the page, and into the open.

And then the superhighway made a left turn into a swamp. She could sense the way forward—almost hear it—but it was chaotic, jumbled. A characteristic interval here, a well-placed inversion there. But it wouldn't come out of her head. She needed a piano.

Her hands were trembling, her blood blazing, and her heart overflowed. With love, with loss. With *life*. She felt Blaise's presence, as if he stood just on the other side of a thin veil—and if she could only get the sun at the right angle, she'd be able to see right through it.

This was what it meant to be a mother: the sense that not even death could separate them. And for the first time, it occurred to her to wonder how Mom felt about the distance between them. Miriam must have hurt her a thousand times with the wall she'd put between them.

Much as she felt the bewildered pain of what Blaise had failed to communicate.

If there'd been anything to communicate.

Again, she was back to that. Miriam scoured her memory of her last conversation with Blaise—the phone call after he won the competition. If there were clues to his sexual orientation, they were buried deep. All she remembered was *Dr. von Rickenbach* this and *Dr. von Rickenbach* that. Thank God, Blaise had been too pumped up to notice the dead silence with which she'd reacted to hearing that name out of her son's mouth.

He adored Gus. Had she been wrong all these years? What if she'd chosen differently?

"'*If*' again. *You know better than that, Sassafras.*"

Teo's voice hit her like a wave: a freezing slap, running away to a limitless ocean. How she wished she could talk through all of this with him. She missed having someone in her corner, someone she could count on to care, to take her side, even if that sometimes meant telling her she was wrong.

She'd just made music out of her own head, built on the bones of Blaise's inspiration. How wonderful—and horrible, and beautiful, and sad. And Teo wasn't here to share it. Every good thing that had happened in her life for the past twenty years, he'd been the first to know. The only time they'd been apart was when he'd taken the kids to Argentina to meet his family. She slept badly the whole time they were gone. When she met them outside Security at the airport, Teo grabbed her around the waist and kissed her in front of God and everyone, and she'd felt complete again. And that night, she'd slept like a log.

Who could she share this moment with now? Who in her life would understand? Gus, perhaps. But given their history, entertaining the thought felt like the worst sort of betrayal.

"Miriam?" A warm hand brushed her forearm. "You okay?"

"I'm fine." Carefully, she hooked the pen over the page and leaned back against the seat, not even noticing the uncomfortable headrest. She was tired. So tired. And something else she hadn't felt since before Teo and the kids got on the plane to go to California.

Starving.

That felt like a betrayal too.

Two years earlier
Atlanta, Georgia

August von Rickenbach

Miriam's finger hovered over the "Enter" key. Every time she typed his name into the search bar, guilt grew another root in her soul. Yet Gus was an itch she couldn't stop scratching. It was a slow torment, seeing his list of accomplishments grow, but as long as his star kept rising—as long as he continued to look happy and healthy—she could reassure herself that she'd made the right choice all those years ago.

She hit the key and watched the circle on the screen spin. In the living room, Blaise banged out a Mozart concerto while Teo strummed his guitar out on the deck. Momentarily, Talia joined from her bedroom, offering up Bach to the din.

Miriam had given up everything for this life. The hours she'd spent at the piano instead of making friends, learning wedding music to pay for her lessons. Running scales and arpeggios while the rest of her family yelled insults and encouragement at the helmeted guys crashing into each other on the TV in the basement. It had given her the skills set to be very good at her parish work, but on nights like this, the distance between what was and what could have been loomed large.

Her parents had tried to get her to focus on something other than music—something that would offer a way out, a ticket to more than a shabby house and a daily struggle for solvency in the Detroit suburbs. They'd never understood: music *was* her out.

At least, it was supposed to be. The irony was not lost on Miriam, because both her siblings had made it out. These days, Jo walked around her corner office in Manhattan wearing designer suits and merging international deals. And Brad, with his liposuctions and face-lifts, made more money than God.

Meanwhile, here she sat, in another cramped bungalow in another fading neighborhood, scrunched between her bed and the corner of the room in the six square feet allotted for an "office," while beyond the crooked door frame, the cello, guitar, and piano tried to drown each other out.

Miriam mashed her hands against her ears. One moment, for the love of all things holy. Was one moment of quiet so much to ask?

The web results finally loaded.

It was always tricky finding the information she wanted. She was drawn to news of Gus's accomplishments like a moth to a flame. But what she needed to know required deeper searching. She couldn't just skim headlines; she had to infer the connections from color details included in unrelated articles.

The door closed, muffling the noise of her children's practicing. "Hey, Beautiful," Teo said. He crossed the tiny room in three steps to engulf her from behind, his lips on her jaw, desire in the feel of his hands running over her breasts.

Sex was the last thing on her mind. She had to force herself not to shove him away; his advances felt like an onslaught. "The kids," she protested, trying to reach the mouse to close the browser.

"They're occupied." Teo tipped her head back, kissing her. She couldn't see the screen.

"Worship commission."

"Doesn't start for half an hour. C'mon, we've got time. How often does it all work out like this?" He reached the tender spot at the juncture of her neck and shoulder, the one that reduced her to jelly.

Except tonight she was so tense, she just giggled. She hunched her shoulders, and he retreated.

"Well, it was worth a try," he said, smiling.

Miriam reached for the mouse then, but it was too late. Teo braced one hand on the back of the chair and the other on the desk, regarding the face on the screen. He sighed. "Again, Mira?"

Miriam squeezed her hands between her knees, staring at her feet. "He canceled a tour. Because his mother is sick." She looked up at her husband. "Breast cancer. It's got a hereditary link."

Teo scratched his head and sat on the edge of the bed, his jaw working. It hurt him, the way she kept picking at this part of her past. They'd come closer to fighting over this than anything else. He looked so vulnerable.

"Mira . . ." He swallowed a few times. "Has it ever occurred to you that maybe there's a reason you feel so compelled to follow Gus's life?"

She swiveled toward him. "What do you mean?"

"This summer, watching the kids with their grandparents and their aunts and uncles and *great*-aunts and -uncles . . . all their cousins . . . it was amazing. They understand themselves so much better now."

"What are you saying?"

"I think it's time."

"No."

"Don't you think he deserves—"

"Absolutely not."

Teo fixed her with a piercing gaze. "Don't you think *they* deserve to know?"

Miriam bowed her head, clamping her fingers behind her head. "I'm scared, Teo. What if it changes everything?"

He leaned forward, his big brown hands warm on hers as he rested his forehead on the crown of her head. "I know. It scares me too."

They stayed there for what felt like a long time, the cacophony of cello and piano fading to a distant, indistinct buzz. It felt safe here. If only they could stay in this cocoon forever.

At last, Teo pulled away. "I have to get over to church." He kissed her temple as he left.

Miriam looked back at the screen, but she no longer felt any desire to know the latest news on Gus von Rickenbach. She hated seeing that look on Teo's face. It made her insides feel like scrambled eggs. Not just because she knew she'd hurt him.

But because she knew he wasn't wrong.

◆ 19 ◆

Sunday, May 1
Benedictine Monastery
St. Louis, Missouri

AT FOUR AM, MIRIAM woke abruptly to an onslaught of memories:

Teo, looking deeply into her eyes, asking, *"Don't you think they deserve to know?"*

"What the hell?" Talia's voice, shaking with fury in response to a Facebook message Miriam never sent.

And a photo of teenage boys communicating heart-to-heart.

Miriam sat up and leaned her head against the wall. The monastery lay quiet, the dim glow from the street light outside her window making a shadowy outline of the crucifix on the wall.

For years, she'd followed the debates over marriage equality, caught between beliefs she'd accepted without question her entire life and the real suffering of good, faithful men she encountered through her ministerial work. Eventually, she and Teo decided it was up to God to sort it out, anyway, so they opted to treat everyone with dignity and leave the rest alone.

The air in her room smelled vaguely antiseptic. On the other side of the wall, a bed creaked as its occupant shifted. Miriam swung her legs over the side of her twin mattress. She rubbed her feet against the no-frills industrial carpet.

Her brain felt fuzzy with exhaustion, but staying in bed was pointless with this vise clamped around her heart. She might as well quit pretending she was going to go back to sleep and embark on the soul searching a place like this invited.

Because if Blaise really had been gay—if he'd lived, if he'd come out—she would have been forced out of her hidey-hole in the neutral zone. She would have had to confront the difficult questions and find a way to reconcile what resisted reconciliation.

She would have had to accept the fact that some people would have looked at her beautiful son as a man in possession of a one-way ticket to hell.

What would people back home say?

Miriam growled. "That is the wrong thing to be worrying about," she said aloud.

She stood, stretching her neck as she pulled out her clothes to get dressed. The best place to look for the answers she sought was in Blaise's music.

The hallways were dark and chilly, but with the help of the light on her phone, she found her way to the chapel, a round brick room with a narrow strip of stained glass windows ringing the top. An electric keyboard sat tucked against the organ console; a single sanctuary lamp burned over the tabernacle. She genuflected before it, her palms pressed to the cold tile as she tried and failed to formulate something better than "Help . . . please?"

But God felt as distant now as he had been the entire past year. He was there, somewhere, and she knew only her own emotional constipation prevented her from finding Him. What she didn't know was how to fix it.

She flipped on the lamp perched on top of the keyboard. She laid out the notes she'd scribbled yesterday in the car and smoothed open Blaise's notebook, then set to work transcribing.

Her brain warmed to the intellectual challenge. She just wished she could write something that sounded more innovative than an eighties pop song. Subdominant, secondary dominant, augmented seventh, half-diminished. Jazz chord, lowered seventh—no matter what she did, it all sounded very . . . instinctive.

She wasn't writing a sonata, she was writing church music.

Miriam threw the pencil on the music stand in disgust.

She'd had such hope yesterday when the freight train of inspiration had run her down. She'd felt connected to Blaise. Not exactly felt his presence, maybe, but still . . . connected. What had she expected to happen in the compositional process? To find a secret code that said, "Yes, I'm gay," or "No, I'm not"?

"Can't sleep?"

Miriam shielded her eyes from the pool of light and saw Dicey walking toward her.

"No. You?"

Dicey cocked her head one way, then the other. "Just dreading the future. All the what-ifs."

Miriam slid the cover over the keys and rested her forearms on it. "It's not so bad. Don't lose hope based on my experience."

Dicey shook her head. "Not that kind of what-if. More like, what if I'm not there when Baby Girl needs me?" Her voice broke.

Miriam reached out to lay a hand on her arm. "There's no need to think that way, Dicey."

Dicey put her elbows on the keyboard console. "Tell me about your kids. About—Blaise."

"What about him?"

"I don't know. What was his favorite song?"

Miriam reopened the keyboard. She started playing the Thomas the Train theme. "That was his first favorite." She segued to Star Wars. "Then that . . . and then this." A Marvel movie theme.

He'd had church favorites too: not just "For the Beauty of the Earth," but praise music and everything in between.

Dicey settled into a wooden chair beside the keyboard to listen.

It was easier to talk about them while her fingers were moving over the piano. The first few years at St. Greg's were a bit fuzzy. She and Teo had traded parenting and work shifts so they didn't have to pay for day care, which meant neither of them slept much.

The twins grew up at church. They'd play with toys on a blanket beside the piano while she rehearsed with cantors. For two years in early childhood, Blaise was fascinated with all things electronic. Once, he'd unplugged a cord in the middle of Mass. What a noise that had made! More than once, he'd shoved the master volume on the soundboard all the way up, causing a feedback screech that embarrassed his parents and enraged the traditional churchgoers, who were already suspicious of music ministry that required guitars and electronic equipment.

St. Gregory's bell tower had always been left unlocked until one day, while Teo and Miriam were training altar servers, Talia had convinced Blaise to climb up to the belfry and have a contest, one on each rope pull, to see who could get the most chimes out of their bell in one minute.

There'd been ice cream at the rectory with Father Simeon on Christmas Eve, and the day the kids had played tag in the gathering space and tripped the crankiest old-timer in the parish.

By now, both women were laughing. "And I thought my brothers were trouble!" Dicey said.

"St. Greg's put up with a lot from us." Laughter felt good. "We had to come down so hard on them, but at night we'd laugh so hard we'd cry." She sobered. "I envy you, Dicey," she said. "You have so many sweet moments coming your way."

Dicey's smile vanished. She spun her blue bracelet around and around her wrist. Miriam tried to get a better look at it, but Dicey sensed her attention and covered it up. "Well," she said, standing abruptly, "thanks for the

distraction. I should probably try to sleep a while longer."
She walked out of the pool of warm light cast by the lamp.

Miriam sighed. She couldn't shake the feeling that
Dicey was hiding something.

But it wasn't her business. She'd be better off trying to
figure out what—if anything—Blaise had been hiding from
her. She wondered if he'd confided in Talia.

Miriam touched the keyboard again, though her heart
wasn't in it. Maybe she should go back to bed too. There
were only so many days she could drive safely on no sleep.

She closed the keyboard and turned off the light,
heading down the darkened aisle toward the exit. She
dipped her hand into the large font in front of the door
and crossed herself, then stopped, breathing the faint smell
of water.

No matter what had been going on in her life, the
sound of water trickling from stone basin to stone pool
always filled her with a cool, clean sensation. And sometimes, inspiration.

Gianna, she thought. Talia's best friend. If Talia had
known anything . . .

Well, it was worth a shot.

She checked her phone. Five forty-five AM. Which
meant almost seven on the east coast. A quick naviga-
tion to her work e-mail confirmed what she thought she
remembered: Gianna was scheduled to serve at Mass this
morning—so she *should* be up.

Miriam tapped out a text message. *Got a minute?*

Pause. *Sure thing.*

Miriam scratched her cheek, trying to decide how to
word it. *Did Blaise ever talk to anyone about what happened at
camp?*

A pause; then a rush of verbiage appeared. *No I never
heard anything and neither did anyone else it's the only thing we
talked about Friday at school counselors religion teachers kids everybody it's crazy*

Miriam hesitated. *Talia never said anything to you?*

A long pause. Miriam squirmed. This conversation felt wrong on so many levels. Not the least of which was the humiliation of having to ask her kids' friends to tell her about the people she should have known best of all.

At last, a reply. A series of them, one right after another:

No but she was different about blaise

Wouldn't talk about him the way she talked about other people

Gossip u know

Like she was more protective of him

Just in general

Don't know if that helps

Mom is calling time for church

Miriam swallowed. *Thanks, Gianna.*

She laid her phone on her leg.

If Talia had had an inkling that her brother was gay, surely she'd have talked it over with her best friend. Then again, the twin bond was unlike anything Miriam had ever experienced. As much as her children fought with each other, they stood united against everyone else. Blaise hated conflict; he thought deeply and quietly and kept most of it to himself. But the one time he'd gotten into a fight at school, it had been because someone said something about Talia. He'd never admitted exactly what—not to Miriam, at least. Just spent the weeklong suspension keeping up with schoolwork and practicing piano while Talia spent every evening doing her homework in his room.

Yes, she could believe that Talia had been more protective of Blaise, and Blaise's deepest secrets.

Her phone, left unused, faded to black. Which left her right back where she'd started: in the dark.

Sunday, May 1
Cahokia Mounds
Near St. Louis, Missouri

MIRIAM SAT CROSS-LEGGED ON the flat top of the larg-est hand-built earthwork in North America. The bottom of Monks Mound was as big around as the Great Pyramid in Giza. They'd climbed a hundred and fifty-four steps above the Mississippi River bottoms, between steep embankments left unmown, with scruffy grasses waving in the spring breeze on either side.

It was so quiet. Quieter than the chapel at the monas-tery this morning before the monks came in for Mass. Yet at one time, fifteen thousand people had lived around the foot of this mound. It was hard to imagine. Did they get snow here? Did little Mississippian boys and girls use this steep hill for sledding? Did they roll down the hills in the summer? Or was this a sacred place, off-limits to all?

No way to know now. Those people were all gone. Vanished. Like her family, taking their secrets with them to their graves.

Miriam stared off to the southwest, where the St. Louis skyline, headlined by the distinctive silver arch, shimmered, mirage-like, in the midday sun.

How many times I saw my western city—

Her phone dinged, overriding the post in process. Miriam's bloodstream electrified to see Gus's number. *I just saw the video* (three bug-eyed emojis). *Are you okay? Are you still in jail?*

Miriam rolled her eyes and weighed her reply—how much did she really want to get into this with Gus, of all people?—but was interrupted by another ding.

I guess if you're in jail you won't see this. The text ended with another bug-eye.

She opted for short and polite. *Not in jail. Everything's fine, thanks for asking.*

She returned to the trip app, but she'd only written one word before she was interrupted by another ding.

I saw you were working on music in that video. How's the sonata coming?

Of course, that was what he really cared about.

She blew out a breath, kneading her forehead. She hadn't made one whit of progress out on the waterfront. She'd never even finished analyzing the chord structure of the existing music, let alone done any real writing.

Somehow, she didn't think Gus wanted to hear that.

But she couldn't lie either. She made a face and typed, *Slowly.*

Happy to help. Just let me know.

Wow. Pushy much? She shook her head. *Will do.* "Not," she murmured as she hit "Send."

She sat tense on the top of the mound for two minutes before she knew he wasn't going to text again. It was like having someone looking over her shoulder.

She returned to Talia's app to finish her post. *How many times, I saw my western city dream by her river . . . Sara Teasdale. #GreatAmAdven.*

She clicked "Post" and turned toward the sound of labored breathing. Dicey lumbered toward her, oversized T-shirt gaping over her belly as she tried to catch her breath.

"A hundred fifty-four steps times three," Dicey gasped.

"Four hundred sixty-two. That's enough. Why don't you stop going up and down those steps and join me?"

Dicey shook her head. "This is the best exercise I've had in weeks. I'd like to get up and down them a couple more times." She coughed hard.

"Sounds to me like you're overdoing it."

"Nope. I'm fine." Dicey gestured at the phone in Miriam's hand. "Are you still trying to deal with those comments?"

"I was just getting ready to."

"Don't."

"I thought you wanted me to look at them."

"I changed my mind. There's starting to be more trash. When we get back on the road, you let me wade through the trolls and read you the ones you actually need to see. How does that sound?"

Miriam was touched. "You'd do that for me?"

"Sure. I gotta pay you back for giving me a ride, right?" Dicey grinned. "By the way, I've been thinking about your next video."

"Just stop right there, Dicey. I'm not doing any more videos. Still photos will be just fine, and they won't go viral."

Dicey looked crushed. Of course she wanted Miriam to do more videos. She was an aspiring filmmaker. "But Miriam—"

"I don't want what happened in Cincinnati happening again."

"We can take precautions. I'll be more careful. We don't have to go live—"

"You're missing the point. I came out here to honor my family. Not to plaster myself all over social media."

Dicey's face tightened. "They're not mutually exclusive, you know."

There it was: the edge that never quite left Talia's voice in the last year of her life. Miriam had wondered if Dicey might possibly be different somehow. If she could go all the way across the country with a girl who might have been her daughter's character clone, and not fall to bickering. Now she knew.

And she also knew she wasn't replacing her memory of her daughter with some Stepford version of her instead.

The quiet morning was ruined. She stood up. "There's no need for sarcasm," she said, brushing off her legs. "I promised myself a soul-searching road trip across the country so I could mourn my family, and instead I'm traveling with a stranger, getting arrested, and going viral. Thank you, no. No more videos."

Miriam stalked along the gravel path to the stairs that would take her back to the Mississippi river bottoms. She was halfway down the first flight by the time Dicey caught up to her and grabbed her elbow.

"Miriam!" Dicey was out of breath, but the exertion of speaking only added force to her words. "Stop. Listen." She punched something on her phone, took two deep breaths, and read:

"'My neighbor just shared your account with me. I lost my daughter to suicide two years ago, and I still have trouble getting up in the morning. Your music moves me. It expresses the joy and the pain of love.'" Dicey glanced up to see if Miriam was listening, then continued. "'You probably didn't expect all this attention, and perhaps you didn't even want it. Still, I hope you'll speak out as well as play. Speak for all of us who've lost someone and don't have the courage to speak for ourselves.'" She looked up. "Don't you see, Miriam? You're making a difference."

The words moved Miriam more than she wanted to admit, but she shook her head. "It's lovely, Dicey, but it doesn't change anything."

"It changes everything." Dicey stood on the step above her, earnest as a high priestess. "Not everything can be controlled. You, of all people, should understand that you *do not squander* life! You embrace it! Even when it doesn't look the way you think it's supposed to look."

"Social media is not life!" Miriam wove her fingers into her hair, praying for patience. "Look. I've been where you are. Trust me, I *know* not everything can be controlled. But I have the right to guard what little I have left."

"You've never been where I am," Dicey said. Her brown face looked pale. "You never had to contemplate doing *this*"—she rested her hands on her stomach—"alone!"

"You wanna bet?"

Dicey's mouth hung open, her next sentence stopped, half formed.

Miriam turned away and started down the stairs. She could feel the whole gloppy mess bubbling up. Maybe if she went fast enough, she could outrun it. The wind whipped her face, but it wasn't loud enough to bury the sound of Dicey calling her name, wheezing as she followed.

Then Dicey shrieked. Miriam wheeled, cursing her own selfishness. The younger woman hadn't fallen, but she was folded over the red railing that bisected the stairs, clinging to it as she tried to catch her breath.

Miriam ran back up and caught hold of her. "I'm sorry," she said. "I'm so sorry, honey." She fumbled in Dicey's bag for a bottle of water and handed it to her.

Dicey coughed hard, as if trying to expel her very lungs. She spit the results in the shaggy grass adjacent to the stairs. Miriam winced and looked away.

Dicey gripped her arm. "What did you mean, 'you wanna bet'?"

Miriam swallowed. She felt very aware of the ground on which she stood: a veritable mountain, built one basketful of dirt at a time. Like the mountain of lies she'd built her adult life on.

"I wasn't married when I got pregnant either," she said. "I was terrified. I know exactly how it feels to think you're going to be doing it on your own."

A wind gust peppered them with dust. Dicey turned her face away until it passed. "Miriam, that makes no sense. Everything you ever said about Teo, he's not the kind of guy who'd—"

"Teo wasn't the twins' biological father."

The words disappeared into the great open space, swirling upward on the wind, as if taken by the ghosts of all the Native Americans who'd lived and worked and died in the shadow of this giant terraced mound.

Dicey gaped at her. "Then who . . ." She stopped, then said hesitantly, "Gus?"

Miriam nodded.

She could see Dicey spinning out the implications of this revelation. "Wow. No wonder you've been so freaked out about him."

Miriam had lived with the weight of this secret for so long, she felt off-balance without it. She gripped the railing, focusing on the edges of peeling paint to ground herself.

Voices approached, a man and woman walking hand in hand. They fell silent, nodding and smiling at Miriam and Dicey as they passed.

Dicey waited until they were out of earshot. "So Teo . . . knew?"

"Of course."

"What about the kids?"

Miriam's throat closed up. "No," she said softly. "I was too scared."

The moment lengthened, the sun warming the top of her head. She'd been angry so much the past year—the inside of her chest like a volcano under pressure, waiting to blow. But shame was different. Shame felt cold. Cold and hard, and capable of binding her heart so tightly, she struggled to breathe.

"Wow," Dicey said. "You really do understand what I'm going through, don't you?" She made a face and shrugged. "Some of it anyway."

They stood awkwardly, looking at each other, not sure what to say. Miriam had never told anyone: not Becky, not her family, not her kids. From day one, she and Teo had conspired to keep it secret. Yet it seemed right, somehow, to tell this young woman who stood now where she'd once been. Maybe now, Dicey would let her help. Who could say? Maybe Dicey could help *her*.

Her phone rang again. She slipped it out of her back pocket, her finger moving toward "Silence," but when she saw who it was, she knew she couldn't ignore it. "It's my mom," she said apologetically.

"I'll . . . um . . ." Dicey pointed down the stairs. "I'll just wait for you at the car." She headed on down the wind-swept stairs and left Miriam alone.

★   ★   ★

When Miriam was little, she loved spending time with her mom.

Maybe it was because her parents worked, and she spent so much time under Jo's supervision, but she craved her mother's attention and approval. Mom gave her little jobs to do, like dusting, which morphed into bigger jobs as she proved herself capable. Eventually, Mom taught her to cook the family recipes handed down through generations of Polish women: pierogi and cabbage rolls and paczki.

She learned not to talk about music; Mom's eyes always glazed over. Mom liked it better when she talked about what she was learning in math or science. Sometimes they'd stop working so Miriam could write things out on paper and teach them to her mother.

Mom's antipathy toward music never made sense to Miriam. Mom had a beautiful voice. She'd pull out two ironing boards and let Miriam help her wash, starch, and iron the altar linens for church. They'd sing and sing: old Latin hymns, *Glory and Praise*, gospel music.

It wasn't that Mom and Dad ever forbade her from pursuing music. It was just that little hesitation every time she talked about it. The deep consideration before they agreed to let her enter a competition, whereas approval for any academic event seemed automatic.

Miriam tried to find something else. She really did. But nothing set her on fire the way music did. Kept her up nights with anticipation and the glow of creation.

And the deeper she went into music, the more the low-grade patina of unspoken disappointment seemed to color her relationship with her parents. By the time she realized that said more about their own unhappiness than anything they felt about her, she no longer felt safe opening her heart to them.

Which didn't mean they never talked. One of the surprises of adulthood was that families could be perfectly cordial while withholding what mattered most. For years, the long drive to Detroit after Christmas was a ritual of family life, like Sunday afternoon phone calls. But since Teo and Talia's voices had begun reminding her of the ways she'd failed them, Miriam had managed to limit most contact with her family to e-mail, where a degree of distance made avoiding the hard topics easier.

Now, standing on the steps of Monks Mound, her secret exposed to the universe, Miriam held her vibrating phone and wondered if she was poised to blow the lid off the fragile equilibrium she'd clung to for so long.

She breathed deep and swiped "Answer." "Hi, Mom." The words came out bright and brittle.

"Mira! Finally. I've been trying to reach you for days. Jo said you'd been *arrested*?"

"I hope she also said I was released, and it was all a big misunderstanding."

"Yes, yes, but are you all right? They didn't hurt you, did they?"

"I'm fine, Mom." Miriam suppressed a sigh. As vehement as Jo had been about keeping their mother calm, she seemed to have done a pretty good job of winding her up instead. "I don't know what Jo told you, but I was never in any danger. No charges, no nothing."

"Well, thank God for that. But you never know. I hope this doesn't cause you problems down the line. Did you check to make sure it's not on your record?"

Miriam tried to swallow her impatience. Probably it wasn't Jo's fault. Mom always gravitated toward alarmism. Most likely, her attention had shut down at the word "arrested." Miriam supposed if she'd ever heard Blaise or Talia had been arrested, her attention might have gotten stuck there too.

Exhaustion caught up with her all at once. "Everything's fine, Mom," she said, sliding to a seat on the stairs. "I promise. I'm already two states down the road."

"Where are you?"

"Near St. Louis." She leaned her head against the railing and gazed across the huge lawn that had once been a busy plaza. At the far end, two smaller mounds stood side by side. One for each of her children. "I'm sitting on a Native American mound, actually."

"Is that legal?" Her mother sounded shocked.

"It's a park, Mom!"

"I wish you'd called me. I could have flown out and driven with you. I could still come out and meet you. It would be safer than traveling by yourself."

"I'm not by myself. I'm traveling with a young woman now. Her name is Dicey."

"Yes, Jo said you'd picked up a hitchhiker. That's at least as dangerous. And what kind of name is that, anyway—'Dicey'?"

"The name her parents gave her, I presume. Anyway, there's nothing to worry about. She's hardly in any condition to beat me up and rob me. She's pregnant."

"She's *pregnant*? That's even worse. Do you really want to be responsible for her health and safety?"

The phone case bit into Miriam's hand. She forced herself to relax. "What do you want me to do, drop her off on the side of the road and say, 'Good luck'? At eight months pregnant? That's a real Christian attitude."

"Don't put words in my mouth. That's not what I'm saying at all. Buy her a bus ticket to wherever she's going."

"Look, Mom. We're headed in the same direction. Why not carpool? At least this way, if something happens, she's with someone who cares about her."

A moment of silence, while it registered to both women what Miriam had just admitted.

I am not replacing my daughter. I'm not.

Her mother spoke again, her voice lower, more gentle. "But there's no one to look after *you*."

Miriam bowed her head. For a moment, she let herself sink back through layers of memory, to a time when a hug from her mother had been the safest feeling in the world. Daughters grew and changed, and they found embraces stifling instead of comforting. Did that pendulum swing only once, from dependence to resentment? Or did it eventually reach equilibrium?

She would never know. At least, not from the perspective of a mother.

All the more reason to mend fences with her own mother. Miriam rubbed her forehead. "Listen, Mom, I know you don't approve of all this, but . . . I'm a mess right now. I need this. Once I get done with this trip, let's talk. Okay? I just need . . . I need to focus on me right now."

For a moment, Miriam heard only the low hiss of static on the connection. Then her mother cleared her throat. "All right, Mira. Just don't forget you still have a family."

When they'd said their goodbyes, Miriam laid her phone beside her on the steps. At the base of Monks Mound, Dicey, now a tiny figure far below, walked slowly toward the parking lot. Miriam watched her and wondered if there really was such a thing as a second chance for mothers.

Part 5

Near Des Moines, Iowa

Life is about surviving loss.

—Mary Steenburgen

Blaise's intro to the High Trestle Trail Bridge

The High Trestle Trail Bridge goes across the Des Moines River Valley. It's one of the longest trail bridges in the world—almost half a mile. It's part of a biking trail that connects two towns called Ankeny and Woodward. I know, you're thinking, "A bridge? Really?" But just wait till you see it. It's a work of art. Like, these things they call "cribbings"—I guess that's in reference to the structural braces they used to use inside coal mines. And it's thirteen stories tall! Enjoy!

✦ 21 ✦

Sunday, May 1
Hannibal, Missouri

FOR THE REST OF the day, Dicey didn't mention Miriam's revelation. She campaigned for and then planned a stop in Hannibal, Missouri, boyhood home of Mark Twain. But on the subject foremost on Miriam's mind, Dicey remained silent.

It was unnerving. Miriam had held her secret so long, she scarcely knew who she was without it. There was a giddy yet terrifying weightlessness, merely knowing another living soul knew it now too. She hadn't realized what a difference it had made, having Teo to share the burden. Now, she waited in agony for the moment Dicey would ask more questions . . . an agony of simultaneous dread and longing.

Touring the cave made famous by Tom Sawyer took her mind off it for a while. So did setting up the tent and air mattress at the adjacent campground. But when she left Dicey to go find a grocery store, it came rushing back.

Miriam returned to find Dicey perched on top of the picnic table, trying to take a selfie while holding a piece of paper that read "Love you forever" in bright pink, outlined in brown. "You want me to do that?" she asked.

"Sure."

Miriam snapped several pictures and then handed the phone back. Dicey continued working on her scrapbook while Miriam started cooking. But still not a word about Miriam's big secret.

Maybe she should take heart from that. If Dicey accepted the truth so casually, maybe everyone else would too.

Not Gus, though.

Miriam closed her eyes and breathed long and slow and deep, a singer's breath, then exhaled even more slowly, listening to the sound of insects in the trees and squirrels darting around in the undergrowth.

"This is so much work," Dicey said. "It'd be easier to go grab fast food."

Miriam opened her eyes. Dicey had set her phone aside and was watching her cook. The look on her face made Miriam smile. The kids used to say the same thing, in the same tone of voice, wearing that same look. "Everything about camping requires more effort. That's kind of the point. To focus on the moment. On the doing."

Dicey rolled her eyes. "Did you guys camp a lot?"

"Had to. We didn't have money to take big trips." Miriam turned back to her work. "I remember this one time, Teo set the fire up on the side of a hill. We didn't realize it until the sausages started rolling off the grate into the fire. He couldn't stop it. The kids were thrilled because we had to go to Dairy Queen for dinner. It was a huge treat."

She rolled the sausages onto plates. "Ready to eat?" She turned to find Dicey munching on root vegetable chips. "Clearly."

"Sorry. Got hungry. Needed salt."

"You and salt. Is this, like, a medical condition or something?"

"It's a none-of-your-damn-business condition."

The words were spoken with Dicey's characteristic biting humor, but they hit Miriam like a physical blow. She turned away.

Dicey wiggled off the table and came over to embrace her. "I'm sorry. That was bitchy. I know I'm kind of sensitive."

Miriam managed a little smile. "You're right, it's not my business." Although the more defensive Dicey got about it, the more suspicious Miriam became. Coughing, salt, and mechanical equipment in the bathroom. It added up to something. She just didn't know what.

But Dicey was already moving on. "I don't suppose you bought ketchup and mustard, did you?"

Miriam groaned. "No, I didn't even think of it."

"Hmm. Well, lucky for you, I keep all my fast-food packets. Here." Dicey opened another zipper on her apparently limitless backpack and grabbed a handful.

"Teo was the one who was good at that kind of stuff," Miriam said as she doctored her bun. She dropped her voice. "One more thing I never appreciated."

Dicey chewed her sausage thoughtfully, swallowing before she spoke again. "You're awfully hard on yourself. Your family died. It sucks. It's not fair. But how is it your fault?"

Miriam's throat sent up a sudden revolt at the taste of the sausage. With effort, she swallowed, then set the rest aside. "It's *not* my fault that they died. It's my fault that—" A hot wave rushed over her. She focused on the roughness of weathered wood beneath her palms to tether her to reality. "I never told them about . . ."

"Their real father."

Miriam's jaw muscles clenched against that phrase, but it was such a relief to have the subject open at last, she let it go.

Dicey scooted her chips around her paper plate. "I'm sure you had a reason."

Miriam nodded slowly. "Yes. But the longer I didn't talk about it, the more it—the more *I* changed." Why had she never realized that secrets harmed the keeper as much as the one left in the dark? "I used to be a good mother, you know. I was never a great wife, but I *was* a good mother. When they were little, I made their lunches, took them where they needed to go. Cuddled them, kissed their boo-boos. As long as they were little, I could justify keeping it from them. I was protecting them. They didn't need to be confused, you know? And we were always so busy. And exhausted. Whole weeks would go by when I didn't even think about it."

Dicey leaned on the heel of her hand, listening.

"But the older they got, the more I could see Gus in them. I couldn't forget anymore." Miriam shook her head. "The talent, the single-mindedness . . . Talia's charisma . . . but they were Teo's kids, you know? In their character. It was Teo who taught them to be human beings. *Good* human beings."

"And you."

Miriam spread her hands. "I don't know about that. Carrying that secret . . . it got in the way. It didn't seem to impact my relationship with Blaise so much . . ." She trailed off. Maybe Blaise had sensed the weight of her secret, and that was why he hadn't come to her.

Or maybe he hadn't come to her because there was nothing to come to her *about*. Trying to know the unknowable could make a person crazy.

Miriam shook her head and continued. "But Talia had a built-in bullshit monitor."

"Also like you."

Miriam smiled wanly. "She knew all the buttons to push. She'd always had these zingers in her back pocket, but it was like one day, they grew barbs. And they were always aimed at me. It was like she *knew* I was keeping something from her."

Dicey groaned. "Miriam."

"What?"

"Aside from the fact that you're being completely irra-tional, you're forgetting something important."

"Which is?"

"Teo knew too. If there's fault here, it's on both of you."

Miriam pondered that. "He wanted to tell them. I was too scared. I'd started doing these concerts and master-classes, and it was stressful on the family. I couldn't imagine adding to it."

Dicey looked skeptical. "So you feel guilty because you didn't tell your kids who their real dad was, and now you're torturing yourself because you carved out some time for yourself?"

She left Miriam to think about that while she pulled open a bag of marshmallows and crouched down to roast one. The sun hadn't yet set, but it had disappeared behind the hulking hill at their back. The glow of the fire pushed back against the gloom that gathered in the shadow of the Mississippi River bluffs.

Was Dicey right? Miriam wondered. The performance career—such as it was—had started while Teo and the kids were in Argentina. She'd rediscovered how it felt to have time for herself, practicing every day until she got her finger coordination back.

When they came home, Teo encouraged her to find an outlet, so she gave a recital at St. Greg's, then reached out to every community concert series within a hundred miles. One of them asked her to do a masterclass for local high schoolers. She enjoyed it so much, she added it to her offerings.

She enjoyed having something of her own, something she could take pride in. But it made life so much harder. They'd felt stretched thin, those last couple of years.

Dicey's voice interrupted her reverie. "So I guess their real dad doesn't know either," Dicey added.

This time, Miriam didn't let it go. "*Teo* was their real dad. Teo's the one who raised them. Changed their diapers, sang them to sleep."

"Yeah, yeah, my stepdad is my real dad too. I get it. But you're ignoring my point." Dicey looked up at her then.

"It's too late now to tell your kids, and it's killing you. The question is, are you going to tell Gus?"

That was the question, wasn't it? The one that had haunted most of her adult life. "I don't know," Miriam said. She could barely hear herself over the crickets. "I was afraid. Of how complicated it might get. Afraid he'd ruin them. They were such good kids, and he was such a . . . cad."

Dicey made a face at the old-fashioned word.

"What possible good could come of telling him now? He's missed the chance to have a relationship with them. I just feel like . . ." She pressed her lips together until the pressure in her throat eased. "I screwed up everything."

Dicey started fiddling with packages of crackers and chocolate. "Maybe you were wrong not to tell them. Maybe you were right. You may never know. But you can't torture yourself about it for the rest of your life. You're a good person."

"What have I done in my life that was worthwhile," Miriam said softly, "except make those kids?"

"Bullshit. Here. Eat this." Dicey shoved a s'more at her.

"I haven't eaten dinner."

"Oh, come on. You know you're not gonna eat that sausage. Might as well have this. It's perfectly toasted."

Miriam smiled and took it. Dicey was right. Perfect. "I thought you didn't camp."

"We have a firepit on our patio. We made s'mores all the time. Anyway." Dicey stared out at the falling darkness as she savored her own dessert. Then she swiveled to face Miriam. "I don't want you to run yourself down, Miriam. You deserve better. Look what you've done for me. That alone proves you're a good person."

Miriam shook her head. "Having you along keeps my mind occupied."

"So what? You think it's only a good deed if you get nothing out of it? You have to be miserable to be holy? How very Catholic of you."

Miriam swallowed without bothering to finish chewing. "That's not what Catholics believe," she said sharply. "That's not what *I* believe."

"Good. So prove it. Tell me one good thing you've done that has nothing to do with Teo or your kids."

The challenge touched a nerve. Miriam leaned on the picnic table, staring at the thick growth of old oak and elm and walnut, alive with the sound of spring insects. The hard edge of the graham cracker inched its way down her throat, scraping open parts of her she'd stopped paying attention to.

"Talia had a friend," she said slowly. "Not exactly a friend. An acquaintance from the civic youth orchestra. A kid from a rough background. Really screwed-up situation. But she was a phenomenal violist. Her dad threw her out of the house before rehearsal that night because . . . never mind; it doesn't matter why. When I came to pick up Talia, this girl was planning to sleep in the park. We brought her home with us instead. She stayed with us two weeks while I looked for a safe place for her. Eventually her dad went into rehab, and she went to live with her grandmother." Miriam nodded slowly. "I felt like I did something good there."

Dicey slapped her hands on her thighs. "You see? That wasn't so hard, was it?" She retrieved her backpack and suitcase and headed for the shower house, leaving Miriam to ponder a word she'd grown up with but never really understood until just now, when Dicey had shown her what it meant.

Grace.

♦ 22 ♦

Monday, May 2
Hannibal, Missouri

IN THE MORNING, MIRIAM woke to a curious sensation she couldn't quite place. It was a coolness in her heart, an emptiness in her mind. It was the sense of being in tune with God and the universe, of absence of anxiety. It was the sound of breathing on the air mattress beside her, reassuring her that she was not alone.

Contentment. That was it. She hadn't felt it in so long, she'd forgotten.

She wasn't supposed to be content. Teo was dead. Talia, dead. Blaise, dead.

A flashback of a scene she hadn't witnessed—only imagined again and again. The coastal highway. The kids talking, Teo's attention split. Crossing onto a bridge over an almost nonexistent creek. Shouting as that monster pickup truck swerved into their lane, crushing their little rental between the truck and the railing. Twisted metal. Screams. Burning.

Miriam sat bolt upright, her head grazing the roof of the tent, gasping for air. Her body was covered with sweat.

The air mattress bounced as she scrambled off it; Dicey groaned. Miriam unzipped the tent and escaped into the blessed chill of a spring morning, crouched down in a primal defensive position, her hands pressed to the dirt.

Sunlight pierced the canopy, laying down long strips of golden luminescence on the worn pavement as she walked to the shower house. Inside, she turned the spigot all the way over and let the water scald away the nightmare vision.

She powered up her phone on the way back to the campsite. Jo had called, and she had three text messages.

She listened to Jo's voicemail first. "Hey, Mira." Her sister sounded ill at ease. "Sorry to call so early, I have a merger to negotiate today so I won't be able to talk later, but I wanted to call, at least." A pause. "I have something I want to talk to you about. About Mom. So, call me tonight."

For Jo, that was unusually not pushy. Miriam navigated to her texts.

Becky: *How are you holding up? We're all thinking of you today.*

Gus: *Your motivational speech for today!* It was a link to a TED talk about working under pressure. "Thanks a lot," she murmured. "That's no pressure at all."

And Mom: *Just touching base. Call anytime if you need to talk.*

Well, she'd asked for space. Her mother was giving it to her without going completely silent. Although it was a little odd that *both* Mom and Jo were trying to contact her the same morning. Miriam suspected a conspiracy.

As if in response, her phone rang. It was her brother. Now she *knew* there was a conspiracy. That or an emergency.

She picked it up. "Brad?"

"Hey, Mira." He sounded half asleep.

Okay, maybe not an emergency. "What time is it where you are?"

"Um . . . five thirty?" Her silence evidently clued him in to the oddity of his calling at such an hour. "I'm in surgery today. I wanted to call while I had a chance. I imagine today's gonna be a rough one."

She was missing something. "Um . . ."

"I figure it was probably all too fresh last year, so this is probably the first one. I know Teo always made a big deal of your anniversary."

Anniversary.

Orange blossom and larkspur. The courthouse steps. Feeling nauseous, and not just from morning sickness. Teo, his hand sweaty, trying not to betray that he was at least as nervous as she was.

Miriam felt like she'd been punched in the gut. She'd come home after the congressman's funeral and canceled the standing order, and she'd never thought another thing about it.

"Mira?" asked Brad. "You still there?"

She heard her voice, faint and breathy, from a great distance. "I hadn't . . . been keeping track of the dates."

"Oh, shit." She could practically see him mussing his hair in agitation. "I'm so sorry. I didn't mean to—"

"Jo called this morning. And Mom texted. I couldn't figure out why." She chuffed, more a hiccup than a laugh. "Imagine Jo remembering when I didn't. What kind of person doesn't remember her own anniversary?"

Silence on the line. Then, a fierce tone. "Don't do that, Mira. Don't do that to yourself. You're on the road. You're off schedule. Besides, Mom probably called Jo last night to remind her."

"Mom never forgets stuff like that."

"Of course she doesn't. And neither do you under ordinary circumstances. I'd place bets you've never forgotten before."

Miriam swallowed. "That's true." But that was because they'd always talked about it together. Planned it together. She'd never *had* to remember it on her own.

The tent zipper buzzed. "Going to the shower," Dicey mouthed. She dragged her suitcase up the drive.

"Mom was hoping to spend this whole week with you," Brad said. "To . . . you know. Support you, or whatever. But she got roped into helping plan some big event at church. You know how she is."

"Yeah." Miriam mustered a chuckle and then gathered her thoughts to redirect the conversation away from herself.

A survival instinct. "Is everything okay with Mom? Jo's message said . . . I don't know—it was weird. She wants to talk about her."

"Oh, you know Jo. She has Mom one foot in the grave. Mom's fine, she's just not fifty anymore. I mean, she's lonely. Like you. I'm sure that's what Jo's thinking about. She sees you both in pain and figures you can help each other. Merger of two struggling entities, you know?"

Miriam smiled wanly. "She does try to make everything fit into a profit loss spreadsheet, doesn't she? Dad would be so proud."

"Wow. That was bitter." Brad hesitated. "Do you have any *good* memories of our family?"

Miriam pondered the question. "We used to have popcorn and soda on Sunday nights," she said at length. "And watch Disney movies. I liked those nights. And I remember doing a puzzle one New Year's Eve."

"Wow," Brad said again. "That's all you remember?"

"I remember Dad on his deathbed, still trying to convince Teo to go back to the accounting firm."

Brad blew out a breath. "I'm sorry, Mira. I wish . . . you know, they really struggled for a while. They kept it from us, but it wasn't easy for them."

Miriam remained silent. They probably did think they'd kept it from her.

"Neither one of them were any good at all that warm fuzzy stuff, and it probably hurt them more than it hurt us. But it doesn't mean they didn't love us. Dad wanted to provide for us, and Mom . . . I think Mom worked so hard around the house because she didn't know how else to show us how she felt. When they were having problems, I figure she was too scared to own up to the hard stuff. She figured she'd just do what she could." He paused. "You're a lot like her, you know, Mira."

"Emotionally constipated?"

Brad uttered a short bark of laughter. "I'm just saying, cut yourself some slack."

Miriam considered. Maybe Mom, too, had dreams she'd had to bury, hopes left unrealized, ghosts unresolved. Maybe she'd done the best she could with what she had.

Brad was right; she *was* like her mother. She, too, had been scared to face the hard parts in her marriage; she, too, had compensated by making sure dinner was on the table and everyone had everything they needed. She wasn't perfect, but she'd done the best she could.

"As far as Jo," Brad said now, "don't worry about it. My theory is, thinking about you makes her feel guilty."

"Jo? Guilty?"

"Sure. All this touchy-feely social justice Catholic stuff you and Teo were into—the food pantries and the refugee resettlement stuff—she can't figure why you'd put so much energy into giving other people a leg up when you always had to make do with so little yourselves."

"She sort of missed the point of all that Catholic schooling." It was getting easier to talk, now that she could focus on something else.

Brad liked it better also. His chuckle was a little too high-pitched to hide his discomfort. "Actually, I think she got the point perfectly well. That's why she feels guilty. But I don't have room to talk. Look what I'm doing with my life."

"Breast augmentations for A-listers?"

"Well, wannabe A-listers, anyway." He laughed at his own expense, then sobered. "I hate it, you know."

"Really?"

"It's awful, Miriam. I mean, I'm good at it. And I like the way I live. I like my house, I like surfing, I like throwing big parties. I need the money to make all that possible. But I hate the work. I always admired you two. What you did . . . it was who you were. They were one and the same. There aren't many of us who get to tie together our work and our identity. I always envied you that. I still wish I knew what I could do to make my life like that."

The surge of affection for her brother surprised her. Growing up, Brad had never been all that supportive. Or even present. He'd left for college when she was in the fifth grade. Mostly, she remembered him teasing her.

"I had no idea you felt this way," she said. "I'm sorry I never asked."

"Oh well, our family never really talked about our problems, did we? Maybe we'd all be happier now if we'd learned to deal with things instead of sitting on them and letting them fester." The line fell silent for a moment. Then he took a breath. "Look, I gotta go, but if Jo gives you any crap, just ignore her. You be you, Mira. And I'll be happy knowing you're happy. Or anyway, knowing you will be again."

"Will I?"

"Oh yes," he said quietly but with conviction. "You will. And you should let yourself be."

♦ 23 ♦

Monday, May 2
Near Des Moines, Iowa

MIRIAM KEPT THE RADIO on all the way into Iowa to discourage conversation and leave space to think. Her unexpectedly profound conversation with Brad had given her a lot to unpack.

Dicey took the hint, breaking Miriam's reverie only to request occasional bathroom breaks. They both stared out the window, drinking in the sight of endless miles of fields. Something about the sight of green tractors sweeping up and down the black fields settled Miriam's soul. *Repetitive work,* she thought. By all indications, boring—yet full of purpose.

They arrived at the High Trestle Trailhead late in the afternoon. It was in the middle of nowhere—not particularly near Des Moines or anything else except a water tower and two tall grain elevators.

As soon as the car stopped, Dicey headed for the trim red building that housed the restrooms. Miriam got out and stretched, breathing deep of the cool, clean air. One thing had become clear in the last five hours on the road: today needed to be about Teo. She might have forgotten her anniversary, but she hadn't missed it. She knew what she wanted to do with this day. She wanted to play Teo's guitar out on that bridge.

She headed for the restroom too, and when she returned, she didn't see Dicey anywhere. She pulled the guitar out of the car and strapped it on her back. As she donned Talia's beribboned hat, she heard Dicey speaking indistinctly. She turned. The young woman sat on a nearby bench, talking to her phone. At first, Miriam thought she was arguing with someone by video chat; she had a fierce, impassioned look on her face. But as Miriam approached, the words became clear. ". . . so that's the first thing I want you to remember. My second would be, always listen to your grandma. She's a pain in the neck, but she knows what she's doing. And the third is this: you are brown, you are beautiful, you are strong. Go change the world for me, baby."

Miriam halted. This was no conversation; Dicey was recording a message for her daughter.

She inched backward, but Dicey noticed her anyway. Her face wiped clean. "Hey," she said. Her phone disappeared into her pocket.

"Sorry," Miriam said. "I didn't mean to disturb you." She hesitated, wondering if she dared ask the purpose of that video. Dicey was by turns totally open and prickly as a porcupine.

Dicey gestured. "You're taking the guitar?"

"I thought I'd go out and play some of Teo's favorite music. Badly."

Dicey grinned. "I don't believe that for a second."

"Well, let's get going. You'll see soon enough."

Dicey hauled herself to her feet, and they started down the paved trail, only to stop at a sign: "High Trestle Trail Bridge: 2.5 miles."

Miriam turned to her companion. Could she safely walk five miles round trip? "Um . . ."

"Come on, we're wasting daylight." Dicey grabbed her elbow and propelled her forward.

Miriam's phone dinged as they began walking. She palmed it and rolled her eyes to see Gus's name. "This is the second time today."

"For what?"

"Gus," she said.

"Really?" Dicey looked thoughtful. "What's he want?"

Miriam clicked the attachment and found herself looking at a program. *Cleaning my desk and found the program from the festival concert. Do you have a copy? Would you like one?* she read. She sighed. "Really, I think what he's doing is reminding me that he wants that sonata finished."

"That's kinda pushy."

"Yeah, well. Gus has never been what you'd call 'subtle.' He's wearing me out."

"Secrets are hard to carry," Dicey observed.

This from the girl who turned every conversation away from herself.

Miriam took the high road, tapping out a short reply: *Sure, thanks.*

She slid the guitar case around her front and slipped her phone into the zippered pocket. "So—that recording you were making, back there? It's for your daughter?"

"Just thinking out loud," Dicey said. "You had a conversation this morning too. Who were you talking to?"

Miriam shook her head, chuckling at the two of them, dancing around subjects they didn't want to discuss. She decided to break the dysfunctional cycle. "My brother."

"Oh? Why was he calling?"

"Today's my wedding anniversary."

Dicey's jaw dropped. "Oh, Miriam." She hesitated. "What did he say about it?"

How to distill that conversation into one topic? "He said I'll be happy again someday. And that I should let myself be."

"Huh." Dicey eyed her appraisingly. "That's surprisingly empathetic, for a guy."

Laughter underscored the heavy, compressed ache around her heart. "How did you get so jaded?"

"I've only ever known one good man in my life—my stepdad." Dicey spread her hands. "Though it seems like your Teo was a good one, I have to admit. And it sounds like your brother's not completely without hope." Dicey winced and pressed her hand to her abdomen. "Baby girl's feisty today."

Miriam slowed. "I'm pushing you too hard. Should we go back?"

"No way. I'm feeling better than I have in a long time. It's just that sometimes I forget for a little while. It's just nice to pretend nothing's changed. But then sometimes . . ."

"Then it hits you all at once, and you can't breathe. You just want it to go away."

"Mostly I just get pissed off." Dicey was already out of breath. "I want to go do something really stupid, like bungee jump or skydive or, I don't know, get trashed. Just to give this pregnancy the finger, you know?"

Miriam nodded, laughing. "I know exactly."

Out of nowhere, Dicey started coughing so hard, she had to stop and bend over. Miriam wrapped her arms around the younger woman, helping her to the ground and holding her while her body heaved.

The tight ache of anxiety that seemed her constant companion these days seemed less burdensome suddenly. It had turned outward.

Tenderness. That's what it was. Talia had contracted food poisoning a few weeks before her final Christmas. Taking care of her, Miriam had felt this same beautiful ache. So often, life with Talia had been a battle. For that fleeting thirty-six hours, Talia had belonged to her again. She was needed—and, more importantly, *wanted*.

Dicey's coughing fit lasted a long time. When it finally slowed, Miriam pulled a bottle out of the bag and handed it over. Dicey drank, coughed again, and drank some more. She was sweating.

A bicycle bell dinged; Miriam scrambled to clear the path so the group could pass by. Then she braced herself and helped Dicey to her feet. "I think we need to turn around, honey," she said.

"No!" Dicey pulled a pill bottle out of her backpack and tossed back a tablet. "I just can't talk anymore. Not while I'm walking."

Miriam regarded her with a focus she hadn't felt in a long time, her own troubles distant and insignificant. "Dicey," she said, "what's going on with you?"

"Nothing you need to worry about."

"But I am worried. I care about you."

"Then help me up and let's get going."

But as soon as she started walking, Dicey clutched her abdomen again. "Damn, that hurts," she said through gritted teeth. "That's been happening more often. Like some muscle's about to snap."

"Oh, I know what that is. Round ligament pain." Miriam took a deep breath to calm her racing heart. Mom's warnings about traveling with a pregnant woman sounded more justified today than she'd given them credit for.

"The fact that you knew what it is from that pathetic description does not comfort me. Is it that common?"

"Well, it certainly happened to me a lot." Miriam shook her head. "Look, it's not worth this. Let's just head back."

"No!" Dicey took several deep breaths. Frustration flitted across her face and then gave way to resignation. "I'll go back. But you need to do this."

For Dicey to admit weakness, she must be feeling wretched. Miriam gripped her elbow. "I'm not leaving you alone."

"Give me the keys. I'll go sit in the car. It'll be fine. You need this time. Take it."

Miriam bit her lip. She did want this. Very much. "Are you sure?"

"Positive. I've got your phone number if I need you. I could use a nap anyway, and there are plenty of snacks. Go on. And don't you rush yourself either! Do this thing properly."

Miriam raised her hands, laughing. "All right, all right," she said, and started down the trail toward the bridge. A hundred yards down the path, she peeked over her shoulder.

Dicey was watching. *"Go!"* she yelled.

Miriam laughed and faced forward.

★　★　★

The trail unfolded beneath Miriam's feet. It was uncannily quiet, with only the crickets and native grasses and trees and the sky for company. Beautiful, but a little lonely.

"Happy," Brad had said. *"You should let yourself be happy."*

She'd be satisfied with much less. She'd be content to walk with her head held high and her heart unfettered again.

How did one simply choose to be happy?

One foot in front of the other. Her feet hurt. Talia's artistically beat-up Mary Poppins boots were not designed for long walks.

She spotted the twin obelisks marking the end of the bridge long before she reached them. They were built of blond stone, wide at the base, tapering toward the sky, with veins of charcoal running through them. As she passed between the towers, she understood why Blaise had chosen this out-of-the-way, uninspiring-sounding landmark as a destination for the trip. The High Trestle Trail Bridge really *was* a work of art. Massive rust-colored square frames, angled in a radial pattern, dotted the crossing and created a tunnel effect in the center of the bridge. These must be the "cribbings" Blaise had mentioned.

A bicycle bell rang behind them. "On your left!"

Miriam hugged the rail. The man passed, followed by a woman with a toddler on a seat behind her. "Beautiful day!" she said.

And it was. Miriam glanced over her shoulder. It was a long way down—and a long way across. The wind kept blowing her hair in her face, no matter how many times she tucked it behind her ears. She pulled out her phone to take a pano of the river bottoms, just beginning to emerge from the spring rise. Patches of grass and black soil peeked from the water. Birds circled low, dipping in to grab dinner. So peaceful. So quiet.

The wind grabbed the tassels of Miriam's scarf-headband and slapped her across the face with them. Miriam chuckled and set off again, now at a leisurely amble. As she walked, she sent the photo to Dicey. Her coiled insides were finally beginning to relax.

On the far side of the cribbings, the bridge deck widened to accommodate twin viewing platforms. She stopped there and shouldered out of the guitar case, letting it rest against the rail as she took in the scenery. Momentarily her phone buzzed. *Wow,* Dicey said. *Wish I could've made it.*

Miriam crossed her hands on opposite arms, rubbing them for warmth. It was chilly here, much chillier than May in Atlanta, but not as cold as May in the Detroit of her childhood.

When she'd had her fill, she unzipped the guitar case and pulled it out, slipping the strap over her neck and checking the tuning. Then she looked around. There really wasn't anywhere to sit. She hoisted herself onto the railing in the corner of the overlook platform, wrapping her feet around the bars for stability.

She closed her eyes, searching the vaults of her memory, and began playing softly, then humming "Georgia on My Mind." How many times had she come home from running kids to practices to hear these chords and Teo's lovely rich baritone, drifting in from the back deck? It was one of his favorites.

Involuntarily, her lips parted, forming the words quietly, an intimate love song to the place she'd lived with her husband.

It felt like forever since she'd sung. At least, sung like this, with the music vining tenderly around her heart, drawing emotion from her soul, thickening her voice. The song ended too soon. The wind gusted as she transitioned to another of his old standbys—the Fauré "Pie Jesu," which they'd often sung at weddings at St. Greg's. Usually, brides wanted the piano or organ, but once in a while Teo convinced someone to let him accompany. It was lovely that way. She closed her eyes, leaning into the music as the cold wind blew her hair around her face. She wasn't nearly good enough to do it justice, but it brought Teo closer.

In some ways, that was worse. This raw, burning ache in her throat—this gaping hole beneath her sternum—those hurt far worse than guilt and self-recrimination.

Her fingers stilled on the strings. She became aware of the low, mournful keening of the wind, the cry of hawks circling on invisible currents. Aware of the wet, dank smell of mud far below. Of the chill against her skin that grew deeper every moment as the watery sun sank toward the horizon.

"That was absolutely beautiful, ma'am," said a voice.

She opened her eyes. Leaning on the opposite rail stood a man with gray hair and glasses. Around seventy, she guessed. "Hello," she said.

"I've never heard anybody play out here."

"It's a long way to haul an instrument," she said.

He smiled and nodded, staring at the sinking sun. "It is, that. But worth it if you play like you."

"You're far too kind." Miriam flexed her butt muscles, which were starting to numb against the metal railing. She had a suspicion what was coming, and it meant she'd be here for a while longer. She was starting to get a sixth sense for people who'd experienced loss.

His next words confirmed it. "My wife was a musician," he said, leaning on the rail.

"Vocal or instrumental?"

"High school choir director. Voice like an angel. We met in a choir, you know. Community choir, for Christmas. Got married six months later."

"When did you lose her?"

"Six weeks ago," he said, shaking his head. "Real sudden-like."

"I'm sorry."

"Me too. She loved this bridge. Walked it nearly every day. We live just over there." He waved indiscriminately toward the far end of the bridge. "I was always too busy. Too tired from taking extra shifts, to give her nice trips, when all she wanted was to be with me."

Miriam nodded. She knew that regret all too well.

"I was taking voice lessons before she died, though," he said. "I was going to surprise her on our anniversary. But we didn't make it."

Miriam's heart went out to him. She opened and closed her mouth, trying to decide whether to tell him her story: the loss, the significance of today in her marriage.

Teo's presence perched on her shoulder, the way it had the day she met Dicey. *"You know what he needs,"* it seemed to say.

"What were you going to sing?" she asked. "On your anniversary?"

He looked surprised. "Schubert. 'Du bist die Ruh.'"

She smiled and nodded. "A good choice. Good pronunciation too."

He smiled. "I had German in high school, you know, a couple hundred years ago."

Miriam smiled too. The query was enough; the man was satisfied he'd been heard. But Teo's presence hovered around her, nudging her to go further.

I'm not good enough, she told it.

"Doesn't matter," he would have said. And of course he was right.

"Would you like to sing it now?" she asked.

He turned to her, startled. "Really?"

"Keep your expectations low," she warned. "I'm a pianist, not a guitarist. But I think I could muddle my way through it."

He raised his shoulders. "Well, I'm a grocery store manager, not a singer, so we're even on that score." He pushed off the wall, assuming a posture that would have made Maria Callas proud. Miriam noodled around a minute, getting her bearings in a song she'd only ever played on piano, and then nodded.

He was right—his was not a trained voice. But it was a beautiful one. Clear and unaffected. The kind of voice people would love to hear cantor at church.

She'd forgotten how beautiful this song was. Or maybe it just meant more, coming from a man who'd undertaken to learn it as a gesture of love. She didn't know German, but she remembered the gist of the translation: a lullaby to absolute trust. A testament of love made all the more powerful by the fact that it never used the word at all.

It was the perfect song to dedicate to Teo on this day.

When the song ended, the man put his hand down heavily on the rail. Miriam's breath felt slightly tremulous.

He looked up, his eyes bright. He crossed the distance between them and hugged her, guitar and all. "Thank you," he said.

Her heart contracted. Bittersweet: yet another emotion rediscovered. A pang, profound and painful, but pure. Not infused with self-recrimination. For once, she'd done Teo proud.

"My pleasure," she whispered.

Part 6

Chimney Rock, Nebraska

I have found the paradox, that if you love until it hurts, there can be no more hurt, only more love.

—Mother Teresa

Talia's intro to Chimney Rock

So, Chimney Rock. This one's way off the beaten path. It's a big rock out at the far edge of nowhere Nebraska, but it looks way cool. It's about 300 feet high, so you can't miss it. And when the settlers were on the Oregon Trail, this was one of the big landmarks that let them know they hadn't gotten lost in all that grass.

It's got a visitors center run by the National Park Service, so you guys can read signs to your hearts' content. Yawn. We'll be having fun at Interlochen.

✦ 24 ✦

Tuesday, May 3
Omaha, Nebraska

WIND FARMS AND FIELDS: western Iowa in a nutshell. Lots and lots of fields. A few displayed rows of tiny, bright green plants marching away into the distance, but most were still bare black earth, striped with planting furrows.

Dicey had given up on the view long ago, burying herself in her scrapbook app, but Miriam found it soothing, a calm counterpoint to the intensity of the last few days. They'd slept in this morning and then gone out for a huge, sit-down breakfast. Now they were getting close to Omaha. Nebraska, for heaven's sake. Never, in all her daydreams about traveling the world, had she imagined visiting *Nebraska*.

Her phone rang through the Bluetooth. Miriam punched "Answer" without looking at the ID. "Hello?"

"Oh, so you *are* alive!"

Miriam smacked the back of her head against the headrest. "Hi, Jo."

"Don't sound so thrilled. I suppose I ought to be grateful you answered, considering you flaked out on me last night."

Miriam gritted her teeth. Apparently Jo's lack of pushiness only had enough staying power for one day. "Look, I did what you wanted. I talked to Mom. I asked her for some space, and she gave it to me. Which I'm sure you know because you talk to Mom all the time. So how about you ease up?"

"All right, pipe down. I didn't call to pick a fight."

Dicey flashed Miriam a look that clearly communicated: *Coulda fooled me!* Miriam bit back a laugh, knowing it would only aggravate Jo further and make whatever this was last longer.

"I only have five minutes," Jo said. "If you'd called me last night when you were supposed to . . ."

"I believe you said something about not picking a fight?"

Dicey gave her a fist pump.

"All right, all right." Jo took a deep breath and lowered her voice. "It's just a crazy day. It would have been much better to do this last night."

Miriam didn't argue, but she knew her sister. Jo worked around the clock; last night, this morning—it made no difference.

"So I have an idea that will help everyone," Jo said. "My firm is opening an office in Albuquerque. I can guarantee you a position as an administrative assistant. You can live with Mom."

Miriam picked her jaw up off the floor. "You're kidding."

"It'll be good for both of you. Mom's seventy-five. She needs someone to look after her, and Brad and I can't relocate. But you can."

"Because my life and my work are so much less important than yours?"

"Miriam." Jo infused the word with deep scorn. "Don't act like a child. You know there's nothing for you in Atlanta now."

"No, thank you."

"See? I knew you'd react this way. Mom thought you'd listen, but I—damn it!"

"What?" Miriam said, making sure her tone communicated her displeasure.

"They're early. I've got to take this call." Jo made it sound like the interruption was Miriam's fault. She spit out the rest in a rush. "Look, I know you don't like change, but think about it. For Mom's sake. And yours. Whether you know it or not, you need this."

"Goodbye, Jo."

"I'll call you later." The phone went dead.

Dicey drummed her fingers on the door. "Well, that was awkward."

"Yeah."

"You know, I'm not entirely sure I like your sister."

Miriam laughed. "I learned long ago the best way to deal with Jo is curl up in a ball and let her bulldoze through. Eventually, she'll run out of steam."

"I have a better idea."

"What's that?"

"Ignore her calls."

Miriam made a noise of opposition. "You don't know Jo. There's a reason she climbed the corporate ladder as quickly as she has. She doesn't roll over when she wants something. You ignore her, she escalates."

Dicey made a face but didn't argue. She pulled out her pink spangled phone and held it up to photograph the state line sign as the Hyundai glided smoothly onto the bridge across the Missouri River. "Nebraska . . . the good life!" it proclaimed.

Miriam's phone dinged again. Dicey sighed as she exchanged one phone for the other. "Boy, she's a real piece of work. Making deals and texting at the same—oh."

"Oh what?"

"It's not her. It's your friend, Captain von Trapp, or whatever."

Miriam winced. "He's not my friend. What's it say?"

"*Just put the program in the mail.* Well, I'm so glad he shared that enlightening and useful piece of information."

Miriam chuckled.

Dicey tapped Miriam's phone on her palm. "Does it seem weird that he's texting you so much?"

Miriam raised her shoulders. "I don't know."

"It just seems like kind of . . . I don't know, entitled behavior, if you aren't actually friends."

Miriam snorted. "Entitled sounds about right."

"So, you want to reply or not?"

Not really. But courtesy dictated otherwise. "Just say, 'Thanks.'"

Dicey complied, coughing into her elbow as she did, and dropped the phone back in the well. But in a moment, it dinged again. Dicey sucked an annoyed breath through her teeth, but she picked it up and read it:

So this is going to sound crazy, but I've been looking at your social media, and you look familiar to me. Have we met before? Or is it just because Blaise looks like you?

Dicey looked at Miriam. "Whoa. If you want to tell him, I'd say that's an opening."

"You want me to tell him by text message?"

Dicey held up her hands. A mile or two of industrial Omaha passed by the windows before Gus's next text dinged. Dicey lifted the phone.

I hope I'm not offending you. It's the last thing I intend.

"He must be wondering why you haven't replied," Dicey said.

"Well, he's going to have to keep wondering."

"Uh, okay . . ." Dicey sounded doubtful.

Another ding: *If it's the e-mail thing, I just want you to know, I had no idea you didn't know Blaise and I were e-mailing.*

Dicey looked over at Miriam. "I think you're gonna have to—"

Ding.

Dicey's sigh signaled her growing impatience with her role in this one-sided communication.

If I'd ever had a son, I think he would have been just like Blaise. My wife pointed out how he pulled in his lower lip when he played. I used to do that.

Shit. "Turn it off," Miriam said. "Turn it all the way off."

"Gladly." Dicey complied and threw the phone in the well. "Something's wrong with that guy. You really think he doesn't know who you are?"

"If he knew, surely he'd just say so."

"He said everything else, that's for sure." Dicey pulled her backpack onto her lap and curled forward over it. "But he's so emotionally involved in all this. It's almost creepy. That lower lip thing."

Of all the things Miriam found troubling about Gus inserting himself into her life, this was the most disturbing. "He's right," she said softly.

"About the lip?"

"Yes. It was one of the first things about Blaise that reminded me of Gus."

Dicey sat up, rubbing her stomach, but she didn't reply, and Miriam didn't prompt her. Traffic was heavier in Omaha than it had been since St. Louis, and the SUV flashing its lights in her rearview alerted her that she'd been in the left lane too long. She gunned the gas to clear the vehicle beside her and merged over. The SUV roared by, followed by a semi that sucked the car to the left and then released it again.

Dicey groaned.

Miriam jumped. "Are you okay?"

"I can't tell if it's Baby Girl kicking or indigestion." She took a deep breath and exhaled slowly. "There. It's better now. Sort of."

Miriam heard her mother's warning again. "Let's find you a quick care clinic," she said. "Just to get you looked over."

Dicey shook her head. "No, I need to get back to California. My doctor there is expecting me."

"Well then, maybe we need to forget this whole flip-a-coin thing and go straight there."

"No. I'm all right. Come on, let's turn on some music." Dicey flipped the radio on and hit "Seek," pausing just long enough on each station to classify it. R&B, hip-hop, country, Christian radio, classical.

Which was playing Gus's movie score.

Not funny, Miriam addressed the heavens.

She reached for the dial, but Dicey knocked her hand away. "No, no, I love this one!"

Of course she did.

"You know this won an Academy Award, right?"

Miriam gripped the steering wheel. "Yup."

"Did you see the movie?"

"I haven't seen too many movies in the last year."

"Of course. I'm sorry."

"It's okay."

The music filled the car. For months, it had been used to promote everything from burgers to Band-Aids. Who would have ever thought Gus, the quintessential ivory tower boy, would explore such plebian territory as a save-the-world-from-certain-destruction blockbuster? People were comparing him to John Williams.

The music ended with a soul-stirring swell that faded into the quiet hiss of the radio signal. Then the announcer came on. "That was August von Rickenbach's Oscar-winning score to *Terminus.*"

"Huh." Dicey rubbed her stomach absently. "von Rickenbach." A pause. "Hang on," she said slowly. "Is this *him*?"

Miriam groaned.

"You're shitting me. The father of your kids is an Academy Award winner? For *writing music*? Why aren't you beating down his door for help with Blaise's sonata?"

"I don't want to."

"Because . . .?"

"Because I don't trust him. That's why."

Dicey rubbed her hands over the swell of her belly for a long moment, thinking. Then she said, "I kinda think you gotta tell him, Miriam."

"What?"

"It doesn't take anything away from Teo. But all those texts—it's obviously bugging him. And it's killing you."

"How do you suggest I have that conversation? Call him up and say, 'Hey man, let's Zoom? You know how you think I look familiar? That's because you slept with me back at the Curtis Institute. And guess what? I got pregnant with twins. Remember me now?'"

Dicey waited out her sarcasm, then said calmly, "I think you have to go see him in person. Take him for coffee. Someplace public, where he can't kill you for keeping this from him for twenty years."

Miriam gaped at her. "Are you serious?"

"You're headed for San Francisco, right? Because that's where they died?"

Miriam tipped her head back and forth. "More or less. It was near a beach south of the city."

"So yes, in other words. You know you'll never have another opportunity like this."

Miriam focused on the roar of vehicles surrounding her, filled with moms and carpools and delivery guys. People with purpose. People with places to go.

"What if I screwed up his life too?" she said softly.

Dicey's voice sounded slightly strained. "We screw up our own lives, Miriam. We don't need any help."

Then she doubled over with a gasp, her teeth gritted, her face pale, her breathing shallow and labored. "Oh, crap. Crap, crap, crap."

"What?"

"Literally, crap. Bathroom. Need a bathroom. Now."

Miriam crossed two lanes of traffic in order to make the next exit, eliciting a honk and the bird from the driver of an SUV going too fast. She careened into the parking lot of a Wendy's. Dicey had the door open before the car came to a complete stop.

Mıʀıᴀᴍ ɢᴏᴛ ᴏᴜᴛ ᴏғ the car. The sweetness of crabapple hung heavy on the warming air. She breathed deep, stretched, and settled into the moment. She'd forgotten how it felt to be idle. For so long, her life had been a hamster wheel, kids' activities chasing church responsibilities in an ever-accelerating circle. Planning weddings, funerals, choir rehearsals—although, truth be told, she'd spent more time winging choir rehearsals than planning them.

She walked slowly along the sidewalk. It felt good to stretch her legs. To drink in the feel and smell of spring, the way it mixed with the aroma of fried food coming from Wendy's. It was like . . . being alive.

Dicey wanted her to tell Gus. The idea was terrifying. What good would it do now? And how much harm?

And yet, to have this weight off her chest . . . it was what Teo had wanted from her. *For* her.

For twenty years, she'd picked at the jagged wound of her unfinished history with Gus von Rickenbach, her emotions numbing as it scabbed over but never healed. As a teenager and young adult, he'd had such a hold on her. He'd been like an addiction, his face behind her eyes every time she practiced, rendering her blind to all others.

If she hadn't been so starry-eyed over Gus, maybe she would have realized Teo had been in love with her from the beginning.

Mom and Jo had seen it. Teo had been living with his uncle for years by then, his parents having returned to Argentina to care for their aging elders. She invited him to Detroit for Thanksgiving the year she was at Curtis. Mom and Dad raised their eyebrows, but Miriam insisted they were just friends.

"Don't you see how he looks at you?" Mom asked the night before Thanksgiving, as she, Jo, and Miriam peeled potatoes.

"He looks at me like he's paying attention to me. He looks at everyone like that. He looks at *you* like that. Because he's a really good human being."

Jo looked up in the act of mutilating a potato while attempting to cut out a bad spot. "I think you're fooling yourself," she said as a potato chunk flew across the room and Mom loudly protested the mess.

Thankfully, the men came in then, in pursuit of a snack, and Mom and Jo dropped the subject. But the whole rest of the weekend had been kind of awkward. And with Mom and Dad tiptoeing around each other, overly polite and falsely bright for Jo's and Brad's benefit, Miriam couldn't help thinking about the guy who'd asked her to prom her senior year. She liked him as a person, but she'd been too nice to him. He'd been crushed when he realized she wasn't interested in being his girlfriend.

She thought too highly of Teo to let that happen again.

So Miriam paid closer attention the next couple of months, and every once in a while, just often enough to make her nervous, she thought Mom and Jo might be right. The night before she left for Boston—the fateful trip where Gus had noticed her at last—Teo had walked her to her car after choir practice. "You've been working so hard," he told her. "Go knock 'em dead. When you come back, I'll take you out to celebrate. I . . ." He hesitated, then forged ahead. "I have something I'd like to talk to you about."

It could have been anything—a recording project, a personnel problem he needed advice on—but something in the way he was fiddling with the loose string on his music bag signaled nerves. Miriam felt a hot flush—half thrill, half dread—which she resolutely shoved down. "Sure," she said casually.

Two days later, Gus noticed her, and the heavens opened. When she came back to the church ensemble, everyone could tell. They were happy for her—even Teo tried to be. But their rapport was all off. They'd always been perfectly in sync, finding each other's styles with ease, bouncing ideas off each other for how to highlight a verse or a nugget of text.

No one really enjoyed rehearsal that night. They all teased her for being on cloud nine. Except Teo. All his usual banter was absent.

She and Teo could talk about anything except Gus, it turned out. She'd never mentioned his name to Teo—not until after. And she never talked to Gus about Teo either. They represented conflicting worlds she couldn't reconcile. And then Gus ripped her heart out, and Teo picked it up.

How much joy she could have had with Teo. If she'd just confronted Gus, it might have been different. A failed relationship was supposed to end in a breakup. It wasn't supposed to just hang there, unresolved, forever.

In this moment of clarity, it was hard to blame Jo for thinking she needed a total reset on her life. Was she being unreasonable to resist?

But the idea of babysitting a phone sounded like the death of her soul.

She powered up her own phone, more from force of habit than because she expected to find anything worth her time. Another text from Gus. This was more what she'd expected from him. She swiped it away unread. The e-mail from Becky, though, deserved her attention.

She'd sent a video of the choir, gathered in the music area of St. Greg's, with one of the other parish accompanists behind the keys. He started playing the familiar melody of "KREMSER," and the choir began singing.

We gather together to send you our blessing
Our prayers and our love are behind you today.
Drive safely, eat healthy, don't text while you're driving,
Remember Father's foll'wing, so watch what you say!

"Happy trails!" they all shouted.

Miriam laughed, her throat thickening. She'd known she was blessed in her volunteers, but it had been a long time since she'd had it demonstrated so clearly.

Nobody at St. Gregory's had hesitated to pick up the slack so she could take this trip. Not even Father Simeon, her boss. They stood behind her a hundred percent, the people who knew her best, the people who had watched her family grow, cheered their successes, and encouraged her when the kids had pushed her to the edge.

She thought of the rehearsals peppered with smart-ass comments and liberally sprinkled with laughter. Of the way they supported each other with prayers and casseroles and cards and hugs. Of the way St. Greg's had opened its arms and enfolded them when she and Teo arrived, young and sleep-deprived, with twin babies in tow, and handed them a small but newly renovated house at a ridiculously low rent. Of Becky, who'd kept Miriam sane for the last year, forcing her to take a break from the busy work she was using to keep the demons at bay.

That community, with Teo, was the only place she'd ever felt she belonged. For the past year, she'd been keeping them all at a distance, afraid to show them her heart, afraid to lean on them as they had so often leaned on her.

Jo was wrong. Miriam had plenty of reasons to stay in Atlanta. This video proved it.

She sent Becky a string of hearts. When she looked up, Dicey was emerging from the restaurant, moving slowly. Her blue bracelet flashed merrily in the bright sunlight.

Miriam wondered again about the significance of that accessory. She'd never seen Dicey without it. "You okay?"

Dicey smiled wanly. "Well enough."

Miriam chewed the inside of her cheek as Dicey eased into the car and reclined her seat. They really should find a quick care clinic. But she could imagine how Dicey would react if she brought that up again.

Miriam got in and slid the keys into the ignition. A phone buzzed. She tensed, but it wasn't hers. Miriam had never seen Dicey ignore a text. "Dicey? Are you sure you're okay?"

"I just need to rest a while."

The phone buzzed again. "That's going to keep buzzing until you clear it, you know."

"You check it, then."

Miriam took it from her. "What's the password?"

"Nine-one-nine-seven."

Miriam punched the code in. "It's your mom. She sent an article. 'Pregnancy and Gastro-Intestinal—'"

Dicey grabbed the phone without looking. "I'll read it later."

Miriam touched the ignition again. They'd spent the better part of six days in the car. Dicey might not see a doctor, but maybe she'd rest for a day.

Miriam could use some rest too. Rest, a piano, and a few uninterrupted hours to immerse herself in Blaise's music.

"Hey, Dicey."

"Yeah?" She sounded half asleep.

"I was thinking. I know we've only been driving a couple hours, but how would you feel if we just stop here for the day? Grab a cheap motel room, and I'll find a place to write. Give you a chance to relax. What do you think?"

Dicey opened her eyes and smiled. "I think that sounds great," she said.

★ ★ ★

Miriam left Dicey asleep at the motel and headed for a Catholic church that looked, from its online pictures, like it had an accessible piano.

The traffic was terrible around the church. She glanced at the clock and smacked her forehead. Of course—the adjacent parochial school was dismissing. She'd timed her arrival badly.

Carefully, she navigated the traffic and pulled into a parking place. Her phone rang as she gathered her things. She glanced down and silenced it. No way did she have the energy for her sister right now.

She headed for the church, dodging parents and children walking hand in hand, the children shouting goodbyes to their friends. Inside, she paused to dip her fingers into the holy water. She breathed deep of the rich, buttery silence unique to the inside of a church. It was as if every person who set foot within its walls left behind a remnant of themselves: joy and peace along with bitterness, anger, sorrow, and shame. Outside, the interstate roared and schoolchildren shouted, but within these walls, everything retreated.

She'd always loved that about churches. One of her earliest memories was of coloring Disney princesses on the floor while Mom sat in front of the tabernacle on her holy hour. She remembered the way Mom's crystal rosary beads caught the light from stained glass windows, sending bits of glitter scampering around the chapel.

Throughout her childhood, that otherworldly feel meant comfort. Safety. On the hard days—that last year of high school, when the chill of her parents' floundering marriage made home seem like hostile territory—she'd bike over to church after school and stay there until dinner. She'd practice or do her homework or just sit quietly and pray. Sometimes she even got roped into helping the volunteer cleaning crew.

In recent years, she'd sort of forgotten. When church became a place of work, Miriam started bringing outside worries in with her. Even so, she would often go into choir practice ready to bite the head off the next person who looked at her wrong, and by the end of the night she'd be laughing again.

Miriam scanned the church, a modern building with pews radiating outward from the raised sanctuary. The light seemed to come from everywhere, streaks of color slanting across the brick wall, as if stained glass were embedded in the roof behind the altar. She spotted the sanctuary lamp burning in the corner and headed in that direction, running her hands along the backs of pews, her footsteps muffled by the carpet.

She paused at the door of the chapel to genuflect and say a quick prayer, then made her way to the grand piano perched to the left of the altar.

The moment Miriam's fingers touched the keys, something inside her relaxed. It felt right. Like coming home after a long absence.

Which was silly. It had only been six days since the congressman's funeral. Then again, a lot had happened since then.

She let her fingers explore, filling the church with songs and hymns: "Draw Near" and "In Every Age," "Taste and See" and "Lord of All Hopefulness." With every new song, her heart opened a little more. This expansiveness, this sense of connectedness with a larger reality, was what had drawn her to church music as a profession. Well, this and Teo. She closed her eyes, remembering how his fingers caressed the guitar strings, picking chords and melodies. Over the years, playing Spanish-language songs had become a well-rehearsed dance. She provided enough structural support for the congregation to feel comfortable singing, but Teo took the lead.

At its best, liturgical music drew invisible threads between hearts gathered for worship. At its best. But Miriam hadn't been at her best for a long time.

"I just want you to be happy," Teo said one night after choir practice as they turned off the lights. *"We have a beautiful life."*

Out in the church, a pew creaked, the sound echoing in the open space. Miriam looked up but saw no one. She'd forgotten the comfort of phantom creaks in a church, as if the spirit of some saintly former worshiper was taking a seat. Maybe, in this case, her husband. Or one of her children.

"We did have a beautiful life," she said aloud, and the air around her seemed to breathe a little more freely.

She pulled out Blaise's notebook and played the first two measures for the millionth time. Now she was certain of what she'd heard back in Cincinnati. There were hints of Gus's compositional style in her son's music.

Miriam flipped to the music she'd transcribed at the monastery. Maybe if she made some headway on a third movement, she could get some momentum going to finish the troublesome second. She played it and started improvising. There. That had promise. She scribbled the notes and moved on.

"*Derivative,*" Gus's voice whispered.

"Go away," she said aloud, but she changed one note in the chord anyway. Ah yes. It still sounded slightly church-y, but if Guillaume Dufay could make a ninety-minute Mass setting out of "L'Homme Armé"—a Renaissance tavern song—it ought to be possible to go the other way too. If she could just get something on paper, she could start experimenting.

Colored beams of light crept across the brick wall, then faded altogether. The back pews shrank into shadows. Five cross-outs or erasures for every three measures worth keeping. Things that seemed to work when she played them but felt cliché when she committed them to paper. Was she remembering them wrong? But even so, forward progress.

"Do you have a phone?"

Miriam nearly fell off the bench, so startled was she by the unexpected voice. A priest stood next to her. A baby priest, Becky would have called him. She stared at him, confused. She'd never met a person in his demographic who didn't have a handheld device at the ready every moment. Why would he need hers? "I—I'm sorry?"

He gestured to the music. "If you have a phone, you can record a voice memo. Then if you get something that works, you don't have to stop. And you don't have to trust your memory. You can come back to it later."

Oh. That made sense. But Miriam's forehead furrowed. How did he know what she'd been thinking?

Then she realized, and her face flamed. "Was I . . . talking to myself?" It had been known to happen when she got lost in the music.

The young priest smiled a knockout smile. "Uh-huh."

"I'm so sorry."

"Don't be. It was entertaining." Baby priest, nothing. Talia would have called him *Father What-a-Waste*. "I haven't seen you around before."

"I'm just passing through. Needed a piano."

"Ah. Well, that's too bad. I'd have offered you a job."

Miriam smiled. "Thanks."

In the deepening shadows, a door creaked. Both of them turned to see a young couple walk in, pushing a stroller. "That's my cue," said the priest. "A group of us get together for prayer on Tuesday evenings."

"Oh. I'll just pack up, then, and get out of your way."

He waved her off. "No, no. We'll be in the chapel. You won't bother us. Although you're welcome to join us, if you'd like."

Miriam hesitated, torn. She didn't want to be rude, but her fingers itched to be on the keys. She hadn't felt so awake in a long time; her soul craved more. "I think I'd better work."

"Of course. Good luck!" He strode down the aisle with a spring in his step as a middle-aged woman entered the church and held the door for an elderly man using a cane.

Miriam returned to work. It was close to full dark in the church now. She flipped on the gooseneck light clipped to the music stand and tried to ignore the rise and fall of voices in the chapel. But writing was a solitary venture, and no matter what the priest said, she felt like she was intruding.

She set her teeth and backed up five measures. Nothing. Played it again. There—that little fragment swirling around in her frontal lobe—that might be something. She tried it two or three ways, picked one, and wrote it down. Two more measures done.

Maybe it would help to get a running start at it. She started at the beginning of the movement. It worked, sort of—she managed to sketch out a melody, and she could tell she needed two more measures to link to the B theme. She reached for her phone to try the baby priest's trick, thinking the music might flow better if she could play without having to stop to notate. But her mojo was gone.

After ten minutes, she gave up. She was starving anyway. And she needed to check on Dicey.

She shuffled her papers together, packed them away, and switched off the light. She stood, the satchel heavy on her shoulder, blinking as her eyes adjusted to the darkness. The voices in the chapel seemed louder now than they had while she was working. They were reciting the Canticle of Zechariah—the end of Night Prayer. She froze. She knew what was coming, but the brief concluding prayer didn't give her time to brace herself or to escape.

"May the all-powerful Lord grant us a restful night and a peaceful death."

Miriam swayed, her hand coming down hard on the piano cabinet. *Peaceful death.* Those words had gone round and round in her head for months before she'd managed to suppress them. *Peaceful death. Peaceful death.*

Her family hadn't gotten that.

The satchel slid off her shoulder and thumped the floor. She sat down again on the piano bench, her fingers trembling with the need to drown out the voice screaming in her head: *Peaceful death. Peaceful death.*

She launched into the first angry thing she could think of: the final movement of the *Moonlight Sonata*, as raging as its more famous movement was placid.

Had Teo seen that big-ass pickup truck cross the median? Had Talia or Blaise? Or had the crash come out of nowhere? Did the airbags knock them out, or were they conscious when their tiny rental car was smashed between the heavy-duty truck and the bridge railing? Did they feel their bones break, their bodies burn?

Miriam pounded the keys until the church was fully dark and deserted. Her underarms were soaked and her voice raw, as if she'd been screaming without realizing it. And when she was spent, she collapsed on the lacquered surface of the piano, calm enough at last to face the truth:

Nothing about her family's death had been peaceful. Not even the days leading up to it.

And in the end, she had no one to blame but herself.

✦ 26 ✦

Spring, one year earlier
Atlanta, Georgia

ON SUNDAY OF THE terrible week, Teo woke up with a toothache that put him down for the count, leaving Miriam to lead all the Masses—including Confirmation Mass with the bishop—on her own.

On Monday, he had a root canal the insurance wouldn't cover.

On Tuesday, a pipe broke, rendering their only bathroom off limits until almost six PM. The kids reacted to the aggravation by fighting over who got the last English muffin, who was playing too loudly for the other one to concentrate on his or her own practicing, and who was hogging the wireless bandwidth.

By dinnertime Wednesday, Miriam had just about reached the end of her rope. "So!" Teo said as she cleared the chorizo platter, "who's got what this evening?"

"Youth symphony, and I get the car," said Talia.

"You always get the car! I have astronomy club!" Blaise protested.

"Well, you should speak up faster."

"Well, *you* should consider somebody other than yourself once in a while."

Talia's phone trilled. She whipped it out of her pocket.

"You're not supposed to have your phone at the table!" Blaise said.

Talia, her thumbs working furiously, ignored him.

"Talia," said Teo in his warning voice.

Sighing, she put it back in her pocket.

Miriam closed the dishwasher. "You two know perfectly well you have to share the car. Dad and I have choir practice, so we don't need it, but you have to figure out how to make it work for you both."

Another sound, this time from Miriam's phone. She glanced to see who was calling. "Uh, I think I need to take this," she said.

Talia made a guttural sound of disgust.

"Miriam! So glad I caught you," said the director of the community orchestra. "Our soloist for this weekend was just diagnosed with cancer. He has to fly out to the Mayo clinic tomorrow morning. I know this is really short notice, but we need someone who can play the Mozart twenty-one. Would you be able—would you *want* to step in?"

Did she *want* to? Of course she wanted to! She already knew that concerto. "It's this weekend?"

"Sunday afternoon."

Miriam squeezed her eyes shut. "I'm supposed to be in California with the kids this weekend."

"Oh, this is the week of nationals, isn't it? Well, it was worth a try. I guess I can call . . ."

Miriam rested her head against the refrigerator as the only good thing to happen all week threatened to slip through her fingers. She'd traveled with the kids to state and regionals. Did she really need to be there for nationals too?

"Hang on, Phil," she said. "Give me half a second, okay?"

She turned to her family, who stared at her, electrified by her mention of the trip, the first real family vacation they'd ever taken, the one for which they were going to miss an entire week of school.

"The soloist is sick," she said. "They need someone to play a Mozart concerto Sunday afternoon."

Dead silence. Wide eyes from her children. A thoughtful look from Teo.

"I could change my ticket, come out right afterward, and meet you guys there." Miriam tried to keep her voice neutral, to disguise how much she wanted this, but she could feel the tremble.

Teo pursed his lips. He rubbed his face and nodded slowly. "We could still celebrate your birthday in San Francisco."

"Are you *serious*?"

"Shut up, Talia," said Blaise, his eyes fixed on Miriam. "Can't you see she wants this?"

"You are so selfish!" Talia shrieked, and stormed out of the kitchen.

And that, right there, was why Miriam needed this. Because she'd given up everything for those kids, and her daughter still called her selfish. "Phil," she said into her phone, "I'll do it. I'd *love* to do it."

It took a couple more minutes to iron out the details. Miriam was only vaguely aware of Blaise moving around the kitchen behind her while she scribbled notes on a piece of scrap paper. When she disconnected, she found him running dishwater, unasked. "Thanks, honey," she said.

He shrugged a reply, not really meeting her eyes as he squirted hand soap into his palm. "Don't worry about Talia," he said. "She'll be okay. You deserve to do something for you."

Blaise didn't try to escape the kiss she planted on his cheek, but he didn't accommodate it either. He just endured it, like a proper teenage boy, and then shuffled soundlessly in his stocking feet out to the living room to practice.

Talia didn't speak to her for twenty-four hours.

But Thursday night, while Teo and Blaise labored outside in the yard, there came a knock on her bedroom door. "Mom?"

Miriam turned away from the computer. "Yeah?"

Talia held a package in her hands, neatly wrapped with a red bow. "I was thinking," she said. "I mean, Blaise and I were talking. I guess I understand why you want to do this. I mean, I guess you should get to do something for you."

The words fell like rain on scorched earth. Miriam couldn't speak; she just crossed the room and enfolded her daughter in her arms.

"All right, all right," said Talia after a moment, but she couldn't quite hide her smile. "Daddy and I have something for you. We were *going* to give it to you—" She caught herself and started over without the accusatory tone. "We were going to give it to you on your birthday, but we figured maybe you'd like to wear it for your concert."

Miriam opened the box Talia handed her. Inside, she found a beautiful dress—crinkled black, splashed with enormous crimson hollyhocks. Cap sleeves and a billowing skirt. A skirt meant for dancing.

"It's beautiful, Talia," she said.

Her daughter beamed. "I've been trying to figure out a whole ensemble. You can borrow some of my makeup, and I think if you do your hair right, you could use my red scarf." She hurried over to the computer. "I know you never put your hair up, but I saw this tutorial—"

Miriam, mesmerized by the soft fabric, didn't register the sudden silence until Talia's voice broke it.

"What the . . . *hell*?"

"Language," Miriam said automatically. Then she realized what her daughter was seeing, and the bottom dropped out of her stomach.

Gus von Rickenbach's Facebook page, with its header photo of a man playing piano with an orchestra. The profile photo showing his hands on the keys. And, especially, the unfinished private message in the bottom right. The one Teo had been telling her for years to write, and which she'd finally worked up the nerve to compose tonight.

"'I wish I'd done things differently'?" Talia read. "'I'd like to see you while I'm in California'?"

Miriam dropped the box on the bed. "Get out of there," she said. "That's my business."

"Your business." Talia's face was white. "Are you *cheating* on Dad?"

"Of course not!" When would she have had *time* to cheat on Teo? "I am not discussing this while you're screaming at me. When you're ready to be rational, you can come try again." Miriam headed for the kitchen.

Her daughter followed. "What is the *matter* with you?" she shrieked; Miriam cringed, wondering how much the neighbors could hear. For some reason, her memory picked this moment to offer up her mother's voice, screaming the word *divorce* at her father. All she could think of was the need for escape, even if the only escape available was work. She pulled out the cleaner and started scrubbing the stove top.

"What are you *doing*?" demanded Talia. "This is no time to *clean*! Don't you care about us at all? You never do anything with us! You just work all the time! It's always dishes or floors or—or stove tops! If you loved us—"

Miriam wheeled. "For your information, young lady, there's a lot of work involved in raising a family!" She sounded just like Mom. She redirected. "I don't ask much from you because I'm trying to make sure you have all the chances I never did!"

"Dad's been so unhappy!" Talia swiped at her eyes, as if angry with herself for caring. "Even I can tell! He deserves so much more—why do you always push him away? And now you're trying to hook up with some guy while you're in California with *us*? Oh, my God, Mom! You're always riding *us* about right and wrong, and look at you! You're such a hypocrite! Such a two—"

"Whoa, whoa, whoa, ladies!"

Talia fell silent. Teo stood there with his arms folded, looking back and forth between them.

"What's going on?" he asked. "What are you fighting about?"

Miriam shot him an agonized look, desperate for rescue, but he didn't know what she needed rescuing from.

Face flushed, Talia flung her hands out. "Nothing," she said. "Nothing at all. You can't fight with someone who has no heart."

With a withering glance at her mother, she stomped to her room and slammed the door.

◆ 27 ◆

Wednesday, May 4
Scotts Bluff, Nebraska

The seams in the pavement passed beneath the tires, *ka-thump, ka-thump*, marking the passage of miles like a metronome. *Ka-thump, ka-thump*, counting the heartbeats between the past Miriam could no longer fix and the desolate future it created.

"Are you cheating on Dad?"

"Why do you think I want a divorce?"

The juxtaposition of her mother's words to her dad, twenty years earlier, with Talia's more recent, anguished accusation sent Miriam's anxiety skyrocketing. Stripped bare of her defenses by the intensity of this pilgrimage, she recognized the fear she'd been running from for the last year.

What if that fight had been, for Talia, a moment as formative as the one that haunted Miriam?

The flowered dress, still unworn, now sat at the bottom of her suitcase, reminding her every night and every morning of the broken relationship with her daughter. A break she'd never get to repair.

She'd tried. A few hours after the fight, she'd knocked on Talia's door, but Talia pretended to be asleep. Miriam and Teo had sat outside on the swing for another hour, trying to decide what to do. Even Teo recognized that the day before leaving for a national competition was not the time to drop a bombshell on the kids.

As for the Facebook message that started it all, she'd never sent it. She'd been grateful for that in the end, when Gus turned out to be the kids' competition coordinator in San Francisco.

"Not like this," Teo had told her on the phone after the awards ceremony, and he'd been right. As he'd been right about so many things. She'd tried to do everything in the wrong order. Gus might have been her unresolved past, but he wasn't the first person who deserved an explanation.

The Bluetooth overrode the soft classical music Miriam had playing. Dicey was asleep, so Miriam glanced quickly at the screen. Jo—again. It was the third time in eighteen hours.

For the third time, she ignored it. She knew she couldn't put her sister off much longer. But telling Josephine Lewis-Thurston no took a lot of emotional energy, and right now Miriam simply didn't have any.

Chimney Rock turned out to be more a photo op than a destination. They stopped briefly; Dicey took Miriam's picture with the distinctive rock formation jutting up in the background like a birthday candle jammed into a giant mole hill. There was a small museum, but Dicey hated reading signs as much as Talia had.

When they realized the bluffs twenty miles down the road offered a more substantial attraction, they decided to finish the day with a shuttle bus to the summit and a hike back down.

Dicey spent the ten-minute ride watching a Latino couple wrestle their whirlwind of a little girl whose perpetual motion made her too slippery to hold onto. When the bus stopped, the girl took off across the parking lot while her parents were still gathering paraphernalia.

"Lena!" called the man. "Wait for *a'pá*! Annamaria, go. I'll get this."

"How old is she?" Dicey asked, when she and Miriam joined the family on the sun-swept plateau.

"Three," said Annamaria.

"Going on thirteen," added the father wryly.

Miriam smiled. She remembered Talia perfecting a teen-worthy eye roll at this age. More than once she'd told her parents, "Talk to the hand!" Where she'd even picked that up, Miriam and Teo had no idea. They came down hard on her, but sometimes it was all they could do not to collapse into giggles. Almost every night when they went to bed, they'd trade Talia stories, laughing until tears squeezed out of their eyes.

Nothing Lena was doing qualified as "going on thirteen," but Miriam refrained from saying so. She remembered how condescending comments from older parents had infuriated her. As if her experiences were without value, her frustrations without justification.

"How much longer?" she asked instead, gesturing to the bump around the woman's waist.

"Fourteen weeks."

"Ah, you're in the good part of pregnancy."

"That's why we're traveling now instead of in June. We're on our way to Omaha. Lena is crazy about zoos."

The wind gusts on top of the bluff made Miriam grateful she'd worn her jacket. Lena buried her face in her father's legs. He picked her up, and she wrapped her arms around him so tightly, it was a wonder she didn't cut off his circulation.

"Give me a break-me hug!" Talia again. That was one of Miriam's favorite memories of parenthood: the warm, chubby arms and legs wrapping her up in sweetness.

"What brings you across Nebraska?" asked Annamaria.

Miriam shrugged. "Just seeing the country."

Dicey shot her a look razor-sharp with disapproval, but thankfully, she held her peace.

"There's a lot to see. I want my little girl to see it all!" Annamaria patted her daughter's back.

"Lena," said the father, peeling his daughter's arms away from his neck, "you can't squeeze that hard."

"But, *a'pá*, I *love* you!"

"Yes, but I can't breathe, chiquita."

Miriam smiled to see how Dicey watched them: hungrily, fixedly, as if trying to see into her own future. Miriam could have told her there was no being ready for parenthood, no anticipating the experience. But she didn't. Some things had to be discovered for oneself.

"I guess I have to tickle you!" roared the father, and the little girl, giggling, made a dive for freedom. She landed on her feet and scampered away, her parents scurrying after her. "Good luck with your trip!" Annamaria called over her shoulder. Little Lena grabbed both her parents' hands. "One-two-three-WHEE!" said the father, and they hoisted her, giggling, into the air.

Apparently every young child was born knowing that game. The twins had certainly loved it. It was a constant battle, the two of them bickering over whose turn and how many swings. Miriam and Teo tired of it long before the kids ever did.

"Bitter grace," Dicey murmured, watching the young family walk away.

Miriam looked at her. "What?"

"Annamaria. It means 'bitter grace.' Although that's a German thing." Dicey took a deep breath. "Never mind, just thinking out loud." She wandered away, snapping photo after photo on her phone.

Miriam took a few photos too, but her heart wasn't in it. She glanced back at the little family. Would Annamaria, too, someday face a daughter who saw only the worst in her? Motherhood could be a bitter grace indeed.

The little girl's giggle floated back on the wind. Talia had such an enchanting giggle. Like audible silver. And such a temper! On her third day at St. Gregory Elementary, she'd tackled a second-grader for making fun of a kindergarten classmate who was crying for her parents. Miriam had been ridiculously proud.

But the best part came a week later, when Miriam walked by the playground and saw all three children playing ring around the rosy. "He said he was sorry," Talia explained with a shrug.

That was her daughter in a nutshell: she'd fly off the handle in an instant, but she was just as quick to forgive.

A wind gust slapped Miriam's face with grit. For a second, she couldn't breathe, her mind processing a realization that had never occurred to her before:

Talia would have forgiven her too.

As bad as things were in her last months with her daughter, there had been good moments too. The hilarity of playing Apples to Apples the night they'd been snowed in—a term that only loosely applied in Georgia. The seamless ensemble as they played Christmas carols at a fundraiser for the children's shelter. The very existence of the road trip app.

Yes, things had been strained, but they wouldn't have stayed that way. Not forever. Talia would have grown. Miriam would have grown. They would have bickered and struggled and eventually found each other again.

What she'd lost when Talia went into the sea was not a lifetime of butting heads, of hurled accusations and simmering resentments. What she'd lost was everything that came after: lunch dates, college graduation, taking grandchildren to the pool.

The wind scoured away the walls Miriam had been hiding behind for so long. The truth was, excoriating herself for her mistakes was less painful than facing the reality of what she'd lost. Here, from this windswept ridge that towered above the vast plain, she could see everything, from the town to the east, to the fields and ridges and undeveloped plains stretching out of sight in every other direction. It was like standing on the threshold of heaven, the world spread before her in all its far-flung beauty, its wounds and pock marks reduced by distance to texture on a vast tapestry. Not flat. Not featureless. Beautiful.

Her life was like that too. Not the wasteland of tedium and obligation she'd perceived it to be, but a richly textured mosaic stretching into a tantalizing unknown.

Except now, she would traverse it alone.

The weight of the word, the sorrow it carried, nearly crushed her. Miriam could feel it pressing down on her shoulders, the gaping emptiness where there should have been a lifetime of experiences yet to unfold. It was too great a weight for anyone.

And she knew, too, that what death had stolen from her and Talia, she'd willfully withheld from her own mother. Jo was right about that, at least.

Dicey had the camera trained on her now. Miriam could see it in her peripheral vision, but she didn't protest. It was only right that this moment should be captured—from a distance. As for herself, she only wanted to settle into the moment, to let it imprint on her memory. It hurt. Oh, how it hurt. But there was peace in it too. Because despite all the dysfunction, Talia had loved her. It was too late to repair that relationship, but it was not too late for Miriam and her own mother.

For now, that was enough.

Thursday, May 5
Scottsbluff, Nebraska

DICEY AND MIRIAM SAT at a table beneath the awning of an old-fashioned drive-in, nibbling burgers and fries beneath a neon sign that read "Scotty's."

"So I decided with such archaic video editing equipment, two seconds and a fade was enough. No need to get fancy. But you were already dead to the world. And you . . . are not paying attention. Earth to Miriam."

Miriam blinked, her finger freezing where it had idly been scrolling her phone. "What?"

Dicey sighed and wadded up her waxed paper. She'd stayed up half the night assembling a video montage of photos of Chimney Rock and Scotts Bluff, and she had a sort of wild-eyed manic vibe going on. "You planning to eat that sometime today?" she said, motioning to the French fry in Miriam's other hand. "Or are you just going to stir your ketchup all day? Excuse me, miss?" She flagged down the teenager who was emptying trash bins. "Do you happen to have salt packets?"

"How many you need?"

"A handful, if you can spare them."

"Sure, back in a jiff."

Miriam shook her head.

Dicey coughed a few times. "Anyway," she went on, "clearly something is eating at you. You never scroll your phone that much. Why don't you tell me what's bugging you?"

Miriam ate the fry. It was soggy from all the ketchup. "Jo quit calling," she said. "And that worries me."

"I think I'd be relieved."

Miriam shook her head. "It means she's moved on to phase two. Whatever phase two is." Her phone dinged. Gus: *Gorgeous video and a gorgeous shot of you. You can use it for the album cover when you record Blaise's sonata.*

Yesterday he'd been all Stevie Stalker, and today he was giving her compliments?

"What's up?" asked Dicey.

Miriam turned the phone toward her.

Dicey raised her eyebrows. "What is *with* that guy? Didn't you say he's married?"

"Mm-hmm. This is totally Gus. It's part of his charm."

"Yeah, you say charm, I hear 'asshole.'"

Miriam smiled. "And you want me to go talk to him."

"Well, he likes my video. *That's* bona fide charming."

Miriam laughed; Dicey touched her phone, and the soaring strains of Dvořák's *New World Symphony* started up. It had to be the fourth time she'd enjoyed her handiwork since they sat down.

The employee came back and dumped a handful of salt packets on the table; Dicey ripped one open and started dipping fries in it.

The sun went behind a cloud. A puff of wind whisked away a napkin; Miriam managed to catch it by stomping on it. The big, billowy clouds racing across the plains were getting closer together. There was something unsettling about the feel of the air. Something that made the back of Miriam's head prickle. As if someone were watching.

She looked around but saw nothing noteworthy.

"Miriam."

"Hmm?"

Dicey leaned forward, resting her elbows on her knees, her legs splayed wide to accommodate her belly. "You're still not talking."

Miriam pulled together their trash. "Dicey, I appreciate that you're concerned, but . . ."

"But it's none of my business."

"I didn't say that."

"You thought it."

"Yes, I did."

Dicey sighed and heaved herself out of the chair. "Well, you're right about that. But crap is easier to handle with help. Trust me on this."

The sun came out as Dicey returned to her phone. Miriam stared at the top of her head. Unbelievable. The girl who turned every conversation away from herself and refused aid—even when she clearly needed it—had the nerve to tell *Miriam* not to go it alone?

Something was going on with Dicey. All Miriam's instincts told her so. The question was, what?

She shook her head. She had enough to worry about. Like this bad feeling that Gus was going to pop out of the bushes to stalk her for real.

It was time to get out of here. "Come on, Dicey. You want to flip the coin?"

"Sure." Dicey pulled out a quarter and slapped it down on her wrist. "Heads," she said.

Miriam tapped the icon on her phone. "Pikes Peak," she said.

"Well, that's unusually predictable."

"You sound disappointed." Miriam got up and tipped their tray into the trash can—and froze. A tan-colored two-door had just stopped abruptly as it passed the restaurant, and was now backing up. "Oh crap," she whispered.

"What?"

"Jo is here."

Dicey looked at her like she'd lost her mind. But she followed Miriam's gaze anyway.

Jo had already parked and was striding toward them. Her sister wore a pencil skirt and pumps, though her French roll hadn't survived the flight. Clearly she'd gone straight from the office to the airport.

"I guess this is phase two?" Dicey whispered.

Miriam raised her shoulders. "Jo," she said. "What are you doing here?"

"You won't answer your damn phone, that's what!" Jo's phone blipped; she silenced it but waved it around as she continued. "Six times I've called you, Miriam. Six times! You owe me an answer."

"Not calling back *is* my answer."

"Yeah, well. Too bad. I told you, whether you know it or not—"

"This is not your business," Miriam said as Dicey tugged on the keys in her hand. Miriam released her death grip on them. She sympathized with her companion's desire to escape.

Unfortunately, Dicey's action drew Jo's attention. "So you're Dicey," she said, looking her up and down.

"Hi."

Jo reached into her purse and pulled out a Visa card. "Here. This has got a thousand dollars on it. You can Uber to the airport and fly home."

It was a breathtaking presumption. Miriam saw the telltale flash of anger in the way Dicey's face tightened, but she kept her cool. "Thanks, but I'm good."

"Well, it's no skin off my back, but you might as well take it, because you're not riding with Miriam anymore. Miriam's going home. I'm riding with her to make sure of it."

"That's not your call, Jo," said Miriam through gritted teeth.

"You made it my call," Jo said. "You made it my call when you decided to go incommunicado. You know I had to follow *her* social media"—she waved her phone toward Dicey—"to figure out where you were? I'm missing three meetings today alone—and at least two of my kids' soccer games by the time we get you back home."

Miriam refrained from pointing out that she was sharing every road trip stop with the faceless e-universe. It didn't matter anyway. "You don't have to miss anything. You can go right back home. I didn't ask you to come out here."

"No, Mom did." Jo dropped her bomb with cool efficiency. "She's worried about you, Miriam. And she's hurt because you don't want to talk to her. You act like you're the only one who lost something. Mom lost her grandchildren."

The catch in her sister's voice stopped Miriam in her tracks. That wobble betrayed love. Deep, fierce, protective love for their mother. A love Miriam had rarely shown.

Her conscience, awakened yesterday on the blufftop, stung. For twenty years, she'd been guarding her heart. Her mother was still waiting for that magical day Miriam would never get with her own daughter—the meeting of adult minds, independent yet devoted to each other. She'd never be able to properly grieve Talia until she made peace with her role as a flawed daughter to a flawed mother.

Sunshine and shadow whirled in tight circles, the wind gusting and quieting depending on which held dominance.

She shoved the keys into Dicey's hand. "Go on," she said. "I'll be there in a minute."

Dicey made good her escape while Miriam tried to redirect her emotions. Jo's abrasive, aggressive personality served her well on Wall Street, but it brought out the worst in Miriam. "You're right, I should have called you back," she said now. "But I needed to sort things out, and it's hard to do that with . . . other voices in my head." It took a lot of willpower to make that a neutral statement instead of an accusation.

She met her sister's eyes. "I know I need to do better by Mom. But I have a life, Jo," Miriam said. "Just because it doesn't fit your vision of success doesn't mean it's not important. It's important to *me*. It's what I'm supposed to do."

Jo was silent for a moment. "I don't get you. Clearly you're a hard worker. Why wouldn't you focus all that energy on something that lets you get ahead?"

"I do what I do because it's who I am," Miriam said quietly. "And if I were to move to Albuquerque, I'd do the same thing there. But I'm not going to move to Albuquerque, Jo. I have a life and a community. I'm going to be all right. And so is Mom."

Jo stared at her, nostrils flaring. But at least she was thinking about it. "You know I can't just leave you here. Mom—"

"Oh, come on, Jo. I'm not ten years old. You, me, Mom—we're all adults now. Mom was wrong to ask you to come. If she needed to talk to me, she shouldn't be hiding behind you."

"She did it because—"

"I know why she did it. But that's on me, not you. None of this is your . . ." *business*, she thought, but what she said was " problem. Go home. Go to your kids' soccer matches."

Jo was tempted; it was clear that the prospect of driving across the country together appealed to her no more than it did to Miriam. "Well, you sound more with-it than I expected," Jo said grudgingly. "So I guess I'll let you go. On one condition."

Miriam held her temper. "What's that?"

"You text me and Mom and Brad at *least* once a day until you're home again."

It was still an unnecessary oversight, but considering she probably should have been doing that all along, it seemed ungracious to refuse.

The sun disappeared again. Miriam looked up; it seemed to be out for the count. A tumbleweed skittered across the street and past them, like something out of a spaghetti western.

She looked back at Jo. "All right," she said.

Jo blew out a breath, looking toward her rental car. "I wish you had called me back so I didn't have to waste the time and money coming out here," she grumbled. "Now I have to go explain to the rental car place why I'm turning in a car I just checked out."

Miriam pinched her lips shut on the apology that tried to worm its way out. She hadn't asked Jo to come. It wasn't her fault.

"Bye, Jo," she said.

"C'mere." Jo reached in and gave her a brusque hug. "Take care of yourself. Let us know when you get there. Wherever 'there' is."

"Pikes Peak," Miriam said, touched despite herself. "And you too."

She headed for the car, where Dicey was sitting in the passenger seat with the door open to take advantage of the stiff breeze.

"You carried the day, then?" Dicey asked with an impish smile.

Miriam returned it. "I think we're working on understanding each other."

"Good for you," Dicey said, closing the door.

Miriam fastened her seatbelt. "Let's get out of here," she said, and pulled out toward a highway that stretched as far as she could see beneath an endless, glowering sky.

Part 7

Colorado

The things that we love tell us what we are.

—Thomas Aquinas

Blaise's intro to Pikes Peak

Yeah, I know. We've been keeping you off the beaten path till now. But, I mean—Pikes Peak! You can't skip that on any road trip across America. You remember that trip we took to Colorado with the gifted program in middle school? This was my favorite part. If the weather's clear, from the top you can see five states. So no matter what coin flips you take, you'll cross Colorado Springs. Anyway, I only have two words for you: high-altitude donuts.

(Talia's voice, sotto voce): That's three words, numb nuts!

◆ 29 ◆

Thursday, May 5
Pawnee National Grasslands, eastern Colorado

THE SIMPLEST ROUTE TO Colorado Springs—not the short-est, but Miriam was sick of impersonal interstate high-ways—took them on a straight shot south, pretty much forever, on US 71. Miriam drove in solitude, Dicey's long night finally having caught up to her. The younger woman slept in the pas-senger's seat, using her backpack for a pillow, leaving Miriam to ponder the unexpected insight she'd just gained into her family.

What if their most annoying characteristics were actu-ally how they expressed love?

Last spring, her family had swept in, picking up the burden she didn't know she couldn't carry. Mom stayed for months. Brad flew up to San Francisco to identify the bodies and bring them back to Atlanta. Jo paid the funeral expenses and never said a word. Miriam didn't even know until months later, when she called the funeral home because she realized she'd never received a bill.

Miriam hated owing Jo. She wanted desperately to repay her, but she couldn't, so she never said anything. Neither did Jo. For a year, the knowledge of the debt had weighed on her heart alongside everything else, smarting, irritating her. She wished she'd thought of it a few hours ago. For the first time, she felt ready to thank rather than berate her sister.

She woke Dicey when she pulled off for gas at the I-80 interchange. The guy smoking a cigarette outside the gas station set the younger woman to coughing like Miriam hadn't seen in days. When she finally recovered, Dicey glowered and muttered about people disrespecting the gift of their lungs.

Miriam texted her family and Becky: *20 mi to the CO border.* A round of thumbs-up emojis followed in short order.

Miriam had been counting on Dicey's company now that she'd had a nap, but Dicey went right back to sleep. Miriam looked over periodically, noting uneasily the pallor of her companion's face and the increasing persistence of the cough.

But her worry about Dicey soon gave way to another, more immediate concern. A couple dozen miles into Colorado, Miriam began to eye the hunkering clouds with trepidation. The wind seemed determined to blow her right off the highway. She checked her phone, but the signal strength wasn't sufficient to bring up her weather app. The sky grew darker by the moment. Then came the rain: first a drizzle, then a steady downpour and finally a deluge, given structure by lightning the likes of which she'd never seen. She slowed down.

At four thirty in the afternoon, the world outside the window looked like twilight. Miriam crept down the highway, hoping to spot a place to get under cover, but she could see nothing. No homes, no businesses, no gas stations, no trees. Just endless miles of prairie grass whipping in the frenzied storm. Come to think of it, she hadn't passed a business in . . . had she seen one since crossing the Colorado border?

A gust of wind pushed the Hyundai into the wrong lane; Miriam jerked it back. She cast her mind backward, searching for some explanation for the isolation, and landed on a brown sign she'd read without processing, preoccupied by the giant wind turbines behind it, not far south of the state line: "Pawnee National Grassland."

National grassland. Did that mean a nature preserve? The kind with no development at all?

And then, both phones erupted in an emergency alert.

Dicey woke with a start, cursing. "What is it? What happened?"

"I don't know. Check your phone."

Dicey scanned the horizon. The sky looked like Dr. Frankenstein's lab gone wild. "Miriam, that is a shitload of lightning."

The car bucked again. "I know." Miriam sounded calmer than she felt. "Tell me what's going on."

Dicey cursed again. "Tornado warning."

"How close?"

"I don't know, I'm trying to find out—just wait a minute! I've only got one bar."

Miriam gripped the steering wheel, knowing nothing she said could make the insufficient connection move faster.

"The map won't load," Dicey said. "I don't know where we are!" She leaned forward and peered into the deepening gloom.

The seconds ticked by. Miriam's fingers ached from gripping the steering wheel so hard, repeatedly wresting back control of the car. The wind was like a living thing, howling against the windows. The gloom settled around them. And just when she thought it couldn't get any worse, it did.

"Miriam . . ." Dicey's voice sounded squeaky. She pointed.

"I see it!" The twister looked like a narrow Play-Doh worm flipping around while God rolled it through the sky. It roared toward them in the midst of a huge debris field. Maybe Miriam was imagining things, but it sure looked like it was getting fatter by the moment.

The prairie stretched, rolling and unbroken, to every side. No ditches to hide in, no buildings to shelter in.

"Don't freak out, don't freak out," Miriam whispered.

Dicey grabbed the overhead handlebar as the car bucked again. "Are you kidding? This is exactly the time to freak out!"

"There." Miriam pointed. "That sign up there. What's it say?"

A yellow triangle flashed past. "Narrow bridge. Narrow bridge!" Dicey said. "We can hide under the bridge!"

Miriam veered onto the shoulder.

The road cut through a low ridge, too small to provide any real protection. They got out of the car; the rain stung as Miriam half dragged, half carried Dicey down the grassy slope at the edge of the road. Her locket slapped her collarbone with every step.

It wasn't much of a bridge—just a short deck enclosed by guardrails crossing a shallow ditch gouged into the prairie by runoff. But at least it blocked the rain. Mostly, at least.

The wind, though, was unstoppable. Dust and debris slapped Miriam in the face. The women huddled up into the narrow angle where the sloping creek bank met concrete. Miriam huddled behind Dicey, putting protective arms around her companion, as if she could possibly ward off a twister. Dicey clutched her arms. Her metal bracelet bit into Miriam's forearm.

The younger woman was mumbling; it took Miriam a minute to recognize the Lord's Prayer. The gut shot went clear through her: it hadn't even occurred to her to pray. Just how much of herself would she lose before this was over?

If she died in the next five minutes, Mom might never know what happened to her.

And what about Dicey, whom she'd dragged along for this ride into hell? Dicey had a mother too. And an unborn child!

Miriam didn't want to die. She wanted to live. Not just exist, mummified in her guilt and regret and loss. But live. Like Dicey, grabbing life by the horns. Like Becky, indispensable to everyone around her.

Please, Miriam whispered silently. *I'll do anything. I'll talk to Mom. I'll tell Gus—somehow. I'll even be nice to Jo! Just keep us alive.*

The tornado roared closer, the wind at its edges skittering up and down in pitch like a banshee. Miriam closed her eyes and added her voice to that of the girl trembling in her arms.

◆ 30 ◆

WHEN THE STORM PASSED and the two women emerged, shaking and battered by debris, from their hiding place, they found the darkness complete. They struggled up the wet embankment in the rain. Dicey got back in the car, but Miriam wanted to check the vehicle's condition before they went on. She walked around it, using her phone as a flashlight. The front windshield was cracked, the driver's side back window shattered altogether. The instrument cases in the back seat were littered with glass, but mercifully it seemed to have missed the front seats. Hailstones covered the rear floor, though. And she had no intention of picking them out. Not with broken glass all over everything.

The outside of the car was pockmarked, the finish rough after being sandblasted by dust.

Becky was going to kill her.

She got in and closed the door. With the back window broken, it wasn't exactly cozy, but it got her out of the rain. "Let's go find a service station," she said.

"Let's hope the car starts."

"It'll start."

Dicey raised her eyebrows, cradling her abdomen protectively. "Just sayin'."

Miriam had always hated that phrase, but she pinched her annoyance beneath her lips and started the car. "See?"

But the moment she pulled forward, she knew something was wrong. The motion felt jerky and uneven. She shut it off again before stepping back into the rain.

She'd missed the flat front tire. A shattered glass bottle lay right behind it. She hadn't even felt the car go over it when she pulled off the road.

Nothing to be done about it now. Miriam popped the trunk and retrieved the tent and the sleeping bag. "Here, spread this out," she told Dicey, handing her the sleeping bag. Then, she started rigging the tent cover around the edges of the back door.

"What are you doing?" Dicey asked.

"We have a flat."

"Don't we have a spare?"

"I imagine we have a donut. But it's buried under all our stuff, and it's raining, and it's dark."

Dicey pulled her phone out. "I have no signal." She sounded scared. "Do you?"

Miriam got into the car and closed the door. "No," she said, anxiety gnawing her insides. She'd just promised Jo to keep in touch, and she couldn't. Jo would freak. *Mom* would freak.

Well, there was not a thing she could do about it now. She relaxed her throat to keep her tone even. "We'll just have to wait for daylight."

"How can you be so calm?" Dicey's voice, normally so dusky, was almost sopranino.

Miriam caught her hand. "Did I tell you my parents worked on car assembly lines?" she said. "My dad knew everything about cars. We weren't allowed to drive until we knew the basics. If I can change the oil, I can certainly change a tire."

"Really?"

"Really. I just need daylight and a break in the rain. It's going to be okay."

Dicey relaxed. "I hope I get to be half as cool as you before I die."

Miriam laughed. "I thought we'd already established that you're way cooler than me."

She spread the sleeping bag over the two of them as best she could. Dicey moved restlessly, this way and that, coughing and spitting.

"You all right?" Miriam asked.

"My back hurts."

"Turn the other way. I'll rub it for you."

Dicey's taut posture relaxed as Miriam kneaded her lower back. It was a terrible angle, and Miriam's thumbs started to hurt, but she kept at it. The wind settled to a low whoosh.

"Deandra," Dicey said quietly.

Miriam paused. "What?"

"Baby Girl's name. I think, at least."

Miriam's breath caught. For the first time, Dicey had let down her armor, here in this deep darkness. "What's it mean?" she asked in a whisper, afraid to shatter the moment.

"Divine protector."

"That's a good meaning."

"I wanted a strong name for her."

"You did good."

Dicey shifted again. Momentarily, Miriam felt the younger woman's hand brush against hers. She clasped it.

The rain continued to patter on the roof of the car. Dicey's breathing slowed; Miriam's insides relaxed.

Teo felt very close in this moment. One snowy night in Philly, she'd fallen asleep on his lap as he read from "What to Expect When You're Expecting." When she awoke, the house was quiet, though the wind blew outside and snow hissed against the windowpane. Teo was sitting awake, still stroking her arm, watching the fire crackle. She'd felt safe. Protected.

Tonight it was her turn. Miriam closed her eyes and drifted, counting the breaths between each of her companion's coughs. Something had changed between her and Dicey just now, and Miriam along with it. She knew she wouldn't sleep much tonight. She was on duty.

★   ★   ★

In the morning, they broke out the last of the snacks Miriam had bought in Cincinnati. They drank Dicey's water bottles dry before either of them felt satisfied. Dicey looked tired and drawn, and her cough seemed worse. Miriam fretted, wondering if she should broach the topic again, but what good would it do? It wasn't like there was a quick care clinic nearby.

She unloaded the trunk and excavated the donut. "Miriam Tedesco, rock star," said Dicey as the first lug nut came loose. Miriam glanced up and saw her recording. "Seriously, Dicey," she said, laughing.

The next lug nut wouldn't budge. She skipped it in favor of starting the remaining ones, then returned, but it proved impervious to the force of the small wrench. She needed a longer lever, but rack her brain though she might, she couldn't think of anything in the car that would work.

She put her body into it, but her shoes slipped in the gravelly mud and she slid partway down the berm at the edge of the road, earning nothing for her trouble except skinned knees and elbows. "Turn that off," she snapped. What good was all Dad's training if she didn't have the tools she needed?

Dicey put her phone away. "So now what?"

Miriam checked her phone again. No signal. She swallowed. All night, she'd kept her cool by thinking in the morning they'd be on their way and back in contact with the world in short order. Being stuck here, literally in the middle of nowhere, was triggering some panic. "I guess we hope somebody comes by."

They sat in the car. With nothing to drink, Dicey's cough got progressively worse. The hacking, choking sound rubbed Miriam's nerves raw.

This could not continue. Dicey needed water.

Miriam opened the door, and a blessed breath of fresh air swirled into the car. "I'm going to start walking," she said. "Surely there's got to be something . . ."

"Miriam!"

She looked up and saw it: an enormous pickup with a tow rig on the back coming toward them. It passed, stopped, turned around, and angled in front of them. A burly, bearded man in plaid button-up, jeans, and boots hopped down. "Morning, ladies," he said, tipping his hat. "Name's Buck Gardner. Looks like you could use a tow?"

Dicey burst into tears. Miriam just sagged with relief.

"My wife and I live down the road a little ways. I got a shop, I can get your tire changed for you. Can't do nothin' about the window, though. Whereabouts you headed?"

"Colorado Springs."

"I know a good guy down there. I'll give him a call here shortly. Toss your gear in the back of the truck there while I get you hooked up."

Buck hooked the Sonata to his rig, and they got underway. He spent the ten-minute trip regaling them with an overview of the night's storms, which pretty much beat the crap out of the entire central plains. Miriam couldn't believe she'd been so stupid. Running off into the middle of nowhere without checking the weather.

The cell signal improved as they went; soon enough, her phone started dinging.

Jo: *I told you to text us!*
Mom: *Please call me.*
Becky: *The Weather Channel talked about bad storms in eastern Colorado. Are you okay?*

The tone of the messages escalated from there; she could practically hear the anxiety ratcheting up in their tone as the messages continued.

The missed calls fell off the bottom of the screen. Jo, Gus, Brad, Mom, Gus again, Becky, Simeon. Gus *again*. Talk about escalation.

Her battery died halfway through formulating a reply; using it for a flashlight had drained the battery. Miriam sighed and slid it into her pocket.

When they reached the ranch house, Buck apologized—"The wife's away for the weekend"—and opened a box of gas station donuts before heading out to change the tire for them. Dicey nibbled at one without enthusiasm. Miriam ate with more relish, but her anxiety to contact her family was stronger than her hunger. She plugged in her phone and stared at it, listening to the buzz of an air wrench outside while she waited for it to power up. As soon as it did, she sent a group text.

We are okay. Both of us. Scary night in the Pawnee Grassland. Close encounter with twister. But we are ok. Rescued by a gallant rancher. Regrouping to go on to CO Spgs.

It took all of thirty seconds for the replies to start coming in. A cascade of them, covering the spectrum she'd expected, from Jo's *I should never have let you talk me into this* to Becky's effusive emoji-laden statement of support.

She supposed she ought to put something up on the app too. Her choir members and Father Simeon were bound to hear about it; better to control the narrative.

She repurposed the text she'd sent her family and posted it through Talia's app as Buck walked back into the house. "All set," he said. "But keep it slow. You shouldn't drive too far on that donut."

"Thank you," Miriam said. "We'll get on the road shortly and be out of your hair."

"Oh, you're no trouble at all."

"In that case, I could use a shower," Dicey said. "A really, really long shower, if you don't mind."

She pulled her entire suitcase into the bathroom, just as she had the first night in Cincinnati. Miriam smiled and shook her head.

Her phone rang. She glanced down, and her body flashed hot and cold: Gus. Good grief. She'd only put up the status update about a minute ago. He really was stalking her.

Her promise to God the night before seemed rash now. She wasn't ready for this conversation. When she'd thought her life was ending, confession seemed a no-brainer. But in the light of day, she was right back to *Won't it do more harm than good?*

But she'd promised: anything, she'd said last night under the bridge. If she got out of this alive, she'd do anything. Even confess to Gus.

Heart pounding, she answered the call. "Hello?"

"Miriam! August von Rickenbach. I just saw your post." Gus gave an awkward chuckle. "Glad you're okay. I have to say, I've gotten a bit obsessed with your little trip the last couple of days. My wife is getting irritated with me. Actually . . . she's not the only one. I was supposed to have some excerpts ready for recording three days ago, but I . . . I can't seem to concentrate."

He almost sounded proud of it. Like it proved his worth as a human being. But surely even Gus couldn't be so crass as to appropriate someone else's grief.

Her silence seemed to get through to him. "I . . . uh . . . I know you must think I'm crazy, taking so much interest in your family," he said. "I can't account for it. It's as if I've known you forever."

Well, if she intended to do it, now was the time. Miriam sank into the plush office chair. "Listen, Gus, I need to tell you something."

"Yeah, I have news too. Guess where I am right now? *Denver International Airport!*"

Miriam's revelation died on her tongue. "What?"

"I know, right? I'm performing with the Denver Symphony tomorrow. What are the odds? Can you come? I'd love for you to come."

"Um . . ."

"It would be so great to meet you in person. Talk about Blaise. I have some ideas I want to share with you. I can comp a ticket for you, if money is an issue."

Miriam gritted her teeth. Money *was* an issue, but having him toss her free tickets like she was some kind of charity case just pissed her off. "It's really not that kind of trip, Gus."

"But it can be!"

"I'm traveling with someone else."

"She can come too."

Miriam's near-death vow warred with the tower of resistance rising up in response to his pushiness. Maybe this was a sign—a humongous, flashing neon sign screaming *"Tell Gus!"* But it didn't feel that way. It felt more like a car with all its warning lights going off at once.

"Listen," she said. "We just got the crap beaten out of us by a tornado. I don't know about Dicey, but I'm really not up for a concert."

"Then I'll rent a car and come down to Colorado Springs on Monday," he said. "I really want to talk to you face to face."

Miriam was starting to feel caged in. "We won't be there by Monday. We don't stay more than a day anywhere, usually."

"But you could." A wheedling tone had entered his voice.

Miriam was starting to feel panicky. What if she screamed, *"Blaise is your son!"* just to shut him up?

Except that wouldn't end the conversation. That would just make it worse.

"Hey, I'm getting another call," she lied. "I've got to go."

"But Miriam—"

"Bye," she said. She punched the red button and slapped the phone down on the desk, then picked it back up and shut it off entirely. She'd fulfilled her obligations to the people who mattered. If past history was any indication, she had at least an hour before Dicey would be ready to leave. It was time to take care of herself.

She needed to get her equilibrium back before she got on the road. Her body itched to feel the burn of exertion at elevation in muscles numbed by fifteen hundred miles of driving.

"Buck?" she called. "Do you mind if I take a walk outside?"

✦ 31 ✦

Friday, May 6
Colorado Springs, Colorado

DICEY SPENT THE DRIVE to Colorado Springs working
on her scrapbook and singing with a playlist off her
phone. The resiliency of youth: a hot shower and all was
well.

Miriam had never been that emotionally agile, not even
at Dicey's age. The phone call with Gus rankled like an
itch she couldn't scratch. Maybe it was guilt. Every time
she passed another highway turnoff, queasiness stabbed her
throat again. That road would get her to Denver. And that
one too. And that one.

Her phone dinged for the sixth time in an hour. Dicey
glanced down at it. "Hey," she said, "it's not Gus, for once!
It's your sister." She held out the phone for Miriam's thumb-
print. "Wow! It's a prepaid hotel reservation in Colorado
Springs."

Miriam grimaced. It was one thing to have made peace
with Jo, but accepting yet more largess from her really
smarted. Knowing her sister, it would be the swankiest
place Colorado Springs had to offer.

"Miriam," said Dicey, seeing the look on her face,
"don't be an ass." She coughed long and hard, reminding
Miriam that she needed a place to rest too. Then she took a

swig from her water bottle. "Only by pride cometh conten-
tion," she said in a singsong voice as she capped it.

Miriam shot her a glare. "What is *that*?"

"Proverbs, Church Lady. Someone didn't have enough
Sunday school."

Miriam tried to scowl but ended up laughing. "All
right, fine. Tell her thank you."

Thunderheads were building over the mountains, dis-
gorging periodic lightning blasts and thunderclaps as the
car sped south along the base of the range. After last night,
the juxtaposition of storm and sunshine was doubly discon-
certing. Especially with the long crack in the windshield
bisecting the view, and the flap of plastic covering the back
window for a reminder.

By the time they arrived in Colorado Springs midaft-
ernoon, Gus had given up texting. Miriam felt inordinately
pleased to discover that she could not only resist him but
outlast him.

It was also gratifying to discover that the room Jo had
booked was, after all, in a modest hotel a few blocks from
the repair shop. She couldn't possibly have known about the
crazy-painted upright piano sitting on the sidewalk outside.
Miriam took it as a sign of divine approval.

"I'm going to run the car to the shop and then go
work on that piano outside." She frowned at Dicey, who'd
mummified herself in pillows. The younger woman looked
drawn and pale. "Are you okay?"

"I'm okay. But I need to stay close to a bathroom."

Maybe not so resilient after all. Miriam wanted to feel
her forehead for fever, but she suspected Dicey wouldn't
take kindly to that.

Dicey's blue bracelet flashed as she extended the remote
to flip a channel. For the first time, Miriam saw the symbol
on the metal. "Is that a medical bracelet?"

Dicey folded her arms, hiding the ornament. "Yes."

"What's it for?"

"Drop it, Miriam."

"Dicey—"

"I said drop it." Dicey's mouth took on a stubborn set. "Don't look at me like that. You are not my mom, and this is not your problem! *Butt. Out.*" Her passion sparked a coughing fit, but when Miriam moved forward, Dicey put up the heel of her hand to block her.

Miriam's anxiety ratcheted upward. She wanted to tell Dicey what a bad idea secrets were. But she knew it wouldn't make any difference.

Maybe she could unravel the mystery herself. She knew all Dicey's symptoms. Could a Google search illuminate a path forward?

Dicey finished coughing. "Just chill," she said, her voice husky. "I'm just worn out. I'm taking care of myself while I have the chance. That's all. I don't need help."

"Says the woman who told me, 'Crap is easier to handle with help.'"

"Piss off." Dicey turned up the TV volume.

"Fine." Miriam put her hands up. "I'm outta here."

"Fine."

She made it to the door before the TV went silent. "Miriam?"

Miriam turned back.

Dicey's voice was small, an echo of its usual bluster. She looked so fragile. "Do you ever regret it?"

Miriam glanced over. "Regret?"

"Keeping the kids. Getting married. Giving up your schooling."

Miriam opened her mouth, then closed it. The right answer was no, but it wasn't true, and Dicey would see through it in half a second.

Dicey picked at a string hanging off one of the pillows. "It's just that . . . my life would be so much easier. In so many ways. If I could've just taken that check, gone down to a clinic, and . . . but I couldn't do it." She swallowed. "You've been where I am. I guess I just want to know if it's worth it. Everything I'm giving up."

Miriam returned to the bed and sat down. "It's worth it," she said. "Motherhood is a terrifying responsibility. And an amazing gift. Yes, I did regret it at times, when it was hard. Sometimes I felt like if I got pulled another millimeter, I'd snap in half. Sometimes I wanted to run away. But I always knew if I'd chosen differently, I would have spent my whole life looking over my shoulder, feeling like something was missing. And now, I just regret wasting time regretting. But I guess that's part of it too."

"It takes a lot. Motherhood."

"It takes everything. I was lucky. I had a good man who loved me. He gave up at least as much as I did, and they weren't even his kids. I'd wish that for you if I were a fairy godmother."

The corner of Dicey's mouth turned upward. "I don't need anybody," she said. "As long as I have breath in my body, I'm going to live and breathe for this baby."

Miriam smiled. Dicey would learn about balance soon enough. "I'll let you rest now. Give me a call if . . ."

"If I go into labor?"

"Definitely if you go into labor." She brushed Dicey's hair back, letting the impression of the wiry, coarse texture imprint on her memory. "I may be gone a while."

"I'll be okay."

Miriam stood, and Dicey clasped her hand. "Thanks," she said.

★   ★   ★

Miriam took the car to the shop and walked back to the hotel, texting an update to her family on the way. She messaged Becky separately: *There's a piano outside the hotel—can you believe it? Going to try to work on the sonata. Send good vibes.* She attached a picture of the garishly painted piano on the sidewalk.

Becky texted back: *I'll do you one better.*

Miriam frowned. What did that mean?

She sat down at the piano and got to work, but people kept walking by. She wanted to move from the theme she'd wrestled out of the piano back in Omaha into a development of all the sonata's themes. It was a sound idea; she could hear how they related to each other, but she couldn't quite catch hold of the string that would tie them together. Having people walk by, pretending not to watch, just added distraction to pressure. The mental clutter buried the tiny voice of grief that desperately wanted to express itself through the music.

A paper cup plunked down on top of the piano, a red straw sticking out of its lid.

"I hear you need a place to write some music."

Miriam looked up. The man was tall and fortyish, with a hint of gray at his temples. "Uh . . . hi?" she said.

"That's for you," he said, gesturing at the cup.

Miriam eyed the cup with suspicion. "What is it?"

"Chocolate shake."

She eyed it, her mouth watering, but shook her head. She could hear Jo, walking down the street with her when she was in kindergarten, murmuring, *Never accept anything from a stranger.* "Um, thanks, but . . ."

"Oh, come on. It's only a little spiked. How can you experience Colorado without a little hash in your shake?" Then, seeing her eyes widen, he laughed. "All right, I'll quit teasing. My name's Hadley Merrick. John's my big brother."

Out of context, it took a minute for the name to register. John Merrick, who'd figured out how to load Talia's app to Miriam's phone. "John . . . from my choir in Atlanta?"

"Uh-huh. I'm not really sure of the backstory—I got it secondhand—but I gather that someone called Becky remembered that John had a black sheep brother in Colorado Springs. John called me a few minutes ago. I was told to get my butt down here and look after you while you're in town."

Miriam laughed. "Leave it to Becky."

"Yeah, she sounds like a person I'm not entirely sure I want to know any better."

"Oh, she's the salt of the earth."

"I'll bet." Hadley had a quirky sort of Harrison Ford-Danny Kaye vibe going on. She could already feel her insides warming to his smile. He must be quite the lady-killer. And so easygoing. A far cry from his brother, who would move heaven and earth to help a person in need, but was wound as tight as a garage door spring. Holidays in that family must be something else.

Hadley picked up the cup and held it out. "Nothing but ice cream, I promise."

Miriam smiled and took it, savoring the sweetness.

"Listen," he said. "I own a dance hall down the street. It's called the Gathering Haus. I have a piano. Seems to me like you could use a quieter place to work, considering what you're trying to do."

Miriam was getting tired of being handled, even by people she loved. She thought of Dicey, pushing back against Miriam's concern, and felt more sympathetic than she had a while ago.

"I've got a couple staff members around too, if that makes you feel better," Hadley added, misinterpreting her silence. "They're prepping the bar for tonight."

Miriam gathered her notebook. "Let me text my friend and tell her where I'm going. What's the address?"

He gave it to her, and she punched it in as they started walking down the street.

The Gathering Haus had a baby grand with an easy touch. A handful of employees chatted and laughed as they set up tables and chairs. They paid no attention to her, so they were not a distraction.

Yet still, the music pushed back against her. The voice of grief was like a stubborn child; denied expression on its own timeline, it refused to cooperate at all.

Miriam blacked out yet another forced transition and laid her head on her forearms, themselves crossed on the music stand. Her melody didn't *want* to be classical. It wanted to be sung, full-throated, by a group of people gathered for worship.

She sat up and punched the "Record" button on her voice memo, then started playing the music the way she'd first heard it in her head. Instantly, the melody relaxed, found a fresh chord progression, and took off. She hummed along, hoping to catch words she couldn't quite hear. She paused to write: a few notes, then a few more. The harmony, freed from ostentation, washed away awareness of all else—the clanking and screeching of metal table legs against the floor, glasses banging on trays, voices calling to each other. She wrote and played, erased and wrote again: a clever rhythmic pattern in the bass, a descant, spicing up trite harmonic progressions with adventuresome accidentals. She experimented with a few words from Psalm 46, Teo's favorite Scripture passage. Be still and know, indeed. Yes, that felt right. It felt *right*.

"Miriam!"

The voice had an insistent edge that spoke of several repetitions. It also sounded totally out of context because it wasn't Hadley. She emerged, bleary-eyed, from the music, blinking a few times to get her eyes to stop playing tricks on her, because she couldn't possibly be looking at Gus von Rickenbach.

But no matter how many times she blinked, the image didn't change. Gus von Rickenbach was standing on the dance floor of the Gathering Haus. In the flesh.

Miriam gaped at him. "What are you doing here?"

"I told you I wanted to talk face to face," he said, grinning at her befuddlement. "I realized if you wouldn't come to me, I'd have to come to you."

Of course he'd come. Of course he thought gratifying his own whim more important than respecting her wishes. She should have been prepared for this.

Gus shook his head. "It's totally bizarre, how familiar you look to me. Are you *sure* we've never met?"

All these years preoccupied with him, and the best he could do was *you look familiar*? Well, Miriam wasn't going to spoon-feed it to him. She stared him down, waiting for the dots to connect, for the tumblers to click into place. Surely it was inevitable now. "How did you find me?"

"Well, I knew you were headed for Colorado Springs, so I took a risk that you'd share your location at some point. You didn't, but"—he twirled a finger above his head—"the owner here did. He tagged you on Facebook." Gus hopped up onto the stage, his eyes fixed on the music on the stand. "Is that it? The sonata?"

She swiveled back toward the keyboard. Shuffled the papers into a stack. He didn't recognize her, she thought, numb. She really *had* been that insignificant on his playboy radar. "No," she said, her throat tight. "It's something else."

She rested her hands on the piano, trying to think. She stood at a crossroads now. Either she took his presence as a sign and opened the subject herself, or she needed to get out of this conversation—fast. The longer he looked her in the eye, the sooner he'd figure it out.

She stood up, hugging the folder against her chest, and braced herself to face him. "What's so important that you had to stalk me all the way to Colorado Springs?"

Gus mimed being stabbed in the heart. "Ouch. I guess I deserve that." When she simply stared, arms crossed over the folder, he spread his hands and dropped the act. "Listen, I only have an hour or so. I have to be back in Denver by eight for rehearsal. Can we . . . can I buy you a cup of coffee?"

She stared back without answering.

He blew out a breath. "Okay, straight to business, then. I need to confess. I haven't been completely honest with you."

Of all the things he might have said, that was the last one she expected. She broke her silence to ask, "About what?"

"Um . . ." He cleared his throat. "Blaise and I talked a lot more than I led you to believe."

Miriam went still.

"When he first contacted me, I thought it was just an inquiry about the school. Pretty routine. But he knew me. My work. That was before *Terminus*, you know. In fact, I was still writing the score at that point. But he knew other films I'd written music for. And he talked about them intelligently. I was intrigued." He couldn't meet her eyes. His hand crept toward the piano as if on autopilot, but he pulled it back. "So I responded. It turned into a regular thing. He'd text me questions about interpretation. Or advice on where to apply for college and what repertoire to use."

Miriam couldn't breathe. All the information Blaise had shared with her had come from *Gus*? She'd assumed he was just doing his homework. Yet all that time, Blaise had been talking to his biological father. Without even knowing it. The enormity of it made her head spin.

"I've never been in such ongoing contact with a potential student before, but it just sort of happened. It was as natural as breathing . . . like, I don't know . . . taking a nephew under my wing. But it truly never occurred to me that you had no idea he'd reached out to me at all. I don't understand why he didn't talk about it with you."

Her body felt like jelly, incapable of holding its own shape. Entitled, arrogant, clueless in his privilege—all these things she'd known of Gus, but this—*this* she couldn't fathom. All these years spent agonizing over what she did or didn't owe him. And now she discovered he'd waltzed in and taken a piece of her son without her consent—without even her knowledge.

"Anyway"—Gus swallowed and squared his shoulders—"I wanted you to know that before I propose this."

"Propose what?"

"What you're trying to do is impossible, Miriam. I know what it takes to write a substantial work. Doing it while you're on the road—it's just not possible."

Miriam straightened, indignant, but Gus—as usual—thought his own words the most important in any conversation. "I've been working on it too. The sonata, I mean. From the copy Blaise sent me. I was totally ready to give it up. To let you do it yourself, even if it wouldn't be as good as I could make it. But if you're struggling, please let me help. The last week, I've been playing with the excerpts in your videos. We could collaborate. You can come to San Francisco. Or . . . if you're ready to wash your hands of it—I mean, you're not a composer, actually—I could do it for you, if you want."

And now, at last, he shut up.

Miriam stared at him, her body on fire with rage. This sonata was Blaise's gift to her—his last gift. Gus had no place in it. Gus, with his monologues and micro-aggressions, the insults he gave without even realizing it.

"Over my dead body," she snapped. The words echoed around the large room; everyone in the Gathering Haus ceased talking and working and turned to stare at them.

Gus blinked. "I'm sorry?"

"Haven't you taken enough from me?" she shouted. "This is not yours! It's mine. Do you understand? This trip, the sonata. *Mine*. You can't have him! Do you understand me?"

He looked genuinely alarmed. He raised a placating hand. "Miriam—I'm not trying to take your son from you."

She snorted. He was like a freight train of self-gratification—so self-absorbed, he had no idea how his actions harmed those he ran over on his way to getting what he wanted.

For this—the feeling of a knife between her ribs and the sucker punch to her gut—she'd run to Teo, and he'd taken her in. And loved her, even though she was so wounded she could never fully reciprocate.

No way was Gus touching Blaise's music. Not in a million years. This music was her love song to her family. Hers. Not his. He hadn't raised these kids, changed their diapers, ferried them to lessons, and worked past the point of exhaustion to keep them safe and cared for. He had no right to take it away from her. Or from Teo.

And she owed him nothing. Especially not an explanation of his true role in Blaise's genius.

"You know what?" she said. "Screw you, Gus."

Miriam took a flying leap off the stage, slinging Blaise's music satchel over her head and shoulder as she strode across the wooden dance floor.

Nineteen years earlier
Philadelphia, Pennsylvania

IT TOOK MIRIAM FOUR years to get Gus von Rickenbach to notice her. And, once he did, despite her determination to stand out from all those other girls, it took him only three hours to get her into bed.

It was the magic of a four-star dinner and an invitation to continue chatting in his corner suite overlooking the Boston skyline. It was feeling like she stood on the cusp of the life she'd always dreamed of. And it was the way he touched her, as if he knew she'd been burning for this moment for years, and he didn't want her to have to wait a second longer.

It hurt, but she'd expected that, and the pleasure leading up to the pain made up for it. She had to leave in the middle of the night to get back to her hotel, pack up, and catch a late-night Greyhound back to Philly. When she arrived, tired and grimy, at her apartment, Gus waited outside, fresh from his much shorter flight. "Where have you been? I've been waiting half an hour," he said, and crushed her lips against his before she could answer.

He came knocking after midnight every night for nearly a week. The pain went away; the pleasure didn't. All day long, her body wound itself up in anticipation of it, even as exhaustion chipped away at the level of her work.

When Gus didn't show up on Monday night, Miriam was almost relieved. But it worried her that she didn't run into him during the day on Tuesday. Or Wednesday. She called him, but leaving a message felt kind of needy. Lizzy Bennet would not be needy.

She squashed the part of her brain that whispered that Lizzy Bennet wouldn't have jumped in bed with him in the first place.

When the knock came that night, Miriam didn't let herself analyze her relief. She simply threw herself into making sure he knew what he'd missed. The next day, she did see him at school. He was discussing recital accompaniment with Kaye Fleming, a soprano a year older than her. "Hey," Miriam said, holding her arms out toward him.

He glanced at her. "Oh, hey, Mira." He gave her a friendly hug and kept walking.

Miriam was a realist. Gus had a way of looking at a girl like nothing else in the world mattered. With a focus in those brown eyes that turned bone into bread dough. He approached the piano the same way. Doors slammed, people shouted nearby, and he wouldn't even twitch. She loved that about him because it happened to her too.

If he could dismiss her this easily, he was already headed for the exit.

But Miriam had no intention of giving up. They were the same, down where it counted: in their commitment to the music. He might not realize it yet, but she'd show him. She had passion to spare; burn hot enough and he was sure to catch fire.

When he came back, she intended to be ready. Miriam went looking for ways to make the sex hotter and the anticipation greater. And it worked. He came back three nights in a row for more. She watched him carefully, look-ing for signs of change, yet every night, when the climax passed, he got dressed, and she watched his brain returning to Beethoven or Chopin or Liszt.

And in the end, the only thing that changed was her.

Twenty-three days after that night in Boston, Miriam entered the venerable arched doorway of the Curtis Insti-tute with no way of knowing it would be the last time. Gus hadn't knocked on her door in three days. Nor could she find him in any of the places she usually saw him during the day. The gnawing in her stomach told her he was avoiding her.

But she had to talk to him. The double line on the preg-nancy test saw to that. She'd seen his name on the recital hall schedule tonight, so she dressed carefully, forced a few crackers down her throat to quell the nausea, and went to find him.

But the hall lay quiet. The door stood ajar; she peeked inside. Gus's music bag rested against the leg of the grand piano, but the room seemed to be deserted.

Until she heard the sounds from the alcove to the right of the stage.

Miriam froze. Then, like a mosquito to a bug zapper, she found herself floating into the room, her body curiously immune to the sensation of walking. In the shadows just outside the light, she saw the figures pressed against the wall of the balcony stairwell. Kaye Fleming, her red hair dishev-eled, her shirt pulled up. And Gus's bare ass sticking out of his jeans.

The moment seemed frozen in time. The pillars of dust circling lazily in the glow of the stage lights. The smell of old building, spicy enough to evoke a sneeze. The way those long, fluid fingers, which had played her body as art-fully as they played the piano, dug into the wall in passion for someone else.

You stupid, stupid twit. You knew better than this. You knew better! And you let him do it anyway!

She'd never felt so humiliated. The meager contents of her stomach crouched on their mark, poised for an all-out spring to exit her body.

She barely made it to the restroom in time.

★ ★ ★

Miriam didn't really sleep that night. When morning came, mocking her with the beauty of spring, she got dressed and started walking in circles around downtown Philadelphia. She watched the buses of tourists queued up at Independence Hall, the pair of women feeding snacks to toddlers on a picnic blanket at Washington Square. She didn't know what to do. She had no one, and she didn't see any way out. Not for a good Catholic girl, anyway.

She wandered aimlessly, but maybe she knew where safety lay, even if her brain was too tangled in knots to see it. Because when she finally came back to the present, she found herself standing in front of a building she'd only seen from a distance. The building where Teo Tedesco worked as a bean counter for some firm with half a dozen names.

For the past nine months, since coming to Curtis, church music had been her "me" time, her refuge from the pressures of living up to her free tuition and housing scholarship. She'd rigorously kept her two lives separate; until this moment, she hadn't realized Teo was the person she trusted most in the world.

The directory inside the lobby pointed her to the fourth floor, where an administrative assistant waved her to a row in the center of a hive of cubicles. "Teo," she said, and when he swiveled in his chair, she knew by the look on his face she didn't have to face this alone after all.

He found a crisis pregnancy center where she could get checked over, and he didn't bat an eye when the staff assumed he was the father.

When they said "twins," Miriam's whole life passed before her eyes. She'd always thought that phrase melodramatic, but now she understood. It was like viewing it all from a great height: every moment she'd spent sitting at the piano, every yard she'd mowed to pay for lessons, every Mass she'd played, and all the nights she'd lain awake with the music churning in her brain. Somewhere in her subconscious, she'd cherished a fantasy of a well-behaved baby sleeping peacefully in a bassinet beside the piano while her real life chugged merrily alongside.

She couldn't possibly do it with twins.

Teo didn't speak as they walked out of the clinic and into the noise of squealing brakes and roaring engines. He had his hands shoved in the pockets of his leather jacket. The May afternoon had grown too warm for it, but he didn't seem to notice the sweat popping out on his forehead.

They walked around Washington Square in silence. The heavenly scent of spring struggled against the stink of diesel. "What am I going to tell my parents?" Miriam said.

He had a strange look on his face, one she couldn't interpret. "Not sure that's the part I'd be worried about."

He had a point. She wasn't yet twenty, and she could only remember fifteen of those years. How could she envision being a mother?

She understood now the temptation of termination. Just erase it all. Hide your screw-ups from the jerks who participated in the process and then revealed their true selves—selves you'd never want around your children.

Children.

She clenched her fists, but she could still feel them shaking. "I can't do this, Teo."

He put a hand on her shoulder. "What can I do?"

"Help me find a place to give them away."

He took her hand. His skin warmed the shaky chill of her own. "Of course," he said.

Yes, that was it. Give the babies to someone who could give them a better life, away from her, and go on with her own. She just had to get through the next nine months.

But—nine months! Maternity clothes! "Everyone will know." She sat down on the edge of the fountain, the single plume jetting upward behind her. Teo put an arm around her shoulders. "Everyone. Even Gus." She pressed the heels of her hands to her forehead. "I can't go back to school. I don't know what to do, Teo. I can't face him again."

Teo's arm tensed, but his voice remained quiet, measured. "You're sure you don't want to . . ." He hesitated, swallowed, went on. "To give this . . . Gus? . . . a chance to do the right thing?"

Miriam paused a long moment. Pining for Gus, living for the crumbs of notice he'd bestowed on her over the past few years, had been a roller coaster: the anticipation, the swoop in the stomach as the car crested the hill and began the drop, the thrill of being out of control. But nothing cleared a girl's head like good old-fashioned humiliation. "He hates kids," she said. "You should hear the names he calls them. 'Snot monster,' 'shriekling'—words I've never even heard. 'Spermlette.' And his family is rich. They'll think I did it on purpose. *He'll* think I did it on purpose. They might try to force me to . . . get rid of them." She rested her head on Teo's shoulder.

Teo's grip tightened briefly. She could feel his pulse against her ear; oddly, it seemed to be pounding. This had to be as awkward for him as it was excruciating for her.

"I can't believe I was so stupid," she whispered.

He swallowed three times in quick succession. "Mira," he said, "are you sure, when the time comes, you're going to be able to give them up?"

Her shoulders hunched. She stared at the ground. "What choice do I have? I can't raise two kids on my own."

Teo rubbed his fingers across his mouth and chin. "What if . . ." He cleared his throat. "Maybe there's another way." He swallowed again, as if his next words would change everything.

And they did.

"We could get married," he said.

She lifted her head, certain she'd heard wrong. Not because he wasn't the marrying type; she was certain he was. But because he would never say such a thing flippantly. "What?" Miriam said, hoping a couple more seconds might help her decipher the tiny spark that had suddenly materialized in the murky despair within her soul.

He took his arm from around her shoulder and turned to face her on the bench, clasping her hands in his. And then he said again:

"Marry me."

✦ 33 ✦

MIRIAM MADE IT TWO blocks from the Gathering Haus before she heard someone calling her name. She picked up the pace. She was still furious, but now that the shock was past, the pounding of her heart had more to do with the fear that Gus might figure out her secret. After his revelation, she'd carry that secret to her grave without a twinge of remorse.

She'd hoped his overinflated opinion of his own dignity would prevent him following her, but the multiple repetitions of her name indicated otherwise.

"Miriam!"

At the touch on her shoulder, she wheeled, swinging her arm back in preparation for the second punch she'd ever thrown in her life, only to realize it wasn't Gus. "Oh," she said. "Hadley. I'm sorry. I thought—"

"It was your friend. I mean"—Hadley shook his head between gasps—"not your friend, I guess?"

Miriam rubbed her fingers across her forehead. "It's complicated."

"Clearly." He held up a hand, leaning down and bracing himself on his thigh while he caught his breath. "Man. I wouldn't normally be this winded, but I had to make sure that guy didn't follow you before I could come after you. John's gonna have my hide if he finds out I sicced some asshole on you when I was supposed to be protecting you."

"I don't need protection."

"Again: clearly." Even out of breath, he had a pleasant twinkle to his eye. He stood up straight. "I'm really sorry, Miriam. I didn't think anything of tagging you in that post. Never occurred to me something like that might happen. When he showed up, I just assumed you invited him."

She wanted to be angry with him, but mostly she just wanted to be angry, and it wasn't fair. She might just as easily have done the same. "Apology accepted," she said, and started on her way.

Hadley gripped her elbow. "Wait a minute!" He ran a hand through his hair, laughing. "Do you always make everything this hard? I'm trying to ask you to dinner."

"Hadley, you don't have to take care of me, no matter what Becky said."

"This has nothing to do with Becky. I don't even know Becky! I'm just asking you to dinner. Because I've been listening to you play for the last two hours, and . . . you're amazing, Miriam. That's all. I'd like to invite you to dinner with the rest of the band, and I'd love for you to come back to spend the evening at the Gathering Haus. Maybe we can even find a use for you on the piano."

"Oh." Miriam had to take a beat to reorganize her thoughts around a totally new thought process. The warmth in his eyes disarmed her anger. It made her feel, for the first time in so long she couldn't even remember, like a woman rather than a mother or widow. "What do you guys play?" Stalling for time. Nice.

"Traditional music . . . bluegrass. A little honky-tonk. Stuff to square-dance to."

"Not much use for a piano in that mix."

He shrugged. "I'm sure we could figure something out."

She bit her lip. "Well, I—I've got—my, uh—my friend, I need to check on her." She wasn't accustomed to being tongue-tied.

"Okay?" There was that gleam in his eye again— amusement? Something about the way his obvious sincerity mixed with that mischievous quirk at the corner of his mouth made her want to say yes. If for no other reason than to wash away the bad taste of her interaction with Gus.

"Okay," she said. "Let me check in with my friend. And I *don't* want to go back there before dinner."

"Just in case?" he finished with her, and they both laughed.

★ ★ ★

Dicey sounded groggy, but she insisted she hadn't been asleep. "You got a date?" she said. "Damn, woman, you work fast."

"It's not a date. I don't think."

"It's a date, Miriam. Anyway, whatever. I'm having a rom-com night. You have fun. But not too much fun."

Dinner with Hadley and his bluegrass band turned out to be the most fun she'd had in, well, a year. Though not at first. For the first half hour, she kept scanning the restaurant, fearing that despite his supposed rehearsal at eight in Denver, Gus might pop out at any minute. It took half a margarita to remember that a place where you could throw peanuts on the floor wasn't really his scene.

Slowly, she relaxed, resting her chin on the heels of her hands and enjoying the conversation. She'd forgotten how much she enjoyed hanging around musicians, trading esoteric jokes and talking in impenetrable lingo. Unlike Gus, these people already thought she belonged. They didn't view her as a charity project, but as a colleague.

At the bottom of her second margarita, Miriam found her abdominal muscles achy from laughter and the world a bit surreal—in the best of ways. This night offered the freedom and lack of responsibility of college without the insecurity of late adolescence.

Four months from now, she and Teo would have been empty nesters. Less, if she subtracted the weeks the kids would have spent at Interlochen over the summer. Would she and Teo have grown into a social life like this?

Her phone buzzed; she pulled it out in case Dicey needed her. But of course, it was Gus.

Please call me. I understand you're angry, but I can't concentrate. That music haunts me. I need resolution to this.

Unbelievable. She slid it back in her pocket without wasting a moment debating a reply. Gus didn't matter. All she wanted to think about tonight was the admiration in the eyes of the man across the table. Hadley wasn't even being particularly subtle about it. She could feel herself lighting up. She was still young . . . ish. Not even forty yet. Maybe Brad was right. Maybe she *could* be happy again.

Impulsively, she pulled her phone back out, clicked "Options" beside Gus's number, and blocked it.

The others ordered dessert, but Hadley took Miriam back to the Gathering Haus for a square-dance lesson before the event got underway.

"I'm not so sure about this," she confessed, standing in the middle of the hardwood floor.

"Why not?"

"I don't know, I just keep seeing *Hee Haw*. All these old women in creepy tulle skirts, and guys with string ties and belt buckles at their collars."

Hadley laughed. "They weren't old, actually."

"Well, they seemed old."

"To a kid, sure. Anyway, those ties are called bolos, and I can't promise you won't see any, but as for the rest, you can relax. This is very casual. Just local people who do it for fun."

The Gathering Haus lay quiet. The bartenders sat outside the back door on camp stools, smoking. They waved as Hadley and Miriam entered, but didn't leave their cigarettes.

Hadley led her to the center of the floor. "You look really nice," he said. "You've got this kind of bohemian Kate Winslet thing going on, with that scarf in your hair." He fingered it, brushing her hairline in the process. Miriam spent a moment savoring the thrill of being touched.

But apparently her hesitation gave the wrong impression. "Oh, I'm sorry," he said. "I mean, I shouldn't . . . I know you're not supposed to compare—"

Miriam, charmed, took him by the hand. "Relax," she said. "You're destroying your whole suave act."

Hadley's eyes widened; then he chuckled. "All right," he said. "Do-si-do."

By nine, the building was full. She'd never dreamed square dancing could be so much fun. Probably didn't hurt to have a couple margaritas in her. Hadley brought her onstage to join them for a honky-tonk set.

At the end of the set, the woman on the fiddle leaned down to murmur something in the caller's ear. "Virginia Reel!" he said. Hadley set his guitar down and held a hand out to Miriam. "Care to dance?"

If she'd met this man two weeks ago, she would have worn her widowhood like a shroud. Or maybe a martyr's crown. Either way, she would have refused.

But not tonight. Tonight, she was alive.

The dancers formed parallel lines; Miriam and Hadley took their place in the middle of the pack, and by the time they made their way up to the head position, Miriam had the knack of it: swinging partners and do-si-dos and all. Arms spread wide and hands enclosed in Hadley's, she slid down the center and back, giggling from the sheer joy of it all—music and bodies moving in concert, the warmth of a man's skin. That last part was at least as intoxicating as the alcohol.

"That's it for us, folks!" called the fiddler when the dance ended. A roar of applause, and the crowd began to wander toward purses and jackets.

The night air held a chill. As the musicians' van rumbled away, Miriam felt strangely let down. She hadn't had this much fun in years, but now what? Who could she share this moment with? The alcohol suppressed her defenses; grief surged forward, with the longing to see Talia skip down that reel, to watch Blaise watch people and analyze the music.

And Teo? What about Teo?

She cupped her palms over opposite elbows, trying to hold back the grief, and looked up into the clear sky, the stars mostly washed out by the downtown lights.

"What are you thinking about?" Hadley leaned on the wall with one boot propped on the brick.

"My family," Miriam said, too engulfed in an alcohol haze to dissemble. "It feels wrong to enjoy this so much, when . . ."

"They're the reason you're here, and they're gone," he finished.

She nodded.

"How did it happen?"

She rested her head against the brick. "Just a drunk driver. The oldest story in the world." She passed a hand over her eyes. "They were on the way to a beach. They'd taken a selfie in the car and sent it to me. That was the last communication I had from them." She shook her head, feeling the bricks pull strands of her hair. "It all happened so fast. So many things I never got to say."

Hadley must be wishing he'd never let Becky and John bully him into tracking her down. Another few seconds and he'd have a crying drunk on his hands, but she couldn't stop talking.

"I'm a church musician," she said. "Life, death, resurrection—my whole professional life is built on those things. But since it happened, I keep thinking, what's the point? You can spend your whole life working toward something, and in one second, it can all be gone. Am I going to spend the rest of my life waiting to be hit by a comet, wondering if I really believe everything I sing about on Sunday mornings? Wondering if they thought of me when . . . when it happened?" Her voice broke.

A car full of whooping college students passed by, followed at a more sedate pace by a sedan. In the distance, a police siren double-blipped a warning.

Hadley pushed off the wall and put an arm on her shoulder. "You know, I remember hearing something on a field trip once. A lot of Native Americans—not all, but many of them—figured it was a waste of time to think too much about death. They kind of thought there was something after death, but since they weren't gonna know exactly what until they got there, why waste time worrying?"

Miriam clenched her jaw, folding her arms to lock him out. "Easy for you to say."

"I lost my brother last year."

Miriam stared at him, her sluggish brain struggling to catch up. If he'd lost a brother, that meant John, her choir member, had lost a brother too. How had she not known? "When?" she asked.

"June."

Last June, she'd still been almost completely nonfunctional. John must have kept his grief to himself, trying to make her life easier. How horrible.

"I think about it all the time," Hadley said. "It's hard not to question, you know? People are always saying it's for the best, God has his plans."

"You have your own angel in heaven. Theological bullshit. People don't become angels. They become saints. Angels are different."

"Um, okay." Hadley's mouth quirked. "I'll take your word on all that."

"Oh, and *'At least you had them for a long time before they died'*!"

His eyes widened. "No way. Did someone really say that to you?"

"They sure did."

He shook his head. "People get so creeped out. You know they're all just praying the shit storm that hit you doesn't hit them next. And they feel guilty as hell about it, but that's the facts, ma'am."

She nodded emphatically.

He stepped forward, putting both hands on her cheeks. "We can't live in the past, Miriam. We have to live for today. For this moment, and this moment alone."

Barely a foot separated them now. Hazel eyes dizzied her, too close to focus on. She closed her eyes and raised herself on tiptoe, arcing into his body. She didn't need to see his face; she could feel his mouth from the surface of her lips to the deep place below her womb where desire was born. And then she fell back against the brick, exploring and being explored with a complete lack of concern for who might be watching.

Hadley drew a shuddering breath. "My apartment's upstairs," he said. "Just let me make sure my people have everything under control."

Miriam slipped inside the door and leaned on the frame, watching the easy way he interacted with his employees. He glanced back at her with a little smile, and her nerve ends lit up in response.

She smiled, her fingers playing with her waterdrop chain, looping it around her fingers, savoring the anticipation. She hadn't felt like this since that morning, how many years ago, when Teo had whispered in her ear . . .

Teo.

The locket burned her skin. She let go, but in all her worrying the chain, it had gotten tangled around her fingers. She had to shake it to get free. What was she doing? She was supposed to be out here to honor Teo, not to hook up with the first available guy who showed some hint that he understood what she was going through.

Inside the building, Hadley murmured to one of his employees. A low reply, a raucous laugh. Was he gloating about his conquest already?

Don't freak out. Not everyone was like Gus von Rickenbach. But suddenly, she felt cheap.

Miriam pulled Talia's sweater tight around her and slipped out the front door. She stumbled down the sidewalk, Teo's words chasing her back to the hotel, a whisper on repeat in her brain: *"You saved me. You saved me.*

"You saved me."

◆ 34 ◆

Twelve years earlier
Atlanta, Georgia

THE DAY BLAISE AND Talia headed off to kindergarten, Miriam and Teo walked them to school and waved until the door closed behind them. Then they returned slowly back home. Miriam stopped at the base of the porch steps. The street felt empty, and so did her body, like a burden had just been lifted, one she hadn't even been aware she was carrying. She tried to remember the feel of tandem nursing them, to recreate the visceral terror, the certainty that those floppy necks would break, that they'd be dead or brain damaged, and it would be her fault. But the sensation was gone as surely as the babies they'd been. All the sacrifices she'd made for such a brief blip on the radar. Plenty of years of parenting remained, but she hadn't expected this milestone to feel so . . . monumental.

Not until Teo's arms encircled her from behind did she feel her body shuddering, the tears sliding down her cheeks. He turned her around and cupped her face, kissed her cheeks, stroked her lips with his thumbs. He'd never touched her like this—with a trembling in his limbs and a sense of power barely restrained. "Mira," he whispered into the juncture of her neck and shoulder, and her body responded without waiting for permission from her mind. She was drowning in his kisses, her limbs wrapped around him, as she floated up the porch steps with her head flung back, blind and deaf from the glory of the newborn sun and the blood pounding in her ears.

The whisper of the air conditioner caused the seashell wind chimes hanging in the corner to shiver. The sunlight slanting through the window hit the water glass on the nightstand and shattered into a thousand points of light that bounced around the room with the vibration of their lovemaking.

Only when it was over, when Teo, flung back against the sheets like a man utterly spent, tried and failed to speak, did Miriam process what had just happened. That was not the intimacy she'd known, these past five-and-something years. What she'd once expected to be painfully awkward turned out to be quite natural—even, at times, enjoyable. But this was like nothing she'd ever experienced. She felt naked—vulnerable—her very soul exposed. It terrified her.

"Mira?" Teo pushed himself up on one shoulder, curling a lock of her hair around his finger. "I don't think I ever told you, but that day you walked into my cubicle, you saved me."

She turned her face toward him, frowning, her skin still hypersensitive to the warmth of the sunlight falling across her bare breast. She'd saved *him*?

"That morning, they'd offered me a place in the management training program. I didn't want it. You know how I hated working there, but it was so much money. More than my parents could ever have imagined. Everything they wanted for me, the reason they left me in America. I felt like I had to take it. I was begging God for another option. And then . . . there you were. You'd come to *me*. It felt like the answer to my prayer."

He caught her hand and pressed his lips to the back of it. "I know this wasn't how you envisioned your life," he said, "but I've loved you since the first summer I met you. I will spend the rest of my life loving you, every moment, if you'll only let me."

It was like a moment from Austen or Brontë. Miriam should have been melting into his arms, but all she felt was dread. Love in real life wasn't like it was in books. Gus and her parents had taught her that. Those "loves" had turned out to be a sham. Why should this one be any different?

And yet she knew Teo deserved better than such jaded thinking. What she saw in his eyes right now was a kind of love she'd never experienced and didn't know how to reciprocate. Why he'd chosen her, she'd never understand. He'd stepped into the mess and redeemed a situation she'd thought unredeemable. He saw the best in her and managed to bring it out simply by being himself.

She wanted to do right by him. She wanted to be capable of looking at him the way he was looking at her right now.

Could she learn? Maybe. Maybe if she worked at it long enough, diligently enough, someday she'd accidentally slip into the kind of unconditional love being offered to her right now.

Teo was still hovering above her, his expression eager. She couldn't give her husband what he wanted. What he so richly deserved. But she couldn't crush him by telling him the truth either.

She reached up and kissed him, praying forgiveness for all that the gesture implied. Praying she'd be able to live up to it . . . and almost certain she would not.

◆ 35 ◆

IN HER DREAMS, MIRIAM was being kissed, a kiss that transported her to the edge of ecstasy. But when she peeked over the edge, she found herself looking instead at an abyss of eternal damnation. It smelled less like sulfur than hot machinery. She heard a noise behind her, like someone blowing up an air mattress, only louder. She turned to see Dicey wearing a black contraption around her chest. Plastic tubes protruded from it.

Miriam tottered on the edge. The hot wind gusting up from the chasm scorched her back, but she focused on the pregnant woman. "What's going on with you, Dicey? Are you sick?"

"It's not your problem," Dicey answered. Her voice was fractured, as if she were speaking through a fan.

Miriam reached out. "Let me help you."

Dicey's visage shifted, becoming brighter and more terrible, like a vision out of *Lord of the Rings*. "Why would I want your help? You almost cheated on your husband!" She grew in height until she towered over Miriam. *"Gu-i-i-i-i-lty-y-y-y!"* she rumbled. Lightning shot from a slim finger. Miriam scrambled back and fell into the pit with a scream.

A gentle touch roused her. "Hey, Miriam. It's okay."

She pried her eyes open to find herself looking at Dicey, who retreated to the other bed and sat with her hands folded.

Miriam had to blink a few times to bring the image into focus: stretchy maternity jeans, sparkly sandals, the pretty, feminine flare of her maternity top. Miriam had never looked half so stylish when she was pregnant.

"Had this weird dream," she said. Her voice sounded like it had been dragged over gravel. She cleared her throat. "You were wearing this black thing that looked like a suicide vest, with hoses coming out of it. It made your voice all funny."

Dicey's eyes widened; she gave a strange little laugh. "Suicide vest," she said. "That's funny. And kinda twisted."

"Sorry."

"You were calling out for Teo."

Miriam groaned and rolled onto her back. The best thing about hotels was the sheets: beautifully tucked in, neat and tidy and untangled. Teo had always pulled the covers untucked. It used to make her crazy. Now, the memory made her smile.

Or would have, if she didn't feel so lousy.

Miriam pushed herself upright. The world swam. Her nose wrinkled. She could smell alcohol. And something else—something mechanical. Like hot machinery. She frowned, but her brain was moving too slowly to put together whatever pieces it wanted to connect. "It *was* a dream, wasn't it?"

"Wasn't what a dream?" Dicey grabbed a bottle of orange juice and two red-coated tablets. "Here," she said, handing them to Miriam. "You must've had some night."

"Some night," Miriam mumbled. As her slow-moving brain began to replace dream images with memories, she deeply regretted putting anything down her throat. Gus. Dinner with the band. Drinking . . . a lot. Dancing with Hadley.

Almost sleeping with Hadley.

She'd known she was a mess, but she hadn't realized just how big a mess.

Dicey cleared her throat. "The auto shop called. We can pick it up anytime. There's a train headed up Pikes Peak at noon. I figured we could catch it."

Miriam nodded slowly.

"But first, you need a shower. Badly."

A shower made her feel marginally human again. Miriam answered the knock on the bathroom door to find Dicey holding out a bundle of clothes. "Here. Figured I'd help you out."

Miriam stared at the black dress, red flowers splashed across it like blood.

"You haven't worn this yet. It's pretty," Dicey said.

Miriam looked up. "I'll get my own clothes," she said shortly, and closed the door.

Dicey showed her disapproval of Miriam's rudeness by barely speaking a word all the way up the mountain. Not that they could have talked much, anyway; the noise of the cog railway all but buried the guide's narration. Still, it smarted.

The sunlight felt stronger on the summit of Pikes Peak. Miriam couldn't tell if that was real, a result of glare off the snow that hadn't yet melted at this altitude, or merely a figment of her imagination. She did know that, no matter what her inner ear wanted her to believe, the ground wasn't actually moving.

She gazed down over the plains. Blaise had promised her a view of five states, but there was nothing to distinguish one from another. She shivered, chilled by more than the cold at fourteen thousand feet.

Miriam swallowed the last bite of her high-altitude donut. No doubt it was as good as Blaise had claimed, but a hangover had a way of making everything taste like dust. A hangover and regret. Regret for last night and for a lifetime of bad choices.

She'd given Gus so much power over her: first as an obsession, briefly as a lover, and ever since, as the ghost in her bed.

She needed someone to talk to. Becky, perhaps, although Miriam couldn't imagine baring the gunked-up depths of her soul to her serene, competent friend. She needed someone who could see her for all that she was, good and bad alike, who would listen without judgment and still love her unconditionally.

In other words, she needed Teo.

The locket burned like dry ice against her chest.

How she missed that man. The way he always pushed her tempos in choir practice and mouthed off when she pointed out the metronome markings. "The Bickersons," her older choir members used to call them, laughing. The way he could figure out how to fix anything with a YouTube video and a trip or ten to the hardware store. The way he'd come home with the tiniest little thing—a vanilla Pepsi or a pint of Superman ice cream, something to show he knew exactly what would make her feel loved in that very moment.

She wished she were more like him—exuberant and effusive, generous with affection. But fixing meals and doing dishes and working out meticulous schedules for a busy family and work life were the best she could do.

How he used to laugh about those matrices, which she'd print out and mark with highlighters once a week. "It never lasts past Monday anyway," he would say. "You might as well make it up on the fly."

Such a gentle man. So kind and considerate. Except that one glorious morning when she'd seen the passion he kept buried. Felt it in every nerve in her trembling body. In that moment, the one time in her life she'd allowed herself to be vulnerable to her husband, Miriam felt loved from the outermost tip of her hair to the deepest, most secret place in her soul.

It scared her so much, she'd never let him in that deep again.

This was the man whose wildflower petals she carried in this locket. She missed him with an ache that eclipsed the cold, the altitude, and even her hangover. Was Talia right? Had he been unhappy? Had he ever known how much he meant to her? Had he ever, in some deep, dark, unexpressed corner of his soul, resented her? Wondered whether she'd come to him that day in Philadelphia, calculating that he would offer a respectable way out of her predicament?

Surely not. *"You saved me,"* he said.

She shivered, as if the words had whispered on the cold wind rather than existing only in her memory. Doubt was a cold and lonely thing.

Teo's locket felt cold in her fingers. The chain swung in the wind, flashing the stark white light at the midpoint of every arc. She didn't remember taking it off, but there it lay in her clenched fist.

The chain whipped her arm. The wind wanted that pendant. If she flung it away, it would disappear into the great, clear blue. It might fall on late snow or newly exposed rock or be carried on a gust to snag on some twisted, tortured pine gasping for breath at the edge of the tree line. Either way, no one would ever see it again except maybe a marmot. She'd be rid of the reminder. Rid of the burden of guilt she'd been carrying around for the last year.

And yet the locket was all she had left.

"Miriam?"

She turned. Dicey walked slowly toward her, her face white. The altitude must be rough on a pregnant woman. "Is it time?" Miriam asked.

Dicey nodded. "The train is boarding."

Miriam slipped the chain back over her head and tucked it beneath her blouse, then slipped a hand beneath Dicey's elbow. "All right," she said. "Let's get going."

"What's in the locket, anyway?" Dicey asked as they made their way back to the red rail car.

Every mistake I ever made. But Dicey wouldn't understand.

Miriam shrugged. "Just some dead flowers," she said.

♦ 36 ♦

Saturday, May 7
3:30 PM
Manitou Springs, Colorado
Cog Railway parking lot

THE COIN ICONS ON the app were unresponsive. Miriam tried three times. She checked social media to make sure her photos had posted, but if that were the problem, Talia's wagging finger .gif would have come up. It just wasn't working. It was as if the app had seen her choices these past twenty-four hours and passed judgment on her for them.

Beside her, Dicey began coughing so hard, the car shook. Miriam put the phone down and rubbed her back. "Dicey," she said, when the attack eased at last, "let's find a quick care clinic."

"What's the matter with the app?"

Not even an acknowledgment. Miriam wanted to shake her, but as always she butted up against the thing Dicey never let her forget: Miriam was not her mother.

She stared out the window at the sunlight on the high elevations, debating. Dicey had made clear how much she valued her baby's life. Surely, if she needed medical attention, she'd say so.

Miriam capitulated. "It's not working." She handed over the phone.

Dicey swiped and tapped for a minute or two, pausing only to cough again. "Hmm," she said. "You know what I think? I think there aren't any more destinations. She never finished putting in the content."

The words dropped, leaden, into the quiet car. A gaggle of college-aged girls walked past, talking over each other about the party they were attending tonight. Miriam stared out the windshield at the pines and aspen rising from the shoulders of the mountain. "You're right," she said. The words nearly choked her. She hadn't realized how much she'd come to depend on those glimpses from beyond the grave, precious for their novelty. For a year, she'd had nothing but memories, fading quickly from overuse. The videos let her pretend there were still depths to plumb and discoveries to be made. It gave her children back to her, alive and well, if only for a minute or two.

That was all over now. Miriam thought back to that last video, in which Blaise had been talking about Pikes Peak. He'd been wearing a sweatshirt, and the background had been unfamiliar. Had he recorded it while they were camping, that last night before . . .?

Miriam put her head down on the steering wheel. It was like losing them all over again.

Dicey rubbed her back. "What do you want to do? Head straight for the coast?"

She should. Whatever was wrong with Dicey, her best bet was to get her to her mother and this all-knowing doctor she kept talking about. Miriam could drop her off and go do what she'd come on this trip to do. Except, when she reached that beach, she would no longer be able to avoid the reality: her family was gone forever.

Grief so heavy ought to come with tears. She had no tears. Only a vast, angry emptiness, ready to rebound on the world as bitterness, as it had when she'd played "Ring of Fire" at the congressman's funeral. Her children had stranded her halfway across the country. Just far enough away to wreck everything familiar. Not far enough to provide answers.

"We can keep going, you know." Dicey gestured with her pink spangled phone.

Miriam shook her head. "The point was to follow the kids' directions."

Dicey made a guttural sound of half-amused disgust. "Come on, Miriam, that was never the point." But at the look on Miriam's face, her bemusement faded. "Is that really why you did all this?"

Miriam sat up. "I did it because I was going to lose my job if I didn't get my head on straight, and I thought maybe if I did this for my family, I'd stop feeling so shitty and get my life back together. But if the kids aren't part of it, what's the point?"

Dicey leaned forward. "To live, Miriam. To find your joy again. Look what you've become, how you've changed. You've . . . you've blossomed. When I met you, you had this cloud of darkness all around you."

"And now I don't?"

"Not like it was. You've had fun out here. When you forget to punish yourself, you're this amazing woman who touches everyone you meet. You of all people know how little time we really have. How precious every moment is. Just embrace it, Miriam. Don't squander the gift."

"The gift. Like the trolls who passed judgment on my son?"

"Screw the trolls. Who cares about the trolls? I just want you to devour this experience! Swallow it whole! Life's too short to live it by halves. That's all I'm saying." Dicey's vehemence overtook her in the form of a brief coughing fit. She unscrewed a water bottle and drank deeply.

Miriam leaned her forearms on the steering wheel, thinking. "How would we go on?"

Dicey opened her phone. "When you said Talia had been working on it the spring before she died, I wondered if we might run out of destinations. I found this site the other day that lists quirky, cool places to see in every county in every state. So I figure, we say heads is north, tails is south, and either way we head west. We make our own destinations." She waited a moment. "Miriam?"

Miriam stared at the mountainside beyond the glass. It would only delay the inevitable, but still, it was a delay. "All right," she said. "Let's do it."

Part 8

Hooper, Colorado

Grief is the price we pay for love.

—Queen Elizabeth II

Dicey's intro to the UFO Watchtower, Hooper, Colorado

H'lo, folks. I know, you're thinking, "Who is this chick?" Well, the name's Dicey. I'm the one who's been making the videos. And just in case there's any question? Yes. I'm totally preggers.

Sometimes you forget that all good things must come to an end. We weren't ready for it, but it turns out the Tedesco Twins weren't able to finish planning the Great American Road Trip before they passed away. We discovered earlier today that we were out of destinations. But never fear, we rose to the occasion. With the help of a little site called Local American Treasures, we're back in business. We've got our nose pointed southwest, toward an itty-bitty town called Hooper, Colorado. A few years ago, a woman decided to become a rancher there. Only, not all acreage is cattle-friendly. So, since everybody is UFO obsessed in this part of the country, she figured, Hey, we'll just go with it.

So tonight, we're camping at the UFO Watchtower. We figured the Tedesco Twins would approve. We'll be sure to report on any and all sightings, in real time. Over and out.

37

Saturday, May 7
Sunset
UFO Watchtower, near Hooper, Colorado

THE CLOUDS GATHERED BEHIND them as Miriam drove south. The radio announcers warned of a major late-season snowstorm bearing down on Colorado Springs, but it looked like they'd dodged the bullet. Gradually, the clouds thinned and the sun reclaimed the sky.

Meanwhile, Dicey slept. And slept. And slept. She'd nailed the introductory video, but within fifteen minutes, she'd crashed. She hadn't moved a muscle since.

Miriam wanted food, but she couldn't rouse her companion. She grabbed drive-thru, figuring if Dicey was that worn out, it was better to let her sleep off whatever bug she was fighting.

Except . . . Dicey had been with her eight days now, and the cough was no better. If anything, it was worse. Her mother's admonition sounded more prescient every time she thought about it. But what could Miriam do, if Dicey wouldn't let her help?

By the time they arrived at their destination, Dicey's burger was cold.

"Dicey," Miriam said, shaking her arm as she drove beneath the square timber arch marking the driveway to the UFO Watchtower. The handwritten sign proclaimed,

"Come on in." "Dicey, wake up. Come on, honey. Please. You're scaring me."

Dicey stirred and took a deep breath—or at least, she tried. She started hacking instead. Miriam had never been so grateful to hear coughing in her entire life.

The watchtower was a small, dome-shaped building with a metal platform around three sides and a rock garden in front. Across the valley, the sun was setting, orange light streaming across the flat ground to bathe the Sangre de Cristo Mountains in a light that made them live up to their name. It looked like something out of a Peter Jackson movie.

Dicey emerged from the car, still coughing, as a sixty-something couple clanked down the stairs dressed in matching jogging suits. "You've missed the lady of the manor," said the man. "She went home for the night. You can pay your two dollars in the mailbox over there, though."

"Is she okay?" asked the woman, peering anxiously at Dicey, who leaned over the hood of the Sonata, still coughing. Dicey held up a hand and nodded, but Miriam had reached her limit. First thing in the morning, they were going to find an urgent care clinic whether Dicey liked it or not.

But for now, she focused on the immediate issue. "You said the owner is gone? I thought you could camp here."

"Oh, you can. She'll let you pay tomorrow morning if you want to set up, but . . ." The woman was still eyeing Dicey.

"What about bathrooms?" asked Miriam, looking around.

"It's primitive camping," the man said.

"Shit," said Dicey, coming up for air at last. "I need to pee. Bad."

Maybe it was a divine prompting to go find a clinic tonight. Miriam gave her a sidelong look. "I don't think we can stay here, Dicey."

Dicey set a stubborn face. "I want to see UFOs. I'm staying."

"There's no water, honey."

"We have a couple bottles left. It won't be any worse than the night of the storm."

"And you're okay with just peeing anywhere?"

"Oh, for heaven's sake," said the woman, taking Dicey by the elbow. "Come use the toilet in our camper. We're staying too. We're going to sit up on the viewing platform until it gets too cold. Care to join us? Only . . . is that contagious? We're on our way to see our grandkids."

Dicey snorted, which led to another, shorter bout of coughing. "Not contagious, no worries."

No worries? Miriam was feeling nothing *but* worry.

The chatty couple, it turned out, hailed from Wisconsin and were on their way back north after spending the winter in the southwest. "You should take a look around the garden there," said the woman, when they'd all returned to the base of the platform. "Supposedly there are two 'vortexes' in there."

"What's a vortex?" asked Miriam.

"Like a portal to another dimension," said the man.

"Or a convergence of spiritual energy." The woman rolled her eyes. "We're not really believers, but we've been driving past for years, and I finally told him we should stop before we get too old to climb the stairs. And we figured if we were doing it, we ought to do it right."

"Miriam, come here!" said Dicey, from the middle of the rock garden.

Miriam joined her. There was a rapt expression on Dicey's face as she surveyed the ground, but Miriam couldn't summon much enthusiasm for the scattered array of junk people had left by way of an offering to . . . whatever. Hubcaps, pens, credit cards. Headless Barbies. "Wow," she said. "That's a lot of . . . stuff."

"This is the coolest thing we've done yet." Dicey's breaths buzzed softly, but the long nap seemed to have done her good. At any rate, her eyes were bright, and her cheeks had some color. "I want to be buried in a place like this."

"That's a bit morbid."

Dicey scowled. "You can't feel it, can you?"

"Feel what?"

"The energy in this place." Dicey spread her arms. "It's amazing." She sighed at Miriam's lack of enthusiasm and held out her pink spangled phone. "All right, whatever. Take a picture for me."

She had another one of her pink-and-brown lettered signs. Miriam framed the photo and then paused, looking between the image on the screen and its real-life counterpart: *Anytime you need me, look in the mirror.*

"Your daughter's going to love this book," she said.

"I hope so." Dicey retrieved her phone and wandered off. Miriam opted to stay put and look beyond the garden. This great, vast emptiness was precisely the kind of desert designed for spiritual renewal. John the Baptist would have felt right at home here.

Miriam, not so much. The quiet settled around her, but worry pushed back against any sense of spiritual awareness. She focused again on Dicey, wandering the pathways lined with trinkets, and gnawed at the edge of her lip. What could possibly cause such chronic, productive coughing and not be contagious? More importantly, how was she ever going to convince Dicey to go see a doctor?

One thing at a time, she told herself.

She left Dicey to the enjoyment of the so-called garden and went to retrieve the sleeping bags from the trunk of the car. She could already tell that at this elevation it would be too cold to sit outside in just their jackets. It was going to be another long night.

★　★　★

Miriam made as comfortable a nest as she could on the wire mesh deck while chatting with the Wisconsinites. They swapped travel stories in the falling darkness, hoping for an unexplained light or two to keep them company.

Although the older couple said they meant to sleep in their RV, they seemed in no hurry to descend. Slowly, quiet fell. The man snored; Dicey buzzed. Miriam thought she was asleep, but then she murmured, "There are so many."

"Stars?"

Dicey nodded. "It gives you a sense of how small we really are."

"Mm."

Dicey snuggled up against her. "Have a favor to ask."

"What's that?"

"I want you to be Baby Girl's godmother."

The shock went through her body, freezing her in place. "What?"

"I mean it."

"I—" She swallowed the thickness in her throat. "Dicey, I don't know what to say."

"'Yes' would be appropriate." Dicey sounded amused.

"I'd be honored. I just . . . are you sure you want me?"

"Why wouldn't I? And don't give me any crap about not loving your family."

Miriam closed her mouth.

Dicey sat up to look at her head-on by the faint, silvery glow of the stars. "That's what I figured." She scowled at Miriam. "I want you to be Baby Girl's godmother because you're an awesome human being. But there's a condition. I don't want to hear you say anything about not loving your family, ever again. I've heard how you talk about them. You loved them just fine."

It took Miriam an unreasonably long time to clear the thickness in her throat. "Okay."

"Good." Dicey leaned against her again. Slowly, her buzzing breaths lengthened. Miriam pressed her cheek against Dicey's head as the younger woman's weight settled into sleep. She'd always loved the quiet in the middle of the night. The peace of it, the knowledge that everyone under her care was safe and at rest. The journey had bonded the women, but Dicey's request tied them together in a lasting way. It was surprisingly emotional.

Out in the scraggly brush, crickets creaked. The wind whispered low, whisking away the day's heat. Dicey's body provided welcome warmth.

Miriam stared up at the sky, her brain fuzzy, yet still vibrating with awareness. The wind died down, and with it all sense of connection to the world. She sat suspended between heaven and earth, anticipating what, she didn't know. She only knew her whole being was holding its breath—waiting—waiting—waiting.

There were no dancing lights over the Sangre de Cristo, but every moment, more stars emerged from the darkness. She'd never seen anything like this spangled velvet swath, tinged cream and brown: the Milky Way. How could something so spectacular hide within what had always seemed, to a Motor City child and Atlanta transplant, a threatening darkness?

Blaise would have loved this. While other preschool boys made lists of dinosaurs, he'd listed constellations. They never could afford a good telescope, and the skies around Atlanta were too washed out anyway, but he'd seemed content to join the astronomy club. "I wish you were here to see this," Miriam whispered.

There was no answer, of course. Below the star-slung sky, the highlands lay silent, save for the hypnotic, metronomic pulse of desert insects and the buzz of Dicey's breaths. Miriam closed her eyes and let herself drift into the space between.

38

Miriam woke to the sound of deep, raw gasping, of coughs without recovery time.

Even before her mind processed the sound, Miriam had both arms around Dicey. In her panic, the younger woman's arms flailed wildly, contacting Miriam's eye, and for a moment, Miriam did see dancing lights above the UFO watchtower.

As soon as she recovered, she maneuvered behind Dicey and pinned her arms to her sides. "Calm down," she said, pressing her cheek against Dicey's to limit her range of motion. The girl's skin radiated heat. "Calm down, Dicey. Just breathe. Breathe."

It felt strange, doing this to a grown woman, yet achingly familiar. This had been the only way to get Talia through medical appointments in the early years.

"You never stop being a mother," Dicey had told her. The truth in those words pierced the darkness with a light that took Miriam's breath away.

She breathed in and out, letting the air pass over her vocal cords. It was Teo's lullaby, the wordless ditty he'd sung to the twins when nursing couldn't settle them, when thunder woke them screaming. She hummed in Dicey's ear until the younger woman began to calm down, her breath still noisy and labored, but less panicked. It was cold, Miriam realized. She hadn't noticed at first because of the heat of Dicey's fevered body, but it had to be near freezing. Above them, the snow-capped mountains were bathed in a star glow that seemed otherworldly. It also illuminated the Wisconsinites, sleeping in each other's arms in the corner of the platform railing. Miriam felt a moment's loneliness, but only a moment's. There was work to do. A mother's work.

"All right, Dicey," she said softly. "Whether you like it or not, you're going to the hospital. Come on. Let's get you to the car."

With effort, Miriam got her down the narrow stairs and into the car. But Dicey wouldn't let her close the door. "Oh two," she wheezed.

It took a minute to process. "Oxygen?"

Dicey nodded listlessly and waved one limp hand toward her backpack.

Damn it, Dicey. But Miriam had no time to indulge her anger. She dug in the bag and found a small canister. Sick as she was, Dicey moved like a pro, attaching the plastic tubing of a cannula and looping the ends over her ears. She pressed her hands against the tubing, her head falling back on the seat, and the light from Miriam's phone illuminated the words engraved on the medical bracelet.

Dicey Smith, cystic fibrosis.

The words socked Miriam in the gut. She'd heard of cystic fibrosis, but she knew nothing about it. Only that anything that required a medical ID bracelet and portable oxygen was bad news.

Miriam stalked to the back of the car and popped the trunk. Unzipping the stickered suitcase revealed more oxygen canisters . . . and a black vest with tubes protruding from it.

So it hadn't been a dream.

Why didn't I make her go to the doctor?

Miriam pulled up her mapping app. The nearest ER was thirty miles away. She spit gravel pulling out of the parking lot.

It was one of the longest half hours of Miriam's life. Every shallow, labored breath Dicey took made her chest ache in sympathy. Dicey needed to cough, but she seemed too weak.

Miriam began singing again. Teo's melody, and then, flowing effortlessly from it in counterpoint, her own. The one she'd spent an hour fighting with at Hadley's piano, trying to make it classical. It had found its voice in Teo's favorite Scripture passage: *Be still and know that I am God.*

They arrived in Alamosa, Colorado, at two thirty AM. The ER lay quiet and empty except for one woman reading a magazine in the corner and another behind the desk wearing, improbably, *Día de Muertos* scrubs. *Muertos* looked up, her eyes widening at the sight of the pregnant woman putting all her weight on Miriam. "Enrique!" she bellowed, and another nurse came out from the door beside the check in window. He removed Dicey's weight from Miriam's arm; Dicey held her wrist up to show him the bracelet. His face turned grave. He turned to Miriam. "Do you have her meds? Her oscillation vest?"

"The black vest with the tubes? It's in her suitcase."

"We'll need it. We'll need everything."

Miriam didn't need to be told twice. She ran out to the car and retrieved all Dicey's belongings. Inside, she shoved them into the arms of the waiting nurse, who turned and headed into the back. Miriam started to follow, but the woman behind the desk stopped her. "I'm sorry, are you family?"

"No, but . . ."

"Then you can't come back. I'm sorry."

Miriam stood there as the door swung closed with an electronic click. *Damn, damn, damn!*

She sat down in the chair directly in front of the door to wait. Stupid privacy laws!

The only sounds in the ER waiting room were the piped-in Muzak and the guy in a shiny suit on the Weather Channel, talking about a late-season blizzard.

"CF?"

It took a moment to realize the voice was addressing her. Miriam looked over her shoulder. Magazine woman. "I'm sorry?"

"CF." The woman nodded toward the closed door. "I recognize the paraphernalia. My cousin died of it when she was nineteen." Perhaps seeing the look on Miriam's face, she added, "But I hear the life expectancy's improved a ton."

Miriam gave the woman a stiff smile and sat down, pulling out her phone to look up everything she didn't know.

. . . *Mucus that's too thick or sweat that's too salty* . . .

. . . *sticky mucus that clogs the lungs and digestive system* . . .

. . . *compromised lung function* . . .

. . . *some people are living into their 40s* . . .

Suddenly, everything made sense: the videos and photos for her daughter, the scrapbook. The loud music and long showers, cover for breathing treatments Dicey didn't want Miriam to know about. Her vehemence about living life fully. The cryptic comments about death.

Miriam clicked her phone off and dropped her head between her knees, hoping the blood would rush to her brain and knock her out. Because the chasm opening in front of her was one she wasn't sure she could crawl back out of.

◆ **39** ◆

Sunday, May 8
5:52 AM
Alamosa, Colorado

THE TV STAYED ON all night. The Weather Channel guys couldn't stop salivating over the storm now pounding the hell out of Colorado Springs. Miriam supposed she was lucky she'd even gotten to see the Milky Way in Hooper. From twisters to blizzards in two days: *#Gr8AmAdven,* indeed.

Somewhere down deep, she must be hysterical, if she was thinking in sharp signs. *Hash tags,* she corrected herself.

"Please," she said to *Día de Muertos* woman again. "Please, just tell me what's going on."

"I'm sorry, privacy . . ."

"Forget the privacy regulations! Just ask her if she wants me to know! Is that so difficult?"

"Ma'am, I need you to calm down, or I'll have to call Security."

Miriam gritted her teeth. She'd never felt so powerless.

"Do you really want to be responsible for her health and safety?" her mother had asked.

No, she replied silently. *No, I don't. But I'm all she has right now.*

Miriam took a deep breath and refocused on the desk attendant. "I'm going to get a breath of air, and then I'll be back," she said. "I'm not leaving."

The woman stared back, expressionless.

Miriam glided out the door, projecting the calm, with-it image she knew she needed in order to have any chance. For heaven's sake, she'd brought Dicey in. Surely that ought to count for something!

As Miriam walked out the door, a helicopter approached, heading for the landing pad in the corner of the parking lot. The noise disrupted the quiet of a small-town Sunday morning. She shivered as she stretched her neck in the cold wind. The sky glowered in the gray pre-dawn. She imagined she could see the blizzard clouds to the north, covering highways she and Dicey had traversed only a couple days earlier.

The chopper powered down. Miriam walked to the end of the drive and then continued. A walk around the block might help clear her mind. So would finding a church to go to Mass. How could it be Sunday again? In the real world, people had gone through an entire workweek, an entire school week, a week of lessons and sports practices. The last seven days had passed in a flash, yet she felt years older.

Miriam set off at a brisk clip. How could she convince them to give her information? Someone had to get word to Dicey's family. Or had Dicey been coherent enough to give the hospital personnel contact info?

She'd been coherent enough to show that orderly her bracelet. The bracelet she'd refused, again and again, to let Miriam see.

What if Dicey had specifically told them not to tell Miriam anything?

"Stop it," she said aloud. "That makes no sense. She just asked you to be her baby's godmother." She rubbed her eyes. In the corner of the parking lot, the landing pad buzzed with activity: one swarm of people loading equipment onto the chopper, another shepherding a stretcher toward it.

Wait a minute. Was that guy putting Dicey's suitcase into that chopper? He closed the door and retreated, and the helicopter powered up again.

Miriam took off running. "No!" she shouted, running toward them, waving her arms. "Wait! Wait for me! Please!"

Too late. The icy wind from the blades sliced through Talia's flowing brown skirt and peasant blouse as if they weren't there at all. In the gray predawn, the chopper's spotlight blinded her. As it banked right and turned, nose-down, into the wind, Miriam blinked repeatedly, trying to clear her vision enough to see the emblem on the side. All she caught was one word, written in black just forward of the tail rotor:

Albuquerque.

Her head spun; her vision blacked over. She sat down hard on the ground, her ears roaring. By the time sight and sound returned, the helicopter lights had shrunk to a point, the noise fading from a deafening roar to a faint murmur. Dicey was gone.

Miriam put her hands to her forehead, the emptiness inside so vast, surely the whole universe could fit inside. Except emptiness shouldn't hurt, and this hurt like hell.

The sun broke the horizon and flowed across the valley, bathing the mountains and everything between them in a deep orange-pink glow. She felt the warmth on the backs of her hands, her eyelids, and the tip of her nose.

And Miriam knew:

She loved this girl.

She'd thought herself incapable of love. She'd thought she'd spent everything she had on her children, an entire life's supply poured out, wasted now that they were gone. She'd thought she had no more to give.

She knew now she was wrong. Maybe she'd buried it, maybe she'd turned her back on it, but here it was, coursing and raging like a river swollen by spring rains, sweeping away all the barriers she'd erected to keep it in and everything else out.

She could feel it now, for the first time since she'd seen Simeon and that police officer coming up her front walk last April. There was *something* out there again, a sense of connection and understanding and wonder at the world and all that existed within it. A sense of being part of something much larger than herself.

Be still, the melody whispered in her mind. *Be still and know.*

How long Miriam stood soaking in the rising sun, she couldn't say. But when she finally moved, she had a purpose again. She was going to find Dicey, whatever it took. Because Dicey had broken her open, and allowed her to touch the best that lay within her once more.

★   ★   ★

Sunday morning text message conversation:

Miriam: *Dicey's been sent to the hospital in ABQ.*
Becky: *WHAT???????????? Details!*
Miriam: *Later. Just pray. Anybody in ABQ have a friend with a spare room?*
Becky: *Your mom?*
Miriam: *Not sure I can deal with that much togetherness.*
Becky: 😓
Becky: *CALL YOUR MOTHER*

★   ★   ★

Texts between Miriam Tedesco and Josephine Lewis-Thurston:

Miriam: *Well, I'm going to see mom.*
Jo: *About damn time.*

Part 9

Albuquerque, New Mexico

There can be no deep disappointment where there is not deep love.

—Martin Luther King Jr.

Miriam's e-mail to her choir members:

Hi, everybody,
First of all, I want to thank you for all your messages on Facebook. I don't think I've ever fully appreciated, until this trip, just how blessed I am to have you all in my life.

I had to stop and nap on the road to Albuquerque . . . didn't sleep much last night. Dicey got very sick, and the hospital in Alamosa transferred her on to ABQ. I can't give you all the details because, frankly, I don't have them, but it looks a lot more serious than I had guessed. So please pray for her.

And for me, because there's something else I have to do there, and I'm not sure I'm ready for it.
Thanks all,
Miriam

♦ 40 ♦

Sunday, May 8
Albuquerque, New Mexico
Noon

Miriam's entire childhood in Detroit, she'd known what to expect when she came home from school: the smell of savory spices on the stove, so strong, even the walls of the house couldn't contain them. That, and the sound of a vacuum cleaner.

It was disorienting to step out of the car in front of a row of identical zero-entry duplexes in Albuquerque and experience exactly the same thing.

Miriam rang the doorbell. The vacuum shut off, and momentarily the door opened. "Mira," said Sallie Lewis, opening her arms. "At last."

Embraces had never been part of earlier homecomings; it added to the foreignness of this one—her first time visiting Mom's new home. How small her mother had become, her frame shrinking, her skin loosening on her bones. Had this happened recently, or had Miriam just been too wrapped up in herself to notice?

Sallie released her, patting both her arms and stepping back to wave her inside. "All right, come on in," she said. "Judging by the looks of that car, you've had a rough ride. I'll get it cleaned out, but Becky's not going to be happy."

Miriam looked behind her. "I'm just grateful it still runs." At this point, it was hard to get too worked up about a car. Becky would feel the same. She hoped.

Her mother bustled ahead of her, deeper into the condo. "Are you hungry? Do you need a shower?"

"Right now I just want to sleep. I've got to try to find Dicey, and I can't even think, I'm so tired."

Her mother pursed her lips. "All right. Sleep first, then eat."

But the smell of pierogi and sausage—Grandma Novak's super-secret recipe that Miriam knew how to make but had never mastered to her satisfaction—grew stronger every step closer to the kitchen, and Miriam discovered she did have an appetite after all. While she ate, Sallie called Jo. "Yes, she's here. No, we haven't talked about it yet. Yes, I'll make sure we do."

Even before Miriam popped the last pastry in her mouth, the starchy food had rerouted all the blood from her brain to her stomach. "Nap," she said, pointing. "Down the hall?"

Her mother, still on the phone, nodded. "On the left," she mouthed.

Miriam padded down the hallway and turned into the open doorway of the guest room to find herself facing a shrine to her siblings' achievements. She could barely see the color of the walls. There were team photos, framed newspaper clippings, and academic awards; Jo's chess trophies, Brad's academic bowl medals, and countless mementos of victories in track, basketball, and softball.

As if she'd needed any more proof of her second-class status in her own family.

Miriam mummified herself under the covers. The room pressed in on her, her heart and throat pushing back, swelling until they ached. How could she feel so hurt when she was the one who had withdrawn from her family?

Her brain was slowing down, sleep washing toward her, heavy and irresistible. On the cusp of dropping off, her subconscious served up a memory she wished mightily she didn't have: the slam of the frying pan and her mother screaming the word *divorce*.

Twenty-one years earlier
Detroit, Michigan

BY THE TIME MIRIAM looked at the clock that May morning, she was already running late. She'd awakened hours too early, but, wound up with anticipation of meeting with a bride and groom—the first ever to consider hiring her—she couldn't get back to sleep. She pulled out Jane Austen to settle her nerves, and the call of Lizzy and Mr. Darcy proved too strong. By the time the two were safely united, Miriam's parents were moving around in the kitchen, as they always did on Saturday mornings, the floor creaking as Dad read the paper and Mom made pancakes and bacon.

Did Darcy and Elizabeth do such boring, companionable things in the mornings? No way. They were probably all over each other.

Did Mom and Dad have sex anymore?

Now there was an image to give a girl the heebie-jeebies.

Miriam focused on choosing the right outfit. It felt like her entire life was riding on this wedding meeting. Mostly because her parents would take failure as further proof that classical music constituted a one-way trip to the poorhouse.

Outside the window, the maple tree nodded in the breeze, its miniature leaves bright green. The roar of the Fisher Freeway bounced along the treetops. After one last glance in the mirror, Miriam ran downstairs toward the clank of dishes and the smell of coffee and bacon. Her parents appeared in their usual positions: Dad at the end of the table, Mom at the stove, as dependable as the sun rising in the morning or the Pistons choking when it mattered most. *As it was in the beginning, is now, and ever shall be, world without end, amen.*

Dad didn't even look up from his paper, but Mom turned her cheek toward Miriam's kiss. "Did you sleep well? Where are you off to so early?"

"I'm meeting with a bride and groom. Remember? If they like me, they'll hire me to play their wedding. Remember?" She hated herself for saying it twice, for the angsty note in her voice, but they'd just talked about this two nights ago.

Dad gave her a sour look and ruffled the paper. "Don't be gone too long. You need to be studying for the SAT, not dinking around on the piano all day."

Miriam grabbed a toaster pastry. Her mother looked up. "Don't you want some eggs?"

"No." She dashed out the door and ran for the bus stop, seething.

They'd all taken piano when they were little, but where her older siblings had fought tooth and nail to quit, Miriam had to fight for the right to continue. It was one thing to pay for half-hour lessons, but when she graduated to an hour and a more expensive teacher, her parents balked. She'd spent the last four years mowing lawns and babysitting to help cover the expense. Doing weddings would be a huge step up. The pressure from Mom and Dad had ratcheted upward lately. Josephine and Brad had already stamped their passports out of the world of time cards and union dues; every week at church, Mom bragged about Brad acing his premed courses and Josephine's steady rise up the floors of a New York skyscraper.

Miriam wanted them to brag on her for earning a hundred bucks an hour as a high school pianist.

She ran over her mental list again: Pachelbel, Schubert, Purcell: the holy trinity of wedding music, her piano teacher had called them. Far from the hardest pieces Miriam had learned. She'd also spent an hour last night, cramming a handful of top forty songs. Just in case.

Wait a minute. She'd left those pieces on the piano.

She sprinted home. The screen door squealed, but her parents, engrossed in conversation, didn't acknowledge her entrance. She grabbed the sheet music off the piano and shoved it in her bag with shaking fingers, barely noticing the measured voices in the kitchen until Mom said, " . . . talked to a lawyer."

Miriam stopped halfway back to the door. What did her parents need a lawyer for?

Then Dad answered. "I assume he told you the same thing mine told me. Stick it out until Mira graduates."

Miriam's feet felt glued to the floor. All her life, her parents had gone to work, gone to church, gone to ball games and school events. Never once did they look at each other the way she imagined Darcy and Elizabeth Bennet would have done. But they'd always been there. Never a major fight, every problem approached with level-headed reason.

The words coming out of her parents' mouths now made Miriam feel like she was looking into a carnival mirror: the shape of everything familiar distorted, reversed. All those words, about separate rent payments and child support, could only add up to one thing, and that thing just wasn't possible. Not in her family.

And they were talking about it practically right in front of her! They must not have heard her come back in, over the noise of the bacon frying.

"Well, I've been making your meals and doing your laundry this long." Mom's voice was tight. "I suppose I can put up with it for one more year. But the minute she moves out, I'm done. You understand?"

Paper crinkled as Dad folded the newspaper and set it on the table. "If it's bothering you that much, draw up a list of household duties. I'll do whatever you want." He sounded weary. "Just hang it in the closet, somewhere Mira won't see it."

The frying pan slammed. "Don't you *dare* play the victim, Phil! You're like a block of ice. How am I supposed to live with that? Why do you think I want a divorce?"

The impossible word cracked the air between the kitchen and the living room. Three months ago her parents had celebrated their twenty-fifth anniversary with silver bells in the middle of every table and a blessing at Mass. The choir had sung a song. Everybody had oohed and aahed over them.

Yet she could also hear Brad whispering in her ear in the middle of Mass. *"They're holding hands,"* he'd said. *"Does that seem weird to you?"*

It *had* seemed weird, because Mom and Dad never touched. Ever.

They rarely fought. But they never kissed either. Not in the morning, not at the Sign of Peace at Mass, not even before bed. Miriam had never questioned it, but now, as she fled the house for a world that made sense, understanding settled in a dull ache on her collarbone, repeating over and over:

I should have known.

◆ 42 ◆

Mɪʀɪᴀᴍ ᴡᴏᴋᴇ ᴛᴏ ᴛʜᴇ rumble of a hot dryer and the smell of Vicks.

She lay with the pillow over her eyes, getting her bearings. It had been a long time since she'd dreamed about the divorce fight. Thankfully, it had been brief—just a flash of the emotion she'd felt in that moment when the iron skillet slammed down on the stove and her mother shouted.

Plenty of her classmates' parents had gotten divorced. Why had that moment felt so monumental to her? Maybe because it happened without warning. As far as she'd known, her parents' relationship was just fine.

She'd spent her adolescence sucking up classic romances—Austen and Brontë, du Maurier and Orczy. Maybe, deep down, she'd sensed there had to be more to love than her parents' well-oiled partnership, dependable but relentlessly and ploddingly indifferent, disguising bitter resentment that sooner or later had to come boiling to the surface.

And yet they'd stayed together, right to the bitter end. It was time to find out why.

Miriam flung the pillow off her head, taking in the shrine to her siblings once more, and swung her legs over the side of the bed.

She found herself looking at her own face.

She hadn't seen this wall from the doorway. The black and white head shot she'd submitted for the competition where she'd met Gus hung among a collage of others: snapshots of her at the piano and the state honor choir; the group photo from her liturgical music camp. A picture of her with Teo at St. Greg's, and one with the kids playing on Christmas Eve. A shelf containing her festival cups lined up in a row in increasing order of size, and a shadowbox filled with high school blue ribbons. Recital programs.

It was a collection that spoke of love.

Footsteps padded on the tile; her mother entered the room. "Oh, Mira, you're up. Good. Are you feeling better?"

Miriam couldn't drag her eyes away from that wall. Her wall. "Um . . . yeah." The Vicks smell centered around her mother, entwining with a whiff of cotton warmed in the oven. The smell of safety. Mom used to lather her with Vicks and pin warm cloth diapers inside her pajamas when she had a sore throat.

"You must have been really tired. It's been hours," Mom said.

"Haven't been sleeping very well lately."

"Well, I'm not surprised. I never sleep well away from my own bed." Mom picked up the shoes Miriam had kicked off before collapsing in bed, and arranged them beside the door. "By the way, I cleaned out the car while you were sleeping. I stacked all the receipts on the kitchen table, so you can decide what you need to keep. You left your phone in the car too."

"No, I didn't, I . . ." She stared at the pink spangled phone case in her mother's hand. Dicey's phone. Dicey must have kicked it under the seat during a coughing fit.

Miriam snatched the phone from her mother's hand. It was dead. She lunged for her charger and plugged it in.

"I have to get cooking," Mom said. "Funeral dinner. You want to come out and talk?"

Obediently, Miriam unplugged Dicey's phone and followed her mother out to the kitchen, where she reconnected the charger and laid the phone on the granite counter. She watched the deft motion of the knife in her mother's hand, slicing through onions with great precision. The carrots on the counter sparked her memory. She knew this recipe.

She pulled out another cutting board and knife and started chopping alongside her mother. The silence grew heavier every second. Miriam cleared her throat. "I'm sorry I haven't called. It's been kind of . . ."

"Busy?"

"Emotional."

"Yes, it must be very fulfilling to share your personal experience with the entire world."

Miriam winced. "I didn't share my personal experience with the entire world."

"Well, you shared a lot more than you've shared with me."

The words stung. Miriam scooped up a handful of carrots and dumped them in the pot. "I'm only just discovering a lot of things, Mom."

"Like?"

"Like I love that girl." Her voice caught. "I didn't think I was capable of love anymore."

Sallie stopped cutting. "Why on earth would you think that?"

"Because I've . . ." Miriam rested her hands on the board. She wished the phone would hurry up and power up. She longed for distraction. "For the past year, I've been trying to pretend I was this poster child for the perfect Catholic widow. But I'm *not*. I'm angry. When I was nineteen, I had all this energy, all this drive. I had goals, I had a future. And then the kids came along, and I had to divert all that into them instead."

"That's what happens when you become a mother."

"You think I don't know that? That's what I told myself for years. I gave the best years of my life, Mom. All that energy, all that time. For what? Nothing. They're dead. What was the point?" She slammed the butt of the knife on the granite. "A person who loved her family wouldn't think things like that."

Sallie's eyes glistened. "Mira. Of course you loved your family."

Miriam shook her head and sat down hard on a bar stool.

Her mother sat beside her and took both her hands. "Talk to me."

She hadn't confided in her mother in decades. The words came slowly, then faster and faster. "Teo loved me so much better than I could ever love him. He was my best friend. I liked living with him. But he deserved so much more, and I could never give it to him. He was this amazing romantic. He could make a gift out of—of wildflowers, for crying out loud." The locket burned against her skin. "And all I did was run around and prepare meals and clean up after everyone and make sure they got to do whatever made them feel fulfilled."

Her mother was smiling. "That sounds like love to me."

And here was the heart of the matter. What pale shadow of love had her parents settled for all these years? Miriam wove her fingers into her hair and pulled, the physical pain dulling the deeper emotional one.

Sallie frowned. "Why are you looking at me like that?"

Miriam swallowed. "I don't . . . know how to ask this."

Sallie folded her arms. "Maybe you should just try spitting it out."

The refrigerator cycled off. The house held its breath. "Okay," Miriam said. "Why didn't you and Dad ever get divorced?"

A split-second pause—just long enough to give the lie to the response. "What are you talking about?"

"Come on, Mom. You and Dad, talking about how miserable you were, but you'd put up with each other until I left home."

Sallie blanched.

"I think the exact words were, 'The minute she moves out, I'm done.'"

Her mother's eyes were wide. "Oh, Mira," she whispered. "I didn't know you heard that."

"I know you didn't!" Miriam clenched her fists on the counter. "Do you understand what that did to me? I thought love meant cooking dinner and fixing drains and gutters and planting flowers, and if you two hardly ever touched each other, so what? But that was all a lie. And you made it about *me*. I spent my senior year trying to decide whether to flunk all my classes so I could keep living at home and keep my parents together a little while longer. Even though I was miserable there, because you'd made it perfectly clear you thought everything that was important to me was worthless! How *could* I ever love Teo? When that was all I had to go on?"

Her mother pressed her fingertips to her lips. They were trembling. "So this is why," she said softly. "Why everything changed." She shook her head. Suddenly she looked old.

"I never wanted to divorce your father, Mira. He just . . . he couldn't hear me. No matter what I said. He wouldn't talk to a counselor. I thought if I brought up divorce, it would shake him out of it. He'd recognize the stakes." Sallie brushed at her eyes. "But he just went and found a lawyer. So I did too. We might have drifted into a divorce by accident, except you stopped talking to us."

"What are you talking about?"

"When you went to Curtis, you never called. Not once."

"I talked to you all the time."

"We called you. You never called us. We had to make all the effort ourselves."

Miriam sat silently, replaying that pivotal year in her mind. She didn't remember. Could Mom be right?

"That was what broke your father," Sallie said, brushing her eyes. "We went on a Marriage Encounter. We figured if the marriage was all we had left . . ." She shrugged. "That weekend changed everything for us. Except you."

Miriam stared at her. If things had changed, she'd never seen it. They'd still never been romantic. Not demonstrative, like Teo.

Had she been right in the first place? Did none of that really matter?

And if so, what did that say about her and Teo?

Her mother's hands were clasped so tightly on the edge of the counter, her fingernails turned white and red. "I tried so hard not to be hurt. I told myself you were just growing up. But it does hurt. Being pushed away by a child you've carried in your womb and given your entire life to."

The words cut deep. Losing a child was a raw wound, a steam burn that just kept sinking deeper and deeper into the soul. How must it feel when loss came not from death, but from a child's own rejection?

"I'm sorry," she whispered.

"I'm sorry too." Her mother's voice was a thread. "Sorry you felt like we didn't value your gifts. We knew you'd spend your life struggling, just like we did. But we tried to support you."

"How?"

At the derision in Miriam's voice, Sallie looked up. "We moved the TV downstairs, for goodness sake. So you and Brad wouldn't fight over the front room every time he came home for the weekend."

Miriam stared at her, blank. Mostly what she remembered about that move was how hateful he'd been. That, and the fact that ever after, her family had spent most of their time in the basement, as far away from her as they could without actually leaving the premises.

But Mom was right; they'd given Miriam the best room in the house.

That realization jarred loose other memories. Cookies in the shape of music notes in her lunchbox. Pristinely ironed concert dresses laid out on her bed on performance days.

What if she'd been looking at everything all wrong? What if she'd spent all these years chasing a notion of love that didn't actually exist?

For the first time, she recognized the terrible, long-suffering patience on her mother's face. "Mom, I . . ."

Dicey's phone flashed an image of an apple, followed momentarily by a predictable cascade of sound effects. Slowly, Miriam reached out and laid her hand on it. She needed to find Dicey, but abandoning the conversation now felt like all wrong.

She withdrew her hand.

"That's hers, huh?" Sallie gestured with the knife. "The girl you were riding with."

"Uh-huh."

Her mother sighed. "Well, it's clear you're not going to be able to concentrate on anything else until you know. Go on. Find her."

Miriam searched her mother's face to make sure she meant it. Then she snatched up the phone. "Be right back," she said.

★ ★ ★

She went out onto the front porch before pushing the unlock button. What was the passcode? Dicey had given it to her a few days ago when she got a text message. *Something symmetrical with nines, right?* She closed her eyes and summoned her muscle memory. Nines alternating with the left side of the keypad. 9291? A buzz. 9197? That felt right.

The screen unlocked. "Yes!"

Miriam scrolled down until she found the text message Dicey's mother had sent while they were in Omaha—five days ago? Already? The article outlined pregnancy and gastrointestinal problems in cystic fibrosis. Miriam felt slightly queasy.

She typed the number into her own phone. It rang four times before connecting.

"Hello?"

"Hi. Um . . . my name is Miriam. I've been . . . Dicey's been riding with me . . .?"

Silence.

"Is this . . . Dicey's mother?"

The reply came out low and trembling. "Yes."

Thank you. Thank you. Thank you. "Did they find you? The hospital?" Oh, Lordy. Could she possibly handle this any worse? "I'm so sorry, she only has 'mom' on here. What's your name?"

"Dayana. Dayana Porter."

Miriam gave a shaky laugh. "I would never have found you. I was going to go through every 'Smith' in East Palo Alto. I had to take Dicey to the ER, and—did they contact you?"

"Yes. I caught a flight in. I've only been here an hour."

"In Albuquerque?"

"Yeah."

"Thank God," Miriam breathed. She rubbed her forehead. "The hospital wouldn't tell me anything. They didn't even tell me they were transferring her." Her voice broke. "I guess I was hoping . . . you might tell me what's going on?"

"What do you want to know?"

"She . . . she has cystic fibrosis?"

"Yes."

Miriam swallowed. "She didn't tell me. I kept asking what was wrong, but she got so mad at me."

Dayana gave a grudging chuckle. Or maybe a snort. "She wouldn't have told you she was pregnant if it wasn't too far along to hide. That girl's got more guts than sense."

Miriam's response came out half laugh, half sob. "Your daughter's amazing, Mrs. . . . Ms. . . ."

"Just call me Dayana."

"Dayana."

"Thank you," said Dicey's mother in a low voice. "I should've bought her a plane ticket, but it wasn't an emergency then. I figured maybe she was a little safer traveling with you. At least, I felt better knowing she had a mother in the car."

The word broke her. Miriam sat down hard on a scrolled iron porch chair, wiping her eyes on her sleeve. She concentrated on her breathing until she had control of her voice again. "So what happened to her?"

"She's got pneumonia." The words were flat with exhaustion. "It happens, you know, with CF. She's on antibiotics all the time. A month on this one, a month on that one. But sometimes it's not enough. This is one of those times. It comes on sudden."

Not your fault, Dayana was trying to say, but it didn't feel that way to Miriam. She sat in front of the quiet duplex, the weight of her decisions settling around her. "I should have put my foot down," she whispered. "I wanted to take her to a quick care clinic, but I let her win."

"CF's a strange beast. You don't want to talk to just any doctor. She needed to get home, to where—"

A sudden commotion: a jumble of voices; white noise, then muffled, as if Dayana had suddenly forgotten the phone in her hand and shoved it in her pocket.

"Dayana?"

More noise. Then Dayana spoke again, hurriedly. "Dicey and the baby are in distress. We're going for an emergency C-section. UNM medical center. Text when you get here." The connection went dead.

Miriam laid her phone on her leg and clenched her fists to stop the trembling.

How long she sat there, she didn't know. When the door opened, she looked up to see her mother. "Did you find her?"

She nodded.

"What did you find out?"

"Pneumonia," Miriam said. Her voice did not sound like her own. "She and the baby are in distress. They're delivering now."

"How far along is she?"

"Thirty-three weeks," Miriam said, and raised a shoulder. "And some change."

Her mother tsked, then sat down beside her.

Slowly, deliberately, Miriam flipped the phone to "silent" and laid it face down on her knee. Dicey had her mother. Miriam's place was here, with hers.

For a long moment, both women sat silently. Then Sallie exhaled heavily. "Go on," she said. "I'll be here when you get back."

Miriam met her mother's eyes, acknowledging something she'd never recognized before: the quiet undercurrent of devotion, imperfectly expressed but always present. Love meant letting go, that look said. Trusting that eventually, however long it took, the beloved would return.

She stood to embrace her mother. "I love you," she whispered, and ran for her keys.

◆ 43 ◆

WHEN MIRIAM FOUND HER way to the ICU, she had to wait outside the mag-locked doors for Dayana to let her in. Dicey's mother was an imposing woman, tall, with skin darker than Dicey's and long braids wound tight on the crown of her head. She led Miriam to a sink to wash her hands. The sign above it admonished her to scrub for two minutes, and Miriam didn't dare short it—not with Dayana staring her down. Miriam knew a mama bear when she saw one. When Miriam finished, Dayana handed her a surgical mask. The precautions made it clear just how serious Dicey's condition was.

She followed Dayana to Dicey's room but stopped short on the threshold. Dicey lay with her eyes closed, her skin so pale, Miriam barely recognized her. Her face was obscured by a mask attached to a tube, and an obnoxious treble hiss flexed and waned in time with Dicey's breathing. Something clipped to her forefinger glowed red. Miriam couldn't identify all the wires and tubes coming off her chest, the back of her forearm, and even out of her neck. The room was a bewildering cacophony of blips, beeps, and hisses.

Dayana beckoned. "Come on in. I know it can be overwhelming."

Miriam tiptoed forward, her breathing shallow and hasty. "What is all of this?"

Dayana gestured. "Antibiotics here, fluids here. This line"—she pointed at the monitor—"tracks her heart rate. And this one is the blood oxygen saturation. It's too low."

Miriam squinted at the number at the end of the curving line. "Ninety-two percent doesn't seem so bad."

Dayana's shoulder twitched. "It's marginal. And she needs the BiPAP to keep it there. As she gets older, she loses more and more of her lung function." Dayana's voice was steady, and Miriam couldn't see enough of her face to tell whether she was as calm as she sounded. Surely she wasn't. "Baby Girl's heart rate was falling," she continued. "If Momma doesn't have enough oxygen, the baby doesn't, either. They did a C-section."

"And maybe it'll be better for Dicey, now that she's not breathing for two?"

"Maybe." Dayana rested her hand on her daughter's, apparently oblivious to the wires. "Nothing to do but wait and see. It's always a crapshoot."

Miriam stared at the mound of braids. *Always,* Dayana said, as if this were only the latest in a long line of ICU stays. Miriam leaned against the counter. "I'm so sorry," she said. "If I'd known . . . if I'd known what she was risking. I tried to get her to go to the doctor, but—"

Dayana's eyes flashed. "Just stop," she said. "I know you mean well, but after everything she's been through the last few days, traveling with you . . ."

Miriam shrank from the justice of the half-spoken accusation, but before Dayana could continue, Dicey began coughing. The pitch of the electronic beep dipped; then an alarm sounded—soft, four chimes, another four chimes. A nurse entered, sanitized her hands, and began monkeying with the buttons on the electronic box connected to the BiPAP.

"What's happening?" Miriam asked, hating the terror in her voice.

"The coughing causes her to desat."

Desat. It took a minute to connect the word to oxygen saturation.

Finally, Dicey's body stopped shaking. The women looked back at the monitor. The oxygen saturation hovered, then slowly began to rise again. Eighty-five percent. Eighty-nine. Ninety. The nurse raised the blanket to examine Dicey's surgical scar, then turned to them. "The doctor's making rounds. She'll be in shortly."

"Thank you," said Dayana, and the nurse left.

Dayana stood with her arms folded. She stared at the numbers on the monitor for a long moment, then took a deep breath and raised an arm to swipe at her eyes. "Lord almighty, help me," she said, and turned to face Miriam. "I'm sorry. I raised that girl. I know very well you can't make her do what she doesn't want to do. My daughter always follows her own path, and all we can do is stay out of the way." She brushed a hand tenderly over Dicey's forehead, her voice dropping. "And be there to catch you when you fall, baby girl."

She sat down, covering Dicey's hand with both of hers, and bowed her head. Praying, Miriam thought. She should do the same.

Slowly, carefully, she lowered herself to a hard plastic seat. She tried to summon the mental presence for a rosary, but her mind just kept repeating: *Please let her be okay. Please.*

The doctor arrived a few minutes later with a crowd of residents in tow. She greeted Dayana and then focused on the task at hand, asking questions of the nurse, examining Dicey's sutures and the data on her laptop. Miriam wondered how Dayana could stand it.

At last, the doctor turned her attention to Dayana. "Do you have questions for me?"

Miriam had a few, starting with *What the hell is going on?* Were they really supposed to have gleaned the situation from all that medicalese?

"The bottom line," Dayana said. "That's what I want."

The doctor hugged her laptop to her chest. "Her pulmonary function isn't what we'd like. Fluid is building up." She crouched, putting herself below Dayana's line of sight, and gripped her hand. "But let's give those antibiotics some time to work. We've got her on the good stuff." Her eyes crinkled, evidence of a smile.

She patted Dayana's hand. "The other good news is the baby is stabilized. She'll be ready for some skin to skin soon, if you want to go down."

"Thank you, I believe I will."

Dayana waited until the room cleared. Then she stood up and leaned over to whisper something in her daughter's ear. She stopped face to face with Miriam. "I'm going down to see my grandbaby. You're welcome to come, but before you do, let me tell you one thing. I've learned you never leave without telling her what you need her to hear." She shuffled out of the room.

Miriam stood frozen. How could Dayana do it? Where did she find the strength to confront the possibility of death again and again?

Miriam had only just dragged herself away from the edge of the pit. She couldn't start down this path again. She had to get away.

Only—where could she run? She was too close to the end now; she couldn't just blithely pick another road trip destination, as if Dicey weren't in intensive care. If she went anywhere now, it was to the beach her family had been trying to reach when they died. There was no escape from the possibility of mortality.

Her ears roared. She couldn't breathe. She needed fresh air. Sunshine. Clouds. Escape from the maddening hum of blowers and the smell of antiseptic and the hushed whispers of thousands of people's pain.

"I'm sorry, Dicey," she whispered. "So sorry. I can't. I just can't." Turning, she fled.

★ ★ ★

Miriam made it as far as the first floor. She could almost smell fresh air when she saw the sign: "Interfaith chapel."

No. Not this time. She would not get caught; she needed to care for herself now. Protect the fragile healing she'd achieved.

Because of Dicey.

She slowed. Stopped. Pivoted. Went inside.

Despite everything, as always, the rich, buttery silence settled around her. The hum of the hospital remained, but it was low, distant, overwhelmed by the density of the prayers and tears and joys left by every person who had ever paused a moment in this tiny room.

She was worn out. Tired of fighting, tired of running, tired of having to psych herself up for every task. She hadn't realized it until she stood at the foot of Dicey's bed and contemplated starting all over again.

How long she sat there, she didn't know. The door opened and closed. People breathed; chairs creaked as they settled beneath bodies and resettled when weight lifted again. People coming, people going. Upstairs, Dicey and her baby fought for life. But here, there was peace.

She felt a touch on her shoulder. She looked up. "Mom," she said, startled.

"I thought I might find you here." Mom settled beside her. "It's Sunday, and you didn't go to church today." Wry humor twisted the corner of her mouth.

Miriam chuffed at her own predictability. "What are you doing here?"

Her mother sat down and set a black case on Miriam's lap. Talia's computer, which Miriam had left at the condo. "Well, it's a funny thing. I was watering my plants and thinking about Talia and Blaise, and how much I missed them. And how much it meant to me to see all those videos. And out of nowhere it occurred to me. Shouldn't there be more? Weren't there two choices for every coin flip?"

Miriam cried out. Fingers shaking, she ripped the zipper open and pulled the computer out.

There were so many.

There had been a southern route and a northern one, with stops in the middle latitudes to bridge the two. Flippant, sincere, read off the phone—it was like a feast set before a starving person. Miriam gorged herself on the sight of her children, even though each video left her gasping for air.

She and her mother clutched each other in the tiny chapel, laughing and crying by turns.

The last video froze with the twins grinning at each other after tag-teaming an overview of something called the Corn Palace, in South Dakota. So beautiful. It wasn't enough—it would never be enough. But it satisfied a deep, visceral hunger.

"I miss them," Miriam said. "I miss them so much."

Her mother hugged her.

"If I had one more day, I would . . . I'd do so many things differently. I wouldn't clean a dish the whole day, I'd just—I don't know . . . hold them so tight. Make sure they knew I loved them."

"They knew you loved them, honey." Sallie pulled back but didn't let her go. "Everybody shows love in different ways. You know JoJo's all about gifts—" She touched the string of pearls around her neck. "And Brad always wanted touch. He was *so* clingy. Sometimes it was all I could do not to scream at him to leave me alone. But you? You're like me. We love by doing. And that's nothing to be ashamed of, Mira."

The words vibrated in deep places within Miriam's body that she'd never even known were there. It broke her heart to realize how many years she'd squandered, thinking herself not good enough. "I'm sorry, Mom," she said softly. "I wasted so much of my life being angry with you for something that wasn't even real."

"Shh." Sallie stroked her hair. "There's no untying that knot now. We were in the middle of a crisis ourselves. We should have realized there was more wrong than teenage rebellion. We were too focused on saving ourselves to save you. There's plenty of blame to go around. I'm just glad you finally told me what's been haunting you all these years."

Well, some of it anyway. For the first time, Miriam thought she might actually like her mother's take on the whole Gus situation.

Gus. Wow. He'd been totally off her radar for the past twenty-four hours. She'd been so angry with him. After the events of the last twenty-four hours, Gus's offense seemed insignificant. So he'd talked to Blaise. So what? If it had been any other musical luminary, she wouldn't have batted an eye.

If she'd just talked to him years ago, like Teo wanted her to do . . .

It was hard to stomach the thought of how much richness she'd closed herself off from all these years out of a fear of confronting the unbeautiful and uncomfortable. How different might her life have been if she'd had the courage to face the difficult conversations ten years ago—or even five, or two? How much less conflicted?

Impossible to know. What was certain was that, somewhere upstairs, Dayana had both a daughter and granddaughter fighting for their lives. A daughter and granddaughter Miriam cared deeply about and to whom she was connected.

We love by doing.

Miriam closed the laptop. "Mom," she said, "I need to go back upstairs."

★ ★ ★

Miriam walked her mother to her car and then headed to the NICU, where she found a window at one corner where she could look in. Tucked between cribs and plexiglass boxes, Dayana sat in a chair with her shirt partly unbuttoned and her granddaughter nestled against her skin. The baby had a tube in her nose, but the blanket wrapped around her hid any other medical attachments.

Miriam tapped on the window. It took a couple of tries to get Dayana's attention. "Five minutes," Dayana mouthed, holding up one hand, fingers extended, for extra clarity.

When Dayana joined her, she said, "I was beginning to think you weren't coming."

"Me too." Miriam winced. "Sorry."

Dayana cocked her head, like a shrug. "Well, you came back, and that's what counts." She stared at her granddaughter through the window and then said, "Dicey told me she planned to ask you something . . . important."

"To be Baby Girl's godmother."

Dayana nodded. She looked sad. It had to be hard, giving someone else a piece of your child when the piece you had was already too small. "I need you to tell me something, and I know it's not my right to ask, but . . ."

Miriam waited.

"We were so close when she was small, you know. You couldn't separate us. She's been out of the house now, so I know what it's like to live without her right there by me. But even so . . ." Dayana swallowed. "I need you to tell me what it's like to lose a daughter. What I need to know."

Miriam shuddered. "Dayana, you can't think about that right now."

"I've been thinking about that since the day my girl was diagnosed. It's not a question of if. It's just a matter of when. We've been on borrowed time for years."

Miriam cupped her elbows in her palms. What she wanted to say sounded horrible, even in her mind. "Does it make me a terrible person if I say I almost envy you? Having had it in front of you your whole life, reminding you to savor every moment and not waste time looking over your shoulder."

Dayana fixed a penetrating gaze on Miriam. "If anybody else said that, I'd punch her in the face. But I guess you know what you're talking about." The braided bun wasn't as tight as Miriam had thought; the plaits bounced as she tossed her head. "Yeah, I guess when you got a child sick for years, you got a long time to prepare."

"But that doesn't mean you're ready." Miriam reached out and tentatively rubbed Dayana's back. "You're never ready." The view blurred. She waited until she could speak. "It's awful," she said. "Like a part of you died. Because it did." Through the window, she watched the nurses move around the cribs, changing a diaper, changing an IV bag. "And there are so many things I wish I'd resolved when I had the chance. Questions I'll never know the answers to."

It would be so easy to give in. To wallow. But right now, what mattered was Dicey, her baby, and the impossibly strong woman standing beside her.

She touched Dayana's elbow. "Thank you for sharing your daughter with me. She's been a gift to me. Every moment."

Dayana looked at her and swallowed three times in quick succession. She nodded with a small smile.

The women stood in silence, looking in the nursery window like fellow warriors in a battle no one wanted to fight anymore. At length, Dayana turned to her with a hand outstretched. "I'm gonna need your help, Miriam. I got two of them here. I can't have Baby Girl's godmother running away. I want your word."

Miriam grasped the proffered hand. "I'm not going anywhere," she said.

44

Tuesday, May 10
Albuquerque, New Mexico

TIME MOVED DIFFERENTLY IN a hospital. Everything took longer than it should. The ebb and flow of crises and the erratic appearances of the doctors stood in contrast to the maddening predictability of nurse check-ins and meds administered at precise intervals. Every moment dragged, yet the clock swallowed two whole days without the passage of time really registering—because nothing in Dicey's condition changed. She lay sedated, inert, except when a coughing fit took her and the room filled with alarms and ICU staff. No amount of staring at the numbers on the monitor could force them to move upward.

Miriam and Dayana traded off sitting with Baby Girl and Dicey, catching snatches of sleep in the vinyl chair in the corner of the ICU, sending updates by text message and phoning the other in whenever the doctors visited. Dayana embarked on a campaign to have the baby brought to Dicey for skin-to-skin time. Miriam was certain she had zero chance of winning that battle, and she was astonished at the older woman's nerve. But after watching a couple of interactions, she found herself more astonished the staff hadn't capitulated on the spot.

"That's not my call to make," said the resident on duty the third time she asked.

"Well, whose call is it? Your attending? The unit manager? The unit manager? How about you stop stalling and call him in here? I know you're all hoping if you just put me off, I'll go away. But let me tell you, I'm an ICU nurse and the mother of a woman with cystic fibrosis. I've spent more time inside an ICU than all of you put together. I'm not going anywhere."

When the resident retreated, stumbling over his apologies, Dayana turned to Miriam, her eyes crinkling above the paper mask. "Time to talk to the ones with the real power," she said.

Miriam began to see where the strength of Dicey's personality had come from. "The unit manager?" she asked.

"Uh-uh. The nurses."

Tuesday morning, Dicey's brothers began arriving, one by one, to boisterous claps on the back and loud greetings cloaked in laughter. The family set up camp in the lounge outside the ICU and began rotating in and out, ordering pizza and sandwiches and Danishes, depending on the time of day. It was clearly a well-rehearsed maneuver.

Miriam laughed until she cried to hear the family's stories—like Dicey, age three, riding the meanest dog in the neighborhood as if it were a horse.

"No change overnight," said the doctor who came Wednesday morning to deliver the update. "She's holding steady, but we'd hoped to see more improvement."

"Maybe you should listen to me, then," said Dayana. "My baby needs her baby."

"We're still working on that permission, Ms. Porter."

"Well, work harder."

"You've got to understand, it's hospital policy. Babies in the NICU—"

"Can travel with a NICU team."

The doctor blew out a breath and put his hands up. "I'll check."

"Thank you."

The team left. The last one out of the room was the social worker who had been their liaison all week. She whispered to Dayana and hurried off after the team.

The lounge felt oppressive, as if all the air had been sucked out of it. Miriam chewed on her lip. The family was uncharacteristically silent.

Then Dicey's oldest brother, Derrick, leaned over the arm of his chair toward Miriam. "She's gonna pull through this, you know," he said softly.

Miriam looked up, surprised. She didn't see how he could speak with such certainty.

Derrick smiled at her confusion. "I know it all sounds terrible, but Dicey's been through worse, believe me. We've had the funeral home on standby a couple times. And she's got that baby to live for now."

Miriam opened her eyes, staring at him with a question on her lips she dared not speak.

"I know," he said. "It's gonna get her eventually. But I know my sister, and I'm telling you, she's not going anywhere when she just had a baby."

The silence felt a little less oppressive now. Miriam glanced around the room, seeing the way the rest of the family had begun to relax and crack jokes again. He hadn't delivered that speech for her benefit, but for his siblings', she realized. She looked up and caught his eye. He winked, and she smiled.

"Speaking of the baby, nobody's talking about a name," said Dwight—brother number three, Miriam recalled. "What are we gonna name her?"

Miriam waited for Dayana to take the lead—surely Dicey had shared her thoughts with her mother—but no one answered him. "Deandra," Miriam said at last.

Everyone looked at her.

"That's what she was thinking when I asked her. Something strong, she said. It means 'divine protector.' And it . . . you know. It keeps the D's going."

They regarded her with surprise. "You got her to answer that question without ripping a new hole in your ass?" said Devon, the youngest of the boys.

Everyone laughed. Then silence fell again as the social worker walked back into the lounge.

She was smiling. "They've signed off," she said. "They're working on a plan to bring the baby up."

The whole room burst into cheers and a round of back-slapping and soft-drink toasts.

"See?" Derrick said, nudging Miriam with his elbow before knocking back his Dr. Pepper like a shot. "Told you. It's gonna be okay."

★ ★ ★

True to form, it took the hospital until noon on Wednesday to figure out how to bring Baby Deandra to Dicey's ICU room. Miriam waited in the lounge with Dicey's brothers for news from Dayana, the only one allowed in the room. It came in the form of a photo of the baby nuzzled against Dicey's chest.

Miriam tried not to expect a miracle, but Dayana's unshakable conviction about the benefits of mother–baby togetherness made realism hard.

But evening rounds brought better news: for the first time, the team was "cautiously optimistic." Miriam had been hoping for something slightly more dramatic, but the family assured her that starting to wean Dicey from sedation was a big deal. And the news on Baby Deandra was much better. Her heart rate, breathing rate, and body temperature were all more stable than they had been before.

Miriam and Derrick had the three-to-six AM shift into Thursday morning. Miriam sat silently, watching the numbers on the monitor as Derrick whispered in his sister's ear. The numbers were definitely better than yesterday. Not an instantaneous healing, but still—motherhood was a miraculous thing. A mother who wasn't even awake and a baby who couldn't hear her mother's voice. Both healing just by having snuggled together.

Miriam sat in stillness, listening to the sound of the hospital, the rumble in the walls, the hiss of air, and the muted blips and beeps that had grown so familiar they echoed in her dreams as well as her waking hours.

She woke when her phone buzzed. She pulled it out. "Brad?" she asked blankly.

"Hi. Mom says you're in Albuquerque?"

"Yes." Miriam hadn't updated the app because she'd had neither the energy nor the desire. Besides, the only stories she could tell weren't hers to tell. She rubbed her eyes and looked at Derrick, who was passed out in the chair on the opposite side of the bed. "Brad," she said again.

"Yeah?"

"This is the second time you've called me at five in the morning your time."

"Um, yeah. Sorry about that."

"I'm not worried about me. I'm up. But this is not like you."

"Yeah, I know. I . . . what's up with this guy who's been commenting on your social media posts? The film composer guy."

Miriam stilled. "Gus has been commenting?"

"You haven't seen it?"

"I haven't been checking my feeds."

"He's kind of obsessed with Blaise's music. And he's . . . weirdly personal." His tone changed then as he backpedaled hastily. "Never mind, just forget it, I shouldn't have called. It's not important right now."

But it was important. It was the last piece of unfinished business.

Miriam sat up and rubbed her itching eyes. "What's he saying?"

Brad cleared his throat. "Well, for the past couple days, he's been talking about Blaise's music and asking you to call him. Here. He says, *I woke up with Blaise's music in my head. I could hear the whole thing for one glorious moment, but I need the original if I am going to do it justice. Please contact me. I'm so sorry. Please believe me.*"

Miriam shook her head, sighing.

"There are more like that," Brad said. "But today, it's just . . . weird. It's just one word. I don't even know how to pronounce it. I guess it's a name. Pia . . . P-i-a-z-z—"

"Piazzolla," Miriam said, and sagged back in her chair. Gus knew.

"Who's Piazzolla?" Brad asked.

"A composer." Which explained nothing. She tried again. "That was what I played the night he finally noticed me."

The connection went silent for a long moment. "Is he the kids' father?"

Miriam gaped. "How did—?"

"He looks like Blaise." Something rustled in the background. "I, um . . . he was weirding me out, so I went and looked him up. It took a while to place. And then I remembered. You mentioned him once, when I called you on your birthday. You wouldn't say anything about him, but I could tell it was important to you. And then you just went radio silent, and next thing I know, you're married to your best friend that you claimed not to think of like that."

The knowledge of how fragile her secret was made her feel slightly queasy. "Does everyone know?"

"No. I didn't even know for sure until just now." A hesitation. "Are you gonna tell him?"

"I've been trying to decide ever since he first contacted me," she said. "But now I think I have to. I mean, he's in San Francisco. I have no excuse not to . . ."

"I'll drive up to be with you."

The tears in her eyes had nothing to do with grief. "Thanks, Brad," she said softly, "but you have your own life. I have to do this myself."

Her brother blew out a breath through his nose. "Just let me know, Mira."

"I will."

She disconnected and let her hand drop . . . and realized she was looking into Dicey's eyes.

She scrambled to her feet, rushing to the head of the bed. "Dicey?"

Dicey's voice sounded far away, indistinct and muffled by the BiPAP. She moved her arm, her slim finger pointing. Miriam looked all over, trying to figure out what she was pointing at. Then Dicey nudged her hand—the hand that held her phone.

"I'm sorry it woke you," she said softly, stealing a glance at Derrick, wondering if she should wake him.

Dicey nudged the phone again.

"You want your phone?"

Another nudge. Miriam extended the phone to her. Dicey swirled her hand. Miriam took a wild guess and unlocked it. Dicey mimed typing.

"Oh!" She opened her note app, and Dicey began to type, slowly.

Sorry

"Sorry for what?"

Didn't tell you

"You don't need to apologize." It was the socially acceptable response, but not the most honest one. Miriam winced and shrugged. "Still. Thank you."

Dicey's eyes crinkled, a telltale sign of a smile Miriam couldn't see. She typed again.

Everyone treats you different bc your family is dead. That's like cf.

She looked at Miriam, her eyes craving understanding.

Miriam nodded. "That's why you didn't tell me." She hesitated, then pulled up the picture Dayana had sent last night: a tiny body, kangarooed in the hollow of Dicey's throat. "Did you know Deandra came to see you?"

Tears welled up and overflowed. Dicey shook her head.

"She's perfect. Derrick said you'd hang around for her sake. I guess he was right, huh?" Miriam glanced over at the tall man, legs splayed, mouth open. "Should I wake him?"

Dicey shook her head and typed again: *Who phoned*

Miriam shook her head. Truly, Dicey was a wonder. "My brother. Don't worry about it."

About Gus?

Miriam gave a half laugh through her nose. "Does nothing get by you? You were sedated, girl!" She raised her shoulders. "Yes, it's about Gus. He figured it out."

Course he did

You gotta go

Miriam shook her head. "Eventually. Not now. Right now you're more important." Even the BiPAP couldn't hide Dicey's scowl. "Okay," Miriam said. "Let me be frank. I promised your mom I wouldn't go anywhere. And call me chicken, but I'd rather stay on your mom's good side."

Dicey's eyes crinkled, but she tapped on the phone again. *I handle mom.*

Miriam laughed. "I have no doubt, but . . ."

Dicey shook off her grasp, typing again.

I'll be here when you get back.

promise

Miriam smiled, her insides relaxing. She drew her lips between her teeth, her jaw trembling, because that, after all, was the only reason she wasn't already on her way to the car.

Twelve more hours. She'd give it twelve hours, to make sure Dicey was really and truly on the mend. Then, she'd go.

"Okay," she said.

Dicey closed her eyes briefly and then typed one last word.

Sing

Miriam stared at her. "Now?"

Dicey nodded. Her eyes were already drooping.

"All right," she said softly. She breathed deep, let her throat relax, and began softly. "Amazing grace, how sweet the sound . . ."

She could swear Dicey was trying to sing too, but it was something more felt than heard. She clasped Dicey's hand as she finished the first verse and began the second.

Suddenly, she wasn't singing alone. Derrick's voice joined hers, his rich baritone adding a layer of harmony.

Tears sprang to her eyes. How long had it been since she'd really paid attention to the richness of singing with another person?

Derrick gripped her hand. Human contact—simple, profound. A warm hand, a shared love. Everything there was to live for. The thing she had withheld from Gus.

From the moment Blaise had reached out to him, this moment had been inevitable. Dicey had realized it days ago. Gus could hardly help recognizing himself in the young man he'd fathered. This was what he'd been instinctively reacting to these past weeks. What he needed now—what he craved—what kept him unnaturally invested in her life at the expense of his own—was a sense of completion, of clarity, of understanding.

Teo had known. *Don't you think he deserves . . .?*

No, she'd said. But she'd been wrong. The time had come to let the truth into the light.

Through many dangers, toils and snares
I have already come
'Tis grace has brought me safe thus far,
And grace will lead me home.

The open road was calling. Only this time, she didn't need to flip a coin to know where she was headed.

Part 10

San Francisco, California

Forgiveness is the final form of love.

—Reinhold Niebuhr

Text message conversation with Brad Lewis:

Miriam: *Headed to SF. Wish me luck.*
Brad: *I have tomorrow off. I'll meet you.*
Miriam: *I would love to see you but after. I need to do this on my own.*
Brad: *You sure?*
Miriam: *Yes.*
Brad: 💪
Miriam: 🖤

45

Friday, May 13
San Francisco Conservatory of Music
11:43 AM

WHEN MIRIAM WALKED INTO the San Francisco Conservatory on Friday morning, she didn't know what to feel. The students walking around, chatting and sipping coffee in the lower atrium, represented everything she'd once wanted. But the memory of Dicey trying to sing along with "Amazing Grace" around the edge of the BiPAP mask put it all in perspective: how small her regrets really were in the grand scheme of things.

She missed Dicey. Missed her company, her no-b.s. attitude, her strength. Above all, her strength. She could use some of that for the meeting to come.

Miriam framed the atrium in her screen and captured the image, then sent it in a text. *Wish you were here.*

Miriam tightened her elbow against Blaise's music bag as she looked over the railing, taking in the building of glass and pale stone stretching above and below, the staircases circling the enormous atrium. The smell of coffee drifted up from the cafe below; hallways and doorways on every level beckoned, offering tantalizing snatches of sound: vocalizations, scales, shouts of laughter. If things had been different, she might have been here today with Blaise, visiting his new school.

But the sound of a piano overwhelmed all: fluid, impassioned—Beethoven's *Tempest* sonata. One of Blaise's competition pieces. The music tugged her forward, around the perimeter, to the open door of the concert hall.

Miriam recognized the towering walls, the recessed blocks on the ceiling, and the pillars on the side walls marching toward the low stage, which was bathed in warm light. The hall looked just as it had on Teo's sketchy iPhone video—right down to the single grand piano in the center of the stage.

She could see them in her mind's eye. Blaise and Talia played off each other perfectly, their comic timing impeccable. She could see herself on that stage too—the performer she might have been. For the first time, it all seemed real. And disquieting. Foreign.

The music stopped. Miriam focused on the pair on the stage: two men, one at the piano, the other carrying a bag of tools.

"So far, so good," Gus said. "Let me check something more melodic." He touched the keys again.

Miriam rested a hand on the seat back nearest her. Somehow she'd expected to find him rough and unshaven, with circles under his eyes. She should have known Gus wouldn't do soul torment the way everyone else did.

In the shock of seeing him so unexpectedly back in Colorado, she hadn't taken the time to really examine him. Here, in his element, it was clear that he was everything she'd imagined him to be all these years: handsome, debonair even in polo and khakis, his dark hair gleaming in the glow of the stage lights, his fingers impossibly fluid on the keys. Older, but only more appealing for the passage of years.

And yet, looking at him, Miriam felt curiously detached. Of the passion that once consumed her, nothing remained. It was a shell, fragile as spun sugar, its empty calories long since consumed. The only thing that ever really bound them together was the one thing she'd withheld from him: his children.

Gus lifted his fingers, and the scowl of concentration melted into the brilliance of that fabulous smile—the one that fooled a person into thinking no one else in the world mattered to him. "Sounds great!" he told the piano tech. "But can you tighten up the action on A3?"

"Sure thing."

Gus shot off the bench and began pacing as the technician stepped in. He never was any good at standing still. His passion, his quicksilver changeability, the intensity of his charisma—it was all the same as on the day she'd last seen him.

Miriam took a deep breath and started toward the stage.

Gus turned toward the movement, shading his eyes against the stage lights. "Good morning . . . can I help you?"

She stepped into the light. "Hi, Gus."

His eyes widened. "Miriam Tedesco," he said. He jogged down the stage stairs to meet her. "Or should I say . . . Mira Lewis."

He stopped, and they studied each other in silence for a few moments while the knock of the technician's tools against the wood echoed in the hall. Then he gave a half smile. "You looked so familiar, but your personality is so different—you're so much more confident than you were then. And—and the clothes. But you called me Gus," he said. "I should have known right then. Nobody's called me Gus in years. Not even my wife. I can't believe it didn't register right away. But when it did . . ." He shook his head. "You should have told me, Mira."

"I should have done a lot of things."

A furrow appeared between his eyebrows. "Your husband said you were sick. Last year, the day of the competition." The words sounded vaguely accusatory.

"We didn't think it was the right time for that discussion—for any of us. You included. Not on a competition weekend."

He folded his arms, perching a hip on the back of an auditorium seat, his mouth tightening. "Just to be clear what we're talking about . . ."

"Yes," Miriam said. "I was pregnant when I left Curtis."

"Blaise was mine."

"And Talia."

A muscle in his jaw twitched repeatedly. One hand ran through his thick, dark hair, a sign that he was rattled. "Why didn't you tell me?"

"I came to tell you. The night before I left Curtis. I found you with Kaye, in the recital hall. Against the wall."

The piano technician rearranged his tools noisily. They both looked up at the stage. Then Gus grabbed her elbow and dragged her to the back of the hall, where the darkness and the distance offered some semblance of privacy. All the color in his face had compressed into two bright spots on his cheeks. "I was an ass in college," he said. "We're all stupid and self-absorbed at that age. Me more than most. I can admit that. But you had such a gift, Mira—Miriam. Why would you throw it away over some dipshit college guy? Even me?"

Miriam could imagine Dicey's reaction; the thought made her smile. "*Even* you."

Gus had the good grace to look ashamed. "I'm just saying you could have told me."

"I could have told you a lot of things. Like what a big deal it was for me to be competitive at Curtis. Where I came from, what I had to do to get there in the first place. I could have told you what *you* meant to me. But none of it would have made any difference. I was just the next girl." She shook her head. "I was stupid, but I wasn't that stupid."

He swallowed several times in quick succession. "But all these years."

The bitterness she'd clung to for so long wanted to beat its way out and bludgeon him. She took a deep breath. "You didn't want children. Don't you remember? We all went out to dinner, and you complained about the kid at the next table. You were never gonna have kids, you were going to do your part to control world population. Everybody thought it was so funny."

He sat down on the arm of a seat, weaving his long fingers through his thick black hair. "That was twenty years ago."

The despair in his voice undid her. All these years, she'd justified keeping the secret by pointing to his antipathy toward children. Why had it never occurred to her that he might feel differently at thirty or forty than he had at twenty-two?

A door opened and closed. Miriam glanced toward the stage to find it empty. That poor piano tech hadn't bargained for overhearing all this.

"I had children," Gus said, as if trying out the words. "I had children." A pause. Then he slumped over. "Kaye and I can't have children. And you never gave me the chance."

Her legs gave out. She sat down hard on the armrest opposite him. That note in his voice was agony. An agony not so different from hers: the deep grief over a reality that could never be altered.

In the face of his pain, her bitterness seemed petty. "I know," she said softly. "I was wrong."

I'm sorry, she told Teo silently. Teo, who grinned at her in her mind's eye, his eyes full of mischief beneath the thinning black hair—curly, not straight—sprinkled with white. That big nose. Those glasses.

The images hit her all at once, then: The front porch, crowded with people on hot, sticky summer nights. Kamikaze June bugs dive-bombing the lights. The smell of mosquito repellent and grilled provoleta. Beat-up instruments, potluck catering, and the most stirring music she'd ever heard.

Teo playing tickle monster with the twins on the living room floor.

Teo nibbling on her neck in the kitchen while Blaise and Talia, giggling, tried to knock them apart.

And the way her insides always relaxed when she walked in the door of that beat-up old bungalow.

Of course she had loved him. She'd worn herself out, taking care of him, because it was the only way she'd dared show him how much. She could not have loved her children any better than she had, and they could not have had a better father. She could not have had a better life partner, for that matter.

In fact, the only person who'd been harmed in this whole scenario was the man sitting before her. The man who, for the first time in her memory, had nothing at all to say.

Miriam reached across the aisle. "I'm so sorry, Gus," she said. "I know I can't fix this. I just want you to know how sorry I am."

He stood, his face a hard, angry mask. "Don't touch me," he said. "Don't you dare."

He slammed the heel of his hand against the door on his way out of the hall.

46

Mɪʀɪᴀᴍ sᴀᴛ ᴏɴ ᴛʜᴇ armrest, her hands on her thighs, struggling to breathe through the weight of her shame. In all the years she'd imagined this meeting, this was one scenario she hadn't considered: Gus, justly outraged, and she, blistered by the certainty of her own guilt.

It couldn't end like this. She couldn't be powerless. That was the old Miriam, the one who played victim and refused redemption. Here, now, she had to do something. Find some way to make amends.

Blaise's music satchel lay on the floor beside her. She didn't know why she'd brought it—some fleeting delusion that perhaps she and Gus could, in fact, collaborate after all. Foolish. It lay there, accusing her. All her botched attempts to finish Blaise's music, mirroring her botched attempt to tell what should never have been hidden.

Could the music be her way to make restitution?

It hadn't helped her solve the mystery of her son, after all. All her plans had gone off the rails; it had been days since she'd thought about Blaise and what had, or hadn't, happened at camp. Was her son gay or not?

Suddenly, she could hear Teo's voice as clearly as if he stood beside her, saying: *"It doesn't matter."*

And he was right.

If Blaise were gay, if he'd come and told her so, Miriam would have loved him no less and no more. Either way, he was the same beautiful boy he'd always been. There would have been difficult and painful realities to face—religious conflicts to untangle—but she would have spent the rest of her life wrestling them by her son's side. Because that was what love did.

She didn't need to finish the sonata. She knew everything she needed to know about her son. And she couldn't do justice to what he had begun.

But Gus could.

Miriam grabbed the satchel and left the concert hall at a run.

The atrium was crowded now, but through the passing bodies she glimpsed a tall form with a distinctive walk. "Excuse me, pardon me," she said breathlessly as she wove through them. By the time she reached the spot where she'd seen Gus, he'd disappeared.

Outside, she planted herself on the sidewalk amid the crowds of people on lunch hour, shading her eyes as she scanned the area. There. Half a block away. He had his hands in his pockets and his head down into the wind. "Gus!" she shouted. "Gus! Wait!"

She took off after him, the satchel bumping her hip and Talia's skirt swirling around her ankles. She finally got within earshot on a wide brick sidewalk shaded by tall trees, newly leafed out, their branches waving in the chilly wind. "Gus!"

A street car rumbled past, its bell dinging. Either he didn't hear her, or he didn't want to.

She put on one last burst of speed and grabbed his arm. "Stop. Please, listen."

He stared down at her. His face gleamed. "You deprived me of my son, Mira."

"And your daughter." She couldn't let him set Talia aside, no matter how enamored he'd been of Blaise.

"I had a right to know."

If Miriam had walked into that recital hall nineteen years ago and interrupted his tryst, she felt certain the outcome would have been the same because Gus didn't value then what he did now.

And because she was meant to be with Teo.

But there would have been closure, and with it, a chance for them both to live in truth, without regret. "I know," she said. "I was wrong. I wish I could fix it, but I can't."

A muscle in his jaw twitched. "Why are you following me, Miriam?"

She pulled Blaise's notebook from the satchel. "I want you to have this."

The crowds flowed around them, but they stood frozen in time. He took the notebook. Opened it. Flipped from page to page to see Blaise's scribbled *Star Wars* doodles, the half-developed melodic ideas, and all her own cross-outs. He met her gaze and held the book out to her. "I can't take this."

"Yes, you can. I can't write that music. I wasn't meant to write it. But maybe you were." Her throat constricted. "He was my heart," she said softly, pressing her palm against her chest. "I don't need it to remember him. You have a right to have this piece of him. Finish it. Do whatever you want with it. It's yours."

He stood silently for a moment. "What about your benefit concert?"

She shrugged. "I'll figure something out."

He cradled the notebook against his chest. "Thank you." He hesitated. "I'll . . . I'll come to Atlanta to play it. At your concert. If you want."

The words got stuck in Miriam's throat. Giving this task over to Gus would raise questions. If he came to Atlanta, those questions would only have to be answered more publicly.

It would mean telling everyone what she'd kept secret for so long.

Gus watched her, the tiny twitch at the corner of his eyes betraying how much he wanted her to say yes. She'd taken a lifetime of parenthood away from him. Surely she could shoulder the personal cost of giving him this gift.

"Yes," she said. "Yes, that would be . . . yes."

The wind swept up the street, swirling the brown skirt around her calves, and Miriam could swear she heard a whisper on it: *Thank you, Mom.*

She dipped her head, pressing her hand against her chest, as if she could stop her heart from spreading into infinity, because here—in this distant, windswept city— Blaise's memory spoke at last.

She tipped her head back and tried to memorize the feel of this moment, the sunlight on her face and the screech of brakes on the street and the hard pavement beneath her feet and the wind tugging her hair out of her headband and pushing it into her face, wrapping her up in the certainty of loving and of being loved.

She almost forgot Gus was there until he spoke again. "Can you come for dinner tonight? I'd like to talk some more. I'd like to know . . . everything about Blaise. And Talia."

She hesitated. She owed him so much. Yet this fragile peace hung on a wisp of a thread. What about Kaye? Gus, being Gus, hadn't stopped to consider the ramifications: namely, asking his wife to accept this bombshell with Miriam standing right in the room.

She shook her head. "We do need to talk," she said, "but I think you should give your wife some time to come to terms with all this first. You guys can stay with me in Atlanta when you come. If you want."

He didn't like it—the tension in his face told her that— but he nodded. "So then, what now? Are you going home?"

She could. She'd confronted her ghosts, made peace with them. She didn't have to keep going. She could go home. Or to her goddaughter.

Yet she could feel them all around her, those who loved her, those she loved: Blaise, Talia, and Teo. Most of all, Teo. All of them beckoning her onward.

"No," she said quietly. "No, I have one stop left to make."

47

Friday, May 13
Carmel-by-the-Sea, California

MIRIAM STOOD IN FRONT of the mirror inside the Star-
bucks bathroom, applying a hint of eyeliner and
some blush and eye shadow. Teo had never been one of
those guys who insisted makeup wasn't necessary, but he'd
always liked a light touch. She let her arms fall and surveyed
her reflection up close.

She'd aged in the past year. No doubt about it. She
could see three gray hairs in her ponytail, and that fourth
one she'd call blond. But she liked the new slimness in her
face. She hadn't realized all those years she'd spent thrashing around, thinking she was barely keeping her head above
water, were transforming her into a real live adult.

She stepped back, smoothing her hands over the dress
Teo and Talia had given her. The one that, until today,
she'd never worn. It seemed fitting to wear it for this, her
own personal memorial. She brushed at the skirt. It had
picked up some lint the past couple of weeks, sitting in the
bottom of her suitcase, but all things considered, the crin-
kly black fabric splashed with crimson flowers had weathered the trip well. Miriam wondered what Talia would say
if she were here.

*You don't look half bad. Although I gotta say, that fluorescent
bulb isn't doing anything for your complexion. There's this great*

little invention they have now, you know. Foundation? Ever heard of it?

Miriam laughed—actually laughed out loud—for sheer joy. Because if she could imagine Talia teasing her, she must be healing.

The silver locket twisted on its waterdrop chain as she pulled out her phone to tap out a text message to Becky and Dicey. *It's time. Wish me luck.*

Becky's response came so quickly, she had to have been waiting. It contained no words, only an emoji of praying hands.

Dicey didn't respond at all. Probably asleep again. Miriam adjusted her red fringed scarf, scooped up her keys, and slipped out the door.

Nearly three thousand miles behind her, and one left to go.

★　★　★

A mile down the highway, Miriam pulled off into a parking place on the shoulder and stepped out of the car. It was an unprepossessing beach, long and narrow, the water so blue it looked painted. The wind picked up the red scarf; the soft fringe tickled her face as she stepped off the hard-packed shoulder of the highway.

Her foot sank into sand mixed with tiny pebbles, black and orange and white, worn smooth by billions of tides breathing in, breathing out. Rolling along, doing their own thing without regard for the cars whipping by or the lovers walking along the beach.

There was a wildness to this place, from the tangle of evergreen and windswept wildflowers across the highway to the endless expanse of ocean. Talia would have loved it. If they'd made it here, Talia would have torn out of the car and run straight for the water, forcing the others to keep up. Blaise would have been more likely to take his shoes off and sit down, digging his toes in like a hermit crab.

If she had been with them, she would have been like those lovers Miriam could see far down the beach, walking hand in hand with Teo.

If she had come with them instead of staying behind to play a Mozart concerto, might they have actually made it to this beautiful place? Maybe she would have seen the big pickup, weaving dangerously up the highway, in time to warn Teo before they crossed onto the bridge where disaster struck.

If. Always if. But if any of those ifs had happened, everything would have been different, not just the ending.

"This isn't how they should find out," Teo had told her. It was the last conversation they'd ever had, the evening before her family died. Teo and the kids had just left the awards ceremony, and the twins had tripped over each other, shouting at Teo's phone, trying to tell her everything at once. She'd never heard Blaise so animated. In their excitement, they'd failed to notice Miriam's stunned silence after Blaise mentioned meeting the famous August von Rickenbach.

"We'll see you tomorrow!" was Blaise's parting shout as Teo had retrieved the phone. "We're going on a beach-hunting expedition, and Dr. von Rickenbach said he'd camp with us tomorrow night!"

Teo had clicked off the speaker. "You'd have been proud of them today, Mira."

But Miriam couldn't focus on her children's success. "Teo—is it really Gus?"

"I assume so." Of course, Teo couldn't know for sure. He'd never met Gus. She'd made sure of it. "Can't imagine another guy with a name that fussy."

Despite feeling overwrought—or perhaps because of it—she'd had to chuckle.

"Ah," he'd said, and even now Miriam could picture the satisfied look on his face at having coaxed a laugh from her. "I've missed that sound. I wish you could have been here, but I'm glad it worked out the way it did. This isn't how they should find out. They need to hear it from us. But Mira, it's time they know. Past time."

"Can they hear you?"

"No, they're off talking to Mr. von . . . Dr. . . . . to Gus." Teo chuffed. "I gotta say, he's a charmer, that man. Even Talia's starry-eyed."

Miriam could hear the vulnerability in her husband's voice. He'd stepped in and raised this family, and now . . . "I'm so sorry, Teo," she'd told him. "It's not fair to you, having to deal with this."

"It's all right. I'll protect my family. But I think you'd better stay home." His voice had changed. Raised a bit, as if for public consumption. "It's only going to get worse if you get on a plane and wear yourself out. We're going on a hunt for the most beautiful beach in California. Some project Talia has in mind—for school maybe? I'm not sure. But it's not weather for someone with the flu. Windy. Cold. Just stay in bed and let Becky force-feed you chicken soup, okay, Sassafras?"

She could hear the protests in the background.

"No, no," Teo addressed their children. "Of course she didn't tell you she's sick. She's your mother. Tell her you love her and you'll see her when you get home."

Only they'd never made it home. It never occurred to any of them, as they'd shouted "I love you!" and "See you soon!" into the phone, that those were the last words they would ever exchange. If they'd realized it, the end of that conversation would have been very different.

But it wasn't. Her family's story had ended twenty-four hours later, on a bridge, on their way to this spot, on a day not unlike this one.

A spray of sand dusted her sunglasses; her locket caught a brief gust of wind and slapped back down against her chest. She grabbed it and held on tight as she walked toward the water, stopping several feet away from the crashing surf. In this spot, North America's final plunge to the Pacific was steep, waves breaking right at the tide line instead of out in the surf.

Her phone dinged. Miriam, startled, released her grip on the locket, only then recognizing the ache in her hand. A text from Dicey:

You got this girl.

Miriam smiled, breathing a prayer of gratitude. She slid her phone back into her pocket and flexed her fingers to work out the pain of clinging so tightly to the past.

The wind calmed. Miriam took a deep breath. "I'm sorry, Teo," she said. "I wasted so much time. I always loved you. But you knew that already, didn't you?" The sinking sun kissed her cheeks, her forehead, and the tip of her nose. She swallowed. "I'll always miss you. And I'll always love you. But it's time to stop looking back."

The warmth spread. Not quite a hug from beyond the grave. But close. "Kids, take care of your father."

The wind picked up again. She closed her eyes. It was time. She lifted the locket over her head and held it in both hands, closing her eyes. She could feel it all around her again, the sense of being part of something vast and beautiful and holy. She couldn't change the past, but she could shift the trajectory of her future. From now on, she would honor Teo—and Talia and Blaise, and her mother and Brad and Jo—Dicey and Deandra—she would honor all those she loved, the dead and the living alike, by her commitment to live free and love fully. That would be her love song. Her gift to the world.

Breathing deep, Miriam lifted the locket over her head. She flipped a thumb over the latch and let the fragile petals fly.

ACKNOWLEDGMENTS

Authors are often told "write what you know," but the reality is that if we didn't step outside our normal lanes, we could only write about ourselves. So this page is for publicly acknowledging those who helped me reach this long-dreamed-of milestone. I couldn't have done it without you!

First shout-out goes to my husband and kids, who have experienced every up and down of this long journey with me.

To Dolores Caron, Emily Brett, and Dr. Melissa Kouba—my thanks for answering medical questions. Jennifer Sutton, you are my long-suffering hero. Thanks for endless Messenger chats about ICU procedures and for reading that critical medical scene again . . . and again . . . and again!

To the Our Lady of Lourdes contemporary group and the St. Thomas More Newman Center 11:00 choir: you taught me what a church "choir" can be. Also to my friends of the Liturgical Composers Forum, who expanded that lesson to the national level.

To Laura St. Clair: your willingness to share the experience of widowhood helped me enter Miriam's world.

My thanks to my Women Fiction Writers Association writing partners—Janet Rundquist, Cerrissa Kim, and Chris Adler; and especially to my top-notch local critique partners—Brian Katcher, Heidi Stallman, Kelsey Simon, Ida Fogle, and Amy Whitley. I thank God for you every day. Special shout-out to Amy for introducing me to travel writing, which undoubtedly inspired the dream that sparked this novel.

Thanks to Uncle Greg, for giving me working-class suburbs near Stanford; to Andrew Collins and Hadley Williams, for helping me get Miriam arrested; to Will McWilliams, for answering financial questions and asking for novel updates at every financial planning meeting since; to John, for telling me about police procedures, even if I didn't end up using them; and to Mike Holstein at the Green Bank Observatory for making time for a debut novelist. Someday I'll get there to visit for real!

To my cousins, Hamilton, Martha, and Avery: thanks for helping me remember what it's like to be a teenager. At forty-something, you think you remember, but you don't—not really.

Thanks to WFWA friends who beta read and/or gave sensitivity readings—Denny Bryce, Micki Morency, and Nancy Johnson. I am so thankful to be part of this community!

Finally, to my agents, Sonali Chanchani and Claudia Cross, my advocates and cheerleaders, and to Jenny Chen, Melissa Rechter, Madeline Rathle, and the entire team at Alcove Press: thanks for giving Miriam wings!